DEATH ON A LONGSHIP

MARSALI TAYLOR

@ttica

DEATH ON A LONGSHIP
Marsali Taylor

Published by Attica Books 2012

www.atticabooks.com

Cover art by Kit Foster Design

Typeset in Bergamo by Ezra Barany and Anselm Audley

ISBN 9781908002433 (epub)
ISBN 9781908002440 (mobi)
ISBN 9781908002457 (print)

DEATH ON A LONGSHIP

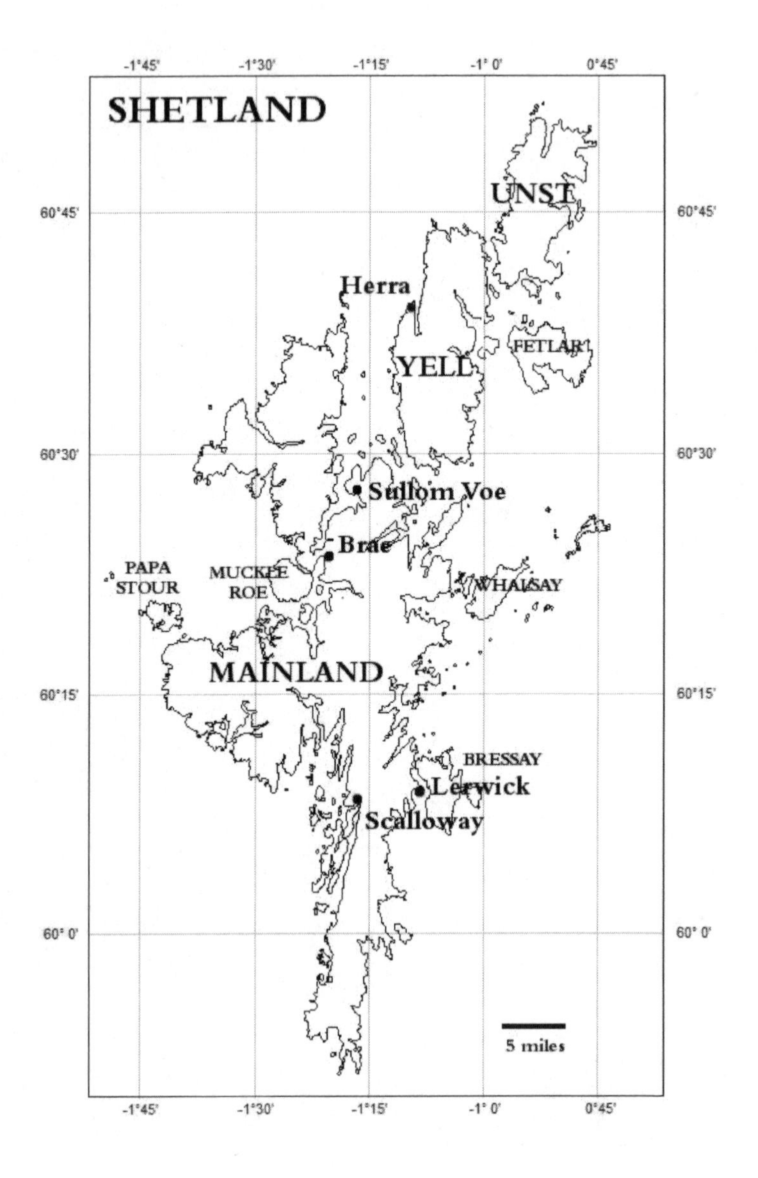
SHETLAND
-1°45'
-1°30'
-1°15'
-1° 0'
0°45'
60°45'
60°30'
60°15'
60° 0'
UNST
Herra
FETLAR
YELL
Sullom Voe
Brae
PAPA
STOUR
MUCKLE
ROE
WHALSAY
MAINLAND
BRESSAY
Lerwick
Scalloway
5 miles

SUNDAY, 8TH JUNE.

BRAE, SHETLAND.

High Water at Brae, 00.48, 2.0;
Low Water 07.09, 0.3;
HW 13.37, 1.8;
LW 19.20, 0.8.

MOON WAXING GIBBOUS.

Chapter 1

She was my longship. She floated beside the boating club pontoon like a ghost from Shetland's past, her red and ochre striped sail furled on her heavy yard half-way up the wooden mast, her painted shields mirrored on the early-morning calm water.

Okay, she belonged to Berg Productions Ltd, but I was her skipper. *Stormfugl, Stormbird.* She was seventy-five feet long, with a carved head snarling in a circle of teeth, a writhed tail, and a triangular log cabin on a half-deck in the stern. Gulls were wheeling around her, bickering among themselves, as if one of them had dropped a fish.

I started *Khalida*'s engine and put-putted across the bay torwards the marina. I wasn't keen on gulls dismembering fish all over my clean decks. I'd hosed them yesterday, after filming. The cameramen, lighting operators, make-up, costume, best boys, grips and all the hundred people that seemed to be needed for even a simple shot had squelched the path from road to shore into dusty gravel, which had clung to the sheepskin boots of my Viking oarsmen. The shore had added a generous helping of sand-laden algae. I didn't intend to start the day re-scrubbing them. I'd fire the gulls' fish overboard, and let them squabble about it on the water.

It was amazing, too, that Anders hadn't heard them. Even someone who slept like the dead, as he did, must surely be woken by them perching on the cabin ridgepole to stretch their necks at each other. I'd have thought he'd have been out to clear them by now.

As we entered the marina I realised that there was a white bundle lying on *Stormfugl*'s deck under the circle of snatching gulls. I turned *Khalida* in a sharp curve and brought her up on the other side of the pontoon. Damn the way Norwegians went for cheap British drink. He'd obviously gone out and got blootered, staggered home and fallen, injured himself –

It wasn't Anders.

I looked at the body lying on the half-deck, one hand stretched towards the prow and felt my newly-won promotion to skipper slipping away. It was Maree Baker, one of the film lot, the stand-in for the star.

I was ashamed of myself for thinking first of me, but I couldn't help Maree now. She lay sprawled on the larch planks like a marionette washed up by the tide, the manicured nails still gleaming like shells in the bloody mess the gulls had made of the exposed hands. There was mottled dirt on her cream silk trouser suit. The red-gold hair falling across her face was stirring just a little in the breeze, as if at any moment she'd shake it out of her eyes and leap up. I looked again at the back of her head, tilted up towards me, and saw the pool of blood spreading out from below her stand-in wig. The gulls had left footprints in it, and across the deck. I'm not squeamish about blood, but I felt sick then. I yelled at the three that had only gone as far as the pier, orange eyes watching me, then looked back at Maree. I didn't want to touch her, but I had to. I was the ship's Master under God; captain, minister, doctor. I curved my hand around the chilling neck and laid two fingers over the vein. There was no flutter of pulse.

I withdrew my hand and reached into my back pocket for my mobile. 999. No, here in Shetland, 999 would probably get me some Inverness call centre three hundred miles away, where I'd have to spell out every name twice. I wanted Lerwick. I dived into the boating club for a phone book, and found the number. There were two rings, then a voice.

'Northern Constabulary, Sergeant Peterson here, can I help you?'

I took a deep breath and wished I was at sea, where the procedure was laid down. *Mayday three times, this is yacht name three times.* 'I'd like to report what looks like a fatal accident,' I said. 'On board the longship *Stormfugl,* moored at Delting Boating Club.'

'The film boat,' she replied, briskly confident even at this hour of the morning. 'Your name, madam?'

'I'm Cass Lynch, the skipper of the boat.'

'Remain with the body, please, Ms Lynch. We'll get a doctor to you as soon as possible. Have you any idea of the casualty's identity?'

ID was Ted's problem. 'She's lying face down. I didn't want to turn her over.'

'We'll be with you in about half an hour. Until then, please ensure that nobody goes near the body. And don't call anyone. We'll do that.'

'I'll stay with the body,' I said, but made no other promises.

I picked up a stone, and scattered the gulls with one vicious throw.

4

Anders should have been on board; it was his night on watch. I went slowly up to the cabin, almost afraid to look inside, but it was empty. My breath came out in a rush. Not even his gear was there, his scarlet sleeping bag, the back-pack he used as a wash bag, and his thermos. There was only the lilo we used to soften the larch planks, inflated and waiting.

I didn't have time to worry about him now. On shore I had to answer to the production company. Was Mr Berg Productions Ltd a captain who'd want to be called at the very first sign of trouble, or one who'd bawl you out if you didn't let him sleep until his life-raft was launched? I slotted his shrewd eyes into my mental line of skippers, and decided the former. I didn't see how even the film world could cover up Maree's death. I wanted to break it myself, in my best Norwegian.

He wasn't happy. 'This was not to do with the filming? What was she doing aboard the longship at night?'

I side-stepped that one. 'I have called the police. They will arrive soon.'

'This will hold up the filming.'

'Perhaps not by much,' I said.

'And your night watchman. Anders. Where was he?'

A good question. 'He does not seem to be aboard.'

He pounced on that. 'You think he is involved in this outrage?'

I hadn't thought of it as an outrage. She'd stumbled and tripped, hit her head with a whack. Head injuries killed. *Alain.* The boom coming over, lifting with a creak then suddenly swinging, lethal – I swallowed the memory away. 'I have every confidence that he is not involved.' Anders had been my choice as engineer.

'I know his father,' Mr Berg said. He would, through the Norwegian businessmen old boys' network. 'Thank you for keeping me informed. Phone later in the day, as this affair develops.'

'Yes, sir.'

I didn't hesitate about phoning Ted, the film's director, because I knew he and his Director of Photography were spending the night on Ronas Hill, filming the sun dipping into the sea and rising again. They wanted the shot for the poster, the western rim of the ocean, with Favelle's face superimposed. I heard two rings, then his voice.

'Cass?'

'Ted, there's been an accident here, on board *Stormfugl.* Maree's dead.'

'I'll come over right now. Have you told the police?'

'Yes,' I said. 'And Mr Berg.' I paused. 'I didn't give a name.'

'Thanks, Cass. See you soon.'

When I'd opened up my phone the screen had said: 1 New Message. Sender unknown; the phone call I'd ignored last night. I looked at it now, and found a message from a dead woman. 'Must talk will come down to boat Maree.'

A wave of guilt flooded over me. I should have answered the phone instead of telling the world to go away. Maree had come to find me in the half-dark, had tripped and fallen. It wouldn't have happened if I'd been here. Hers was the second death I'd caused.

I'd just pocketed my phone when a car scrunched down the gravel below the boating club. The brisk, elderly man who got out had been my doctor when I was a child. He felt her pulse, and shook his head. 'Dead. What happened, Cass?'

'I wasn't here,' I said. 'I presume she tripped and fell.'

'Was it you who moved her?'

'No,' I said, surprised. 'I just felt for a pulse at her neck.'

He gave me a sideways look, eyes lifting, falling again. 'The police will need to see her as she is.'

I could feel my heart beat in the silence. 'Didn't she trip and fall?'

He didn't answer, and I could see it for myself. She might have tripped on the gangplank ridges, but she'd have had her hands to save herself from coming a real cropper, and it hadn't been a metal boom with the strength of a Force 5 gybe coming over to crack her unprotected skull, but a stationary wooden deck. It should have meant a bump, a black eye, a bleeding nose, not death.

Death meant questioning and suspicion. 'Can you tell us exactly what happened? How do you know what the wind speed was? Who was in charge of the boat at the time?'

We were all in even deeper trouble than I'd thought.

We heard the first police car then, its engine echoing across the water as it charged north up the dual carriageway, slowed to come through the township of Brae and speeded up again for the westward straight along to the boating club. Soon the whole pier was swarming with officers cordoning off the area with blue and white tape. It seemed, though, that they weren't to touch anything until the forensic team and the Inverness detective officer arrived.

I was taken aside by Sergeant Peterson. She was younger than I'd expected, with blonde hair sleeked back in a pony-tail and the eyes of a mermaid, ice-green and indifferent to human follies. She took my mobile off me, 'Just a precaution, madam,' then escorted me upstairs in the boating club and made me a cup of tea. 'The Inspector will want to question you, madam. It may be a bit of a wait, I'm afraid.'

'That's my boat beside the longship,' I said. 'I could wait there.'

She shook her head. 'We'd be grateful if you'd wait here, madam.'

She went out to join the white-coated men erecting a tent around poor Maree, and left me to more waiting, and more, which gave me time to think about the implications.

At least I understood now what Maree was doing on board *Stormfugl* in the middle of the night. She'd come along the pontoons to where *Khalida* was usually berthed, seen the empty space and known I'd gone out for a sail. She wouldn't have hung around openly on the quayside, but gone into *Stormfugl*'s cabin to wait, out of sight, discreet to the end, until someone had come on board and killed her. Anders was missing, but why should Anders want to harm Maree?

Why should anyone want to harm Maree?

In the end I took one of the first-aid blankets, lay down on the settee by the window, said a prayer for Maree, and closed my eyes. I didn't sleep deeply, though; I must have surfaced every ten minutes, realising each time with a shock that she was dead. Cars came and went, and the people outside talked on their radios. At tide-turn I woke to Ted's voice protesting, and a murmur answering, and looked out. His white limo was parked at the entrance to the marina, the driver's door left open. He was trying to talk his way through a phalanx of police officers. I could read their lips. 'Not until the Detective Inspector arrives. Sorry, sir. Identification can wait. Very sorry, sir, those are our orders. If you'd like to come inside and wait, sir .

They led him out of my sight into the club. I heard chairs scraping on the other side of the partition wall.

At last there was more movement within the boating club, a sudden rush of voices, Anders replying, startled and defensive, footsteps on the stairs, then the door opened, and an officer escorted Anders in.

He'd obviously just come out of the shower. His silver-gilt hair was darkened and combed, his tanned face shining above the neat beard. His eyes met mine, alarmed, then he looked past me, out of the window. His round eyes widened as they took in the cars, the ticker-tape, the officers, and then his whole face sagged as he saw the body sprawled on the deck. He spoke in rapid Norwegian: 'Cass, what's happening?'

The officer cut in. 'No talking, if you please, sir. Just sit down. I'm afraid we'll have to ask you to wait here until the officers from Inverness arrive. Would you like a coffee?'

He nodded and joined me at the window, sitting five feet from me, and lowering himself like an old man. His eyes met mine again, filled with dread, then returned to our ship. I was left trying to make sense of that. Where had he been, that he hadn't come back via the boating club drive with full grandstand view of the proceedings? Answer: the only place he wouldn't have seen what was going on was in the windowless downstairs of the boating club itself.

For some reason he seemed to have slept in the showers.

ᛋ

Outside, the sea had slid away from the concrete launching slip, then begun to sidle back. At last there was a bustle and stir downstairs. The officer looked up. 'That's the Inverness officers arrived. Not much longer now.'

We looked below us at the two people who got out of the car. One was Sergeant Peterson, getting her impressions in first. The man was older, mid-thirties, and what I noticed most about him was his air of alertness, like a sea-eagle on its eyrie, high on a cliff but seeing every bird that flew past below, every fish that came to the surface. This man stood by the foot of the gangplank, just looking, and the busy scene suddenly focused around his stillness. He must have stood there for a good ten minutes, immobile in the middle of the bustle around him, just looking. Behind him, two local officers exchanged dismissive shrugs. I smiled to myself. They'd learn; there'd be no skylarking on this man's watch.

He moved at last, coming out from the other side of the police car, and I realised the other reason for the dismissive shrugs. He was wearing a kilt. Shetlanders were more Viking than Scots, so the kilt up here was imported for weddings only and associated with fancy socks, ornamental daggers and white-fringed sporrans, all considered very sissy by the Shetland male whose native dress was the boiler suit and rubber boots.

At last he turned back towards the clubhouse. A camera began flashing, and four spaceman-suited figures came forward, a white ring closing around Maree's still form. Sergeant Peterson spoke to the Inspector again; he glanced up towards the club house windows, then strolled towards the lower door. I heard light, even footsteps on the stairs, and in he came.

He wasn't particularly tall, five foot seven or eight, and compactly-built, with strength behind the slightness. Tanned – no, weathered, the complexion of a man who preferred outdoors to in. He had russet hair, cut long enough to rumple around his ears, and it stood up on the top of his head, as if he had a habit of running his hand through it. His nose was slightly skafe, as if he had fallen out of too many trees in his youth. His kilt wasn't wedding-fancy, but a workmanlike affair in one of the sober green tartans, with a plain leather sporran. I'd have betted there was a clasp knife in there, wooden-handled and notched with use. The top button of his shirt was undone because it was missing, and the elbows of his green tweed jacket were bagged. If he hadn't been a policeman I'd have taken to him: a reliable watch-leader.

He paused two steps in to give a long, slow look round the room, as if he was comparing it with his local and noting things to be copied when he got home. He spotted the map of Busta Voe linoed onto the floor, and walked round it gravely. 'We're here, are we no?' His accent was pure Highland, that shushing, lilting note with a downward turn on the question that you only hear west of Inverness. One brown hand pointed. Sergeant Peterson stepped forward.

'The club's here, sir, at the top of the voe.'

'Aye, aye.' He nodded to himself, went over to inspect the whiskies behind the grilled-off bar. 'Tallisker, Highland Park, Scapa Flow. No bad, no bad.'

Sergeant Peterson cleared her throat with barely-restrained impatience. 'Ms Lynch, sir, and Mr Johansen.'

He turned to look properly at us with disconcertingly wide-open eyes, honest-looking, a clear sea-grey. I stared, incredulous and hurting, unable even to nod.

This man had Alain's eyes.

The Inspector nodded to himself again. 'Now you'll be the captain of this ship. I'm Detective Inspector Macrae, from Inverness.' He shook my hand briskly. 'Cassandra Lynch. No, Cassandre.' He pronounced it correctly, French-style. 'The first thing we need is an idea of who the poor lass lying out there is. Can you help us with that?'

'She's the actor who doubled for Favelle last week.' I'd leave Ted to fill in more details if it became necessary. 'Maree Baker.'

I sensed, rather than saw, the startled look Anders gave me.

'Maree Baker,' the Inspector repeated. 'Sergeant, go and see what you can find out.'

'M-a-r-e-e,' I said. Sergeant Peterson wrote it down in her notebook and headed out.

'Thank you for that, Ms Lynch. That lets us get started. Mr Johansen, if you'll go with my colleague here, Inspector Hutchinson, he'll take your statement.'

Anders gave me a look I couldn't quite read, somewhere between puzzlement and warning, and followed the officer like a man about to walk the plank. DI Macrae opened a regulation black notebook. The writing was in dark blue ink, an untidy hand: *age 29, father Dermot Lynch, ex Sullom Voe, director Shetland Eco-Energy.* He watched me read down the page. *Mother, Eugénie Delafauve. Opera singer, France.*

Maman. A specialist in the seventeeth-century composer Rameau: Greek costumes and period instruments presented to small audiences in fancy chateaux.

Grew up Shetland, sailor. France with mother, ran away.

It had been a combination of luck and planning. The Tall Ships were doing La Rochelle to Edinburgh, and I'd half-emptied my bank account for a berth as a trainee aboard a Russian barque. I'd got the train to La Rochelle. Sea. Scottish soil. Sanctuary.

He lifted the notebook, turned a page. 'You argued that you were sixteen, and independent in Scotland, if not in France. You had a British passport, and the Scottish police failed to persuade you. End of that record.' He looked back at the notes I couldn't see, and I braced myself. Alain's death, on a yacht half way across the Atlantic. But he didn't comment, simply nodded again, closed the notebook and put it back in his sporran. 'So here you are, a teenage runaway, in charge of a film company's Viking longship. Fill in the gap.'

'Jobs,' I said. 'In the summer, any sailing I could get. Delivery crew.' I'd begged and blagged and even slept my way on to yachts and gaffers and sail training ships. 'In the winter, supermarkets. Waitressing. I worked my way up the RYA courses, and that got me working in sailing schools in the Med. Then I did my first Atlantic crossing.' We'd been on the way back when Alain had died. If he wasn't going to talk about it, that suited me fine.

He gave a nod, as if working on boats was an entirely normal career, then looked back at his paper. 'Local gossip is you got the job fitting out this longship through your father. Tell me about that.'

It took serious effort to shrug. 'Not exactly. I was working in Bergen, and met the directors of the Norwegian firm who were sponsoring the film.'

ᛋ

Met wasn't quite accurate. I'd been waitressing in a fairly up-market restaurant in one of the main streets in Bergen. It did silver service for tourists and well-heeled locals. It was a quiet Thursday night, so the three Norwegian businessmen at the table by the stove were getting my full attention, especially when they began talking about *Stormfugl.*

I knew about her, of course. She was an exact replica of the largest of boat burials, the Gokstadt ship, and she'd been built three years previously to demonstrate that Leif Erikson could easily have gone to America. He might have; the modern-day Vikings hit bad weather coming up to Shetland, *Stormfugl* was blown ashore and the whole project had to be put on hold.

Shetland. My heart tugged like a hooked fish.

'There is another replica in America, of course,' the youngest man said. The oldest of the three, in his fifties, with a pointed Drake beard below a lean, pink face, shook his head.

'The American one is a warship, light and fast. Nobody would ever believe a voyage to America in something so shallow. The *Stormfugl* is deeper-bodied, a trading ship, with a half deck aft, and a small cabin. On top of that, Ted says that Shetland will do for Norway, for Labrador, for Iceland. It will be cheaper, he says, and he will make it look authentic.'

'But what state is this *Stormfugl* in? How much will it cost to make her seaworthy?'

Good cue, I thought. 'Excuse me,' I said. They gave me that blankly polite look you give a waitress who interrupts an important conversation for bread rolls or more coffee. 'I can tell you a bit about *Stormfugl,*' I continued. 'She wasn't damaged when she went ashore, or not badly, it was a good sandy beach she was blown on to, and they re-floated her straight off. She's only had two winters ashore, uncovered, so the rain will have kept her timbers swollen. You'd need a surveyor's report, but I'd expect her to be sound.'

I had their attention now. The younger man gave me a narrow-eyed look.

'What's your connection with Shetland, Ms–?'

'Ms Lynch,' I said. If there was a job here, blagging might get me in. 'I grew up there, and my father lives there still. I know the Shetland waters well. I'm a yacht skipper.' I gave them a rueful smile, charming enough to interest them, but not so charming that they'd write me off as a dolly-bird. 'Not in winter, of course. I was one of the crew on the *Sea Stallion*, the longship that went from Sweden to Dublin a couple of years ago, and that and my Shetland background made me interested enough to follow *Stormfugl*'s story.'

'Ms Lynch,' the man with the beard repeated, in a thoughtful way that would have set alarm bells ringing if I'd not been so determined to make them consider me for any job going. His eyes were shrewd, assessing me; I looked straight back.

'I'm a qualified RYA Ocean Yachtmaster. You'll need a skipper for your longship if you're going to film aboard, as well as someone to oversee the repairs and fitting out in Shetland. I could do that for you too. I know folk who do that kind of work, reliable ones.'

There was one of those long pauses, then the oldest one smiled. 'Ms Lynch, you don't look much like a skipper right now. Why not clear the table and bring us our coffees for the moment, and, here–' He felt in his pocket for his wallet, brought out a card. 'This is my firm, Berg Productions Limited. Come tomorrow at ten, and we can talk about your qualifications.'

ᛋ

It wasn't a propitious week, with the silver disk of the moon draining away, but at least the sea was pulsing into the Bergen channel. A flowing tide was a better omen. I was there at ten to ten, with my RYA cards in their see-through wallet, and references from a couple of Caribbean outfits. It was Mr Berg's office I was shown into, a symphony of pearl grey and ivory. Just the depth of the carpet I waded across told me this was a megabucks outfit, and if I hadn't been there in front of him I'd have turned tail and run, but faint heart wins no command. I straightened my shoulders inside my best navy jacket and hoped my plait was still neat.

He motioned me to a seat. 'Let me tell you more about this project, Ms Lynch. The film is about Gudrid, the first European woman to reach America, the sister-in-law of Leif Erikson, and we are one of the sponsors. Favelle Baker will play Gudrid, and her husband Ted Tarrant is the director.'

This was big-time stuff. Ted and Favelle were one of Hollywood's golden couples. She'd been a child star, and Ted Tarrant had been her leading man in her first teen movie. It had been love straight away. They'd got married between movies, made two more together, and then Ted had moved from acting to directing, a series of eco-aware films starring Favelle as a feisty activist taking on big business on behalf of the planet. I'd been particularly impressed by the Greenpeace one, where she'd really slung into the oil companies and fisherman who were making a desert of our seas. The way she'd scrambled over rigs and in and out of high-speed rubber inflatable dinghies had made me feel she was a woman after my own heart.

Furthermore, Ted Tarrant had been my teenage heart-throb. Before he'd become her romantic lead, he'd done a War of Independence swashbuckler where he'd played John Paul Jones, one of the world's great seamen. That had sparked off a run of biopics: a supporting athlete in a movie about Roger Bannister, and one about cricket, and another where he was a round-the-world cyclist. The publicity was that he'd done all the stunts himself. It would be amazing to meet him.

'Naturally,' Mr Berg continued, 'most of the film will be shot in Norway, but Mr Tarrant is keen to use Shetland as a location for the sailing scenes because Favelle is to do some publicity for your green energy firm there, Shetland Eco-Energy, and as we have links with them too we are happy to co-operate. You will know all about this, I am sure - there have been some objections to their proposed wind farm. Favelle is to publicise the importance of renewable energy.'

It was the first I'd heard of it. I nodded, with the air of one who talked wind farms at breakfast.

'Hence the need for a longship that is already in Shetland. If the *Stormfugl* is usable then Mr Tarrant will get the outdoor shots he wants and we will be saved a good deal of time and money. Now, your brief would be this. You'd recruit the skeleton crew necessary to get the boat fitted out, hire extras for the oarsmen and be in charge of the sailing while the shooting is going on.'

A pause, then he looked straight at me. 'Tell me why you think you could do it.'

Knowing that I could do it made me confident, and this time fortune favoured the bold, waning moon or waxing. By the end of the interview I'd got my first ship.

If I'd been alone, I'd have turned a cartwheel on that thick ivory carpet. As it was, I smiled and thanked him, and walked demurely out into the street, only letting my face break into a broad grin when I was safely outside. I wanted to sing, and shout and celebrate. I bought a bottle of bitter lemon from the next supermarket and swigged it straight away, then got out my mobile. Contacts, Anders, select. As it rang I could see him, very serious, green boiler-suited, a smear of oil on his right cheek, a spanner in his left hand, fumbling the phone's buttons.

'Goddag?'

'Anders? It's Cass.'

He was in his father's Bildøy workshop just behind the pontoon where *Khalida* was moored; clangs and drills reverberated behind him. 'Yo, Cass.'

'Can you meet me at *Khalida* this evening, after work? I've got a job for you.'

A single-minded bloke, Anders was. 'Is it your injectors again?'

'Much more exciting. I'll tell you when I see you – bye.'

Mr Berg wanted me to go to Shetland as soon as possible and make him a full report of what needed to be done. I wasn't going to take a plane when *Khalida* was waiting in her berth with her sails bent on. The restaurant would have to take three days notice. If Anders could make it, and if the forecast held, we'd leave on Wednesday.

Shetland. *Alain.* If his ghost was going to haunt me, it would be there.

I wasn't going to think about that, nor about my Dad, nor about the home I hadn't seen for fourteen years. I was going back in triumph as the skipper of the Viking ship in a high-profile film.

My heart sang all the way to Bildøy. I'd have a command to my name. Never mind that she was a replica longboat that'd been wrecked and abandoned. She was the proof that I could do it. Superyachts in the Med, yachts to be delivered to the Caribbean, skipper of charter ships in Australia and New Zealand, now I'd be eligible for them all.

There was no sign of Anders at the marina. I unlocked *Khalida's* wooden washboards and clambered down the four steps into my little world, this eight metre long fibreglass hull, lined to window height with amber wood. My eyes danced at me in the brass-framed mirror. Maman's moulded French cheekbones, Dad's stubborn Irish chin. Dad's curls on Maman's glossy dark hair. Maman's smooth skin, weathered to Dad's brown complexion. The long scar across my left cheek was Alain's legacy. Only the sprinkling of freckles across the bridge of my nose was my own.

I'd broken free from Dad wanting me to go back to college and take the qualifications I'd thrown away in France, free from Maman's wish to make a pretty girl out of me. I'd go back on my own terms.

All the same, I wished *Stormfugl* had fetched up in Iceland.

Chapter 2

Of course I didn't say all that to the Inspector. 'Mr Berg was impressed with my qualifications and gave me the job,' I finished.

DI Macrae nodded. There was a silence; I could feel his eyes on me. Then he fished a battered tin box out of his sporran, and opened it. Inside was a glinting of hooks and little weights, and a coil of clear nylon line. I watched, incredulous, as he chose a hook and weights, laid them on the table, took out the line and put the box away again. 'Tell me about your crew on this Viking boat.'

His hands were busy on the line, distracting. He lifted his eyes, grey and sharp, waiting for me to reply. I looked away from the deft, brown fingers.

'The engineer is Anders Johansen, who came over from Norway with me.'

'An engine?' The eyes that were so like Alain's crinkled in a smile, and I wanted to howl in protest. 'Not very authentic, surely.'

Dear Lord, I wasn't going to be coaxed by a ghost. 'Inauthentic but safe,' I replied. 'The insurance company and I agreed on that.'

'What's he like, Mr Johansen?'

'He's not tall, about five foot seven, and compactly built,' I said. 'Blond hair, seaman's beard, blue eyes, very good looking.'

'A ladies' man?' The old-fashioned phrase surprised a choke of laughter out of me. That's what he'd meant to do; I saw a gleam of satisfaction in his eyes. 'Yes?'

Anders was my crew, to be protected against all comers. I gave my most annoying French shrug, the one railway officials or hotel clerks use when they've lost your booking and can't be bothered to find it. DI Macrae nodded as if I'd spoken. 'Why did you sign him up?'

Easy. 'He's a good engineer, and a keen sailor.'

We'd met when I'd first come to Norway, three years ago. *Khalida*'s engine had started making knocking noises. I tried the basics myself, but had to concede that it was a professional job, and took it to the Johansen yard. Anders had fixed it, at speed and at a reasonable price, and so thoroughly that it didn't go wrong again. Most impressive of all, he'd assumed I'd wanted to know what was broken. After that, I'd taken all mechanical problems to him and acted as second mechanic, repaying him with a sail out through the islands and into the North Sea. He'd developed a taste for wind power, much to his father's disgust, passed his Day Skipper and Yachtmaster Theory qualifications, and was always keen to log up sea-miles for his practical. I hoped he'd jump at the chance of a trip to Shetland.

I was just giving him up when I felt *Khalida* rock to steps on the pontoon, and looked out to see him approaching. His fair hair was hidden by a dark cap, and he was still wearing his green boiler suit. He paused by the cockpit. I saw a bulging movement at his right shoulder, then a pink nose whiffling out; the pet rat who accompanied him everywhere. I didn't mind Rat at all. Apart from his unfortunate way with ship's biscuits and nesting in the sails, he was far less bother than a dog. I opened the washboards.

'Hi, Anders. What're you doing, working this late?'

'A fishing boat needed to be finished for tomorrow.' He gave me a kiss on each cheek, French style. Most women got to the other side of the room at this point. Rat snuffled my cheek and leapt nimbly on to my shoulder, then swarmed down my front, tail hooked out for balance, and went off to investigate the bilges. He'd come back with his white patches rather oily, but that was Anders' problem.

'Now, beautiful Cass, how's it going?' A Frenchman might have got away with 'belle Cassandre' but it just sounded uncomfortable in Norwegian, like a ship tackling a cross tide. Then the nerd took over. 'You said it wasn't the injectors again.'

'I've got a job,' I said. 'Have you time for a dram, to help me celebrate?'

'I always have time for a dram,' he said, grinning. He sat down on the couch that ran the length of *Khalida*'s starboard side, tilting his fair head back against the bookshelf to show off the tanned throat running down to muscular shoulders. Such a waste. I rose, fitted the little table between us, and took out two glasses and the boat's bottle of port.

'*Khalida* and I are off to Shetland,' I said. 'Two hundred miles of sea and sky.'

'Single-handed?'

'Could the yard manage without you?'

'Now that fishing boat's out of the way. The next job is a wooden yacht, giving her new decks. My father won't need an engineer for that.' Now his eyes were sparkling, and the would-be sophisticated banter was put to one side as he rose back to his actual age of twenty-six. 'Two hundred miles, and there are always Norwegian boats going back and forward. That would leave me only – let me see, seven hundred to go.'

'Could they do without you till mid-June?'

'I'm not so sure about that.' He grinned again, showing beautifully straight teeth. 'I couldn't do without money for a couple of months, Cass. Rat has to eat.' Then he went back to being florid. I wondered if he lay awake at night thinking up compliments. 'Not even for you, beautiful Cass. I must visit you at bedtime more often, if you are going to greet me with drink, and your hair loosened.' I gave him a reproving, big sister look, which turned him practical again. 'Unless you're trying to soften me up. What's this job, then?'

'It's a paid job, for a film company.' He brightened. 'How d'you fancy fitting an engine into a Viking longship?'

His eyes lit up with more genuine enthusiasm than he'd managed for me. 'What size of ship, Cass, what size of engine, and is it for main power or auxiliary? How fast does it need to go?'

'She's seventy-five feet long, and we don't need a turbo charger,' I said. 'It's for a range of fifteen miles at six or seven knots. It should be an easily driven hull.' He made a face, unimpressed. 'For all that, though, it needs to have enough power to get us out of trouble.' I lifted Rat off the floor before he left little oily footprints everywhere and set him on the table to inspect the dregs in Anders' glass, whiskers twitching thoughtfully.

Anders took the glass from him and considered, his eyes resting thoughtfully on *Khalida*'s little two-ring burner. Rat hitched himself up to the shelf and began washing his whiskers. 'We might have just what you need. There's a boat replacing its engine in the yard right now – the old one is good still, and it could be brought over by fishing boat.'

'Is that a yes?'

'And Rat can come too, of course?'

'He's completely your responsibility,' I said. 'No stealing the ship's biscuits, no sleeping in the spinnaker bag, no falling overboard, and you explain him to the Customs if we see any.'

Anders lifted his glass. 'To the Viking longship's beautiful skipper. I accept your job, with pleasure.'

We shook hands on it. His palm was sticky with grease. He gave me a belated apologetic look, wiped it on his overalls. 'When do we leave?'

'As soon as the wind's right. As soon as we can. We've got a lot to do if we're to fit out a half-derelict longship before mid May.'

He rose. 'I'll warn my father he'll have to do without me until then. I'll be ready to go from the day after tomorrow – no, not Sunday. On Monday.'

'Thanks,' I said.

He raised a hand and shuffled away.

4

We set off a week later. I'd spent the time checking every inch of *Khalida*'s rig and stocking up with stores for the voyage. Anders arrived the night before, just after I'd got back from an evening God-speed Mass in the Cathedral. We had a bacon-and-egg supper together, and a perfunctory game of Scrabble in the burnished glow of the oil lamp. An erratic player, Anders; sometimes he'd plonk down the obvious, sometimes he'd brood for several turns, working towards some coup worth a zillion points. That was the nerd coming out. I wondered what he was like as a chess player. After that they both withdrew to the forepeak, behind their curtain, and made themselves at home. It was strange to have someone else aboard like that. I lay awake for a while, listening to his breathing and Rat's scufflings, then willed myself to sleep.

We motored out of the Bergen channel on the first of the ebb tide, then set our course almost due west, aiming for the centre of Shetland. *Khalida* could do five knots, making it a thirty-hour journey. For the daylight hours we kept two hour watches, one of us above in the cold, the other below keeping warm and passing up hot cups of tea or coffee. The last grey slush of snow in the streets of Bergen was left behind, and the neon-lit clatter of the restaurant. I had *Khalida*'s tiller under my hand once more, the wind against my face, the smell of salt filling my nostrils and the great saucer of pale-blue sea around me under the winter-fretted sky, and my heart sang to the murmur of the water.

We passed our first oil rig just after six, as the sun sank down below the horizon in a glow of peach and pale rose. Anders took midnight till four while I slept, then I took over. Rat stayed to keep me company for a bit, like a plush neck-warmer, then whiffled his way back to his sawdust nest in the forepeak. The stars dazzled around the ribbon of Milky Way, the sails were ghostly above me, and the waves surged below *Khalida*'s forefoot and broke gleaming-white at her beam. We sailed into the darkness until at last the first pale glow appeared on the bowl of sea behind us, and as it grew lighter I began to see a faint mistiness on the horizon, which thickened to a shape like the longship we were going to sail. From here Shetland seemed one island, over a hundred miles long, curving up at the south to the high cliffs of Sumburgh Head, and rising again to Hermaness at the north, with the snow-cone of Ronas Hill in the middle. When Anders came up with a breakfast cup of tea I set him to identifying lighthouses and checking our heading on my rather primitive GPS while I double-checked the tides. Yell Sound at mid-tide was no place for a small yacht, but it was our quickest way through to the west side.

'We're just about right,' Anders reported. 'This course will take us exactly in, and we're thirty miles off. Six hours.'

'Slack tide three o clock,' I said. 'Bang on.'

Anders took over the steering, and I made us a bacon roll each, with an extra rasher for Rat, then went back down for another snatch of sleep. The water flowed at my ear like a lullaby, but for once I wasn't soothed. Alain had been a Shetlander too, half-French, just like me. His father taught French in Mid Yell Junior High, and his mother was a born-and-bred Shetlander with a croft in the south of Yell. I'd written to them, and I should have visited, but I hadn't known what I could say. I still didn't know. Perhaps I could just stay around Brae, not go near the isles, and slide off before they even knew I was there.

Yeah, right.

When I woke, we were in Shetland waters. I made us a cup of soup and a sandwich each, then came up to look. We'd passed the Out Skerries now and the point of Henga Ness was off our starboard bow. The low heather hills were weathered chocolate brown, with camouflage patches of fawn grass. Lower still, the line of cottages followed the shore, each one set facing the sea in a vertical strip of field. The more recent road ran above the houses and down to the shop, to end in a forecourt and petrol pump for the changed way of getting around. The shore glistened olive-brown with kelp thrown up in the March gales.

We motored through Yell Sound at still water, dodged the crossing high-speed ferries and began the long run up the length of North Roe towards the top of Mainland. Now we were giving a cautious distance to spray-black cliffs, topped with fields of stones thrown up by the winter storms, and with pairs of kittiwakes white against grassy ledges slicing along the knobbled volcanic rock. Once we'd rounded the last cliff, topped by the Eshaness Light, we were nearly home; only eight miles to go, diagonally across St Magnus Bay.

Below, Anders was twiddling the radio. A hiss of static resolved itself into a solo fiddle tune, one of the traditional airs with an aching melancholy that pulled me straight back into the world I'd been torn away from when Dad had accepted that job in the Gulf and I'd been sent to Maman. Oh, I could talk to my new French classmates, because Maman had always insisted I spoke French to her, but I didn't have anything to say to them. They were land people, and I was plunged in among them like the selkie wife who'd lived as a seal among currents, suddenly married to an earthling and having to talk of supermarket prices and new sofas with the other wives. I'd made an effort at first; there'd been several nice looking boys in the school that I'd pretended to fancy, and I'd gone shopping with the girls for short skirts and vest tops, but they'd known I was just pretending. They couldn't understand that I was heartsick for the tide flowing past in jagged waves, the sucking noise of the breakers on the shore, the tell-tales fluttering white on *Osprey*'s red jib. When the fiddle tune ended and the announcer's voice began, Mary Blance of Radio Shetland, a great wave of homesickness swept over me and the shore that curved away from us blurred. I blinked the tears away before Anders could see them, and flicked on my mobile phone.

'Does the marina guide give a number for Brae?'

I punched it in as Anders read it out. A Shetland voice answered, Magnie who'd been one of my instructors when I'd been learning to sail. I found myself smiling and going automatically into my native tongue.

'Magnie, is dis dee? It's Cass, Cass Lynch, you mind me? I'm on my way home. Can you find a corner o dis new marina for a peerie yacht that's come ower fae Norroway?'

He gave a great roar of laughter. 'Cass, well, for the love of mercy. Norroway, at this season? Yea, yea, we'll find you a berth. Where are you?'

'Comin round towards Muckle Roe. We'll be wi you in twa hours.'

'I'll be waitin wi the lines,' he promised.

I laid down the phone to find Anders staring. 'Is this Shetland dialect? You sounded as if you were speaking English with a Norwegian accent.'

'Just about what it is,' I agreed.

'And what is 'peerie'? I do not know this one.'

'Small. A little boat.' I unhooked the autopilot and set *Khalida*'s nose for the channel past Vementry Isle. Now I was in home waters, but I didn't look up at the house I'd grown up in. That was enough memories raised. *Khalida* slid on past the island, and into the inlet that led to Brae, a two-mile-long inverted U with a cluster of grey roofs at its end. I could have sailed up to the Boating Club blindfold. Magnie was standing there on the end of the dinghy pontoon, resplendent in an eye-catching Shetland gansey of the old-fashioned seaman's type, a dull blue background with alternate vertical stripes of cable pattern and anchors in white. We paused to drop the mainsail and roll the jib away, then turned into the marina entrance and slipped into the berth he indicated.

'Welcome home, lass,' Magnie said, once we'd tied the last rope. 'How are you doing? Here's a swack young man you've brought wi you.'

I introduced Anders, pointedly saying he was a friend who was crewing for me, and tried to put the kettle on, but Magnie was having none of it. He had a half bottle of Grouse in his pocket. 'We need to toast you comin home at last.'

The three of us squeezed into *Khalida*'s cabin. Magnie looked more tired, drawn about the face. I'd never thought much about ages when he'd been teaching us to sail; he was one of the adults, which simply put him in the ancient bracket. Now I guessed early sixties. His eyes were set in pouched eyelids, his cheeks as rosy as ever, but less round, his curly fair hair more tousled, but he still had his own air of cheery good humour, a man who was never too hurried to stop and have a yarn. 'Here's your good health.' He drained his half-glass of whisky straight off and poured himself another. My whisky burned as it went down. I leaned back against *Khalida*'s wooden shelf and let my breath out in a long sigh.

'So, you're come across to take over the Viking boat,' Magnie said.

I should have known better than to be surprised. Magnie showed rather yellow teeth in a broad grin. 'You're no forgotten me brother David works to the salmon farms at West Burrafirth, where the boat's stored?'

'Ah,' I said.

'I'm been expecting you this three days. I didna ken you were coming by boat, but I shoulda thought o it.' He nudged Anders in the ribs. 'Never went on the land when she could go by sea, our Cass. Now, you'll be wanting a key to the clubhouse.' He fished in his pocket and handed me a key with a wooden label marked MARINA 1. 'You'll see a few changes there. We had this inter-island games, oh, twa-three year ago, with money flowing like water to upgrade our facilities. You could hold a dance in the changing rooms now.'

'Hot showers?' I said.

'Yea, yea. Underfloor heating, even. Now, I'll leave you to settle in. You'll maybe come along me later and tell me all the news wi you.'

'I'll do that,' I promised.

He swung himself over the guard rail and paused on the pontoon arm, his face reddening. He spoke with self-conscious formality. 'I was sorry to read about your man's death. That was a bad thing, a bad thing.'

There was no condemnation in his face or his voice; these things happened at sea. Suddenly I realised I needn't worry here about someone putting my name together with that old report in *Yachting Monthly* or the screaming headlines in the tabloids. The *Shetland Times* would have written a simple report, and everyone in Shetland would have read it. I couldn't evade or pretend it had been someone else. For a moment the thought was terrifying, then liberating, as though I'd pulled clear of a tide race and was sailing free.

Magnie nodded at me, raised a hand to Anders and headed back along the pontoon to his car.

'You don't have drink driving laws here in Shetland, no?' Anders said, watching it pull slowly up the gravel slope by the clubhouse.

'Oh, yes,' I said. 'We just don't have many policemen.'

CHAPTER 3

Over DI Macrae's shoulder, I could see the pier was swarming with police officials. I hoped Magnie'd lie low until he'd pass the breathalyser. The Inspector was entirely unruffled by my silences. He finished tying his line and lifted it up to let the hook dangle, scrutinising the knots against the light, then changed tack. 'I believe you don't get on well with your father, is that right?'

'Not at all,' I said. 'I've just not been in Shetland recently. We speak regularly on the phone.' The bills would prove that: twenty minutes a fortnight, or so.

'You get on well with him, then.' I didn't reply. He made a loop around his finger, and drew it tight. 'I'm sure you were hoping to see a bit of him while you were here, make up for the lost years.'

'Of course.'

'But not to stay at his house? It must have been pretty cold afloat in spring.'

I gave the French shrug again. '*Khalida* is my home.'

ᛋ

We'd spent the next couple of days settling in. Anders was very impressed with Brae's facilities; as the nearest town to the huge oil terminal of Sullom Voe, it had benefited even more than most. The original village of Brae could still be seen running along the U of the shore: a number of small cottages, most of them extended and refurbished within an inch of their lives, the stone-built manse and the kirk beside it, a large house that was now a B&B, the old school, become the community hall, and the former pier, shop and post office, converted into houses. Behind the road that swooped around them were Norwegian style wooden houses, council owned, and a number of new houses, then, sprawling back to the hills, the little boxes that had earned Brae the name of 'toy-town'. There was a population of over a thousand now, and no shortage of things for them to do.

The Boating Club itself had originally been built for the men of the camp, and donated to the village. It stood slightly out of the main village, past the curve of the U. Back in the centre was the leisure centre, with 16m swimming pool, fitness suite, gym and squash court, and, beside it, the school. Brae children could go from nursery to university applications under one roof. Up above the school were the Care Centre for the elderly and the astro-turf football pitch, handily beside the Mid Brae Inn. There was a Fire Station and Police sub-office. There were even Britain's most northerly fish and chip shop and Indian take-away and restaurant. I resolved to sample both while I was here.

For those who preferred to cook their own, there were two shops, the garage and the local community-owned Co-op. I headed along to the garage for Shetland specialities like flaky water biscuits to be eaten with spread-on Lurpak and cheese, and thick Voe oatcakes, and clove rock. The girl behind the till was new, but she turned out to be the peerie sister of a lass I'd been at school with, and the manageress remembered me fine. Then I called at the Brae Building Centre, which sold every tool and DIY aid known to man or even woman, and the owner greeted me as he'd done all through my sailing career, as if I'd never been away: 'Well, now, Cass, is it that time of year already?'

I laughed and nodded. 'Next thing you know, the shalders'll be back.'

Shalder was the Shetland name for oyster-catcher, a large wading bird with an orange beak and evening dress. I used to know it was time to get the varnish out when I heard their peep, peep, peep down at the shore.

'Lass, they're back already,' Neil said. 'They come in February now, the ones that bother to go at all. It's this global warming. We hae geese overwintering an aa, and a fair mess they make o the parks. Folk'll be getting the shotguns out, and having goose for their Christmas dinner.'

'Sounds good,' I said. 'I'd better stay a bit longer, then.'

'That's your own boat that you brought over? Norroway, was it? You'll no be after paint and varnish this time.'

'Not for my boat,' I agreed. I had no doubt at all he'd already been down to the marina for a good look at her. 'I'm going to need gallons of everything for the longship, though. Can we do a deal for a bulk order?'

'I think we likely can,' he said, and prepared to haggle.

After that, I went back twenty yards to the other Brae garage, where I'd helped out on Saturdays as a youngster. Bus transport in Shetland was only any use if you worked nine till five in Lerwick. I needed to buy a car. Hiring wasn't an option, because for that you need to produce a driving licence. I could drive reasonably well at a sensible speed; that would have to do.

'It only needs to last me three months,' I told Angus, and he produced a white ZX that he'd got as part-exchange from someone upgrading to a Berlingo.

'They're very popular in Shetland, you can get six bales of hay or a dozen bags of peats in the back. I don't know how many sheep, nobody's mentioned that.'

Naturally, the first thing Anders and I did once we had wheels was to inspect *Stormfugl.* She was bigger than I remembered, made of dark wood with a high, blind-headed prow, not the traditional long-nosed dragon but a sinister head with an inner circle of screaming, open-toothed mouth. She was much deeper than the *Sea Stallion*, her sides ten feet high as she sat on the ground, and there was a good deal of water sloshing about in her bottom; we let it out in a long, muddy stream and spent the next hour trying to shove a pen-knife into her timbers. All sound. She'd need new rudder hangings, and we'd go over the rigging, but there were no expensive repairs. I phoned the good news to Mr Berg and left Anders to organise his engine while I calculated quantities of anachronistic paint and varnish and talked to the chiefs of the nearest rowing clubs, Eid, Delting and Northmavine.

After that I'd no more excuses for avoiding a visit to the home of my youth. Three miles away. Fourteen years ago.

I drove out of the marina, turned left and left again and drove slowly along the single-track road that led to Muckle Roe. This was the road I'd gone to school on, sandwiched between Inga and Martin in a rattling minibus. Every twist and turn was familiar, although there were more houses than I remembered, spaced out at hundred metre intervals on each side of the road. The banks were lined with clumps of grey-green spikes, daffodil leaves with the first yellow splitting the long buds. I drove below the modern standing stone the roadymen had set up when they'd re-tarred the road, and above the older one set out on its headland to guide the Neolithic fishermen home, past the corbelled white height of Busta House Hotel, and at last, a mile from the boating club, across the cattle grid and into proper country. Below me, the green fields sloped down to the pebbled shore and the polished steel water; above the road was the dark green of the first heather shoots. There were a number of hill sheep grazing, traditional coloured Shetland sheep, not much bigger than a collie dog, and black, rust-brown, speckled. A good number of them were down at the road verge, enjoying the new grass and putting paid to the first primroses. No lambs as yet; they wouldn't come till late April, although I'd spotted one or two earlier cross-breeds in sheltered green parks.

I drove across the Muckle Roe bridge and along the single track road until the Y-shape of Swarback's Minn opened out in front of me, with the voe down to Eid clear and open, and the deep channel of the Rona ahead, and the Atlantic breaking on my right hand against red granite cliffs and sea stacks. I drew into the next passing place, switched the engine off and sat there a moment, arms across the steering wheel, chin resting on my hands, and looked out.

Now my childhood was spread before me. Behind me was the long arm of Busta Voe, where Martin and I had sailed my Mirror dinghy every summer day, launching from the red-sand beach just ahead. I'd paddled in that burn spreading across the sand, caught little fish in my lime-green net, and scooped up jam-jars of frogspawn, which Maman had made me pour back. *'Je ne veux pas de grenouilles à la maison.'* Inga, Martin and I had made housies in the roofless walls of the old croft, and lit fires on the beach with purloined matches. We'd gone swimming on summer days, teeth chattering after three minutes in the water, and skimmed the flat beach stones to try to beat Martin's record of nine bounces.

It was up this hill that I'd stormed until I was breathless when Dad had suddenly announced that the oil company had asked him to go to the Gulf, and I was to leave all my life and friends here and join Maman. The raging hadn't done any good, of course.

Dad had got more authoritarian and I'd got more angry, and we'd stopped speaking by the time he marched me onto the Sumburgh plane. By the time he'd got back from the Gulf, I was in Scotland, going from one ship to the next.

After Alain's death, I'd phoned him. Not to talk about that, just because. But I hadn't gone home.

Our drive-end where I'd waited for the bus day after day was fifty yards ahead. The grey tarmac of the single-track road went on past, to Inga and Martin's house. After them there was only the wide Atlantic. I wondered now if that was part of what had driven bourgeois town-dwelling Maman away. She'd been the selkie wife in reverse, brought up in the chalk-silver Poitevin countryside of fields fringed by elegant, upright poplars, and suddenly trapped by winter storms that frothed the sea up and threw the spray at the windows until they were white with encrusted salt. Perhaps she'd have stayed if Dad had built his beautiful new house with all mod cons in Brae, where the shops and leisure centre were within walking distance, and Lerwick was only twenty-one miles of dual carriageway away.

No. She'd never have stayed.

I walked briskly down to the open front door.

I'd expected to find it smaller, and so it was, in the disconcerting way of a cliche come true. I crouched slightly and it became familiar again, the brown-tile lino, the white-painted walls with the shelf for the postman to leave the letters on. Radio 4 was playing, and the house smelt of lemon polish. I called 'Hello' and Jessie Matthewson came out to greet me, a duster in one hand and another slung over her round shoulder, making an orange splash against the pink-checked nylon overall. There were two cans of spray in the pouch pocket, Pledge and Windowlene, just as there had always been.

Jessie had been our cleaner as far back as I could remember. She lived overlooking the marina, in a big, square-built house called Efstigarth that had once been the farm for Busta House, and was now a B&B. Maman would tell me to keep out from under her feet, and Jessie'd echoed her, 'Now, lass get out from under my feet!' but with a smile that told me she didn't really mean it. She'd tell me stories as she worked: about the time she'd spilled ink on her jotter at school and got the cane, or how her father had taken her out fishing and helped her land a skate as big as herself. She'd talked about her mother and father, her grandparents, her aunts and uncles, her cousins all the way to fourth cousins once removed and her neighbours, to say nothing of the strange habits of her B&B guests. She'd follow the stories with a sweetie and a hug, then chase me out so she could mop the floor.

Now she'd gone from resolute middle-age to discouraged elderly, as if she'd decided that nothing good would ever happen to her. The curly hair that I remembered as glossily black was an indeterminate fake-fur brown, and there were tired lines running from her nose to the corner of her rather small mouth. Bruised shadows gave a blue hollow under her rather small, dark eyes, which widened and brightened at the sight of me standing there.

'Now, then, Cassie! My, what a bonny lass you've turned out. Come in, come in. I wasn't sure when you'd come over. I thought it might be yesterday, and I'd miss you.'

Damn it, I wasn't going to apologise for not going hot-foot to Dad's door.

'How are you, Jessie? It's good to see you again.' I gave her a kiss on the cheek, which seemed to please her.

'Oh, doing away. Busy, you ken. I'm still cleaning here, and at the school every evening, and then I go once a week to Mrs Cheyne over at the Grind, and once to Inga Anderson, Inga Nicolson that was, that was used to be your best pal at the school, to keep the peerie thing for her while she goes to the swimming pool and the gym, although I don't know if I'll keep doing that much longer.'

'Inga's got a baby?' I said.

'Lass, she has three – the two lasses are well through the school.' A sideways look, as if she was checking whether I'd heard some rumour. 'Her man's Charlie Anderson, he's a cousin o mine through my midder. But–' Her nostrils flared in disapproval, and she gave her head a little toss. I wondered what this Charlie had been up to – another woman? She'd always been very strong on keeping marriage vows: *It's no just for a fun, du kens, du has to tak the rough wi the smooth. Things dinna turn out the way you expect when you're young, and you just have to get on wi them.* 'Well, never mind, never mind.' She finished hastily, as if sorry she'd started on that one, 'Now, how did you find your longship? What condition is she in?'

'Fair,' I said. 'A bit of work needing done, but nothing too major.'

'I'd heard that, yes. You'll be pleased to be in charge of her. That's a good chance for you, and a fine thing for the place, that's what your dad said when he heard about it being filmed here. "A lot of jobs," he said. "Repairing the boat, and crew for her, and the film crew will all need accommodation and catering. Early season, too, so there should be no bother finding space for them."'

'Have you many coming to you?'

She flushed; a fleeting, furtive look crossed her face. 'I'll likely be busy later.'

'Everyone'll be busy later,' I said, 'once the film lot arrive. By the time the camera crew and best boys and sound men and all are squeezed in, there won't be a spare bed in the place.'

'You're fairly right,' she agreed, but didn't expand on it, as I'd have expected, with the numbers she'd got, and full details of each person that their mother could hardly have bettered. Instead she went pink, shot a nervous glance towards the sitting room and began twiddling the duster round in her work-worn hands. 'I have just the one, this Baker lass, she's taken the whole house – but you'll likely ken all about that.' Her cheeks went from pink to crimson. 'Now, your dad's just through by. He'll be pleased to see you.'

She bustled me through the kitchen into what Maman had called the *salon* and Dad the living room. It hadn't changed either. The square-cornered leather suite, the moss-velvet curtains, the Chinese rug, had been made to last, and Maman's baby grand piano still took up a quarter of the room. Dad was sitting in his usual armchair, reading the business section of yesterday's *Irish Independent*. All I could see of him was the long legs, black trousered, and shining black shoes.

'Now, Dermot, look who's arrived.'

'The prodigal daughter,' I said cheerfully. 'Hi, Dad, how are you?'

The newspaper was lowered instantly, folded and laid aside in one quick movement. Nothing had changed him either. His hair was dark and thick as ever above his rather beaky nose, and he sprang up like a two-year old.

'Cassie! Now, then, girl, it's good to see you!' He gave me a bear-hug, slightly awkward, then stood back to look at me. 'Well. Well now. It's good to see you. You're looking well. Did you have a good journey from Norway? How did you find the *Stormfugl?*'

It seemed everyone knew what I was doing better than I knew it myself. I sat down on the edge of one of the leather armchairs, facing the picture window that gave a sweeping view of the sea. 'She's good.'

'That's fine, that's fine. We have to toast this.' He rose and went to the glass-fronted drinks cabinet, took out two glasses. 'A gin and tonic? A sherry?'

'I'll have a whisky with you,' I said.

He poured himself a generous measure and me a lady's finger. 'Jessie, you'll drink with us, won't you?' He poured her a sherry. 'To your new command.'

'Your good health,' I countered.

Now I had the chance to get a good look at him, I could see tiny differences. His face was heavier than I remembered, harder, as if the businessman had taken over, the jaw and neck thickened to a stubborn line, the set of the brows determined. If I was meeting him for the first time now, as my new skipper – and I didn't see him being satisfied with mate - I'd walk warily. There were white hairs at his ears and in his brows. His blue eyes, that blazing Irish blue I'd inherited, had faded to the misted blue of the far horizon, but they were quick, alert, ticking off the changes in me. His voice was as vigorous as ever, bouncing cheerfully off the glass of the cabinet and setting the piano wires buzzing, and he was grinning with satisfaction.

'Now, girl, it's fine to have you back home. Fine. Where are you thinking to sleep?'

An odd, sly eagerness about the way he said that. I'd been wondering if I should be asking if we could move into the house, for Anders' sake, because *Khalida* was still pretty chilly at night, but suddenly I decided against that. I'd broken free, and I'd stay that way. The nights were getting warmer, and I could always buy a fleece blanket.

'Aboard, of course,' I said.

'Of course, of course.' I couldn't read his face. 'Have you got a crew for *Stormfugl* yet?'

'Anders and I,' I said.

'Anders, that's your young man?'

I was going to get very fed up of correcting that one. 'My engineer,' I said clearly.

There was a fleeting look of disappointment, followed by a smooth recover. 'I bumped into him at the Co-op – well, someone pointed him out, so I introduced myself. Nice young man. Seems to know what he's talking about when it comes to engines.'

As if Dad did. I reminded myself that I came home as a conquering heroine, and swallowed the '*Dad*, I know what I'm doing' that rose to my throat. 'I need to get one more crewman, a general deck-hand. Someone well used to boats, maybe a retired fisherman.' I could afford to throw a sop to Cerberus. 'You don't know anyone?'

He looked at Jessie. 'Well, it happens I do. Jessie was just wondering about that the other day, weren't you? Her husband's at a bit of a loose end these days since he gave the boat up.'

Jessie nodded. 'Under my feet.' She reddened again and spoke stiffly. 'He heard about the longship on the wireless and thought I could maybe mention that he'd be interested, if you were looking for someone. He's been a fisherman all his days, until this Government quota nonsense. Conserving fish stocks, as if there weren't just as many fish in the sea as ever there were.'

'He worked a shellfish boat too for a bit, didn't he?' I said. An intimate aquaintance with the cliffs and stacks around Swarback's Minn could be very useful. I tried to act like a skipper. 'I may need to advertise the post, but tell him to come along and talk to me at the marina. I'll be there this evening, if he's free. Here.' I scribbled my mobile number on the telephone pad and gave it to her.

'Then that's sorted,' Dad said. 'What time is it? Here, Cassie, let me take you out to lunch. Busta Hotel or the Mid Brae?'

I went for Busta, and we drove the two miles back towards Brae. Busta House Hotel

still felt like someone's home inside, in spite of the board with advertisements for wildlife tours and the little reception hatch with its brass bell. The hall was hung with watercolours of local scenes, and opened up into a wider space, with a substantial carved staircase leading upwards. A Jacobean chair in black oak stood in one corner, and an array of waterproofs hung on the pegs by the back door, with their rubber boots lined up in pairs beneath them.

Dad motioned me into the bar, where tiny windows were set in thick, whitewashed walls, and blackened beams gloomed above our heads. We sat down at one of the beaten copper tables. Dad nodded to an older couple facing each other at the table across from us, and received a nod in return, but with a slight reserve, I thought, as if he'd done something unpopular recently – maybe they'd come out the worse of some business deal he'd been involved in, or maybe it was just the Shetland dubiousness about 'oil folk fae sooth' lingering more than forty years after the first barrelfuls had flowed on to Shetland land.

'So,' I said, once we'd discussed the menu, Dad had ordered steak, I'd gone for local scallops in cheese sauce, and Dad had chosen a bottle of red, 'what are you up to now? Are you still involved with Sullom Voe?'

He spread his hands. 'Oh, from time to time, when they need a consultant in my area. No, I'm one of the directors of a totally different company now, Shetland Eco-Energy.'

The name rang a bell. 'Green energy?'

'Wind farms. That's the future, girl, not oil, and Shetland's the place for it. A turbine here will produce double, three times the electricity of one on the mainland. We're developing a proposal to site Europe's biggest wind farm right here. We're negotiating with the Government right now to lay a cable to take the power down to the Scottish mainland, and once we've got that assurance we can get going. It's not just Shetland that'll never need oil or coal again, we could fuel half of Scotland. Just think of that.'

I'd done the older couple an injustice. The prejudice against incomer oil men had died out long ago. This was a new fight.

'Where,' I asked, 'is this wind farm to go?'

'Along the central spine of the mainland here.' Dad drank half of his glass of wine in one go. 'We're not trying to hide anything. It will be big. The turbines will be visible, and some folk aren't happy about that.' He leaned forward, the businessman pushing the deal through. 'See, girl, times have changed. It's not a matter of spoiling the countryside, it's more important than that. What the folk who are against it aren't seeing is that it's a matter of survival. Things could be desperate if the political situation changed just a little bit. Where do people on the mainland get their gas from, for their central heating and cooking? Russia, the bulk of them. It all looked dodgy for a bit after that diplomat was murdered. It wouldn't take much to get the cold war back, and then where'd they be? Power rationing.' He turned his head towards the older couple, raised his voice slightly. 'Renewables, that's the future, but tide turbines aren't half as developed as wind power, and we need that power too soon to wait.'

Then he turned back to me, with a sudden change of mood. 'Now, we're celebrating. No business talk. Have you heard from your mother recently?'

'Not very recently,' I said.

'What's she singing just now, *Zais*? I think that's this month. One of the castles, Chenonceau, Azay-le-Rideau, one of those. She's a Sybil, the great priestess of love. They made a recording, you should listen to it.'

I wondered how he knew, imagined him googling Maman's name to find her next performance. 'Life's too short,' I said.

He shook his head at me. 'Now, now, Cassie, you've not to be like that. I won't say it didn't take me a while to get into the style of it–' His Irish accent was strengthening now. I wondered if he habitually drank this much in the middle of the day. 'But singing to her is like the water to you. It's in her blood. I knew that from the first moment I clapped eyes on her.'

I'd heard this bit already. He'd been supervising the work at the new Lille Opera, and he'd seen her in the chorus.

'It was her life, you know. Pretty as a picture, she was, with this cloud of dark hair around her face, just like yours would be if you didn't tie it back, and a waist that tiny I could span it with one hand. You wouldn't want her to give it all up and come back home just as she's making a name for herself, now, would you?'

I wasn't sure if he even believed it himself. He must have seen my scepticism, for he changed tack quickly.

'But of course it's hard being alone, very hard on me.' The confident voice went suddenly uncertain, and I thought of the way Jessie had glanced at the sitting room door as she'd spoken about her lodger. *Just the Baker lass – but you'll likely ken all about that.'* Was he trying to break the news of a new girlfriend? Perhaps that was why he'd wondered about where I'd be sleeping; not reeling me in, but fencing me out. Well, that suited me.

If he was, he bottled out. 'Now, then, are you still getting to Mass?'

'Of course.' It was one part of my upbringing I'd kept, regular attendance somewhere between Dad's rather fierce determination and Maman's more casual approach, as if she'd just happened to drift by the church as the bell was ringing, and come in on spec. 'My local's the cathedral in Bergen. How's the parish here going?'

'Growing, girl, growing. We've got a whole community of Poles here now, even read the Gospel in Polish as well as English. Couldn't make head nor tail of it at first, but I'm starting to pick out words now. Fine bunch of people, a real asset to the community.' Dad had all sorts of strange prejudices, but xenophobia wasn't one of them. 'Shall I pick you up on my way past?'

No way. 'I'm not sure what I'll be doing on Sundays, but I've got the car, if I'm free.'

We ate in silence for a bit. It was my turn to choose a topic. 'Has anyone seen poor Barbara Pitcairn recently?'

Dad gave me a blank look.

'The ghost here. Looking for her child.' It was a sad story. The penniless young cousin who'd married the son and heir had had her marriage lines taken from her by his mother, and she'd been treated as a servant. When she'd had a child, Madam Busta had taken him too, sent Barbara to live in Lerwick, and raised him up as her own.

'Oh, that,' Dad snorted. 'Girl, there are people here who'll see anything after the second whisky.'

'Inga saw her, when she was working here.' I hadn't meant to get into an argument, couldn't stop myself. 'A white-faced girl in old-fashioned clothes, searching in the room. She just vanished when Inga came in.'

Dad shook his head. 'Imagination. Liver. A touch of the sun.' I had to admit, too, looking back, that Inga could have been just winding me up, to see how much I'd swallow. She'd had a sly, secretive streak that meant you couldn't totally trust her, and at the time I'd been more and more involved in sailing, leaving her to find her own pals at the weekends. Natalie What's-her-name, who'd wanted Inga to be her best, her only pal, and edged me out. I tried another topic.

'Are their puddings still as good as they used to be? Do you suppose they still do cranachan?'

'We can ask,' Dad said, and called the girl over. They did, and it was as good as I'd remembered, the smoky taste of the whisky colouring the cream, and the raspberries tart in the oatmeal. I ate every last scrap and vowed to myself to try it aboard ship, while we were moored in the marina.

I had a salary now, and wanted to pay the bill, but Dad wasn't having it. 'Now, Cassie.' His face twisted, vulnerable. 'You've not been home this long time, girl. You invite me over to your boat, now, and make me a meal there.'

He'd been over thirty when he'd had me. He was over sixty now, an old man. I felt ashamed of my hardness, and took my credit card back. 'That's a deal.'

In the car park, he paused with one hand on his car door-handle. 'You have fun with your longship, now. I told Berg she'd be a good buy. His company's involved with ours, you know, so when you talked to them in the restaurant of course he linked you up with me, and gave me a ring.'

Shetland Eco-Energy. Dad's company. I stood stock-still, a cold fury swelling inside me. Miracles didn't happen, after all. Berg had recognised my name, in the Shetland context. He'd gone back to his house and phoned my dad, and dad had praised me up, and probably called in a favour or two, and it hadn't been my brass neck or my qualifications which had given me the job, but the old boys' network. It was a bitter pill to swallow.

And as if that wasn't bad enough, Berg would have told him where we'd met. 'Your daughter was waiting at table in our restaurant.' Just as Dad had predicted all those years ago, taking all sorts of menial jobs to keep myself afloat in between charters. Not a success story but a failure, desperate enough to beard total strangers in restaurants.

I forced my shaking legs to move again. 'I'll have fun,' I said. And he'd manoeuvred me into inviting him for a meal. He could damned well take me as he found me. 'I'll give you the grand tour of *Khalida*, once I've got the longship repairs under way.'

'I'd like that,' he said. Only a suspicious daughter would have heard the smooth satisfaction in his voice, the businessman who'd sneaked the deal across.

He got back into his 4x4 and started the engine. 'Empires to run, girl, empires to run.'

It might be through him that I'd come home, but I resolved, as I shut the car door, that I'd make damned sure he didn't run me.

ᛋ

I hadn't tried to phone Dad earlier, because I knew he'd still be out cold, after last night's bender. I was sorry now that I hadn't just kept ringing until he'd answered. I should have told him myself that Maree was dead.

Chapter 4

I didn't say that, but I'd said more than enough. It was the way the Inspector sat there, looking like everybody's favourite bosun, tying his flies with the air of someone who had all day to hang around.

He nodded. 'Now, once you'd had a look at the boat, *Stormfugl,* you hired–'Another glance at his notebook. ' - Gibbie Matthewson as an extra hand and brought her round to the jetty here.'

It was a relief not to have to stonewall. Crew or not, I didn't care what I gave away about Gibbie.

'The world's worst grump,' I said. 'Dad's cleaner's husband.'

ᛋ

He'd come round to *Khalida* the next evening. 'Jessie told me you were looking for an extra hand.'

'We'll need someone once we get the longship launched,' I agreed. I wasn't sure I wanted it to be him though. He had one of those faces my Irish gran used to say would turn the milk sour just by looking at it, with a long nose that twitched as if he was smelling something dead under the floorboards. Like Magnie, he wore a traditional Shetland jumper in shades of blue and stripes of dazzling white, and beneath his face it looked like a clown's waistcoat on an undertaker. He was very tall, and strong-looking, with big, calloused hands that clenched and unclenched as he spoke. His voice had that flat tone of poor hearing. Beneath the sleeked-back hair his eyes were grey and quick, darting here and there, focusing on me, flicking to *Khalida*, back to me again. If it hadn't been for the memory of Jessie's years of kindness I wouldn't have had him nearer *Stormfugl* than a sea-league, but I knew what it had cost Jessie's Shetland pride to ask for a job for him, and I couldn't knock her back. I had no doubts about his ability as a seaman, or his knowledge of the area, and that was what I needed him for.

'It'll just be a deckhand post – I know that's well below your qualifications.'

A shrug. 'You need a man who knows the area, Dermot was saying. This longship of yours is just the size of my *Azure*. I'm well used to handling something that size, taking it into smaller bays.'

'We're still getting her ready for sea – it'd be good if you were able to help with that. After that, we'll do the sea trials, and bring her round to Brae.'

He was a good worker, but after the first couple of days both Anders and I made sure we were in another part of the boat, so as not to have to listen to his running commentary. He seemed to spend his evenings watching TV just so he could disapprove of the example these soaps were setting to the bairns with their bad language and immorality, the strange things people cooked, in his day he had mince and tatties and glad of it, the way politicians were running the world. He was worst on Mondays. It turned out he was the caretaker of the local hall and so the person who had to clear up after discos. 'Floor just clarted with dried beer. Spewings everywhere and worse. They sell condoms in the lasses toilets now, did you ken that? If my faither could have seen that–'

We quickly learned not to mention the EU. He blamed them with an intensive hatred for the loss of his *Azure*. 'No fish in the sea, there's plenty o fish in the sea. This Spanish and French trawlers, they come and fill their holds, don't they? You don't hear any bruck about quotas for them. When I fished first, in the sixties, well, you could barely get a berth in Lerwick or Scalloway for the boats. Peterhead, Buckie, Stonehaven, Portree. The whole north of Scotland, the men lived by the fishing. Now you're not going to tell me all those fish got wiped out. Na, na. It's this foreign boats. If this Westminster government was any use they'd take control of our waters again. I'm telling you, I'm voted for Jo Grimond all my days, but this last two times I went for the SNP. We need our own government, and a strong line on what belongs to us.'

It was odd he'd wanted the job. I was a woman skipper, and Anders was young enough to be one of the bairns whose parents didn't know what he got up to. Maybe Jessie wanted him out from under her feet. I didn't blame her. Anders and I gritted our teeth over tea-break and lunch, and quoted him to each other in the privacy of *Khalida* of an evening, and with him working too then *Stormfugl* was ready for the sea in the first days of May.

We launched her on the fifth of May, when the forecast had promised us our first real summer day. The crane lifted her, belly swinging above us, and lowered her, inch by inch, back into her element. Father Michael said a blessing over her, then we all clambered aboard. My dozen rowers stood to their oars; I took the helm, and Anders started the engine and pumps. Cameras flashed. We headed out through the sectored lights and past the reefs into the Atlantic curve of St Magnus Bay. Ah, they were seamen, those long-dead Vikings. She breasted the waves as if she was rejoicing in the sea. We raised the yard, and the ochre and red striped cotton sail billowed out, caught the wind, and *Stormfugl* rose with it, the helm suddenly lightening. I looked forward at the milky horizon, at the great curve of sail above me, and sent up a thanksgiving for the day.

There was a flotilla waiting for us at the mouth of the Rona, local boats; one even had a miniature brass cannon aboard, and gave us a gun salute as we entered Busta Voe. We sailed up to the club with them clustered around us, white-sailed yachts, fibre-glass motor launches, Mirrors flying their coloured spinnakers and the pink-sailed Picos from the newly-started sailing classes, with Magnie circling them in the guard boat. We rolled the sail well clear of the marina, Anders started the engine, Gibbie hung out the fenders and, heart in mouth, I edged her into the pier. She didn't like the engine, but she was too well built not to go where she was steered. A touch of reverse, and she halted exactly where I wanted her. Gibbie stepped onto the pier and began tying up. Anders and I exchanged triumphant grins. We'd made it. Then we laid the gangplank and invited everyone aboard.

The boaty people were first, of course, and the reporter and photographer from the *Shetland Times*, but there were local folk there as well, including an old school-friend, Dodie, whose dad had had a job at Sullom. His family had come from Yell to stay in Brae for his secondary school years, and his only ambition then-a-days, to the despair of our teachers, had been to be a ferryman on the Yell ferry. If anyone suggested going further afield, he'd concede that the Unst or Fetlar ferries might make a change, so long as he didn't have to stay overnight. Now, it seemed, he'd achieved his ambition. He was working full-time on *Daglion*.

'Now, then, Cass, it's fine to see you. I saw you going up Yell sound. Well, I didna ken it was you at first, but I spoke to Jamie o the Coastguard over the VHF, and he was able to tell me whatna peerie yacht it was that had come over from Norroway.' He looked around at *Stormfugl*'s shining varnish. 'This is a fine boat, this.'

'Come down when your shifts allow,' I said, 'and we'll take you out.'

I left him to inspect, and looked over the crowd for other people I ought to know. I wouldn't have noticed the dark woman with the pushchair if her toddler hadn't made a break for it, racing towards the ship in a flurry of dungareed legs and golden curls. I stopped him before he could go over the edge of the pier and offered him my hand for the gangplank. He clutched his little arms tightly around himself and shook his head. 'No hand.'

'Then you don't come aboard,' I said. 'No hand, no boat.'

He peered up at my face, and saw I meant it. One grubby hand came out to clutch mine. His mother abandoned his empty pushchair and came after him.

'Thanks, Cass. He goes so quickly.'

I found myself looking at Inga.

Older? Yes. Her velvet-dark eyes were the same, round and liquid, like a seal's when it pops its head out of the water to watch you, but her skin had coarsened from the teenage wild-rose I remembered to a weathered fawn, and there were a dozen lines running across her forehead. She was curvily plump under her Lycra t-shirt. The make–up she used to spend hours applying had been abandoned, and the dark hair she'd straightened with tongs and sprayed to a glossy shine had been cut short. The wind had tousled it back to its natural curl, and the sun brought out that purplish sheen of dye.

'Inga!' I said.

She nodded. 'Admit it, if I hadn't spoken you'd not have known me. I've grown old and fat. That's what domestic boredom does for you.'

'What's your peerie boy's name?'

'Charlie, after his dad.' She made a grab at him as he started towards the side of the boat. 'Come here, Charlie.'

'I'll take him to look over,' I offered. 'Hand again, Charlie.'

The little hand clutched mine again, and I felt a pang of longing. This was what Inga had, this small hand coming so confidently into yours. Someone who loved you and trusted you; someone you'd always be there for. I held on to him as he clambered onto one of the rowing benches and stood looking down at the water glinting below him. 'Nice,' he said clearly.

'Yes, it is nice,' I agreed. He gave me an intelligent glance, pleased that I'd understood, and launched into a babble. I managed to distinguish 'boat' in among it.

'She's a Viking boat,' I said. 'A longship.'

'You're so lucky,' Inga said. 'I heard the interview on Radio Shetland. It sounded as if you'd been all over the world. I've never been anywhere.'

'Not even Scotland?' I asked.

She shook her head. 'Only visits. I didn't go to uni. I got married instead, and had children. Oh, they're great, of course I wouldn't be without them, but there are times when I'm stuck in the house all evening, and Charlie – big Charlie, my husband–' Her voice snagged like a kink of rope reaching a block, then straightened itself again. I tried to remember what Jessie had said. Charlie was having an affair? 'Well, he's at sea all this month, and I canna leave the house, no even for five minutes, because of the bairns. I'm even taking an interest in the garden–' She made a face, mouth turned down incredulously, then laughed, one of Inga's lightning changes from grumble to gaiety. 'Listen to me complaining. I wouldn't change my bairns for all the tea in China. Peeriebreeks here'll be at toddler group soon, and I'll be able–' There was that flash of something furtive again. 'Able to go for a swim or a game of badminton and get my waist back. Then once he's at school I can go back to work.' Another laugh, a quick glance at Anders. 'I may not get your perks, though. He's like something out of a Norse myth. Is he..?'

I shook my head. 'Just a friend.'

'Always a good start. Or is there someone else?'

I thought of Alain and forced the thought away. 'Nobody special.'

You can't lie to someone who knew you at school. She flicked a quick glance at me. 'Tell me another time. Which is your boat, the one you sailed from Norway?'

I pointed. 'The little one at the end of the pontoon. *Khalida*. Come and have a cup of tea aboard once this circus is over.'

'I'll do that.' She gave me a quick, intent look. 'I was wanting to have a word with you anyway, about–' The dark lashes lifted. She gave a tiny tilt of the chin towards Gibbie. 'Will you be about tomorrow, say about three?'

I nodded.

'I'll come over then. Come on, peeriebreeks.' She scooped Charlie up, tucked him under one arm, his legs flailing behind her back, and headed briskly back across the gangplank. The screams intensified as she strapped him into his pushchair, then diminished as she marched him off.

We sat in *Khalida*'s cockpit the next day, the sun warm on our faces. Anders had gone for a walk along the shore, taking Rat with him. Peerie Charlie had stomped off below; he'd tried out each of the berths in turn, and was now taking all the tins out of one locker and laying them in a line on the floor. That seemed a harmless amusement, so I left him to it.

'I just wanted to warn you to maybe keep an eye on Gibbie Matthewson,' Inga said. She looked far more like her old self again today, with a fitted fleece in slimming charcoal, and full war-paint emphasising those dark eyes. Her skin was smoothed over with foundation, and her lips pillar-box scarlet. I didn't think it was for my benefit. She had that something-nice-happening-today air; she stretched back against the cockpit rail like a seal basking on its rock. 'My mother-in-law, see, she's some kind of cousin of Jessie's. She said Jessie was really unhappy about asking you for a berth for him, but Gibbie nagged her into it. Insisted.'

'But why,' I asked, 'should it be so odd that he wanted to be a crew aboard?'

'Eco stuff,' Inga said. 'He's rabid about it, haven't you noticed?'

'No,' I said. 'We've had the youth of today, and the Government, and the EU.' I was trying to remember if we'd ever spoken about eco matters in front of him. Probably, given the film's sponsors. Yes, we had, and recently; we'd been speaking about Favelle's Grenpeace film. Unusually, Gibbie hadn't commented at all, just grunted, drunk his tea and been the first back to work.

Inga grimaced. 'Eco stuff is all those rolled together, with him. He blames the Greenpeace lot and the do-gooders and the tree protesters for 'all this bruck about no fish left in the sea'. He was particularly angry about that film Favelle did. You know, the poisoning the seas one that really highlighted the issues. It was after that the Government got tougher on quotas.'

'I think that's a coincidence,' I said. 'I don't see the Prime Minister saying, 'It was on a movie, we need to act now.'

'Gibbie puts the two together,' Inga said. 'Cass, I feel I'm being right melodramatic here, but he's got this hatred of all Favelle stands for, and the only reason I can think of that he'd be so keen to be involved is that he's out to make trouble in some way. If I was you, I wouldn't let him work on anything important – I mean, nothing that would sabotage a day's shooting or something like that.'

'He could do that so easily,' I said. 'Suddenly letting the sail down in the wrong place. Sticking the engine out of gear.'

'But you could watch him, now you know,' Inga said. 'I don't have any proof of anything. It's just really odd he should want to be involved. *He's* really odd.'

I'd talked to Anders about it, that evening. Gibbie was sleeping at home, of course, so once he was off the ship the next day we went over all the rigging with a fine tooth comb.

'Did you find anything?' the Inspector asked.

I shook my head. 'Nothing I could prove. Just odd things, a block rigged the wrong way round, and a sheave jammed with a small piece of cloth. After that we never let him work alone on the boat, and we took it in turns to sleep aboard *Stormfugl* so that there wouldn't be any funny business at night.'

'I wondered about that,' the Inspector said. 'Why you needed a night watchman, up here.'

'Gibbie,' I agreed.

'Obsessive,' the Inspector repeated. 'Did he know the dead woman?'

The truth sounded bad; I gave it, reluctantly. 'She was staying in his house.'

There was a silence, broken by the officer who'd been interviewing Anders coming in. The DI rose in one smooth movement. I listened to the rattle of the ice maker behind the bar, and wondered what Anders had said.

When he came back in, though, the Inspector's face still had that air of friendly good nature, a peaceable soul with all the time in the world. He fished in his tin once more and took out a little packet of new hooks, the barbs steel-bright. 'There's a brown trout in our river that I'm determined to lure out. Well, now, I'd need to know more about the dead woman, and the other film people. The Second Unit arrived first, in late May, is that right?'

I nodded.

'I've never been a film star, so you'll need to tell me a bit more about how it all works.'

'Money,' I said. 'The big star, the big director, they cost. What the studios do is shoot as much as possible before they arrive, using another director and stand-ins. That's the Second Unit. In this case, they did most of the shots of the boat, and some background scenery shots as well, I think – I wasn't involved in these.'

He made the Mmhmm assent sound. 'Lend me your finger for a moment, would you? Just for this first knot.'

I put my finger on the slippery line. He asked, as he was tying the knot around it, 'This Maree Baker arrived with them?'

I nodded. The clear line closed around my finger. I slid it free.

'What was your first impression of her?'

'Her height,' I said. 'How long her legs were. I was sitting down on the pier, so I was looking up at her, and that was my first impression.'

ᛋ

The Second Unit was directed by Michael Ashford, and they arrived in a white transit van an hour before low water, straight off the overnight ferry from Scotland. It rattled to a halt and a dozen scruffs in tattered jeans and bright jumpers got out from the tail doors, all clutching large black electronic boxes or trailing flexes, and eyeing up *Stormfugl* as if she was a cross between an adventure playground and a problem to be solved. The man in the passenger seat strode down the pier and put his hand out.

'Cass Lynch? I'm Michael Ashford. Pleased to meet you.'

I was hard put to it not to go 'Wow!' Michael was like a hero from *Pirates of the Caribbean* era, with glossily brown hair falling in a smooth curve to his shoulders, an oval face, dark eyes under arched brows and a faint hint of moustache over sensually red lips. No, not a pirate, a doomed cavalier or a romantic poet. There was intensity in the dark eyes, a melancholy curve of the lip. The likeness was finished off with an open-necked white shirt and a dark brocade waistcoat. 'It'll be a pleasure working with you, Cass.' The voice was south London, overlaid with American. He held my hand just a fraction too long, and I felt my cheeks go hot, blushing like a schoolgirl. Get a grip, Cass. You're too old for a holiday romance.

'How d'you do?' I managed. 'This is Anders Johansen, *Stormfugl*'s engineer.'

He gave Anders a long, thoughtful look, the same intense handshake. Anders' cheeks reddened. I moved quickly to Gibbie, standing silent and sullen behind me.

'Gibbie Matthewson, our local waters expert.' Gibbie gave a sour nod, his hands staying in his pockets.

Michael turned to look behind him as a rattle and thump across the boating club cattle grid announced the arrival of an articulated van with 'Lighting Systems' blazoned along the side. 'Great to meet you all. Now, we'll just get started.'

In ten minutes he had his crew spread out around the boat, and then seemed to be everywhere at once, indicating a light here, another there, and conferring with the cameramen on how exactly they'd achieve the shots in his storyboard. I watched for half an hour or so, partly out of interest, partly to check that they were leaving operational bits of the ship alone. I didn't want to lower the sail and find five thousand quid worth of camera dropping with it.

Various cars were coming and going, so I didn't particularly notice the Bolts car hire firm red Fiesta come down to the hard standing. I was watching from the pier, back against one of the bollards, legs stretched along concrete that was almost warm in the May sun, when a Gone-with-the-Wind voice behind me said, 'Hey.'

Maree.

My first thought was how tall she was. She was wearing those really skinny jeans, and her legs seemed to go on for miles. Above them was a big, loose jumper, equally designer, with a v-neck that slipped towards one tanned shoulder. Then, of course, I noticed her likeness to Favelle: the same oval face, with that long, curved, enigmatic smile, but Maree's upper lip was fuller, redder, and her green eyes were cat-like under dark arched brows. The biggest difference was that she had short, dark curls instead of Favelle's trademark long red-gold hair. Her hands were the same elegant shape as Favelle's, but tanned with short nails, the hands of someone who's willing to do things aboard a boat. She was expensive and groomed in her wave of perfume, and she made me feel like I'd felt on my first school day in France, a scruffy sailing-mad teenager suddenly dropped among elegant French girls who blow-dried their hair every morning.

'Hey,' she said again. Her voice was gruff, like a boy's when it first starts to break, quite different from Favelle's musical alto. 'You must be our skipper. I'm Maree, the double for Favelle. I sure am looking forward to going to sea in a real Viking boat.'

'A lovely day for it,' I agreed. I stood up and held out my hand. 'Cass Lynch, her skipper.'

Her eyes widened, startled. 'Cass Lynch? Are you any relation to Dermot Lynch, who came over to the conference in California?'

Oh, yes? 'His daughter,' I said.

I got a thoughtful look, then a slow, calculatedly charming smile. 'Hi, Cass, pleased to meet you.' She looked past me along *Stormfugl*. 'It's some boat. I hadn't realised they were so big, the Viking ships. No wonder they came across the pond.' She dropped down beside me, perching herself on the other bollard. 'We're not doing many scenes on the actual ship, are we? Just the long shots, and a few close-ups. Most of it's done already, on blue-screen.'

I tried a smile. 'Technical stuff.'

'Oh, you know. They film you doing whatever in the studio, in front of a blue screen, and then substitute the real background.

Most outdoor stuff's done like that. It saves bother with sound.' She gave a long look round. 'It's so bright here. The sun on the water, and no pollution. I hadn't expected that. How far away is that? Those houses?'

The long fingers flicked towards the white houses of Eid standing out against their green background. 'Six, seven miles,' I said.

'It's clear as anything. Home, you're lucky to see six hundred yards. So where is your house?'

I thought I'd see just how interested she was in Dad. 'Oh,' I said airily, 'I live aboard my *Khalida.* The little white yacht at the end of the middle pontoon, there.'

She sighed, and slid down the bollard to sit on the pier, long legs stretched out, then smiled again, and this time I smiled back. 'Sounds real neat. I work in a bureau in LA – my firm's involved in the same area as your Daddy's, eco-research and alternative energy. I get really fed up with it, you know?'

'I thought you were Favelle's double,' I said.

'Sure.' She ran a hand through her dark hair, making it stand out like a halo. 'Sure, but that's, like, a vacation job. Makes a change, you know?'

'I do waitressing sometimes,' I agreed.

She grimaced, then smiled.

'An interesting life. Tell me all about it sometime.'

'You're the second person to say that, recently,' I said.

A sideways glance from those eyes, the colour of the sea over sand on a sunny day, astonishingly clear, fringed by dark lashes. I'd have betted those weren't natural, in spite of the dark hair. 'Was he good looking?'

'Life doesn't revolve round men,' I retorted.

'Oh, honey, doesn't it? How old're you, Cass?'

'Twenty-nine,' I said.

'Just older than me.' She gave my old jeans a sideways assessing look.

'Very few Shetland women wear make up,' I said equably. 'And they definitely don't get their noses fixed, or their boobs done.'

She stared, genuinely horrified. 'You're kidding me? Don't they wanna make the best of themselves? No wonder your–' She bit off what she was going to say. 'Didn't your Mommy help when you were a kid, about that kinda thing?'

Maman filled the house with crystal clear notes. She didn't do motherly advice. 'It's not a motherly thing here.' Seeing she was still lost for words I added, 'They get their teeth fixed, though. The school dentist comes round once a year.' I was lucky; I'd inherited my dad's good teeth. Inga had been unlucky, and spent two years with a brace that she could barely speak through.

It had given her an opening, though; she tacked back to her original idea. 'Does she stay here, your Mom?'

'No,' I said, 'she has a flat in Poitiers. France.' You never knew, there might be a Poitiers, Ohio. 'She's a singer. Opera.'

'You're kidding me?' I could see her thinking it: a Shetland housewife wouldn't have been competition, an opera singer might be harder to supplant. 'With a particular outfit?'

'She's pretty famous, in Sun King music circles,' I said. 'Eugénie Delafauve.'

'They're separated then, your parents?'

I'd had enough of being cross-questioned. 'I don't quite see what that has to do with the price of fish,' I said.

She looked satisfyingly blank for a moment, then smiled. 'You're telling me to mind my own business, right?'

I was saved from answering by Dad's 4x4 coming round the curve and down to the boating club. He was dressed to kill in a dark suit with a polo-neck under it, Roger Moore style, and he came straight over to us, to Maree, and held his hand out.

'Good morning, Maree. It's a pleasure to see you again. How was your journey?'

'Long,' she said, and made a face that had him laughing.

'Hi, Dad,' I said. I didn't bother to get up.

I was pleased to see a faint tinge of red in his cheeks.

'You've met my daughter Cassie, then. Maree was such a help to me in LA, Cassie, she was my right hand woman.'

'That's nice,' I said equably.

'Maree,' Dad said, 'come and talk to me about Favelle's publicity plans. Are we going to use the ship for the windfarm shoot too?'

He led her off, his hand on the small of her back within ten paces.

ᛋ

To kick the film off we were all invited to a meal at Busta. Dad was up at the top table, between two other suits, with Maree further down, though not out of eye contact distance. I was level with the salt, with Anders a bit lower, and Gibbie lower still. I'd hoped he wouldn't refuse the invitation, in spite of the blight he'd probably cast over everyone; he'd been in such a glowering mood all day that I wouldn't have been happy leaving *Stormfugl* unguarded. I had Michael on one side and a young man with an American tan hiding severe acne on the other – one of the technicals who'd been swarming all over the ship. He gave me a nervous glance and ducked his head away. That suited me, but I was out of luck for shipboard romances. Michael was more interested in Maree, constantly drawing her attention and laying his hand over hers. Oh well. I grimaced at Anders and concentrated on the food. It was a pretty good spread: a starter of toast and local smoked mackerel, presented with the fish nestling among neatly-made tomato roses and curling lettuce leaves. My Norwegian restaurant boss would have approved. It was followed by local roast lamb, then a lemon souffle, sweet and creamy with the zing of the lemon lingering after the mouthful had gone.

There were several bottles of wine on the table, and by the time the coffee arrived voices were louder, faces redder. People began to move around, introducing themselves. I got stuck with a middle-aged man from Detroit who kept putting his hand on my arm. Maree did a circuit, working her way steadily towards Dad. Michael went from one suit to another, going back to Maree for a minute or two between each. Dad radiated local businessman host charm in the centre. When Gibbie grunted a goodbye and slipped out, I exchanged a glance with Anders, and he slid out after him.

Maree looked across at Dad until their eyes met, then excused herself. Five minutes later Dad left too. Michael was enthusing to a suit about the wonderful Shetland light; he kept talking as Dad passed him, but his dark eyes followed Dad through the door. Five minutes more and he too was gone, letting the door swing shut behind him with a bang that caused a sudden, uneasy silence.

Trouble hung in the air then like that over-bright light before a storm strikes. Prince Rupert's men thought they were invincible in their laces and satins, but when they realised they'd lost they preferred glory to safety, a suicide cavalry charge, taking as many of the enemy as you could before they hacked you down. How was a dazzlingly handsome cavalier going to take losing his mistress to an older Roundhead? It would be a nasty shock; perhaps enough of a shock to make him lash out.

Chapter 5

Lash out with what? I hadn't thought about a weapon. There had been nothing near where she lay. I'd have noticed something out of place, even under the shock of finding Maree's body. I asked abruptly, 'What was Maree killed with?'

DI Macrae's head came up. His grey eyes met mine, sharpening. 'That's the first question you've asked me.'

'I didn't think of it before,' I said.

'Something hard, probably larger than hand-sized,' he said. 'More like a stone than a stick. Is there anything like that aboard *Stormfugl*?'

'No,' I said positively. 'A block – a pulley, I mean – would be just what you're looking for, but she only has wood and leather fastenings. I'm pretty sure there's nothing–' I paused at that, for there was something tapping at my brain like the ship's carpenter testing the mast for rot.

His hands stilled on the fly. 'Something wasn't right?'

'I don't think it was that kind of thing, though. Not something about the boat.' I tried to visualise it, but all I could see were the bloodied hands. 'No, it's gone. Sorry.'

'Let me know if it comes back.' He looked up as Sergeant Peterson came in. She had two sheets of A4 in her hand, covered with small, neat writing, and I could see she was fretting with impatience that he was still here talking to me when he should have been everywhere. He leaned back and read them through, like a computer considering information and slotting it into its place: tidal vectors, wind speed, current. There was a long pause, then he turned back to where we had been.

'They arrived in late May and you spent a week filming aboard the ship, with Maree doubling for Favelle.'

I nodded. 'We did the establishing shots first, with the ship being rowed by local folk from the yoal teams. The cameramen did close ups of straining bearded oarsmen and Vikings hauling on ropes, and the sail falling from the yard to catch the breeze. Everything had to be repeated over and over.' I grimaced. 'It took two days before Michael was satisfied he had enough shots in different lights and wind strengths. After that, Joe from the Boating Club took the cameramen and Michael out in the inflatable, and we went into the Atlantic for another day of sail handling with that buzzing around us.'

'You don't sound as if you're smitten by the glamour of the movies.'

'It all started out good fun,' I conceded, 'with us remembering to present our best profiles to the camera, but it soon got tiring. We'd just get the sail up and *Stormfugl* going nicely when we had to stop again, and hand the sail. By the end of the first day my arms felt like spaghetti from hauling the yard up and down.' I leaned forward, getting interested now. 'It was like on the *Sea Stallion*, where they made us hang around and hang around, and then we got caught in a gale and damn near foundered. Real Vikings would have taken the weather window and been safe up a creek burning and pillaging.'

'Maree was in these scenes?'

I nodded, and had to be fair. 'She was good on board ship, in spite of the long dress. Game for any shots.'

He turned Sergeant Peterson's top paper over, tilting it just enough so that I couldn't read it. 'Why wasn't she staying at Busta House Hotel with all the other film people?'

Answer 1: because she wanted to avoid her current lover and screw my dad in peace. I wasn't going to walk into that one.

Answer 2: because part of her job was to avoid being friendly with anyone who was going to stay on and be part of the main unit, Ted's unit, once the second unit left. I'd leave Ted himself to explain that one, if it became necessary.

I shrugged. 'Maybe she wanted peace and quiet in the evenings.' Then I did my best trying-not-to-yawn face. 'Sorry, I've been up half the night–'

The brown fingers added another loop. 'Not much longer now, Ms Lynch.'

I kept quiet. Two could play at the waiting game.

His mobile rang then. Sergeant Peterson stood to attention, head up. He laid the hook down and fumbled in his pocket, rising at the same time. 'DI Macrae. ... Yes, ma'am.' He turned his back, went into the kitchen, and I could breathe again.

ᛋ

It was Inga who'd mentioned Maree first, on a sunny late afternoon, when the crew had gone off up to the bar after a hard day's rope hauling, and Anders and I were relaxing on board *Stormfugl* before getting on with clearing up. Peerie Charlie was scrambling happily over the rowers' benches playing his newest game, which consisted of shoving his panda off the bench, picking it up again, sitting it down on the bench and saying, 'Much better' to himself, in tones of immense satisfaction. Rat watched him warily from the edge of the half-deck, whiskers twitching; the toy and he were a similar size and colour.

'So,' Inga said, 'do you have any idea of who this mystery woman is?'

'Mystery woman?' I said, blankly.

'Jessie's lodger.'

I remembered Jessie's unusual reticence on her next lodger: *This Baker lass – but you'll likely ken all about that.* Maree, of course. 'Why's she a mystery?' I asked curiously.

'That's the village speak.' Inga stretched her brown legs out to the sun. 'This weather's amazing. Look, I've got a tan already. Yeah, Jessie's not saying a word about her. I mean, *really* not a word. When she comes over to clean and mind Charlie, normally I head off as quick as I can, so I don't get half an hour on what her lodgers are like. This time, I deliberately lingered. Zilch. Not a cheep.'

'Maybe she keeps herself to herself.' Jessie's fluster and disapproval was explained now too. Dad had talked her into housing his girlfriend.

'Nobody,' said Inga with conviction, 'can keep themselves to themselves with Jessie about. Not that she's malicious, mind, she's just really interested in people, and the woman's been there nearly a week now. Easily enough time for Jessie to get her whole life history. Also, she's hired the whole house. All three B&B bedrooms.'

'Oh,' I said. That did seem odd. 'Are you sure? Maybe it's just happened that Jessie doesn't have any other bookings.'

'Ah, well,' Inga said. Her cheeks flushed pink. 'I was curious, you see, hearing the other women at the playgroup speaking about it. So I said I'd got a friend coming up, and might she have room, and Jessie said no, she was booked up full right until mid-June.' She drew her legs up, settled into gossip pose. 'Then there's what she looks like. We had a confab about it at the playgroup. Lilian saw her coming out for a walk one day, as she was driving past, and slowed down to look. Marie met her coming out of the Co-op, and Julie negotiated round a passing place along the Muckle Roe road with her, and I'd seen her pulling out in front of me. We're all agreed on tall – not giant, just tall, five-nine or five-ten.

'Not a hiding supermodel, then.'

'Hair colour unknown – she wears one of those headscarfs, tied behind her neck so her whole hair's in a bag.'

'Recovering from chemotherapy,' I suggested. What was Maree up to?

'No, there's hair in there, probably shoulder-length. Lilian looked specially. We'd thought of the chemo theory as well. She goes running every night too, and you don't do that if you've just had chemo. Clothes, big and baggy, but she's probably slim underneath them.'

'Face?'

'She wears dark glasses, the large sort that cover half her cheeks as well. Oval chin. Nicole Kidman style pale skin, suggesting she's either blonde or a red-head. I'd go for red. Eye colour unknown, obviously.'

'In short,' I said, 'someone from the city who doesn't realise how much she's doing to attract attention out here in the country.'

'That's about the size of it. And Jessica said hello to her, and she said hello back, in an American accent.'

'Aha,' I said. 'Do you think she's something to do with the film?'

'Well, actually,' Inga said, 'she seems to be a friend of your dad's. She's visited him. That was where I saw her – coming out of your driveway.'

Rumbled. 'His girlfriend,' I said resignedly. 'Maree.'

Over the weeks we'd been fitting out the longship I'd got into the habit of dropping in on Dad from time to time. I won't say it was a cosy father-and-daughter chat, but he had the tact not to mention how he'd got me the job aboard *Stormfugl* and I avoided awkward stuff like my future career. Instead I filled him in on some of the fun I'd had to date in various exotic places, and invariably he'd know them too, so we'd exchange impressions. The third time he'd asked if I still played Scrabble. The game had started off a bit stiff, with him still pointing out good word-spaces as he had when I was ten, so I stuck 'azure' with the z on a triple letter score and the whole on a double word score.

'Oh,' he said, then set out to play in earnest. He won, but only by three points.

I enjoyed going back like that, to the days after Maman had left, when we'd drawn the curtains against the winter dark, eaten Jessie's casserole at the kitchen table, then spread out the board and focused on it. I'd considered staying in Shetland for the summer. Perhaps Mr Berg would let me lease *Stormfugl* to run as a tourist attraction. *Trips around scenic St Magnus Bay in a genuine Viking longship!* I'd even contemplated moving into the house for the winter - thoughts of a waxing moon, as the night sky filled with light once more.

So it was a shock to come in two days after the film crew had arrived, when the moon had almost dwindled into darkness again, and find Maree in the kitchen, stirring onions in a frying pan. A chopping block lay on the table, white-wood new with a lethal-looking knife beside it, a fan of carrots and peppers, and a plastic bag of mince, along with a packet of tortillas, a block of cheese, and a lettuce in cling-film.

'Oh–' I said, startled.

Maree gave me a malicious three-cornered smile. 'Hiya, Cass. Your dad just went down to the store for a bottle of wine.' She gave the onions another stir, came to the table to cut open the mince. 'He won't be long.'

'Oh, okay,' I said. I looked at her making our kitchen hers, and felt rage swell within me. I'd been thinking about coming back – what right had this unknown woman to take over? But

I'd learned to keep rage in. I spoke as coolly as she had. 'It wasn't anything important. Say hi for me.'

'You're welcome to stay,' she said. 'There'll be plenty.'

The condescension did it. 'My room's here,' I said. 'I know I'm welcome.'

The stirring hand paused. Her head turned and our eyes met. She gave me a long, cool stare. I tilted my chin up, stared back. She smiled, sweetly.

'We might need to redecorate that room.'

I stiffened. How *dare* she? Then she delivered the knock-out blow.

'For a nursery.'

My eyes went to her stomach, back to her face. She smiled again, sweet and patronising.

'Your father's always pleased to have you visit, you know that.'

I wasn't going to visit with her in charge. 'Say hi for me,' I repeated, and I would have left her to it, except that Dad came in then.

'Well, well, Cassie, girl. You know Maree, of course.'

'Of course. Nice to see you off set, Maree.' I gave a smile every bit as false as hers, then turned to Dad. 'Can't stay, Dad. See you later.'

He followed me out to the car. 'Cassie, I've been meaning to tell you–'

'I worked it out for myself,' I said coldly. He had that bounce people get when their sex life has suddenly improved.

'Maree would really like to get to know you better.' In a pig's ear she would. 'Come over for Sunday lunch after Mass.'

Mass. 'Aren't you still married to Maman?' I asked bluntly.

He looked shifty. 'Cassie, you're not a little girl now. A man can't be expected to live on his own – see, your mother's away in France now, and we didn't always hit it off. Maree and I are something special.'

'So I see,' I said. He took that at face value.

'I knew you'd understand. I'm looking forward to the pair of you getting to know each other. Now, how are you placed for Sunday? Maree's a fantastic cook.'

'The film people don't do Sundays off,' I said. 'I'll come another time.'

He tried to press me for a day, but I used the film company as an excuse. 'How about I just phone when I get an evening free?'

'That'd be grand. We'll see you sometime this week, then.'

I had a long, hard think about it during Mass, kneeling in the pew with Dad beside me, and ended up feeling ashamed of myself. I knew my dislike of Maree was jealousy. I'd never done elegant; I was practical Cass who sailed boats and mended engines. Give me a problem and I'd fix it.

I thought of Maman's curtains on the windows, and Jessie dusting her grand piano, and of Dad sitting in the house and looking round him, night after night. I remembered how rarely I'd phoned. Now he had the chance of a new life. What right had I to interfere?

The angry voice inside me said, 'You were thinking of coming home – he wouldn't have been lonely any more.' The more honest voice added, '*You* wouldn't have been lonely any more.'

I'd chosen the life I had. I knelt down and focused firmly on prayer for Dad and Maree to be happy, for things to work out for them, and at the end of Mass I asked Dad if I could change my mind and come to lunch after all. I was on my best behaviour, and so was she. We stuck to trivialities, the weather, and the tulips, and how the film was going, and Dad grinned like a Cheshire cat to have his women one on each side.

When I went back to *Khalida* that night, I plugged in my laptop and checked my e-mails, just to remind myself that I had a life too. Sheila and Max were in Sydney now, Petra was working her way round the Cape. Alistair was becalmed off Labrador, and Graham and Stelle were sunbathing in Santa Lucia. Each e-mail was addressed to a dozen people, and the nearest it got to personal was Sheila's final 'How are all you guys? Let us know what you're up to, love, Sheila and Max.'

Friends. Thanks to the wonders of the Internet, I could touch a button and contact any of them, all of them. 'I'm here in Shetland, skippering a Viking longboat for a film.' The news would go all round the world, to people I'd worked with for two months, or berthed alongside, or met at a couple of parties. People who would say, 'Oh, Cass, yeah, I remember her, *Khalida*. Nice little Van de Stadt, good sea boat.' People who would say, 'Cass?

Doesn't ring a bell – oh, hang on, she was on the *Sorlandet*, six years ago.' People who wouldn't remember me at all.

When you're single, when you're always moving on, that's the kind of friends you have. I snicked the computer off, lit my candle, and found my good book, but it was a long time before I slept.

ᛋ

Three days after that Sunday lunch, Maree had come over to *Stormfugl.* It was my night on watch, and Anders had gone off to join the Busta House lot partying. I was lying on my sleeping-bag with the wooden half-deck warm under my crossed arms. It was a soft, soft night. The force 2 that had fretted the sea all day had fallen away, and I could hear the last peep, peep of the shalders settling themselves in the field. The hills on the west of the voe were already in shadow, but the eastern ridge was dusted golden by the last glimmer of sunlight.

The Second Unit were all going tomorrow, by boat and plane, leaving the beds at Busta clear for Ted Tarrant and the crack troops. Everyone was relieved, because the Maree / Michael thing was creating strain on all of us. The second the cameras stopped rolling he'd be going over to her and repositioning her with maximum body contact. I felt my old distrust reviving; hadn't she told him about her and Dad? Or was she running them both? But I had to admit I was doing her an injustice there, you could see she didn't like it, and by the end of the second day the Viking oarsmen got a sweep going on how soon she'd smack him one. If there was a bust-up, though, it wasn't done in front of us. Maree gritted her teeth and moved away from him, and smiled Favelle's smile for the cameras.

Of the Second Unit, only Michael was staying. I'd expected Maree to be cooking Dad a last five-star meal, so I was surprised when I saw her coming down the grass from Efstigarth, dressed in lycra shorts and a vest top. I remembered what Inga had said about her going for an evening run. She looked across at *Stormfugl,* called 'Hey?' I half raised myself on my elbows and waved.

She came down the pier, across the gangplank. 'Hi, there, Cass.' She took off the large sunglasses and folded herself down on the rough deck.

'Hiya,' I said. 'Come in.' I leaned behind me, into the cabin, for my thermos. 'Cup of tea?'

She shook her head. 'You don't have any orange juice?'

'Sorry.'

'I was just setting off for my run when I saw you aboard, and thought I'd come and say 'hey,' she said. Her long legs were uncomfortably tucked under her, and she sat bolt upright, not staring around but keeping those wide, green eyes on me. Her dark hair was hidden under a head-square, palm-tree green with a rust print.

'It's nice to see you,' I managed.

She took the will for the deed and flashed a Favelle smile at me. 'I hope Sunday's chilli wasn't too hot for you.'

'It was great,' I said, truthfully. 'I thought I'd a cold coming on, after all that hanging around, but there's nothing like a good chilli to sort out a cold.'

Now the smile changed to her own. 'My golly, it sure was freezing, wasn't it? I had thermal underwear on under my costume and my teeth were still chattering in the close-ups.'

'How long have you done doubling work?'

'Since we were little kids.' She raised one slim hand at my look of surprise. 'Honey, did your dad not tell you? We're twins – she's my little sister.'

I felt my mouth fall open. 'You're Favelle's sister?'

Maree was laughing now. 'Identical twins, Cass. You didn't wonder how we came to look so alike?'

If anything, I'd vaguely wondered why the double hadn't tried to look more like the star, grown her hair long, and bleached it to Favelle's red-gold, instead of having to wear a wig.

She followed my look. 'Dyed. I was so sick of the whole world doing a double-take every time I walked in. I wanted a life of my own, you know?'

For the first time, I felt a flash of sympathy. To live always in your double's shadow, never to be recognised as you... 'How did you get into acting?' I asked.

Maree wrinkled her perfectly straight nose and pulled the head-square off, ran a hand through her hair. The slanting sun caught the purple sheen of dye. 'Mom. It was Mom who was keen. The movies, you know, it was her dream.' That figured. Child success meant a driving parent – in my case literally, with Dad driving me to regattas, *Osprey* trundling and creaking behind. 'We got started right off, with commercials and then straight acting – it has to be twins, you know? Anything with kids. You can only work a kid so long, but the camera needs to keep rolling.' The mascara-dark lashes fell to veil the green eyes. 'We spent the whole day in the same place, doing the same thing, but we only saw each other at bed-time. Once they saw she was better than me at expressing herself, they did the emotional bits with her, and the boring stuff with me. That twin movie we did, when we were eight – you know? The Disney one, *Double Trouble.*'

I shook my head.

'She was the fun twin and I was the good girl.' I could hear the hurt in her voice, like the drag of a fouled rudder. 'When Favelle landed *Pollyanna,* Mom was so pleased. All her work – she used to recite it off at us. Getting us up and dressing us nice and feeding us good so our hair would be shiny and our complexions clear. Making sure we got our beauty sleep. Organising all the auditions – we didn't have an agent then, Mom did it all.'

'What about your dad?'

'My golly–' Her face softened again. 'Pop was great. It didn't matter to him the way it did to Mom. He didn't care about me not being as good as Favelle. 'More time to spend with me,' he'd say, and take me off to the movies, or the drug store for an ice cream soda.' She gave me a sideways look, curious, almost shy. 'Like your pop would have been with you, after your mother left.'

I thought of movies and ice-cream sodas. 'We watched movies in the winter,' I admitted, 'if Dad wasn't working late, but in the summer I was mostly busy sailing. We'd go for chips after a regatta, or an Indian in Brae on the way past.'

'But he wasn't driven about it.' She spoke jerkily, on a short breath: 'You didn't have to win to be loved.'

I thought about the bronze medals, and the silvers. The year he'd gone to Iraq would have been my last year in the Mirror

Nationals, and I'd been determined to get the gold. I think I would have, too – but that was water under the bridge.

'It must have been difficult,' I said, 'keeping liking Favelle. I'd have been so jealous.'

'I did suffer from suppressed jealousy,' Maree agreed. 'But actually I was kinda relieved too. She could get on and be a star, and I could just have a normal life, until she got *Pollyanna* and Mom insisted I could be her stand-in. It wasn't fun like this. I hadda do all the really boring bits. Measuring the distance for the camera, focus, lighting, all that. I stood there for an hour while they fussed around, ignoring me completely, like I was a dummy, and then she came on and did the lines.' Her mouth twisted. 'I didn't hate Favelle, but I sure as hell hated Mom for that. Then the TV follow-up bombed, and for a while we got to go to normal school, instead of the school on the lot, with a dozen other narcissistic kids. I really loved that. I was the star there. I was a cheerleader, and in the athletics team, and I learned fencing. Favelle was hopeless at all that.'

'I'd have thought she'd be good,' I said. 'It's what everyone knows about her, Favelle the action-woman. In that Greenpeace film she was scrambling all over the place, driving motorboats, climbing rigs, all that.'

Maree turned her head away, a quick, startled movement. 'Yeah, of course, all that. But she's – well, I don't know how you'd say it here. My analyst said she was a late developer. I'd had my periods for two, no, three years before she had hers.'

Too much information, Maree.

She gave me a wry smile. 'Favelle wasn't good at making friends. Half the time you felt she wasn't there. What she's good at – well, you've seen her on the screen. You give her a feeling, a situation, and she'll *be* it. Tears, smiles, betrayal, love, uncertainty.' She paused, then rushed on, as if she'd thought it, but never dared to say it before, as if it was being drawn out of her by the stillness of the night, and the soft apricot of the sky. 'It was like she'd never had real emotions, just what she was given to do. All her life, she'd only done pretending. Even Ted, well, he was her leading man in her first contemporary story, after all the swords and sorcery stuff. The director told her to fall in love with him, and there they were, the latest 'Hollywood Golden Couple'. He never fooled me, but–'

She stopped, abruptly. 'Hey, though, I'm just talking on about my life, and Favelle's. You'll meet her soon, and anyway, I'm giving all that up. I've had enough, and Ted'll just have to lump it. Really, what I wanted - ' She turned her head towards me, eyes uncertain in the dimness. 'I wanted to get to know you better. Dermot's so proud of you, you know? Tell me about your life. It sounds real exciting, from what Dermot's said, going all over the world on sailing ships. Have you been round the Horn?'

'Mmm.' I nodded. 'Both ways. Once in the *Statsraad* – that's a Norwegian barque – and once in a forty-footer. That was mad.' Confidence for confidence; but I wasn't going to tell her about Alain. Instead, I told her about some of the skippers I'd worked for, trying to give her a picture of life at sea, and she listened like someone who'd spent her life in a cage, eyes shining.

'My golly, I'm envious. Will you take me out on this boat sometime? To spend a night at sea, under the stars?'

'If you like.' Now it seemed natural to ask. 'Are you staying much longer?'

She flushed, the colour rising like a flood tide up her neck and cheeks. 'Yeah, I'll be here a while.' She rose, still graceful even in her hurry. 'My golly, it's getting dark.'

'Here,' I said, 'let me give you my mobile number, and if you get a chance for a sail, ring me.'

'That'd be neat.' She pulled out her own phone and programmed my number in. 'Are you coming to Sunday lunch?'

'Depends on the filming schedule,' I said. 'I don't know how organised they're going to be, for me to let you know in advance.'

'Oh, don't worry, they'll be organised.' Her mouth turned down. 'Elizabeth's in charge of this unit. Ted's secretary. Desperately in love with him, of course, and hates Favelle like poison, but too valuable to sack.' She swung herself ashore. 'Thanks, Cass. Sleep tight.'

I watched her stride up the grassy slope until the dimness swallowed her. I wasn't ready for bed yet, though; I sat on in the cockpit, watching the soft apricot fade to rose, then to a yellow-blue, then at last to night blue, with the stars becoming sharper and sharper, and thought about parents and children. About my father who'd driven me to so many regattas, like a son. About Maree and Favelle, and their mother, who'd wanted two stars, and had had to make do with one. Hadn't she seen the way she'd taken the chance of being sisters from them? Poor little rich girls ...

ᛋ

Suddenly, from below us, outside on the pier, there was an inhuman wail. Sergeant Peterson leapt to her feet, and the Inspector came in from the kitchen. He was at the window as quickly as I was, and then out of the door. The white-suited figures had left their ring around Maree's body and were struggling with a man who thrashed ineffectively at them, then sank to his knees, reaching one hand through the mesh of arms towards Maree, and wailed again.

'Dad?' I said, and then he raised his head to look up at the windows, and I saw that it was Ted Tarrant, his chiselled face distorted with despair and shock and grief.

I saw the red, misshapen hands again, with the long nails gleaming shell-pink, and knew what it was that had given me that sense of wrongness. Maree's nails were natural-coloured.

It wasn't Maree lying there. It was the star herself, Favelle.

CHAPTER 6

Ted and Favelle had arrived the day after Maree's visit. They'd taken their private jet direct to Scatsta, the oil terminal airport, and for an hour before they arrived, the pier was thronged. They'd come straight to the ship, his secretary Elizabeth had said, to get set up. I got Anders and Gibbie busy adjusting the running rigging, to give the mast a very slight rake, and I was watching and saying, 'Let out a bit – back a bit.' It was a nice, captainly pose to be discovered in.

They had a police escort from the airport. The white limo nosed its way down the gravel path. I straightened and braced myself, then strode across the gangway and onto the pier. It was all very well for Anders, doing a mock-salute at me.

There was a pause, to let a pair of photographers get set up, then the lead car's driver door opened, and Ted Tarrant stepped into a flurry of camera flashes. He had that American smoothness – think Gene Kelly, or the good-looking one of the A-team, very charming, but with something just a bit dodgy about him. He had dark chestnut hair, gleaming teeth, an implausibly sincere smile. He wore an open-necked shirt and Chinos, and he bounded out of the car like a man trying to prove he could still cycle up to Machu Picchu if he wanted to.

It was really odd seeing him in real life. What surprised me was that he looked exactly the same as he did on the big screen. Every move, every gesture was just that little touch too precise, as if he was an actor playing himself. He waved at the crowds, then walked around the bonnet of the car and opened the door for Favelle, who oozed out in full film star rig-out: a long, pale coat trimmed with soft jade sheepskin, a Cossack hat covering the famous red hair, a pair of mirror shades. As if it was a signal, the doors of the following cars opened. A scurry of suited flunkeys engulfed them for a moment before they posed for photos,

Ted smiling that confident smile, Favelle on his arm, lips curved enigmatically. That done, Ted took a couple of strides forward, held his hand out to me. His voice was warm and soft as a summer evening.

'Hi, you must be Cass. Glad to know you.' He caught up my hand in one of those double-handed Clinton shakes, green eyes looking directly into mine. They were flecked with hazel, and his eyelashes were as long as a girl's. 'This ship looks wonderful. I could see her from all the way along the bay, I couldn't take my eyes off her. Favelle sure will have to look to her laurels if the *Stormfugl* – did I say that right? – if the *Stormfugl*'s not to upstage her.'

'Yes, she's turned out well,' I agreed.

'She's a real beauty, exactly what I want.' He turned to gaze down the sunlit voe. 'Such a feeling of space, you know? Norway's beautiful, but it's all too high. Here in Shetland you've got the sea, and this narrow strip of land, and the sky. It's just made for widescreen. And the light – Michael's been raving about it all week.'

He turned back to me, confidential. 'What I'm going to do here is do for Shetland what Dr Zhivago did for Russia, or Lawrence of Arabia did for the desert. This movie's going to be epic. In thirty years time you'll still be putting it on your CV, just so people can say, 'Wow, you worked on *Sea Road*?' It's a totally new departure for Favelle. She's done the action girl bit, the dedicated campaigner. Now she's going to be the big heroine. Think Vivien Leigh, think Julie Christie. That's what this story is, one woman's journey in a changing world.'

'We're all ready to go, Mr Tarrant,' I said.

He gave me the benefit of the dazzling smile that had left my teenage self weak-kneed. I was annoyed to find it still worked. 'Ted, please, Cass. How did it go in the old man-of-war days, a master for the ship and another for the fighting men? Equal ranks. Well, you're the ship's master, and I'm in charge of the army.'

'Ted,' I said, smiling back, 'we're ready to go whenever you want.'

'That's my girl,' he said, and turned his gaze on my crew. 'Anders? Glad to meet you. Cass here's told me what a lot of work you've done on the engines. Gibbie. Your experience's going to be invaluable.' He half-turned, motioned me forward towards the group by the limo. 'Now, Cass, come and meet Favelle. Favelle, honey, this is Cass Lynch, our skipper. Dermot's daughter, you remember.'

'Of course I remember,' she said, in the husky voice so familiar to cinema goers all over the world. 'I'm delighted to meet you, Ms Lynch.' One perfectly manicured hand went up to the shades; she pulled them away in one graceful gesture and smiled at me.

It was like seeing Botticelli's Flora come to life. There was the perfect oval face held on the slender column of neck, the heavy-lidded almond eyes framed by dark lashes, the long, straight nose, the arched brows, the serene three-cornered smile. Her pale skin was so perfectly made up that it seemed to be blush-rose velvet. Her green eyes seemed almost too wide open, as if she was trying to look interested in you while really thinking about something else. I stared, and couldn't think of anything to say.

She was used to that of course. 'You're our skipper. She's a beautiful ship, I sure am looking forward to going on her.' She turned to her husband. 'Are we using the ship for Dermot's advertisements too, honey?'

'In port,' he said. 'The interviews, perhaps. Definitely the publicity shots.'

She gave me another of those wistful smiles. 'I love boats, but of course back home in LA I don't really get the time to indulge that. I'm looking forward to this shoot. And the costumes are marvellous, lovely heavy velvet in a to-die-for shade of green, specially dyed to match my eyes.'

'That's nice,' I said inanely, suddenly feeling as if I was talking to Inga's peerie Charlie. Then she suddenly flared into life. 'I'm playing the first white woman in America, Gudrid.' The blank eyes sharpened, the whole face focused into seeing a new land, and for a moment I could believe the illusion.

'Well,' Ted said, 'I must get my troops organised for the morning.'

He fumbled in his pocket for his famous silver cigar case. I took a deep breath. 'I'm really sorry, but you can't smoke on board *Stormfugl.*'

He gave me an astounded look. 'Cass, I smoke everywhere.'

'She's wooden,' I said, 'saturated with tar and a bit of diesel from the engine, and sheep-grease on the ropes. One still-lit butt and she'd be ablaze.' He was still staring at me. 'I'm sorry,' I finished.

A moment's silence, then he flung back his head and laughed, the light gleaming off his white teeth. 'Very well, then, skipper. No smoking aboard. I'll make sure all my crew understand that too.'

'Thanks,' I said.

He clapped my arm and headed off. I was about to follow when there was a familiar rattle of pushchair wheels among the crowd that had gathered to see the stars arrive, and a little voice shouted, 'Dass, boat, Dass, boat.' Peerie Charlie burst out of the crowd, with Inga in pursuit, and stopped dead in front of me. 'Dass. Boat.' He was just holding up his hand when he saw Favelle.

They say you're never too old to fall in love. You're never too young either. Charlie was instantly smitten. He gazed up at her in total silence for a full minute, ducked his head away, watching how she reacted out of the corners of his eyes, then looked straight at her and gave his most beaming smile.

Favelle's eyes lit up. 'Oh, my,' she said, 'you're a little darling. What's your name?'

Charlie ignored that. 'Boat. Hand,' he stated, and held out his hand to her.

She took it like she was mesmerised. 'You want to go on the boat, honey? Come on then.'

Charlie led her over to the gangplank. I took an involuntary step forward. The tide was as high as it could go, so the plank was at a steep angle. Then I remembered the Greenpeace film. The Favelle who'd clambered over those oil rigs was well capable of controlling a toddler on a four-foot gangplank. I'd reckoned without her film star shoes and coat, though; she tottered up, hanging on to the side rope, and I stood at the edge of the jetty, ready to jump into the water and get Charlie if need be. He was steadier than she was, though, and safe aboard the ship while she was still mountaineering.

'Boat!' he shouted triumphantly. I felt a stupid pang of jealousy run through me. All the fun we'd had, with me chasing him around the rowers' benches or on all fours playing peek-boo in the cabin, was forgotten beside a pretty face.

Favelle had clambered aboard at last, and took his hand again, looking around. Her gaze fell on Anders, went from his flaxen head and blue eyes to Charlie's. 'Hi there! Is this your little boy?'

'Ders,' Charlie affirmed.

Anders looked horrified. 'No, ma'am,' he managed, as if Favelle was royalty. 'He's Inga's.'

She turned to see who he was indicating, looking first at me, then at the woman with the give-away pushchair.

'Hiya!' she said. 'Your little boy seems to have kidnapped me. May he play here for just a short time?'

Inga nodded, and in a couple of minutes we were both forgotten, as Charlie initiated Favelle into his favourite game of jumping from seat to seat. I didn't think she had children herself, but she must have friends who had, for she seemed to understand what he wanted, and even deciphered the joined, waving hands and word 'pider' that was a request for Incey Wincey.

They were on their third repetition, with Favelle giving the spider her Oscar'd all and Charlie shrieking with laughter, when Ted went past. Favelle put out a hand and caught his sleeve. 'Ted, honey, look at this darling boy. You know how we cut the part of Gudrid's little boy, well, couldn't we put it back in? *Please?* This little angel would be so cute.'

The spasm of annoyance crossed his face so swiftly that I thought I must have imagined it. 'Sure, if his mom has no objections.'

'Mind having her little boy star in a movie? Of course she won't,' Favelle chirped. 'How would you like to be my little boy? I still don't know your name, do I? Can you tell me?'

Inga moved forward stiffly. 'His name's Charlie, and no, I don't mind.' It was obvious that she did.

'Then that's settled,' Favelle said, and went back to Incey Wincey spider.

'Okay,' Ted said. 'I'll tell the writers he's back in.'

His tone was casual but his back was rigid as he turned away from us, and Inga, beside me, breathed very steadily, as if holding words in.

Ted was busy conferring with Michael, and Favelle had given Charlie back and gone off with her entourage to be dressed, when a brisk, blonde-haired woman came up to me. 'Ms Lynch? I'm Elizabeth Sparkes, Ted's secretary.'

She'd been the one who'd sent me most e-mails, detailing what was to be done, where, when and how; the one Maree said hated Favelle like poison.

'I'm pleased to meet you,' I said, holding out my hand. Her shake was quick and firm. 'I don't know where we'd all be without your organising.'

She disclaimed the compliment with a wave of one beautifully manicured hand. She was in her mid thirties and glossy, with platinum-fair hair looped up in a clasp at the back, and cut with long strands that framed her oval face in front. She had manicured brows, eyelashes with just the right amount of mascara to look groomed, and yard-arm-straight teeth and nose. She wore a dark blue suit, the jacket like a man's, the skirt a flowing Fifties swirl, and cradled a navy clipboard. I wasn't sure how easy she'd be to work with in the flesh, with the briskness of her e-mails translated to a brusqueness that suggested no shilly-shallying would be tolerated. I hoped the weather gods would continue to be kind to us.

She was looking over my shoulder at the longship, her eyes alert, then they flared, and a little smile curved her lips. She relaxed the clip-board breastplate and nodded to Ted as he came up alongside us.

'I'm just introducing myself to Cass here.'

'Great,' Ted said. 'Elizabeth is my right hand woman, Cass, I couldn't do anything without her.'

'He flatters me,' Elizabeth said, smiling, cool. Ted nodded to us both and walked on, and her eyes followed him for two seconds, not more, then flicked back to me, all poise and purpose. 'Now, have you got the filming schedule for today?'

The afternoon was spent doing still shots in the middle of the voe. We let the anchor down and just sat there while Favelle posed. Medium shot of Favelle leaning her head against the rigging. Close-up of Favelle with bucket. Favelle gazing out into the distance. Favelle walking between the rowers, smiling her famous smile at each of them. Our hardy Vikings wilted before her like picked buttercups. I even saw one gazing dreamily at her shadow lying across his foot.

I did end up admiring Favelle's unruffled patience, pose after pose after pose, followed by a long wait before the next sequence. She took it all in her stride, drawing her green coat around her, and picking up her knitting – a baby coat, from the looks of it. Maybe playing with Charlie was practice.

He and Inga came out on the inflatible, to do an hour's filming.

'Cute child shots,' Anders said resignedly, coming to lean beside me in the stern. 'They'll be lucky if he has half the patience she has.'

'A quarter,' I agreed. We'd reckoned without Favelle's influence, though. He was happy just to stand there by her, to look out where she pointed, or clap hands and smile over a game of pat-a-cake, or take her hand to walk between the rowers. He even accepted a drink of juice from a pewter beaker, rather than his own cup with the cat in the bottom; if any of us had tried that, there'd have been a major tantrum. Inga stood by ready to coax when wanted, but Charlie didn't even look back to check she was still there.

The hour had stretched into an hour and a half when Charlie began to show signs of restlessness. Inga scooped him up. 'Home time, baby.'

'No,' Charlie said, and began to scream.

'He could stay a little longer,' Favelle said.

Charlie held his arms out to her, over Inga's shoulder. 'Stay! Down!' The chubby legs kicked furiously, dislodging Inga's red-amber scarf. Inga twisted him so that they flailed the air, caught her scarf with the other hand and spoke firmly.

'It'll be his teatime by the time we get home. We need to go now.'

Favelle blew Charlie a kiss. 'I'll see you tomorrow, honey.'

Charlie wriggled furiously. He'd end up in the water at this rate. He gave Inga a slap across the face with the full force of one angry arm, and she responded with a sharp smack on the nappied bottom which stilled him for the time it took to hand him down into the inflatable. I heard Favelle gasp in horror. His wails turned to heart-rending sobs which echoed back across the water at us even over the roar of the inflatable's engine.

4

We had the helicopter back for the following day, to take more 'at sea' shots with Favelle prominent on board. She'd got her sea-legs now, in spite of the long kirtle that trailed across the decks and hid the uneven planks beneath her feet. We had luck, too; just as we were about to break for lunch, a school of dolphins came tumbling alongside the boat, grey bodies gleaming. The inflatable stilled its engine; the cameras circled Favelle as she leaned over the side, almost touching the largest dolphin as it leapt up from under the ship, rode the bow wave and dived again. Favelle was laughing with delight, eyes wide with the wonder of it. Michael came forward and talked to her. She nodded and clambered precariously up the side of the ship to perch behind the dragon head. I moved over to Ted.

'She's not wearing a lifejacket, Ted, and that dress would drag her down fast.'

He shook his head. 'It's a perfect shot. She won't fall, Cass.'

When the dolphins went, Favelle leapt lightly down from her perch. Her voice was breathless, more childish than yesterday. 'That was so cute. I'd love to be a dolphin, just swimming on and on and on.' Her face clouded, and her voice became older, more like Maree's. 'Except their sonar gets confused by our pollution, and they drive themselves ashore, or they get cut in half by ship propellers, or tangled in tuna nets. If the world doesn't do something soon our children will never see dolphins the way we just saw them.'

There was always a little crowd when we returned to the pier. Favelle looked up and gave them the dreamy smile, and a little wave, and when two girls came forward with photos for her to sign, she said, 'Sure, honey.' They asked if they could pose with her, and she smiled again and stood with them while the girls' father snapped away, the two children awed and admiring beside her. It suited her, the green dress, the soft velvet clinging to her high breasts and rounded belly, then falling in long folds to the floor. She posed with them, then turned and posed again for a press photographer, with *Stormfugl* behind.

Ted saw that too. He gave her a sharp look but didn't say anything, just swung down the gangplank and offered his arm, and they went off to the limo together in a fusillade of camera flashes. The look left me puzzled, though. Why shouldn't she be posing for photographers? Maybe she had some sort of contract with a particular firm, though how you'd enforce that when every six year old had a personal mobile phone, I didn't know.

I watched idly as the long white limo went round the bend above the marina and along towards Busta. It stopped just above Jessie's house; sheep on the road, I supposed. I wondered what Ted made of driving in a place where sheep had right of way.

The third day of filming was dialogue scenes aboard the boat. Only Anders, Gibbie and I were needed for that. We took her out under engine and anchored, ready to spend the day keeping out of the way of the waiting actors, grips, best boys, make-up girls and all the other people that seemed vital for filming even a simple conversation between two people. Scene 53, take 1. Take 2. Take 3. They'd all looked identical to me. They'd do three lines of dialogue several times without the camera, then roll it with cameras facing in different directions, ready to be cut together. Ted would look at the versions in a little hand-held video, and then they'd either re-take, after a long, intense discussion between Ted and Favelle, or move on. Moving on meant a long wait while they re-positioned the cameras. Scene 54. Scene 55. Anders lost himself in some swords and sorcery epic, and Gibbie gloomed. I wished I'd brought a book.

Favelle was good, though. One scene involved a quarrel with her husband, and she spat at him for the camera, then instantly returned to her placid self, knitting in hand, for the next half hour wait. Ted's face wasn't as mercurial as hers, or he couldn't snap in and out of character the way she could, for the defensive look he'd put on for the camera stayed put in between takes too, and he spoke to her roughly when he was moving her position from one scene to the next.

The inflatable buzzed out with Busta sandwiches for lunch, and mid-afternoon tea and cake. There were pizza wedges in an insulated tray at six o clock, along with paper plates of Caesar salad. I made a cone of my plate, and Anders and I saved our walnuts for Rat, left sulking in his cage aboard *Khalida*.

By eight the light was yellowing, so Ted wrapped it up. The mist that had been hovering to the east all day began to creep towards us. The film crew all headed for the boating club bar, Gibbie climbed into his old Fiat and grumbled off, and Anders and I were left in peace. The next day was our big sailing scene, the landing in Greenland, so we'd need to spend the evening getting decks scrubbed, every inch of rigging inspected, and the sail re-stowed. Rat came out of his cage and ate his walnuts with relish, Anders nipped into the bar by the back way and got us a pint of Belhaven each, and we sat on deck listening to the lap of the waves, and terns chittering on the shore, and the distant hubbub of film people knocking back boating club Chardonnay.

'Gibbie,' Anders said. 'I'm not happy about him, Cass. He is beginning to feel–' He made a circular gesture with his hands. 'His cooling water intake is blocked.'

'Oh?' I said.

'He goes over to the rigging, and then he turns and sees I'm looking at him, and he goes very still, then moves elsewhere. I think your friend was right. He is a little crazy. I do not like him on board ship.'

I nodded. 'It's an awkward one. Not much longer, though, two days of filming with Favelle, a couple of days of windfarm publicity, then that's us. Job over.'

Anders made a face. 'I was enjoying this. I wanted to stay on in Shetland, but my father says my replacement has no feel for engines.'

'I don't know what I'll do,' I said. He gave me a quick look, opened his mouth, then shut it again and rose purposefully.

'Bacon roll?'

'Sounds good,' I said. 'I'll just look at this.' I gestured at the letters he'd brought with the Belhaven. 'Half of them will be for the film lot – I wish the postie would take them to Busta, instead of dumping them at "the film boat".'

'I'll bring it over.'

'Thanks, Anders.'

He went off with Rat on his shoulder, and I flipped through the letters. There was a brown envelope for me (the Inland Revenue, noting my arrival back in the UK), half a dozen for Ted and a handful for Favelle, including an official-looking typed one in a white envelope. I wondered if I should take it over this evening, but couldn't be bothered. There were two for Michael, one of them in a blue-ink feminine hand. I refrained from turning it over to look at the address on the back. On board ship, when you were living so cheek-by-jowl with others that every trip to the toilet was a public performance, there were strict rules about that kind of thing.

I put the letters together and leaned back. Gibbie was a problem. I'd been aware of the suppressed rage too, like a head of steam building up, which showed in the roughness he put to the simplest unscrewing of a shackle. For tomorrow, I'd put him on to mooring-rope handling with a couple of the reliable Vikings.

It was my night to keep watch on *Stormfugl.* After we'd made her ship-shape Anders headed off, and I took my sleeping bag and a pillow up into *Khalida*'s cockpit and made myself comfortable. I could smell the ebb weed in the dimness, and hear every sound: a pony tearing grass in the park above the marina, the trickle of the road overflow, a TV set in one of the new houses past the clubhouse. I'd just got settled when a light shone out above me from Jessie's house: a door opening and closing. I tensed. Gibbie?

Two darker shapes moved against the grass that led down towards the shore. Voices murmured, intense, then, as they came nearer, I recognised Maree's walk. They stopped at the fence; the man with Maree looked back up, towards the house, as if wary of being overheard, then leaned towards her. The words floated towards me over the still water.

'*I'll* tell her.' It was Ted. 'Not yet, though, wait a bit.'

Maree's voice was vehement. 'I'll tell her, if you can't work yourself up to it.'

'You can't just spring something like that on her, for Chrissake.'

'Ted, it's not going to go away. The longer you leave it, the worse it'll be.'

'I'm warning you, Maree.' His voice was ice-hard. 'Keep quiet, or–' His tone softened to reasonable. 'Look, something like this could knock her haywire. Let her get the filming over, and the publicity stuff. A couple of days, what difference will that make?'

'I'm not prepared to keep this to myself.'

'You must. For her sake, you must.'

Maree made an annoyed sound, turned and strode away. The rectangle of light winked. Ted waited, leaning forward on the fence wire, looking across the marina; I kept very still, and sensed, rather than saw, the moment when he drew a long breath and turned away. A light flicked on in the house, framing a silhouette Maree looking out over the still water.

CHAPTER 7

We set off before first light to arrive at the Hams for half past seven. Mist still wreathed the eastern hills, but here on the west side the sun shone wrinkled gold on Atlantic swell. Seabirds wheeled overhead, squawking indignantly at this invasion of their territory; the salt spray stung on my cheeks and smelt sharp in my nostrils.

I fretted gently all the way around Muckle Roe. This would be my big test as skipper, to bring the ship in to shore without an engine, just as the Vikings had done, and in this place too. Hams came from the old Norse 'hamar', a landing place. I liked that idea.

We'd walked the ground last Tuesday morning and decided exactly what line *Stormfugl* had to follow into the bay, and where she had to beach, then gone back the following evening with *Stormfugl* under engine, and I'd taken meids, shore features that I could line up one above the other to get me in just the right place. It would be harder under sail, when the wind puffed and curved around the cliffs and fell suddenly when you came into their shadow. That was the problem of working with non-sailors; Ted had this picture of the boat appearing under full sail and just gliding up to the beach.

'We have to make it look easy,' I told my oarsmen. 'You know the line, from the other night, and a good few of you know the Hams, and the way the wind funnels around then dies completely. You'll need to be quick in trimming the sail and handing it before we hit the beach – you can backwater the oars there, so we don't hit it too fast.'

Nods; they knew what I wanted.

'And of course there may be last minute changes.' I grimaced at the headset I had to wear under my felted hat. 'Good luck,' I finished, squeezed the headset on and pulled my hat on top. 'Cass here. We're ready.'

There was a crackle in my ear. 'Just receiving you, Cass,' Michael said. 'Coverage isn't good here, we're having to go back to hand signals. We're all set up for your entrance. Ted and Favelle are setting out now.'

The motor launch bounced across the waves and curved to a halt beside us. Anders held out a hand, and Favelle climbed aboard, moving with confidence in spite of the encumbering dress. Ted followed her and they took up their positions on the swaying deck: the explorer and his wife looking ahead at landfall a thousand miles from home.

'Got them on board,' I reported. I turned to my Viking troops. 'Okay, let's go.'

As soon as *Stormfugl* began to move my nerves fell away. My crew handled this ship as if they'd been born raiders. The red and ochre sail fell without a flap, bellied out, and we began to move smoothly forward towards the narrow entrance between two cliffs. It looked like a dead end, a brown-sand beach two hundred yards on, with no shelter from the northerly swell, but those who knew the place turned hard a-port into a perfect anchorage, sheltered by cliffs from the north, with a sickle of pale gold sand for a landing and water so clear you could see your anchor among the cauliflower weed and fanned mermaid's hair.

The wind today was coming from the south, funnelling down the valley below the old house they were using to hide the cameras in and curling around the cliff to gather in strength as it came over the water. I expected a gust as we came around the headland, and I'd positioned one of my Vikings ready to take the strain on the tiller with me.

I felt the wind on my cheek before *Stormfugl* responded to it. 'Now!' The rattle along the side of the boat quickened, and I felt her heel away from the wind. Four hands moved together on the rope, spilling the wind from the sail without it flapping, and she came upright again. I put all my weight against the tiller. 'Now. Heading up. Sail in.'

Stormfugl's nose came around until it was pointing for the golden beach. 'On course now.' The great sail slid in, taut against its hemp ropes. The faces turned to it were intent. My next mark was the cliff on my right. My hands were wet; I wiped each on my velvet tunic and grasped the tiller two-handed again. 'Start easing the sail.'

The old house was in my view now. 'Bearing away. Keep easing. Oarsmen ready.' We were still going faster than I wanted. 'Dip oars.'

Favelle was at the prow, every line of her eager for this new shore. The cameras whirred in my ear. The ruined house was dead above her now. 'Dip oars – backwater.' At last we'd come into the still water that echoed the shoreline. The sail deflated and hung lifeless as we slid towards the beach. 'Lines ashore.'

Two Vikings leapt over the side and caught the prow, then ran up the beach to loop the lines around the rocks. Ted swung ashore after them, then held his hand back to Favelle, the first woman on this new land. Charlie was too wee to work all day, but one of the Vikings had a little boy of similar age and blondness, and Favelle lifted him over the side and set him down on the beach. They came up the sand together, heads high, looking around, and paused at the high tide mark.

'And cut,' Michael's voice said in my ear.

'Cut,' I repeated. My Vikings cheered. Anders clapped me on the shoulder. Favelle was instantly enveloped in a wrap by her personal make-up woman and led to the shelter of her own little marquee which had been put up out of shot. Ted went up to watch the video with Michael, and came back to report that it was fantastic, just what he'd wanted.

Then, of course, we had to do it again, with Michael on board for close up shots, and again, for luck.

ᛋ

I'd brought the mail with me so that I could give it out at lunchtime. I stopped Favelle as she headed for her little marquee, and waved the bundle at her.

'Favelle, this came for you.'

She was huddling her Viking cloak around her and ducked her head away from me, as if she didn't want to be looked at when she was at less than her best. 'Elizabeth–' she said vaguely, then paused, looked at the typewritten one on the top, and held out her tanned hand for the pile. 'Thanks, Cass.' Then she dived into the tent, leaving me staring at the canvas flaps trembling behind her, with a sense of something not right.

The landowner had opened up his agricultural shed, catering had made pizza and burgers, and we all fell on it like starving wolves. As I ate, I went round with the mail. Michael looked at the feminine handwriting, went a dull pink and disappeared up the hill to the old house. Ted flipped through his and handed them all to Elizabeth.

I wondered, though, if Favelle's letter had been bad news. When she came out to join us for lunch she seemed preoccupied, and when Ted called us all back to work she insisted on finishing all of her special still mineral water before coming down to the beach. Only Anders got the famous smile. She seemed to have taken a shine to him today, perhaps because of his resemblance to Charlie. I wondered if he would call her 'beautiful Favelle.' I should have dared him.

Gibbie was the death's head at the feast. Anders was sticking close to him, and Favelle was glued to Anders. Gibbie's mouth turned down as if there was a bad smell under his nose, and when Favelle laid her delicate hand on Anders' arm and stood on tiptoe to murmur in his ear, he started as if he'd been stung. Then he eyed the pair of them up as if he was calculating something, and his sour mouth stretched into what, for him, could pass as a smile. If he'd been younger I'd have expected him to whip out a mobile phone, take a photo and send it to the tabloids, but rumours about Favelle and a handsome Norwegian wouldn't stop the film going ahead.

I turned away from Gibbie and found myself face-to-face with Elizabeth.

'Hi, Cass. That went fine. Ted's so pleased – it's going to be one of the key images of the film.' Enthusiasm lit her voice for a moment. 'It was real swell, watching the boat come in. I felt like I'd gone back in time. Have you seen the rushes?'

'Not yet,' I said.

'The film's sent south for developing, but they send a video copy back up. You should ask Ted to let you see it.'

'I'll do that,' I said.

Her gaze drifted over my shoulder again, then sharpened to flint. I didn't need to look behind me to know what she was seeing; Favelle smiling up at Anders. Her eyes came back to mine and her top lip fell again, hiding the pointed teeth. She gave a cold smile, then glided to Ted's side, gestured with her clipboard.

'Ted, for the afternoon shots–'

The afternoon was close-ups of the arrival. Charlie wasn't the star he'd been the day before; he was naggy and out-of-sorts, and Inga was correspondingly tight-lipped. He consented to a couple of shots of being swung off *Stormfugl*, but Favelle seemed to be tiring, for the second time she came near to dropping him, and her movement aboard the boat was clumsier, the long velvet skirt tangling on the ends of oars and between the lines of rigging. We were all relieved when they'd done the disembarkation bit. Viking belts were surreptitiously loosened, and an illicit half-bottle began doing the rounds. I kept an eye on it, even though we'd be returning under engine with life jackets on. I didn't want drunken accidents.

After that, Elizabeth's neat plans went awry. Stomping up a hill towards an uninteresting pile of stones wasn't Charlie's idea of an afternoon at the beach. He did it once for the rehearsal, then flatly refused to leave the sand, and when Favelle tried to pick him up he screamed blue murder. I was still in costume, so I offered to keep him on the shore, in shot, so that the audience knew he hadn't been forgotten. Charlie cheered up so fast at the suggestion that Ted agreed rapidly, over-ruling the historical expert. I promised not to use any plastic spades or buckets, and took him down to the beach. I wasn't Favelle-beautiful, but I could make a mean sandcastle with a moat and a drawbridge, and towers for him to stamp on. He was soon his sunny-tempered self again.

Because of that, Ted changed the script. Rather than a known ally, the owner of the house became an unknown quantity. Ted strode ahead, hand on the pommel of his sword, and Favelle leant on the film captain's arm for the steep bits as they made their way up the hill. They went up once as rehearsal, had a cigarette break, then Ted led them all down again for a final address to the troops, swapped them around a bit, and told the cameras to roll.

I was keeping an eye on Gibbie and the boat, ignoring what was going on behind me. Suddenly, there was a bang and a shout,

'Clear set! Clear set!' It was Ted's voice, loud and urgent. There was a rumbling sound and a series of thuds, a scream from Favelle, several male yells, and Inga shouting 'Cass!' all on top of each other. I rose, turning and catching Charlie's hand in one movement and felt my breath snag within me.

A great squared stone was tumbling from the old house and down the hill towards us, gathering speed as it came, bouncing on the uneven ground. It seemed to move in slow motion. I saw the knot of actors scatter away from it, Anders lifting and swinging Favelle in her long dress. It gave an extra heavy thud as it passed where they'd been and continued down to us.

I was moving in slow motion too, catching Charlie up in my arms and scrambling desperately out of the way, the sand sucking at my reindeer boots. Inga was screaming and running towards me, arms outstretched, but she was too far away, and the great boulder was gathering speed, just as they do on the movies, only film boulders were papier mache, and this was bone-crushing granite.

It was almost on us. I flung myself forward, shoulder down to take the impact, Charlie still in my arms, and rolled with him crooked there. The ground trembled under us, and the sand scraped beneath my cheek. I drew my feet up just in time, felt a numbing blow and a stab of pain as my right foot was wrenched sideways, then it was gone beyond us, straight down the beach towards *Stormfugl,* heavy enough to smash in even her solid stem post with its high, blind head.

I lifted my head, fighting for breath. Three of my Vikings were leaping out of *Stormfugl*, ready to shove her back, but they were too late, the stone was pounding across the sand with heavy thuds, slowing as it went. It was going straight for her.

At the last minute it hit a boulder buried under the sand of the beach. The sharp click of stone meeting stone echoed, and the falling boulder checked and cartwheeled again, but with a slight slant which gathered to a swerve. It splashed into the water not a yard past *Stormfugl*'s dragon head and lay still. The noise echoed around the cliff wall, and when the last whisper of it had died into silence the world was suddenly empty. I stood Charlie upright and levered myself to my feet, resisting the temptation to clutch him to me.

'Noise,' he said. 'Splash.'

'Yes,' I agreed, 'splash.' My voice didn't sound like my own, and my hands were trembling. He looked at me and burst into tears.

Inga came flurrying over and scooped him into her arms. 'Baby, it's all right, it's all right. Nobody's hurt.'

It had been close though, and at tea-break the whisper ran through the cast: sabotage.

'There was a flash,' Anders told me, 'and a bang, like a firework, and Ted said that was what it had been. The rock was on the old house, on the top of one wall, balanced on other rocks, and when the firework went off it tilted that last degree, and it fell.'

'A firework,' I repeated.

'I saw it go. There was the flash, and then Ted shouted, and it toppled like death coming towards us. I pulled Favelle out of the way, and then I saw it was heading straight for you and Charlie–' His face was white under the tan. 'I could not look away – but you moved so fast.'

'So did you,' I said. 'Sailor's reactions.' My hand was cold on the polystyrene mug of tea. 'So whoever set the firework could have lit it and got out of the way, to look innocent.'

Anders nodded. 'I have been trying to remember who was up there. The cameramen, of course, and Elizabeth with her clipboard, and that man from the local film club, the one who asked if he might take pictures of a real film crew in action.'

'Kevin,' I said. 'Inga's pal. Gibbie was on the boat.'

'Lunch break, though,' Anders pointed out. 'We were all milling about. Several of the men went up to the ruin to pee.'

Men. I made a face, but refrained from comment. 'It could have been anyone.'

'Not any of the actors,' Anders said. 'You wouldn't set up a boulder that size, and know it was going to fall, and then walk towards it.'

'If you were waiting for it, though, and were prepared to jump.'

Anders shook his head. 'I would not do it.' He leaned in to me, so that his beard was tickling my cheek. 'You hear of people who stalk film stars. Favelle's very famous, she might attract such a one.'

'It wasn't a very good attempt.'

'No, but if we had been closer–' Anders looked blankly ahead. 'I think that is what Ted thought. He said something to Elizabeth about *letters* and I thought she had perhaps been threatened. Favelle did not hear.'

'She took it very well,' I said. I'd expected major hysterics.

'Ted told her it had been an accident. She did not believe him, she gave him a cold, angry look, but she did not want to quarrel in front of everyone. That marriage will not last long, I think.'

'It's lasted a good time already,' I said, surprised.

Anders made a face. 'There is trouble.' He changed the subject. 'Cass, I was wondering whether we need to keep watching all night. It is not comfortable, and I have found these filming days tiring.'

'Knackering,' I agreed.

He shot a quick look forrard to where Gibbie was watching with an air of gloomy disapproval as the Vikings passed their bottle round, and lowered his voice. 'There has been no sign of him at night.'

'No,' I agreed, 'but I don't trust him. He could easily have set that firework. He could have made sure he was the last to leave the old house, lit it and gone off, all innocent. Only another four days, Anders.'

He opened his mouth as if he was going to keep arguing, looked at me and shook his head. 'I can see that you are very tired too. Aye, aye, skipper.'

'Thanks,' I said.

We took our back-to-shore pint down to *Stormfugl.* The film lot had already colonised the bar, and faces were redder, voices higher, than in previous days. Kevin Manson, Inga's pal, 'that man from the local film club who asked if he might take pictures of a real film crew in action', lifted his pint and followed us.

I barely knew him, as there wasn't room for any extra bodies aboard *Stormfugl.* He had been in the inflatable, his height marking him out, and he'd been one of the phalanx of camera-operators filming today. He reminded me of a heron, tall, gangly and hunch-shouldered, with grey-black hair that stuck out behind, and bulbous pale eyes with red corners, as if he had hay-fever. He was in his mid-thirties but born middle-aged. Little Charlie ran rings around him, so goodness knows how he coped with twenty plus obstreperous teenagers.

Inga had waxed suspiciously lyrical about the hard time he'd had with his ex-wife. 'She had an affair with one of the other teachers, meeting in the school, can you believe it? She took him to the cleaners, he's never got over it.' Michael had been equally expansive about him one evening, when he'd had enough pints to drop the doomed cavalier image and reveal himself as a rather bolshie character with a chip on his shoulder about amateurs.

'You set up a film set anywhere and you're over-run with them. Bloody tourists with hand-sized videos. Now Ted gives permission for a human spider to get under my feet. PR, he says. All right for him, down there acting. It's me left trying to keep him out of shot. I've warned him. Stay twenty yards behind the direction the lens is pointing, or I'll break both your legs.'

Kevin's legs had remained unbroken, so he must have taken the warning. Now he followed us aboard *Stormfugl*, and sat down on one of the rowing benches.

'What happened up there?' I asked bluntly.

'It was strange.' He had one of those voices that sounded as if he was talking through a bamboo tube. 'I've been thinking about it. It must have been someone involved in the film, you know.'

Anders nodded. 'I have been thinking the same thing.'

'I don't see why,' I objected. 'Everyone knows where the filming's going on. All the rowers, for a start. Any of them could have told their wives and families, who could have told the entire neighbourhood.'

'There was a road block,' Kevin said. 'A road block.' He had that annoying teacher's habit of repeating everything. 'You came round by sea, so you didn't see it. You didn't get stopped.' He sat up straighter, dipped a finger in his pint. 'Look, here's the island of Muckle Roe, right, with the bridge just past Busta, on the mainland.' I refrained from saying that I'd spent a good deal of time looking at the much clearer Admiralty chart. He drew a line out around. 'You came round this way, round the outside of the island and into the Hams, at the back. We drove from Busta, over the bridge–' more damp-finger indicating–'and that's where the road block was. All but local people were stopped from going across. Another of the film folk was left at the end of the tarred road, to ask walkers not to disturb us. The only people with access were the film folk.'

'And nobody could have come by boat either,' Anders said thoughtfully. 'The motor launch that brought Ted and Favelle stayed out of sight at the bay entrance to stop anyone from spoiling their nice shot of a Viking longship in eight-whatever AD.'

'CE,' Kevin corrected automatically.

'There were of course you and your companions of the film club,' Anders retaliated. 'Why would we want to harm Favelle?' Kevin said defensively.

'Why do you think it was Favelle who was meant to be harmed?' Anders countered.

Kevin floundered. 'Well, I naturally – of course it could just have been sabotage of the film, but who would want to do that?'

'Someone who had a spite against Ted or Favelle,' Anders said, watching him. 'That would be someone in their own crew or entourage, I suppose. Someone who disapproved of films and film actors. That's more likely to be an outsider.' His voice was smoothly guileless. 'Maybe someone who disapproved of the windfarm, and wanted to stop Favelle doing the publicity for it.'

Kevin's reedy voice shot up even higher. 'That's a ridiculous suggestion. Why should the windfarm objectors have anything to do with it? They're sensible people, not thugs or vandals. That's a smear by the developers.' He gave me a sideways look. 'Shetland Eco-Energy.'

'No,' Anders said, 'it was my own idea.'

'Well, I think it's ridiculous,' Kevin said, and huffed off, leaving his pint behind. Anders picked it up.

'Well, well,' I said. 'Did you know he was a windfarm objector, or was that guesswork?'

'He was trying to press pamphlets about it on Favelle yesterday,' Anders said. He lifted the pint. 'It's a good thing this film's nearly finished. They are all edgy as hell along at Busta. Did you hear they saw the ghost last night?'

'Really?' I said. 'Who saw her?'

'One of the make-up girls. Suzanne. She got up to go to the lavatory, and walked straight into her.'

'Literally?'

'No, not through her in best story-tradition. It was a little woman, in old-fashioned dress, with a white, white face and shadows under her eyes, who sidled past her, then vanished. Suzanne screamed to awaken the whole house, then went into a fit of hysterics. So this morning they are all talking of the film being jinxed.'

'And the rock is part of that.'

You are worried, no?'

'Yes,' I admitted.

'Then I will finish this up in the club,' Anders said, and slid towards the gangplank. 'Please don't scrub too much hot water over my poor engine.'

I made a face at him, and he went off laughing.

CHAPTER 8

Skippers evolve their own way of coping with worry (the skipper madness rate is legendary). One, on a tall ship I crewed on, organised mast-climbing practice. Another used to pipe all hands and do a massive sail-shifting rope-coiling exercise. He thought we didn't notice that at the end of it the sails were generally set exactly as they had been. Me, I scrubbed decks. There was something very soothing about the froosh, froosh of the scrubbing brush, the hosing afterwards, playing the gush of seawater into every corner and seeing the particles of dirt chase each other around in a circle, run for the scuppers and leap overboard.

It didn't work this time, though. There were too many people acting unreasonably for motives I couldn't even begin to fathom. I wanted to talk it through with somebody. Dad sprang to mind, even if it meant I had to have Maree too. He was used to handling a construction site filled with people. It was only eight o clock. I told Anders I was going, washed the clothes I'd worn for scrubbing the decks and hung them up on the pushpit while he gathered his night-watch gear together, then fired up *Khalida*'s engine and headed off.

The mist was reaching the near hills as I chugged along, a blind grey fungus creeping over the crest of the hill then pouring itself down into the valley, stifling the hill beneath. Sailors don't like fog. Even knowing the moon had turned didn't cheer me much. Maybe this film had been doomed from the start.

I tethered *Khalida* at the pier and trudged up the hill. I'd been right; I would get Maree too, her Fiesta was parked in front of the garage. Oh well. I was almost at the house when there was a smash from inside, as if somebody had thrown a plate, followed by shouting. I couldn't distinguish words, but Maree was angrily pushing some advantage, and must have been in the right, for Dad was getting louder in a blustering push-the-blame away fashion.

It wasn't the time to pay a social call. I was just about to slink off when the door slammed open and Maree stormed out, her coat flying behind her, and her eyes blazing. Dad was following, put a hand on her arm. She threw it off. 'This is what I get for taking up with someone old enough to be my father!' she spat, stumbled into the car, revved it up and spun off in a scattering of gravel.

Dad made a half-run after the car, then turned back, shoulders slumped. I gave it a couple of minutes, took a deep breath and followed him into the house.

It had been a mug, not a plate. It lay as jagged shards in a pool of coffee on the kitchen floor. I called 'Hello,' and went on through.

The living room was in half-darkness, with only the little lamp by the telephone casting a soft circle that lit the empty armchair and one arm of the couch. Dad had gone straight for the whiskey, and he must have downed one fast and poured another, for he looked drunk already, one arm sprawled along the back of his armchair, feet planted square on the floor. He had a glass tilted in one hand, the pale liquid diagonal against the tube of glass, and a half-empty bottle of Redbreast Single Malt on the table in front of him. He glanced up with an odd mixture of hope and shamefaced apology as I came in, then turned his face away again.

'Dad?' I said.

'Now, Cassie.' He motioned vaguely at the couch. 'What're you up to tonight? Have a dram.'

A drink seemed a good idea. I fetched myself a glass from the black wood cabinet and poured myself a generous slug. I'd have preferred the smoky peat taste of Laphroig, but the Redbreast burned nicely in my throat as it went down.

Suddenly Dad sat upright, blazing with self-righteous anger, and launched in. 'You were doubtful about Maree, girl, and you were right. You'll never believe what she did. Never believe it.'

'What?'

'Had my sperm tested. Have you ever heard the like?' Generations of affronted Irish male shouted in his voice. 'Tested! She must have taken some–' He reddened, remembering it was his daughter he was speaking to. 'She sent it off to a laboratory and had it tested, to see if I was able to father children. How old does she think I am? I'm telling you, girl, I've never been so insulted.'

It did seem a very odd thing for her to have done. Besides, I'd thought, with that crack about needing my room for a nursery – but she hadn't actually said she was pregnant. Maybe that had been an expression of longing. She liked Dad, she wanted a life of her own, but didn't want to risk being tied to him if he couldn't still have children.

'And me with you grown up under her very eyes, and the boy–' He broke off, re-filled his glass.

'What a strange thing to do. How did you find out?'

He reddened again. 'There was this letter. Saying these were the results of the tests on the sperm. If I was a violent man I'd have knocked her down there and then.'

'But – presumably she didn't just show it to you?' Maybe this was standard American pre-marriage practice. Check the fertility of both parties and put it in the pre-nup. What would I know?

Dad wouldn't meet my eyes. 'She's so much younger than me,' he mumbled, 'and there's that cameraman, Michael - so when I felt the letter in her coat–'

Dad had the old-fashioned habit of helping a lady on and off with her coat.

' – well, I went back and read it. Just stuffed in the pocket of her coat, it was, as if it wasn't important. I wouldn't have gone through her handbag, or anything like that.'

'So,' I said, with daughterly bluntness, 'you read a private letter.'

'It wasn't private,' Dad said. 'It was about me. Testing *me.* Without my consent. If she'd asked, if she'd made such a point of it, well, I'd have put her mind at rest. But to go behind my back like that, I had a right to know, didn't I? It was my letter as much as hers.'

He had a point, but I knew how I'd feel about someone taking a letter of mine from my pocket.

'So I asked her, straight out,' Dad said. 'What d'you mean,' I said, 'by getting me tested like that, without so much as a word?'

'What did she say?'

'Gaped at me. Then she asked what I was talking about, and I said it was in the letter, in her pocket. Then she threw a real wobbler – how dared I search her pockets, that kind of thing. And, well, I said a few things too, and it ended with her throwing a mug at me and storming out.'

It all made me glad I was single. Dad drained his whiskey, poured another. 'And right enough I shouldn't have read her letter. I know that. But she had no right – no right–'

'No,' I agreed, 'she hadn't.'

There was a long silence.

'I always wanted a son,' Dad said suddenly. 'She knew that. Your mother didn't want children.'

I didn't want to think about that, that the goddess in her white Grecian robes with her shimmeringly clear voice and no human frailties, didn't want me. For her, being married, being a mother, was like being marooned on dry land for me, stifling, something dying. It wasn't personal. The words burned like the whiskey.

'That's why she went,' Dad said. 'She thought I didn't know. She said it was her singing, and I believed her, but when she came back, he was gone. She went to France to–' The glass slammed suddenly on the table. 'My boy.' He lifted the glass, drained half of it and set it back. The soft light glinted on a single tear that oozed itself from the end of his eye and rolled slowly down his cheek. 'My boy.'

Suddenly I was very cold. 'Maman went to France for an abortion?'

'A mortal sin.'

With the cold came nausea. I knew enough about abortion to visualise the little limbs being torn apart by suction, the minute human remains being dumped in a sack in a hospital waste department. My brother, my flesh and blood. I would have dandled him and sung him songs. I would have taught him to speak, and taken him playing on the beach, and raced chocolate wrappers down the burn with him. He'd have come out in the boat with me and learned to trim the jib. We'd have shared a taxi for discos, and run from France together. 'When was this? How old was I then?'

He answered in his own way. 'He'd have been twenty-five. His birthday was to be July. He was Patrick, after me father.'

Two children stifling that clear, cool voice. Four, I'd have been. Inga's baby sister had been born that year. Patrick would have been mine, just as little Saskia was Inga's. I'd have taken his hand on the first day of school, and waited for him going home, and protected him from bullies in the playground. I'd have helped with his first snowman. In the two minutes since Dad had told me, he'd become as clear in my head as if he'd been born after all, and lost again, killed on the roads, maybe, running out in front of a car, in spite of the times I'd told him. I shook my head to clear his image away.

'Dad, he wasn't born. You mustn't think of him as if he'd lived.'

Dad turned on me, suddenly fierce. 'Don't you let me hear you say that, girl, as if you don't know any better. Sure, he lived. He has a soul just like you and I, and before God his name is Patrick, and he's with the holy souls in innocence right now.'

'I didn't mean that,' I said.

'I'm ashamed of you, now, forgetting Father Peter's teaching like that.'

'I didn't mean he didn't have a soul,' I persisted. 'I meant–' It wasn't good for Dad to mourn a child that had never quite been there in the first place. I moved onto the couch beside him, laid my hand over his. 'It's a shock for me, this.'

He nodded. One hand came up to brush the tear away, then clamped round the bottle. He poured us both another drink. I hadn't planned on a tumblerful of whiskey and I knew I would regret it in the morning, but for tonight I didn't care. I took another swig and screwed up my face as it went down.

'You shouldn't be drinking that,' Dad said suddenly. He sat up straight and took the tumbler from me. 'That's not a lady's drink.' He stood up, swaying. 'Sherry.'

I watched him go to the cabinet. The glasses chinked as he fumbled among them for a little goblet and filled it too full, so that it spilled over his fingers as he brought it to me. It must have been the last of the Christmas sherry, sticky sweet. I took a mouthful, set it down. 'I'm not a lady.'

'Time you learned to be,' Dad said. He leant back, closed his eyes. I thought he was going to fall asleep, but then the eyes opened, bright as a Siamese cat's. 'How old are you now, twenty seven?'

A sharp pang of jealousy shot through me, that he knew that lost brother's age so exactly, yet could not remember mine. 'Twenty nine.'

'You're leaving it late. Time you gave up this sailing and found yourself a fine man, now, and had children. You could give me a grandson, how about that?'

There was no point in arguing about it. 'That would be fine,' I said peaceably.

He nodded, and his eyes closed again. I'd not manage to get him to bed, but I could find a blanket to spread over him.

The airing cupboard still smelt of Maman's mother's pot-pourri, and when I looked up the lavender heads were hanging in their spiked wheat-head bunch above the top shelf. I wondered that they still retained any fragrance. Perhaps it was just memory re-creating the smell for me. There were no blankets here, just sheets and pillowcases and Maman's summer curtains. She had gone in winter, and they had never been hung again.

There used to be blankets in the big wardrobe in their room. I took the three steps down the corridor and opened my dad's bedroom door, feeling like a trespasser.

It was startlingly unchanged. The only trace of Maree's hasty departure was the white lace runner of the dressing-table dragged sideways under Maman's glass bowls, water-clear on the polished wood of the dressing table. Her little china clock stood beside them, its hurried tick loud in the silence. Even her dressing-gown still hung from its padded hanger on the back of the door. I went softly to the wardrobe door. The dresses hung there, the full skirts stirring a little in the draught, just as they'd hung when my four-teen year old self had gone to look, to make sure she was coming back.

Strange, this ghost house where Maman might walk in at any moment to find her lavender hanging above the clean sheets, and her dresses still in the wardrobe, and the piano tuned and waiting, and her husband brooding still over his lost son of so many years ago. It wasn't healthy, any of it. He needed to do a clean sweep, give all these dresses to Oxfam, sell the piano to whoever wanted it and throw out her lavender and her waiting curtains. It would have been easier if she'd died, instead of walking off with a shrug of her elegant shoulders, leaving these obsessions and tangles behind her.

I banged the door on her dresses and tugged the bottom drawer open, took an armful of blankets. No doubt they'd not been touched for fifteen years either. Be damned to the lot of them. If Maree didn't come back, then whatever Dad said I'd be in here with a black bag before I left Shetland.

As I laid the blankets over him, he stirred. His eyes opened, not quite focusing on mine, and his rough hands drew the wool up to his chin. He said clearly, 'Sorry–' before his head rolled sideways, his mouth opened, and I knew he was out cold till morning.

I went slowly back down to *Khalida*. One whiskey. The mist hadn't reached the water, but stayed clinging to the sides of the eastern hills. Just as I reached the pontoon, the sun suddenly blazed from amber to scarlet, too bright to look at, then a veil of cloud turned it blood-orange: trouble ahead.

There was a breath of wind yet. I hoisted the main, unfurled the jib and shoved her away from the jetty, holding the main out to make sure it filled. Soon the water was trickling under her bow and we were moving steadily seawards. The noises of the land gradually fell away and the western horizon lay before me, still with a last stripe of creamy sky above the shifting sea. Tir nan Og, the isles to the west, Paradise. *Khalida*'s navigation lights patterned the sails with white reflection. I set her nose towards the Atlantic and hooked up the autopilot, then went forrard to lean my back against the mast, legs stretched out along the foredeck. The water was a pathway of palest blue, fretted in the centre. A single star shone to the west; Venus rising.

When my mobile rang in the cabin, I didn't move. I wanted to sail on, away from the messiness of human contacts. Maree and Dad, Michael; Ted and Favelle, Elizabeth; Maman and the child who hadn't lived to be born. I wanted to lose them all in the vastness of the ocean, where the stars hung like nightlights above *Khalida*'s white sails, and the mareel flashed green and silver on the water. It was only when the dark bulk of Papa Stour came close enough for me to hear the waves breaking on the cliffs that I turned *Khalida* around, swinging the boom out and setting her on a reciprocal course. Back to civilisation. Back to prison. Give me the open sea any day.

It was as I turned that the thought I'd lost earlier returned. *'Thanks, Cass.'* Favelle didn't know my name; she didn't know anyone's name. She called us all 'honey' to save trying. That hadn't been Favelle who had ducked away from me, clutching her Viking cloak around her; that had been Maree.

Click, click, like rudder pintles slotting into their sockets. Maree's voice, the other evening: *'I was a cheerleader, and in the athletics team, and I learned fencing. All that stuff. Favelle was hopeless at it.'*

Jessie: *'only the one, the Baker lass, she's taken the whole house - but you'll ken all about that.'*

Jessie's house, nicely placed between Busta and the marina. A white limousine stopping just above it, yesterday, for just long enough for one person to get out and another to get in. Maree. Favelle. Maree, the athlete; Favelle, the emotional actress. Favelle, who'd made her name in movies as an action-woman. How long, I wondered, had this substitution gone on?

Now I thought about it, I knew by the way they moved on *Stormfugl* which was which. The close-ups at anchor, with the long green dress tangling around ropes: Favelle. Yesterday with the dolphins, the at-sea takes this morning, the woman who wasn't scared to perch up on the prow: Maree. The woman who'd posed for photographs and signed autographs: Maree. No wonder Ted had looked so grim; a good close-up of the wrong Favelle could ruin everything.

I had another thought. Michael must be in on it of course, waving us all back out of shot so that only he was close enough to tell. Dad must know too; he'd hired Jessie's whole house to keep the secret safe. A wave of sympathy flooded through me. Poor Maree, the invisible woman, living a half-life behind dark glasses in a motel carefully chosen to be between Favelle's swanky hotel and the filming location. A limo pausing to let one person out and another in. Openly, she could be the double where every star had one; hidden, hers was the intrepid derring-do that had made Favelle famous.

Poor little rich girls, living their lie.

ᛋ

It was getting on for 3 o clock. The early sun whitened *Khalida's* mainsail and dusted the land, making the marsh marigolds a gold river down each little cleft in the low hills of Vementry, and turning the pink-orange granite of Muckle Roe to fire-red. It was so still that I could hear the suck of each wavelet on the pebbled beach at the hill foot. The surging movement as *Khalida* breasted each slope of Atlantic swell was the only sign that we were moving on the glassy water.

I hooked up the wind vane and limped below to make a mug of tea. As I'd expected, my ankle had stiffened in the night. While I waited for the kettle to boil I eased it in circles.

As we came around the point into Busta Voe, the yellow-spotted seal on his rock raised his head to look at us, then spread his tail up to dry it, like a Spanish lady displaying her fan. Now the land world began to enclose me again, the smell of summer grass coming green from the hills, starlings gossiping among the low sycamores around Magnie's white crofthouse, the rattle of a lone car coming along the single-track road: Magnie, returning from his Saturday night binge. He clambered out of his car and stood a moment, looking around, then raised a hand to me. I waved back.

He was the only one awake. Film stars and saboteur alike were sleeping as we glided past the white bulk of Busta House. The modern houses closer to the rock arms of the marina were silent under the sun's gilding. Even the sheep were tufted rocks in the emerald grass, with their knobble-kneed lambs gleaming white beside them. The standing stone above the marina glowed gold, and below it, like a ghost from Shetland's past, was my Viking ship, with the white gulls wheeling around her.

It was then that I found the body.

Chapter 9

It was half an hour before DI Macrae came back. He sat down in the same position, just as if he'd gone to the toilet for five minutes, unruffled as ever, and for the first time I was afraid of him. The gentlest swell on sand can break a beached yacht to pieces, just by persistence.

'Was it Favelle?' I asked.

He didn't bother to answer. The hook was still lying on the table; he took out the tin and put it away, then leaned forward. 'Take notes, please, Sergeant.' His shoulders were broader than I'd realised. Dark brows hooded the sea-grey eyes.

Sergeant Peterson flipped her book open. The case had moved into another league for them - not an unknown woman dead on a boat in a remote corner of Scotland, but Favelle, murdered on her film boat. The world would be watching them, and they had to get a suspect arrested quickly, for the honour of the Scottish police. If, of course, they were allowed to keep the case. The death of Favelle would warrant the biggest of big brass.

You and me both, boy. Fighting for survival.

'But – what on earth was Favelle doing aboard *Stormfugl?*' He didn't reply. 'She did die on board, didn't she? I mean, she wasn't brought there after her death?'

He gave me a reflective stare. 'Now why should you ask that?'

I remembered the head pillowed on the arm, the curved back, the lower leg drawn up, the outer stretched down, and the other arm flung out behind. *Was it you who moved her?* 'It was the way the body was lying. Too tidy.'

DI Macrae nodded. 'She died on board, we know that, and someone moved her after death, or as she lay dying.'

'But *why?* Why was Favelle on *Stormfugl*?'

'Had you or Anders any particular connection with her?'

'No,' I protested. 'She'd only just got here. We were introduced, we got on with sailing the ship.'

'But then,' he said, gently, 'you weren't knowing she was Favelle.' He looked down at Sergeant Peterson's notes, then back at me. 'You thought she was your father's girlfriend, Maree. How did you feel about your father taking up with an American thirty five years his junior?'

'Dubious at first,' I admitted. 'But it was his life – ask him, he'll tell you! I went along for lunch last Sunday, and everything was fine.'

'We will be asking him,' DI Macrae said. I bit my lip. The boyfriend. The first suspect - no, not the first suspect for killing Favelle. She was his windfarm's golden goose.

'Dad had no motive for killing Favelle,' I protested. 'She was all set to do the publicity for his firm's wind farm.'

'He could have mistaken her for Maree. As you said, what would Favelle be doing aboard the longship at that time of night?' He took out my mobile, pressed some buttons and turned it to show me Maree's text.

'I didn't get it till after I found the body,' I said.

'What did she want to talk to you about?'

I shrugged.

'Can you give me an account of your movements last night?'

Not without dropping Dad straight in it. 'I was restless, so I went for a sail. We went out at eight fifteen –

'We?' DI Macrae came in quickly.

I answered clearly, '*Khalida* and I.'

He gave me a sceptical look. 'You would normally be counting your boat as an active partner?'

'It's a single-hander's habit,' I said. 'You and the boat, you often talk about 'we' did this or that. The boat and I, we.'

He still didn't believe it. 'You went out at eight fifteen.'

'We came back in at ten to four.'

'Very exact times,' Sergeant Peterson commented.

'I was at sea. I kept the log.' I realised it would show my stop at Dad's. I added, 'I called in briefly at Dad's house, to say hello, then kept going.'

'I'd have thought,' DI Macrae said, 'that you would be too tired after a day's filming to want to go for another sail.'

'I was pretty bushed,' I admitted. I looked straight at him, and Alain's grey eyes pulled me to try and explain. 'But I'm not used to so many strangers around me. These film people, I'm an alien among them. They've come from all over, but they all know each other, and talk all the time about people I've never heard of. I needed to get back to my own world. I just went out into the Atlantic and looked at the stars, and listened to the waves for a bit, then came back in. That's when I found Maree.'

'And you were alone.'

I nodded.

His face hardened. 'I've had a word with Inspector Hutchinson. That's not what Anders says.'

'Anders?' I echoed, startled. *Now* what was the boy up to?

'His version of the evening is quite different. Would you like to change yours?'

I wasn't going to be tricked that way. 'No.'

'Why should Anders lie to us? We're foreign police, so it's not a good idea. He's smart enough to know that.'

I thought about why Anders might lie. What had driven him to spend the night in the boating club? Probable answer: a body. He was scared he'd be blamed, panicked and run for cover, leaving me to do the official discovery in the morning. Thanks, Anders.

No; that wouldn't work. He was on watch. Favelle couldn't have come aboard without waking him.

'He says,' the DI continued, 'that you spent the night together, aboard your boat.'

My mouth fell open. Spent the night *together?* That had better not mean what I thought it did. How dared he? I was about to burst into angry denials when I caught the DI's calm eye, assessing my reactions.

'Why,' I asked, 'would I lie about my alibi if I had one?'

'To get him into trouble? Very good-looking, if a bit younger than you. You fancied him, he didn't fancy you, you want revenge. Frame him for the killing.'

'You can't have it both ways,' I retorted. 'If we spent the night together, why would I want revenge?'

'Maybe you don't want to admit to being a one-night stand. Did anyone see your boat go out and come back?'

'This is *Shetland,'* I said, exasperated. 'Of course someone did.' My voice rose slightly. DI Macrae remained poker-faced, but I caught a gleam of triumph in the glance Sergeant Peterson shot at me. I lowered my voice. 'Just ask along the road there.'

'And coming back?'

I shook my head. There was no point in mentioning Magnie. He'd been two bottles away from being a reliable witness. *The local drunk, m'lud.* Furthermore, he wouldn't be at all pleased by being called as a witness. 'Co-operating with the police,' I could hear him saying, 'I'm never done such a thing in all my born days.'

'In short, Ms Lynch,' the DI said, 'it doesn't look good. She was killed on your ship. You thought she was Maree, who'd asked you for a meeting, and who you had reason to dislike.'

'Maree lived just up above the marina, and she'd come down to visit me once before!' I protested. 'It was a perfectly natural mistake to make.'

'Maree, I'm told, has short, dark hair. Favelle had very noticeable long red hair.'

'Maree wore a wig for being Favelle's double. I thought she was wearing the wig.'

'Why on earth would she wear her wig away from filming?'

'I don't know. I didn't think about that. I just took the body to be Maree.'

'Perhaps,' he said, in that soft Highland voice, 'you wanted it to be Maree. You were jealous of her relationship with your father, and you wanted rid of her.'

That was nastily psychological enough to be plausible. Maree'd got rid of herself, though, getting Dad tested like that. It had been careless, to leave the letter in her pocket – I wondered if she'd done the testing before she'd come here. Had she had a fling with him in LA, got him okayed, come back ready to continue the affair? Even for film people it seemed a bit strange.

'And?' DI Macrae said. I looked up. 'I can see you're thinking something through. Care to share it with us?'

I shook my head. If in doubt, say nowt.

'Okay,' he said. 'Let's go back to the start. You came off set – when?'

'Just after six.' I thought of a ball I could safely throw to distract him. 'We were all a bit off balance because of the rock – oh, you maybe don't know about that.'

Faster than thought, he slammed his palm down. Sergeant Peterson's pencil skidded a Z. 'Don't try to play games, Ms Lynch. I'll come back to this rock. After six. Then what?'

Very well, no nonsense. I straightened my spine. 'Anders and I had a pint. Kevin joined us, Kevin Manson, he's a local man, filming the filmers. Then Anders went up to the bar and I scrubbed the decks and checked *Stormfugl* over. I finished that around eight, had a shower, and washed the clothes I'd worn.'

'What did you do with them?'

'I pegged them out on the pushpit rail. They're still there.'

A glance sparked between the two officers. DI Macrae nodded. 'Go on.'

'Then I went along to see Dad. He was there, Maree wasn't. We had a whiskey together. A nightcap.'

'A bit early for a nightcap, wasn't it?'

Damn. 'Dad's evening dram.'

'What did you and your father talk about?' Sergeant Peterson asked. 'How you'd got on that day?'

I hadn't even mentioned the rock, and it had been the big thing of the day. I didn't want to give them the truth; I had to. 'We talked about my mother.'

'An odd thing for him to talk about, surely, with Maree around?'

'She wasn't there,' I repeated.

'Don't try to be clever, Ms Lynch,' she said. Now I had two bad cops on my quarter. 'What brought the subject of your mother up? Were you trying to put him off Maree? You're a Catholic, aren't you? How do you feel about divorce?'

'If Dad was serious about Maree he'd have to divorce Maman, I suppose,' I said.

The DI came in again. 'You've made it quite clear you knew he was serious. What brought your mother up?'

'I can't remember.'

'Was it he who first mentioned her, or you?'

I shook my head. 'I don't know.'

'What were you saying about her?' Sergeant Peterson asked.

I didn't want to give them this. 'I learned that she'd had an abortion when I was little. She'd gone off to France to sing, and when she came back the baby was gone.'

'Why did he tell you this?'

'I suppose he was thinking about my mother – about setting Maree in her place. This baby would have been a boy.'

'How did he know that? They didn't have the technology then, not for a foetus young enough to be aborted.'

I hadn't thought of that. Had Dad just persuaded himself it would have been a boy, or had the baby been older than I'd envisaged, twenty weeks, twenty-four? I thought of the scan photo of Charlie that Inga kept in her purse and couldn't bear it. 'I don't know how he knew. But it upset me to know about it, even though it was all that time ago.'

I hoped he'd leave it alone then. Naive, Cass. 'Not a happy topic from a man with a new, young girlfriend he could have children with. Was all well with Maree?'

'As far as I knew.'

The DI leaned forward, half-smiling. 'You're a very bad liar. Try again.'

'We didn't talk about Maree. We talked about my mother,' I said doggedly, 'and that upset me.'

'Thou shalt not bear false witness,' he said softly. Then, harder, 'That's not just not incriminating others, Ms Lynch, it's telling lies of omission.'

I shrugged.

'So,' the DI continued in that soft, lilting voice, 'a sum-up: you went to see your father. This rock had upset you, so you went to talk to your father about it, but you didn't tell him. Instead you talked about your mother's abortion over twenty years ago. Did you put him to bed before you went?'

'Dad,' I retorted, 'is six feet tall, and strongly built. I couldn't put him anywhere.'

'He *was* drunk, then?' Sergeant Peterson put in swiftly.

'I told you, we had a whiskey together.'

'Had he been drinking before that?'

'He usually had a glass of wine with a meal,' I conceded. 'He had one whiskey while I was there.'

'How drunk, Ms Lynch?'

'I didn't say he was drunk.' Drunk meant he could have been angry enough to strike out at Maree, kill her without meaning it.

'That's right, he'd just had a nightcap. At half past eight. Then what?'

'Then I kept going. I just went out to sea until dawn, almost to Papa, then turned round and came home. You can see the log for yourselves, it's aboard *Khalida.* I got back in and found the body.'

DI Macrae nodded to the Sergeant. 'Go and fetch the logbook.'

'It's lying on the chart table,' I said. 'A dark blue book.'

She went out, and there was silence. The DI leaned back in his chair, studying me. I wasn't going to do an out-staring contest, as if I was six. Instead I watched the Sergeant walk down the pontoon between *Stormfugl* and *Khalida.* I was unprepared for the wave of rage that swept through me as she stepped clumsily over our guard rail and clambered into the cockpit.

'You don't look like a murderer,' the DI said suddenly. 'Stubborn and self-contained, yes. So was Madeleine Smith, the nice Victorian girl who killed her French lover. You don't look like a sailor either. You're small and wiry, not tall and strong-looking, although I bet you have arm muscles that put mine to shame. But Ellen MacArthur doesn't look like a sailor either, she looks like a primary school teacher. I don't go by appearances.'

Sergeant Peterson came out of the cabin, the log-book in one hand.

'Do you know yet when she was killed?' I asked.

'He gave me a level look. 'She died around the time you arrived.'

That meant I could have killed her. I took a deep breath. 'Look,' I said, 'can I tell you about the rock? It could be important.'

Sergeant Peterson came in and laid the log-book in front of him. He flipped it open. There was last night's sail, with time, compass heading, boat speed, distance covered, wind direction and speed, sea state, cloud cover, visibility, and a line of comments in logbook shorthand: Busta abeam, full sail, port tack. It was written in ink pen, and he could see it wasn't tippex-ed anywhere.

'I agree,' he said, 'that if you didn't go for a sail this looks well-faked. You could do that easily enough.'

I didn't say anything.

'Finish off your story before we begin on your saboteur,' he said. 'How about your Dad? Where did he go?'

I saw the trap at last. If he was drunk, he might have done the murder out of temper.

If he was sober, he could have gone to meet Maree after I'd gone, quarrelled again and killed her. It wasn't me they were after. It was Dad.

ᛋ

I'd have liked to tell the truth and have faith in Scottish justice, but nobody was that naive these days. Even though I didn't accept for a moment Dad would have killed Maree, I wasn't going to risk it. Yet, if I didn't tell now, when I'd not spoken to him, then he wouldn't be believed when he told the truth. I could certainly testify that he was out for the count when I left, beyond driving, beyond waking to quarrel with a returned Maree. I thought about how I could begin: 'When I went over Dad had just had a blazing row with Maree–'

I couldn't do it. Not unless Dad looked at me and said, 'I've told them the truth.' Then I'd corroborate. Not before. For now, I had the right to silence.

Stupid! I had the right to a lawyer.

'I want to phone a solicitor,' I said, abruptly.

The DI's face hardened. 'You have that right, of course. We can interpret this request as we choose.'

I sat up straight again. 'Please. Let me tell you about that rock, yesterday. You're after incriminating my Dad, assuming Favelle was killed by mistake for Maree–' Suddenly, I saw that Dad was off the hook. My mouth fell open. I looked at the DI and smiled.

'It's okay. Forget the lawyer.' I looked him straight in the eye. 'Look, when I got over, Dad had just had a row with Maree. That's why I was stalling. He's a lot older than she is, and she wants to have children, so she had him tested. He found out and had an absolute fit. A slur on his manhood, you know. She stormed out and he got drunk. He told me about the row and then he talked about Maman and the baby, and then he flaked out cold. Believe me, I've put enough drunks to bed.' It was a perennial problem of shore leave. 'I couldn't shift Dad, but I put a blanket over him, and I wouldn't expect him to have moved till morning.'

'Drunks can revive,' DI Macrae said. 'You know that too, Ms Lynch. Maree comes back, he wakes up, hits her.'

I shook my head positively. 'He was hoping she'd come back.' I remembered his face when I'd come in, that mixture of shame and appeal. 'He knew he was in the right, she shouldn't have done it, but he was in the wrong too. He wanted to make up. Of course he was angry – no, that's the wrong word.' I groped for the Shetland. 'Black affronted. How dare she doubt his virility?'

I leaned forward. 'Listen, though. As drunk as he was, he knew me. If he'd woken with someone else coming in, Favelle, say, coming to look for Maree, or coming to smooth things over, though I can't see her doing either of those things, well, he'd have known her. Of course he would. He had a light on in the room, and I left it on. It's like you said: Maree had short dark hair, and Favelle was a redhead. He couldn't possibly have confused one with the other, no matter how drunk he was. So there. He wouldn't have killed Favelle in the house by mistake for Maree, because he'd have seen who she was, and he couldn't have killed her on the longship by mistake for Maree, because he couldn't have driven there. If he'd woken, and got in the car to go and look for her – and I grant you, he might have done that, because he wanted to make up - he'd have been in the ditch at the first bend. He *would*, now. If you were to send someone to take a reading of his blood, I think that would corroborate that.'

He gave me an intent look, then nodded. 'That's better, Ms Lynch. Sergeant–' He scribbled on a bit of paper, and she went out of the door with it. I heard her voice phoning, but couldn't distinguish the words.

DI Macrae pulled the hook out of his pocket once more. His face had gone back to that friendly, good-natured air.

'Do you do much fishing?' I asked.

'A bit, a bit. When I can. There's a river, not far from where I live, with sea trout. I caught a twelve-pounder, just last week.' He gave a sudden smile, like the sun coming out on a shallow river. 'It's not the fishing that I go for, it's the quiet. Sitting by the river, with the wrens flitting from the moss-covered boulders, and sometimes, if I'm still enough for long enough, a deer.' His eyes narrowed. 'Do you ever see strange things at sea, alone, on a night watch?'

I nodded.

'Well, only once, down at the river, I saw one of the Kellynch cats. Big and black, it was, with a tail the length of itself, and with eyes green as copper flames. It came down to drink. It must have been the size of a Labrador. The world's a stranger place than the experts believe.'

I could see it in my mind's eye. The man, still and silent against the silver-trunked birches, and the river running, and the great black cat, raising its head to stare with those burning green eyes, then slipping away with only a waving of curved fronds to show it had been there at all. If he hadn't been a police officer, I'd have told him about my mer-horse, off Fiji, with a glistening neck and blind, saucer eyes, but I wasn't going to be cajoled into an alliance with the enemy. He saw my face close against him, laid his hook down.

'Now, tell me about this rock of yours.'

'Yesterday,' I said. 'We were filming at the back of this island here, and there's an old house up above the beach there. A firework went off and tumbled a sizeable rock down towards us. Something like an old lintel, it was rectangular, it cart-wheeled rather than rolled.'

'A firework?' He glanced at Sergeant Peterson's notes.

'That's what Anders said afterwards. Someone had balanced the rock so that it a touch would put it over, and put a firework under it. When the firework went off, the rock fell.'

'Simple. Ingenious. But it's not firework time of year, so traceable. Did Mr Johansen mention timed fuses?'

'No. Somebody will have kept the bits though, so you'll be able to see them. The other thing is, it had to be somebody who was there, and there was only us.' I explained about the road blocks, and the motor launch on guard.

'Sabotage,' DI Macrae said thoughtfully. 'Or was it aimed at Favelle?'

'Yesterday, I didn't think so,' I said. 'Today, though–' I paused, wondering just how wild my surmises were. A man who'd seen a big cat would accept wild surmise.

He nodded. 'Don't worry if it sounds far-fetched. Leave us to sift that out.'

'It could have been a murder attempt,' I said. 'Elizabeth stuck the running order up all over the place. That shot, the one with everyone going up the hill, well, it was obvious that Ted and Favelle would be in the lead at that point. It was the big 'landing in a new world' scene. So they'd be the likely ones to be hit.'

'Likely, but rather a hit-and-miss method. A murderer who didn't care if he got it wrong.'

'Favelle had a long dress on,' I said. 'Green velvet, floor-length, very heavy.' His eyes, Alain's eyes, sharpened; I could see he was thinking as I was. 'I can't believe the real Gudrid went anywhere near a ship wearing something like that. It tangled round ropes and trailed everywhere.'

'So,' he finished, 'she would be slower to get out of the way.'

I nodded.

'How did she escape?'

'She nearly didn't,' I said. I could see it all in my head, Anders scooping Favelle up in a swirl of green velvet. 'She was stumbling over her dress, and the rock was coming straight at her. She had Anders beside her, and his reactions are like lightening. He just swung her up into his arms, as if it'd been rehearsed, and carried her out of the way. Otherwise I think it would have hit her.'

'How did she come to have Anders beside her? You just said she and Ted should have been in the lead.'

'The other unexpected factor,' I said. 'Peerie Charlie. The little boy that's their boy in the film.' I smiled. 'He wouldn't leave the beach, so they had to re-jig the story and change the order. Ted went ahead, and Favelle came with Anders.'

'Whose choice was that?'

'Ted,' I said positively. 'She was leaning on the captain's arm, but he was too tall for her and it didn't look right. Anders was shorter. Anyway, that delayed the start of shooting the scene, rearranging the people. Not by much, but by enough for the cast to be at the bottom of the hill, furthest away from where the rock fell, instead of at the top, right underneath it.'

My memory gave a little kick. 'They had a cigarette break in between rehearsals, up at the old house. Could you light a fuse with a cigarette, like on the movies?'

'Let's assume you can. Who was last back on set?'

I tried to re-visualise it. 'I wasn't really watching. Ted would know, he was rounding them up. Elizabeth, Michael, the other cameramen, they stayed up there.'

Elizabeth. Once the cameras started rolling, everyone else would be glued to the viewfinder. She could easily have lit the fuse then. I thought of the hunger in her eyes as she watched Ted, the way they changed from cool efficiency when she was talking to him to blatant adoration when he turned away. She hadn't known about the change-over. The film captain had reactions like tar. He wouldn't have saved Favelle the way Anders had.

Had Elizabeth's hatred of Favelle risen to such a pitch that to get rid of her she'd have risked Ted's life?

CHAPTER 10

Sergeant Peterson came back in then, nodded confirmation at the Inspector, and sat down again.

'Ms Lynch is telling me about her rock, Sergeant,' he said. 'Of course it could have been general sabotage of the film. From what you say, there was a reasonable chance that the people would get out of the way. Could it have been aimed at your longship?'

'I suppose it could. They all knew exactly where she'd be beached, from the rehearsal, and it came straight for her.' I remembered the wind and the bang of it passing by, glanced down at my ankle. The bruise was an interesting blue.

He followed my gaze. 'It hit you?'

I shook my head. 'It missed me.'

I drew my foot back under the chair. 'I thought it was going to smash *Stormfugl*'s bows in. It hit another rock at the very last minute, and that deflected it just enough.'

'Would wrecking the boat put paid to the film?'

I considered that one. 'Not now, I don't think. I'm sure they'd have enough shots to be able to cobble something together in a studio.'

'So that's a less likely motive.'

'Yeah–' I said slowly. 'But we had two more days after that, of Favelle doing a promotional video for the windfarm, and one of the protestors was up there too.'

He looked across at Sergeant Peterson. 'Mr Lynch's company wants to build a very large windfarm here on Shetland,' she answered.

He nodded and made a note. 'Who would have a list of who was on set?'

'Elizabeth,' I said. 'I can give you a list of my rowers.'

'You haven't mentioned Maree – was she there?'

That was a good question. She'd gone from the tent into Favelle's white limo, and been driven off for the swap. At Jessie's, she'd have taken off her wig and her film-star coat. After that she could have come back as herself, walking over the hill or flashing her film ID photo at the police road block, in which case she'd have been there, able to go up among the camera-man at the old house for a quick fag while the actors were down below. She could have pressed the lit end of her cigarette against the fuse that would smoulder up to the granite boulder and make it fall towards her double, the woman who robbed her of a life of her own. If she hated Favelle enough to kill her, she wouldn't have cared if Ted died too.

Michael would know if she'd been there.

I didn't want to spoil the friendlier atmosphere by going back to evasion. 'Can I ask you to talk to Ted about that? I'm not sure how much I should be saying about Maree's role in the film.'

'The police can be discreet,' he said. 'You've made up your mind to be helpful now; keep going. If it doesn't concern the murder, I won't spread it further.'

'It's surmise on my part, you understand that?' I glanced at Sergeant Peterson. 'Please don't write it down. Maree was the official double for the filming before Favelle arrived. That's standard practice. The big stars like Favelle only do the close stuff. But I think she was still doubling for Favelle in the scenes on board the boat when we were at sea, unofficially, because Favelle was no good aboard boats, and Maree was the athletic twin. They were alike enough to pull it off. I've no proof of it, though, and Ted may well deny it. He wouldn't want to spoil Favelle's reputation.' Suddenly, a wave of disbelief swept over me. Favelle, living and beautiful on widescreen, had become a crumpled body aboard *Stormfugl.*

'Has anyone told Maree that Favelle's dead?' I asked.

He looked across at Sergeant Peterson. 'We've tried to break the news ourselves, sir, but it's spreading like wildfire. I think all of the people staying at Busta know now.'

'She's not staying at Busta,' I said. Michael would have let her know, if he knew himself. No, Michael had been on Ronas Hill filming the midnight sun with Ted. Michael thought Maree was dead. 'She's staying at the B&B just above the marina here,

Efstibister. That way, they could swap Maree and Favelle on the way to filming.'

DI Macrae nodded. 'Very well.' He smiled again, and this time I smiled back. Entente cordiale. 'If you think of anything else you want to tell me, you can contact me through any of my officers.' He stood up, and I followed, stretching. How long had I been sitting in that chair? My back felt stiff. 'However–' He was interrupted by a rattling at the door downstairs and Dad's voice, in determined businessman mode. An officer came in.

'Gentleman downstairs, sir, a Mr Lynch. He has his lawyer with him, and insists on seeing Ms Lynch.'

'That's fine,' DI Macrae said. 'Bring him up.'

There was no sign of a hangover. Dad was impressively corporate in a dark suit, his hair sleeked back and his club tie giving off 'solid citizen' signals at fifty paces. He was accompanied by a younger man, short and round-faced, with gold-rimmed glasses. Dad came straight up to DI Macrae.

'Dermot Lynch, Inspector. Cassandre's father. This is my lawyer, Mr Cheyne.'

DI Macrae rose and held out his hand. 'I'm pleased to meet you, Mr Lynch. Perhaps you'd like to give us your statement now, and then we won't need to trouble either of you further.' He turned his head back to me. 'Except, Ms Lynch, as I was about to say, that we'd like permission to search your boat.'

'Stormfugl?' I said. 'I'd assumed that'd be automatic, as she's a crime scene. But, yes, of course.'

'No,' he said. 'Your own boat.'

I felt like he'd poured a bucket of icy water over me. 'Search *Khalida*?''

'Your warrant, sir?' Mr Cheyne said sharply.

DI Macrae shook his head. 'With Ms Lynch's permission, of course.'

'You don't have to give it,' Mr Cheyne said to me.

'If Ms Lynch will let forensics examine her boat,' the DI said, 'it's a further step in clearing her of all involvement in this crime.'

Mr Cheyne bristled like an indignant guillemot. 'There is no suggestion, sir, that Ms Lynch is involved in this crime. Any examination of her boat will be entirely a gesture of goodwill.'

'If it'll help clear me,' I said, 'go ahead. May I be present?'

'If you wish.'

'Anders is living in the forepeak, though, and I can't give you permission to search his stuff. You'll have to ask him.' I hoped Rat was stashed away somewhere safe.

'We'll ask him,' DI Macrae said. He turned to Mr Cheyne. 'As the person who discovered the body, Ms Lynch will naturally be of interest to the press. I would have no objection to her speaking at the police press conference later, should she wish to make a single statement.'

'I'd prefer that,' I said.

He gave me an approving nod. 'The conference is set up for two o clock.' He gave the clock above the bar a quick glance. It was ten to one. 'Can you find suitable clothes for Ms Lynch before then, Mr Cheyne? We'll want to take what she's wearing.'

Mr Cheyne nodded. 'Cassandre, both the girls are about your size. Why not come back to my house for breakfast and a shower, and let Frances see what she can find for you?'

'Off you go, Cassie,' Dad added, 'and get your statement thrashed out.'

I didn't like leaving him in the hands of the police, but there wasn't an alternative. I'd told the truth; I hoped he'd do the same.

The press conference was hellish. We'd had enough bother driving out through the cameras on the way out, and the number seemed to have doubled in the time I'd been at Mr Cheyne's house. I ducked my head back behind the car door frame, and wished I was wearing my own navy jacket instead of Mrs Cheyne's disconcertingly elegant green blazer and cream top. I'd washed my hair, looped my plait up on my head and even added a touch of make up, but instead of giving me confidence, it only made me feel more ill-at-ease. A policeman took us to the committee room, where DI Macrae was twitching the cuffs of his green jacket. He looked grim and tired. I wondered if he'd been woken at 4am, if he'd be glad or sorry if the case was given to somebody more senior.

He turned as I came in. 'All set?'

Just as I nodded there was a stir at the door and Ted entered. His tanned face was lined and grey, and there was such a bleak desolation in his eyes that even looking felt like an intrusion.

We went in single file up the stairs: DI Macrae, another policeman, Ted, me. I clutched my paper with sweating hands. We went through the door labelled 'No wet clothes in the clubroom', and into the scrum.

They'd set out tables in front of the fireplace wall, and there were four rows of faces leaning towards us, eyes avid. A phalanx of cameras bristled behind the chairs and in the aisle to each side. I remembered the press after Alain's death, and wanted to be sick, but now wasn't the time, any more than you had time to lean over the rail when you were at the helm, however strong the rolling and pitching got.

DI Macrae did an opening statement in a fusillade of flashes, and then introduced me: 'The skipper of *Stormfugl,* Ms Lynch, who discovered the body, will now make a statement.'

I read out what we'd prepared as naturally as I could. 'I was returning from a night sail. I found Favelle lying dead on board *Stormfugl.* I phoned the police, then remained with the body until they arrived.'

Of course they weren't satisfied with that. 'How did you feel finding the body?'

'It was very upsetting,' I said. 'A shock.'

Then they all began speaking together. 'What did Favelle look like dead?' 'Is there any truth in the rumour that the gulls pecked her hands off?' 'What was she like to work with on set?'

I grasped at the last one. 'She was very good to work with. Completely professional.'

'What was she doing on board your Viking boat? Did you sleep there?'

DI Macrae cut in there. 'Investigations are proceeding on that point. We can't say any more at this stage.'

A greasy-looking man in the front row leaned forward. 'Cass, did you see any tension between Favelle and Ted?'

I shook my head. 'None.' Smile, charm them. 'Except when they were acting.'

It got a brief laugh.

'Cass, do you have a boyfriend?'

'What?' I asked, startled.

'How did you get on with Ted?' a voice asked from the back.

'My concern was with the boat side,' I said. 'He gave very clear instructions.'

They found this funny. I heard their penguin cackle echo round the room and wished the floor would swallow me.

Ted rescued me. 'Cassandre has been a great skipper. The success of the ship scenes was very much in her hands.'

That diverted them. 'Ted, how do you feel?'

'Devastated,' he said simply. 'Not just my personal loss – I can't talk about that yet – but at the loss to cinema too. Favelle was a great star already and she was taking off in a new direction. Who knows what she'd have created if it hadn't been for this tragedy.'

'What was she doing on the longship?'

DI Macrae came in smoothly. 'Investigations are on-going with regard to that.'

'Where were you when she was killed, Ted?'

I straightened indignantly.

'My Director of Photography and I were filming up on Ronas Hill,' he answered. 'We were getting footage of sunset and sunrise on the ocean horizon. It was a perfect night for it.' His voice faltered and died; he ducked his head away and covered his eyes with one hand.

It didn't stop them. 'Ted, are you going to release the film?'

He lifted his face, the tears glinting in their flash guns. 'It'll be her memorial. The shooting here in Shetland was the last piece, and it was all but finished. We can make her immortal–'

He broke down then, and they filmed avidly as Sergeant Peterson came forward and led him away. DI Macrae leaned forward.

'Ladies and gentlemen, thank you.'

Dad was waiting when I got out of there, my heart beating as if I'd just reached port after a rollercoaster dead run.

'Cassie, I can't get hold of Maree at all. Her mobile's switched off, going straight to answer-phone. She left Jessie's last night, just said she'd be away a few days. The DI's checked the boat and airport, and nobody of that name has left Shetland today. She's just gone.' His face was drawn. 'Cassie, I'm afraid the murderer's taken her.'

It wasn't like Dad to give way to panic. I thought of the way he'd waited for my mother all these years, and realised he'd switched all that longing over to Maree and the possible son.

'We have no reason to believe that, sir,' DI Macrae said from behind me.

'Then where is she?' Dad retorted. 'Her sister's death is being blazoned all over the wireless.'

'There are still people who leave the TV and radio off during the day,' DI Macrae said.

'Come on, Dad,' I said. 'Let's get home. That's where she'll phone, when she hears the news.'

But we waited in the house all that long afternoon, and the phone remained silent.

I hadn't forgotten about Anders though. We had a lunch of toast and paté, then I took my mobile into my bedroom.

Time-warp. Whatever Maree had said, the redecoration hadn't started yet. It could have been just yesterday that I'd dragged my kitbag out from under the bed and flung the minimum into it. Posters of a fleet of old Gaffers racing in the Thames estuary were still blu-tacked beside a sixties-bearded Robin Knox-Johnston arriving home. The trophies sat in their row on the chest of drawers, in front of my well-thumbed copies of *Swallows and Amazons* and *Missee Lee* along with my later reading, Bernard Moitessier, *The Last Grain Race,* Elvestrom's *Dinghy Sailing.* My buoyancy aid and my dry-suit still hung in the cupboard. The same duvet cover was on the bed, and the little folding clock with the beep-beep-beep alarm was set neatly in the middle of the bedside cabinet, its battery long since dead. I sat as I used to sit on the window-seat, one leg curled up beneath me and the voe spread before me. The wind was rising; Papa Little was ringed with white, and the near lines of mussel buoys had waves breaking over the black sea-serpent humps.

I wondered if the Inspector had really seen a black cat. It would be nice to know that in this crowded Britain there was a breeding population of large cats. Maybe, though, he was softening me up, using a sprat to catch a whale.

Anders. I took out my mobile. There was coverage here; three bars. A tinned voice buzzed in my ear: This phone is switched off. Try later or send a text.

I wrote a new short message: Where r u? Khalida 2 b searched must talk c.

I called Mr Berg next, before he saw the press conference. 'I am sorry to report,' I said, 'that the woman who died aboard *Stormfugl* was Favelle herself, and that it does not appear to be an accident.'

'I have already been visited by the police here in Norway,' he said heavily. 'I am considering what to do. Ted wishes to finish the film.' His voice lightened, sounded almost smug. 'I will contact you again.'

End of conversation; probably end of job.

ᛋ

Later, after Dad and I had silently shared a what's-in-the-fridge casserole, I phoned Maman. I needed the Olympian perspective of Juno, chief goddess. I thought she might be at a rehearsal, but the phone gave its single echoing buzz only three times before there was a click.

'Eugénie Delafauve, allo?'

'Salut, Maman,' I said.

'Cassandre. I was just about to phone you. I saw you on the news, ten minutes ago. The death of a film star.' She didn't sound surprised. Film stars were a lesser breed, prone to sudden death, unlike singers, who had to go on no matter what. 'Upon your ship, it seems. That is unfortunate.' Although it was also not surprising, as ships, although orderly in conception, had to contend with disorderly waves and wind.

'Very,' I agreed. 'It will not do my métier as a skipper much good.'

'And the police? You are not antagonising them?'

'Au contraire. I am even letting them search *Khalida*.'

'Qui ça ? Ah, your boat.' There was a frowning pause. 'Does that mean you are under suspicion?'

'I think so,' I said. 'You see, I didn't recognise her. I thought she was the star's twin sister.'

'And so?'

'It's a bit complicated.'

'Explain, then.'

'The twin, Maree, whose body I thought it was, she and Dad are friendly.'

'Ah.' It was a soft sound that would have reached the leaning-forward students in the gods. 'Serious?'

'That's complicated too. Yes, I believe. Except Dad's made a mess of it. They had a massive row the night she died, and his alibi depends on me so I'm not sure the police believe it. On top of that, she's gone missing.'

'Yes.' She left another considering silence. 'You are not likely to be arrested imminently?'

'I hope not.'

'Good. I have arrangements to make. You are at your father's house? Do not make anything worse, either of you. I will telephone in half an hour.'

It was nearer three quarters of an hour. 'Cassandre? I will arrive on the last aeroplane tomorrow night. I will stay with you and your father, naturally.'

Naturellement.

'I have arranged a concert in the Town Hall, on Saturday.'

'How did you manage that?'

I could see her immaculately curved eyebrows rising in surprise. 'I telephoned the head of your Shetland Arts, of course, and told him I was willing to perform. He was most delighted. One would not wish to look as if one was rushing to the defence.'

I didn't expect DI Macrae to accept that on face value. And what was Maree going to say when she turned up? Come to that, what would Dad say? I was torn between relief that Maman was taking over, that this whole mess would receive a dose of efficient French commonsense (nobody would arrest us, I thought illogically, with Maman in charge) and irritation at myself for being relieved. A good skipper didn't need her mother as *dea ex machina*.

'Now, the important thing,' Maman said ominously. 'Your clothes. If I am to present you as my daughter, you must be better dressed. I will bring something of a proper cut to the airport, for you to change before we meet the press. What shoe size are you?'

'Five, I think.'

'What is that in Continental size? No, never mind, the shoe-shop will know. Black brogues and sandals suitable for a dress.'

'A dress?' I echoed, aghast. *Assieds-toi, joue avec tes poupees.*

'You cannot impress in jeans. But I will bring you properly tailored jeans and a jacket. I cannot think what possessed you to wear that one for the television. Awful. I will see you tomorrow at ten past seven. Do not alert the Press, my agent will do that. Now, you had better pass this phone to your father.'

I took it through. 'Maman.'

Dad's eyebrows shot upwards. He attempted at a smile. 'Eugénie? How are you doing, girl?'

A flood of accented English from the phone. I left them to it.

My mobile did its text-bleep at last. Staying with friend. Search okay rat out. Meet up tomorrow over and out a.

Over and out. Our shorthand for 'I'm just going up the mast' or 'taking the autopilot off' or 'the wind's blowing up'. I'm not answering any more calls.

I suddenly realised how little I knew about Anders. His routines, yes. He was a morning-shower person. Breakfast at 7.30: a bowl of cornflakes with one spoonful of sugar and half a pint of milk, followed by toast with cold meat on top, salami for preference, and a slice of that sweet Norwegian cheese, then a pint glass three-quarters full of orange juice, drunk in a oner. He'd work until his midday cup of tea, with milk and two sugars. He was a steady worker, not pausing to chat all the time. Lunch break, more bread, cheese and salami. Evening meal, whatever was going. Curry acceptable; British chips, not.

I could tell you what he would be doing at any hour of the day, but I didn't have a clue what was going on in his head. He'd mixed well with the film crowd, chatting up the girls with superficial success, since Rat had had to be left aboard, but I hadn't noticed him actually getting anywhere with any particular one. He'd presumably slept aboard *Khalida* on my watch-nights, since he'd been there for breakfast. He'd been in the cockpit or, these warmer nights, on *Stormfugl*, for his watch-nights, and if anyone had joined him there I hadn't noticed signs of their presence.

Staying with friend. A sudden memory gave me the *where. Did you hear they saw the ghost at Busta ... Suzanne screamed to wake the whole house, then went into a fit of hysterics.* He'd been on the longship all day, and fully occupied with Favelle during lunch; the only way he'd know about that would be if he'd been there, at Busta.

I was sure he hadn't been at Busta last night, though. He genuinely hadn't seen what was going on and he would have if he'd returned from there. He'd have been on watch aboard *Stormfugl* for the first part of the night at least. What had made him take refuge in the boating club? I couldn't see what would have panicked him so much that he'd had to cobble together an alibi.

Spent the night together, indeed. He'd got some explaining to do.

It had been a hell of a day. When I lay down I felt heavy, earthbound. I tried to remember when I'd last slept ashore. That hostel the police had taken me to, a dormitory with a dozen beds. No, it had been in the Med, those box-sized chalets they'd called accommodation.

Not since I'd bought *Khalida.* I gritted my teeth. Until Mr Berg sacked me, I was still skipper. There had been a murder aboard my ship, and under God I'd see the murderer brought to justice.

Paranoia or what.

I lay awake and thought. What on earth was Favelle doing aboard *Stormfugl?* The only answer that I could think of was that she was looking for Maree. She'd tried to find her at Jessie's, and failed, because Maree had already lit out. Perhaps she'd tried ringing Dad, and got no answer. So her next thought was to try the longship, or *Khalida.* I considered that as logic, and decided it would hold.

Now, why was she looking for Maree? Given the secrecy of their set-up, it had to be something pretty urgent. Well, the big thing that had happened that day – yesterday, only yesterday - had been the rock falling. Favelle had been angry when Ted had dismissed it as an accident. Did she have reason to believe it wasn't an accident?

Hang on, the other thing that had happened was the letters. I'd given Maree a handful of letters, and she'd gestured towards Elizabeth. Then she'd looked at the top one, the typewritten one, and taken them after all. Then at lunch-time, Favelle had been distant, annoyed.

Did all that get me anywhere? Suppose, just suppose, she'd been receiving threatening letters, threats she thought were being carried out when the rock fell. That would explain her anger with Ted when he took it lightly.

Yes! That conversation between Maree and Ted, the day before the rock fall. Could it have been about anonymous letters?

Ted had been warning Maree to keep quiet, and Maree had insisted Favelle was to be told. *'I'm not prepared to keep this to myself.'*

Ted's voice, equally determined. *'You must. For her sake, you must.'*

Maree wanted Favelle told. If she'd recognised that type-written letter as a threatening one, she'd have made sure Favelle got it. In the meantime our threatener followed it up with the rock.

That didn't mean Maree herself wasn't the threatener. Suppose she was. She made sure Favelle read the letter, but said she couldn't discuss it just now, she had to get off set. 'Don't come to Jessie's house. Meet me at the longship, after dark.' Then –

My reasoning broke down. Then she legged it in a way calculated to draw attention to herself, instead of sitting put and acting upset, or going back to Dad for a grand reconciliation and acting ignorant. Besides, she hadn't legged it far. DI Macrae had told Dad she hadn't been on a flight or the boat – not under her own name, anyway. If she'd carried a faked passport, then this was a long-laid murder plot, which didn't fit with the affair with Dad. All the same, I considered it. Getting his sperm tested did seem an odd thing to do, and you could safely expect him to have a fit about it. All you had to do was make sure he read the letter.

No, it was all needlessly elaborate. There was no need to drag Dad into it at all, except as a double-bluff too elaborate for even the skipper who made us re-set all the sails into identical angles. And she'd *liked* Dad. I envisaged her again in his kitchen, humming to herself as she chopped onions, her face lighting up as he'd come in. That hadn't been a fake.

Besides, I couldn't think of any reason why Maree would kill Favelle. Finance? No, her husband Ted would, I presumed, inherit the bulk of her estate. Deep laid resentment against her star of a sister was possible, but she didn't like the film star life, she couldn't be bothered with film people, and she was getting out.

Very well then, assuming Maree was innocent, *where was she?*

Dad had been waiting for her to come back. It hadn't been final, just an argument, but serious enough to make Maree wonder if she really wanted to take on a man who was a generation away. She'd have wanted peace and quiet to think it through, but she'd also have wanted to be able to meet Dad for a reconciliation if that's what she decided to go for.

Peace and quiet in Shetland. Jessie had copies of the magazine *Shetland Visitor* in every room. I'd have looked for a self-catering cottage in the back of beyond, and phoned the owner, calling myself Jane Smith and paying cash. I'd have switched my mobile off, so that nobody could bother me. If the cottage was small enough, it might not have a TV or radio, so I wouldn't see the news. Maree wouldn't care about missing a day or two of riots in the Middle East and rows over oil prices.

Tomorrow, I decided, I'd work my way through the pages of the *Shetland Visitor.* I'd phone each landlady and ask if they'd had a sudden booking from a single lady the night before last.

If Maree was still in Shetland, I'd find her.

Chapter 11

DI Macrae had set the search of *Khalida* for ten the next morning. I was pacing the pontoon at quarter to. The tide had only just begun to flow back. *Khalida*'s sides reflected white in the water, and the sunlight rippled along the hull. They'd taken my key, so I could only peer in at the varnished wood and swinging lantern of my home, my sanctuary.

He arrived with three spaceman officers following him. I could feel curtains twitching right round Brae. To make it worse, Ted's white limo drove past, and I saw the pale blur of his face turning to look. I didn't want him to think I could be responsible for his wife's death.

Behind the officers there was someone in a coastguard uniform, presumably an expert in checking boats for hidden compartments. Well, there were no smugglers' holes in *Khalida*. He was a tall, dark bloke of around my age who walked with a familiar, unhurried stride. Then he turned and I saw it was Martin Nicolson, Inga's brother, who used to crew for me.

I'd thought then that he'd end up good-looking. Like Inga, he was a "dark" Shetlander, with black, black hair and brown eyes, Inga's moulded cheekbones, a firm mouth and determined chin. He'd been a damned good crew, reacting before the puff of wind or fall-away; the trophies I'd won had been half his, and we'd shared them month about.

'Martin!' I said.

He ducked his head sideways, gave me a shy smile. 'I wasn't sure you'd remember.'

'Not *remember*?' I turned to DI Macrae, who was frowning at this possible compromise to his search. 'Martin was my crew in my Mirror.'

'A fine time we had too,' Martin said, grinning his old grin. 'I'm never had as much fun since.' Then the grin faded. 'I'm sorry about this, Cass. They asked the coastguard for someone who knew about the construction of peerie boats. I didna ken it was yours they were searching.'

I managed a shrug. 'The more thoroughly they search, the more thoroughly I'm cleared.'

'Then we'll get on with it,' DI Macrae said, and nodded to one of the officers. 'Prints, then we'll come in.'

I eased my toes out of my flip-flops and sat down on the pontoon, bare feet dangling in the water. Its touch soothed me. 'I don't know how you all plan to squeeze in,' I said.

'I'll stay outside,' DI Macrae said equably. He crouched down beside me, the pleats of his kilt brushing the wooden walkway. 'Thank you for being so sensible about this, Ms Lynch.'

'It has to be done,' I said. 'Like I said, go ahead and clear me.'

He could hear the confidence in my voice, shot a quick glance sideways. 'It doesn't clear you that much. If you killed Favelle, why would you bring a blood-boltered weapon to your own boat when you could just drop it overboard?'

I looked into the darkness beneath *Khalida*'s white side, down to where the brown kelp waved. 'Dropping it overboard wouldn't be clever. The water's not deep, and it's clear.' A starfish gleamed on the bottom. 'Look, you'd see it.'

'Not,' he said gently, 'if it was a stone, just like the others.'

'Divers could tell a newly-dropped land stone,' I said. 'I'd think of that.'

A white flash from within *Khalida* made me jump. I could see the spacemen moving like ghosts. In the cockpit, Martin began taking items out of the lockers: the bucket with spare anchor chair, the life-raft, the light-weight sails in their bags, put aft out of Rat's way, fenders and mooring warps, the winch handle for the main halyard, a bottle of water. He swung himself into the biggest locker, and came out again, shaking his head.

DI Macrae watched for a moment, then looked back at me. 'I can tell you that you didn't leave any footprints on *Stormfugl*.'

There was a suspicion of emphasis on the 'you'. I lifted my head. 'Oh?'

'There were a man's footprints, gravelly, going onboard, underneath the body, and to the engine. Larger feet than Anders, by a good three sizes.'

I jerked upright. A little wave crept coldly up my rolled jeans. 'A stranger aboard?'

Now Martin went into the cabin. I could see his shadow checking there were no dummy bulkheads.

A cold suspicion was growing in me. If Anders hadn't been there, then *Stormfugl* had been left unguarded. It could have been Gibbie down below, tinkering. I resolved to check every inch of her before leaving the pier again.

DI Macrae was watching me. 'An idea?'

I shook my head. 'Nothing important.'

'Everything's important just now.' He waited for a moment, but I didn't say anything more. He gave a nod, accepting that. 'Would you like to know about alibis?'

I turned my head to him, surprised. The sun made his thick hair the colour of a stag's ruff. 'If you're telling me.'

'The Ronas Hill group, the ones up filming, they're out of it. They were wandering all over the hill looking for the best views, but their car was parked by a camper-van, and the people in it are willing to swear it never moved until four, when you phoned Ted Tarrant. Tarrant, Michael Ashcroft and the other Director of Photography, James Green, are all in the clear, unless I can work out a way of going twenty miles on foot in three-quarters of an hour, which is the longest time any of them was away from the others. The rest of the film people, well, there was a party at Busta that night, and Favelle and Elizabeth were the only ones who didn't go to it. The whole crew took over the Long Room and stayed up till well after midnight, messing about with ouija boards.'

'Film folk don't seem to need sleep while the shooting's going on,' I said.

'Nobody was absent for longer than it took to go to the toilet or the bar. None of them had any grudge against Favelle; none of them knew her. She was out of their orbit.'

'When was the last time anyone saw Favelle?'

'Elizabeth looked in on her just after half past ten, to see if she had everything she needed. She was sitting at her dressing-table taking her make-up off. She was very calm, Elizabeth said, not in any way different.'

'Was she wearing make-up when you found her?'

He nodded. 'Good, Ms Lynch. Yes, she was. Not heavy make-up; just enough to go out in. But then, we know she went out. She walked aboard your longship.'

'And Elizabeth? What did she do?'

'Went to the party for half an hour. Found the ouija board stuff very childish and went to bed. Alone.' He paused for emphasis. 'The net's closing, Ms Lynch, with only a few fish left in it. Your father, the missing Maree, Mr Johansen, and you.'

Elizabeth, in love with Ted. Gibbie Matthewson, with his obsessive hatreds. Kevin, to stop the wind-farm. There were more fish than he knew, but I wasn't going to tell him that.

He let the silence hang, then, when I said nothing, stood up. 'I'd better see how they're getting on.'

Khalida rocked gently as he climbed aboard. I'd been right about him being used to boats; he went over the guard rail without fumbling. Sergeant Peterson came out to sit beside me, curling her legs underneath her like the Copenhagen statue of the little mermaid.

'You keep your boat very tidy,' she said.

'I have to,' I said. 'When you're at sea the boat's liable to be lying on its side at any moment.'

'I've finally managed to buy my own place,' she said, with good cop friendliness, 'but it's absolutely tiny. I had to weed out everything. One casserole dish, one pan, one frying pan. As for my clothes–'

'But it's yours,' I said.

'No landlord on my back saying I can't do this, can't do the other.' She re-settled herself, keeping her polished shoes well above the salt-stain waves. 'Funny thing is, now I don't want to cover the walls with posters any more. I went to a car boot sale and bought framed pictures, and a bedspread.'

'Nowhere to put a bedspread on *Khalida*,' I said cheerfully. 'She's not one of these aft cabin island bed jobs.'

'It looked cosy, your bed,' the Sergeant said. 'If you're away on your own, though, how do you sleep and keep a lookout for cargo ships running you down?'

'I cat-nap and pray,' I said. 'It's a big ocean. They'll probably miss me.'

Overhead, the terns swooped and screamed. The water lapped at *Khalida*'s side as the men moved around in her. I could see the search in my head. They'd take the covers from my bed, lift the mattress, and see that there was nothing but water-tank and fuel lines underneath. They'd inspect the engine cavity with a flashlight: the prop shaft stretching into darkness. The next compartment, under the chart table: spare clothes, in a polythene bag. One of them was at the cooker. I could hear the clatter as he lifted out the pans from beneath it. Another would be taking out the books from the starboard-side shelf, checking there was nothing behind them, then going down to the compartments: tins, packets, cold store with butter, cheese, yoghurt and fruit. There was a clunk as someone shut the sink stop-cock. I supposed they'd take samples to make sure no murderer had washed off blood in it. The forepeak would be last, with Anders' sleeping bag and gear and the anchor chain in its locker. There was a rattle as someone lifted the tool-box. *Hand-sized, more like a stone…*

Tool box. Gibbie. I turned to Sergeant Peterson. 'When will we be allowed back on board *Stormfugl?*'

'When forensics have finished. It takes as long as it takes.'

'Will you be leaving someone aboard overnight?'

Her brows rose. 'Do you think that's necessary?'

I shrugged. 'I just wondered.'

She gave me a narrow-eyed look. 'I'll tell the officers on patrol to keep their attention on her.'

Gibbie. He'd have come in the darkness, not at 4 am. "Did Favelle die straight after she was hit?'

I got the glare again. 'Why do you ask?'

I remembered touching the still neck. It had been chilly, not cold; the life-warmth not completely gone from it. 'She wasn't long dead when I found her, but I saw no sign of anyone around.'

There was a pause, then a sideways glint from the green eyes, hard as glass. She threw another sprat to catch a whale. 'She was struck on the back of the head, and the blow didn't kill her immediately.'

I didn't ask how long she'd lain there on the half-deck, dying. I didn't want to think about it.

DI Macrae came out again at last. 'Thank you, Ms Lynch.' He gave me back the key, with its monkey's fist ring that Alain had made. 'A clean bill of health.'

'No blood-boltered weapons,' I agreed.

'We've set aside some clothing we'd like to go to forensics.'

'Be my guest,' I said. The clothes I'd washed that evening. I was sorry to see

my favourite gansey in the plastic bag. Even if I got it back, I didn't think I'd want to wear it again.

ᛋ

DI Macrae was just turning away when the white limo came down the gravel track in a spurt of dust and pulled up beside us. Ted leapt out. He had a light blue file under one arm.

'Inspector, I saw what looked like a search of Cass's boat. Surely she's not a serious suspect?'

'We have to consider all avenues of investigation,' DI Macrae said stiffly.

Ted gave me a warm smile. 'I don't believe it.' He turned back to DI Macrae. 'Inspector, Cass had no motive to kill my wife.'

'I think the police case,' I said, 'is that I mistook her for Maree.'

He didn't ask why I should have wanted to kill Maree. Maybe he heard more gossip than I gave him credit for. 'You couldn't mistake Favelle for Maree. They looked quite, quite different.'

No they didn't, Ted, I thought. You're protesting too much to protect Favelle's secret.

'The main difference was in the hair length and colour,' DI Macrae said. 'We have found a white beret which I was hoping, sir, you would identify as Favelle's.'

Ted's long eyelashes flew up. 'Found it? Where?'

'Did your wife wear a white beret, sir? The sort of knitted job a woman might tuck her hair up into?'

I betted the 'sort of knitted job' was a milliner's creation costing half his monthly salary.

Ted nodded. 'She had a beret like that, yes, sir. Although you'd need to show me the actual one.'

'In good time, sir. But you see, if she'd tucked her hair up into it, then she could easily have been mistaken for Maree.'

Ted shook his head very definitely. 'No, sir. I'm certain it was Favelle he was after. I shouldda taken him seriously. I wanted to spare her worry–' He pulled the file out from under his arm, fumbled it open. 'She'd been receiving anonymous letters.'

I gave myself a mental gold star.

DI Macrae took the file from him. 'How many people have handled these, sir?'

'Just myself,' Ted replied.

'Not your wife as well?'

'No. That's what I said – she didn't know about them.'

'They came by post?'

'The first few, yes. I opened the first one in error, and after that Elizabeth looked out for them. I didn't want Favelle to know about them. She's so – she was–' He closed his eyes for a second, mouth twisting. 'There were half a dozen of these letters, if I remember aright, but I've only got two here. We keep them all from her. She needs – needed – to believe everyone loved her.'

'Is that what you quarrelled with Maree about?' I asked.

His head jerked around. 'How d'ya know about that?'

'I was in *Khalida* here,' I said. 'Sound travels over water.'

He hesitated for a moment. 'Yeah,' he admitted. 'Maree wanted to tell her. She was afraid Favelle might be in danger. I didn't agree, but after that rock fell on set I decided I'd take them to the cops. I was gonna come in yesterday, and then–'

DI Macrae opened the front flap of the file and tilted it to look at the letter inside. I was too far away from him to be able to read any of it. 'It's a pity you didn't keep all the letters, sir. When did the first one come?'

'April, if I remember aright. There was a paragraph in the papers about her coming here, and the first one came shortly after that. There were another couple, no, maybe three, while we were still in LA. I'm pretty sure she didn't receive any in Norway. Then, when we came here, I found one lying on her dressing table, not posted, just put there, and there was another one the next day. That's what's in that file. I didn't like that. Someone here was responsible.'

'You've no idea who, sir?'

Ted shook his head.

'What did the envelopes look like?' I butted in. DI Macrae gave me a look.

'Have you any reason to ask that, Ms Lynch?'

'She received a letter that last day,' I said. 'I wondered if it had upset her. A long, white envelope, typed, official looking.'

Ted gave me a surprised look. 'That was it. A white envelope, and the address typed, like a business letter.'

'Did you keep the envelopes too, sir?' DI Macrae asked.

Ted shook his head. 'The two I found weren't in envelopes. They'd been printed on one of our office printers – well, that's what it looks like.'

'And who has access to the printers, sir?'

'Everyone. People are always printing things off, script revisions, timetables, letters. notices.'

DI Macrae sighed. 'Very well, sir. Thank you for that. We'll try fingerprinting them.' He turned towards the drive by the Boating Club. 'Thank you for your co-operation, Ms Lynch.'

'Inspector,' Ted said, 'we need to get the cameras rolling again. The insurance people are on my back. Last night Michael and I had a look at what we still have to shoot, and we need another day of the longship.'

'You can tell your company, sir, that the ship is under forensic investigation.'

Ted looked as if he was going to argue that one. The Inspector spoke drily. 'We'll let you proceed as soon as is possible.'

Martin held out his hand. 'Good to see you again, Cass. Listen, are you going up to see Inga?' He spoke casually, but the tone took me back fifteen years. Martin looking under the jib, watching for the moment to put in a fast tack that would leave our opponents at a loss: *Now, Cass.*

I picked up the cue as quickly as I'd flipped the helm over. 'Yeah, I was thinking I'd call along, tell her what's going on down here.'

His smile didn't reach his eyes. 'I was along her last night, but I forgot to take over a thing I had for peerie Charlie. Can you tell her I'll be over later?'

'Sure,' I said.

I watched them go around the marina and into the clubhouse. I'd have liked to move *Khalida* to her own berth, take possession once more, but there was no time. Martin wanted me to go to Inga as soon as possible. Something was wrong.

4

Inga, Charlie and the bairns lived in one of the new crofthouses built in the eighties, when the arrival of the oil meant that Shetland became rich. Charlie's father had built himself a large, open house with a big kitchen-sitting room whose picture windows framed a panoramic view of Busta Voe. Inga couldn't quite see her childhood home from her married house, but she was close. She could see her primary school, and her secondary school, and the hall where we'd gone to discos through our teenager years, and the garage shop where she'd had her first Saturday job. I looked out at it and saw our history spread before us, and was half glad I'd gone out into the world, and half sorry.

Inga had bruised circles under her brown eyes, as if she'd not slept for a couple of nights, and her dark hair was scraped back in an untidy bundle. She wore old jeans and a T-shirt, and had a carrier bag in one hand, with a thermos sticking out.

'Hi, Cass. We're just heading for the hill. Fancy seeing if you can still raise peats?'

'Sure,' I said.

'You don't actually have to work, just talk. Sorry, but I really have to get these done. The forecast's for rain come the end of the week.'

'Chocs,' Charlie stated, as she added a packet of Penguins to her bag.

'Once we've done some work,' Inga said. 'Come on, boy.'

We set off at Charlie pace up the gravel track behind the house, and soon arrived at the top of the hill, a stretch of level moorland furrowed with rain-streams and tussocked over with pine-green heather. There was a honey-smell as the old stems crunched under our feet. Little birds flitted white tails at us and a Shetland sheep escorted its rust-brown lamb away in a spurt of gravel. The view was breath-taking: the dazzling blue of Busta Voe, with the houses scattered along the shores, and the marina cradled in its rocky arm. Even as I looked, though, I saw reminders of the serpent in Eden, a line of police cars with yellow-flashed roofs heading towards Busta.

Inga's peat bank was right on the crown of the hill. The peats hadn't been long cast; the face of the bank was still smoothly black, oil-shiny, below the chequered wall of cut peats on its head. In front of the sliced bank, in the greff, lay a rummle of bigger peats, the first to be cut. I remembered the greff as being the worst bit, because of the peats being big lumps of moor. That was where you started, though. Inga put the thermos and biscuits down, and we set to.

It didn't take long to get back into the rhythm of stooping and swinging, lifting the heavy blocks and setting them upright against each other. My arms and back were soon aching. Inga was quicker than me, planting her feet apart in a circle of peats and bending from the waist to catch up and place the misshapen rectangles. She worked with a suppressed anger that made me wonder if this was her way of smashing mugs, and soon a row of miniature wigwams trailed behind her. Charlie pottered about peaceably, poking his fingers in the front of the bank and sploshing in the burn. He'd need a complete change when he got home.

Inga straightened when we'd done about half the bank. 'Teabreak.' I glanced at my watch and was surprised to find only half an hour had gone by. 'Charlie, do you want a biscuit?'

'Chocs,' he yelled, and came charging over, feet stumbling on the uneven heather. 'Mine.'

'Of course yours,' I agreed, and patted the wiry grass beside me.

He sat down with little feet sticking straight out, and began to unwrap his biscuit with total concentration. I was given the silver paper, a bit sticky, and he launched into the biscuit.

'So,' I said, 'what's wrong?'

She gave me a hesitant look, weighing something up.

'Go on,' I said. 'Spit it out. I wouldn't believe you killed her if you told me so.'

'I didn't,' Inga said. She paused, then added vehemently, 'But I felt like it. She was a wicked, *wicked* woman.' Her eyes moved to Charlie, intent on covering his face and both hands in chocolate. She lowered her voice. 'Her lawyer phoned and said she wanted to adopt him.'

'Adopt him!' I echoed.

Inga's dark eyes snapped with anger. 'That's what I said. 'Adopt him?' I said. 'The boy has a father and mother who love him. Of course we're not going to let her adopt him.' And then the lawyer started on about all the advantages he'd have. Best opportunities, best education, best of everything. Well, I wasn't having that. 'And I suppose,' I said, 'along with that goes the celebrity lifestyle and the paparazzi and fear of kidnapping and the drug taking the second he's a teenager? All the advantage he needs,' I told him, 'is to grow up here in the country, where he can run free and have fun, with his own family around him. And as for education,' I told him, 'the schools in Shetland are among the best in Scotland, you just look at the league tables in the papers. *And* we're never yet had bairns shooting each other.'

She paused for breath.

'And then–' Her voice rose in indignation. Charlie looked around, and she softened it to a vehement hiss. 'This lawyer had the cheek to tell me I wasn't bringing Charlie up properly. 'I'd been seen to use physical violence on the child,' he said, 'and was I aware that could be reported to the authorities?' *Well*, 'I've brought up three children,' I said, 'and nobody's so much as hinted that any one of them's been ill-treated. That physical violence Charlie got, as you call it, was a warning to him to behave. I was passing him from the boat into a rubber boat, and he was wriggling so hard he was liable to fall in, and if you call it good parenting to let a child of two fall in the open sea, well, I don't. Furthermore,' I told him, 'if you've ever seen a child of two that doesn't have tantrums, you've seen a child who gets its own way in everything. No child of mine's going to be brought up like that. And then – you're not going to believe this–'

I was finding it hard to believe it already. Had Favelle really thought a child was just ask and have? I thought of other celebrity adoptions and supposed that, yes, she did. From her point of view it was a selfish parent who'd stand in his way. She wasn't a mother; she didn't understand.

'*Then*,' Inga continued, 'he offered me money. *Money*. For Charlie. Oh, he didn't call it that. He oozed on about expenses, and allowances, but that's what it boiled down to. She thought

I'd sell him. I'm telling you, if I'd had her there in front of me, I'd have–'

She broke off. The fan of red hair in the pool of blood swam across my eyes.

'So, Inga finished, 'I told him he was offering blood money, and we wouldn't touch it. Even that didn't stop him. He said he could see the idea was a shock, and he'd write it all down and send it to us. I told him if I heard one more word about it I'd go straight to the papers and tell them Favelle was trying to steal my child.'

'Nice one,' I said. Charlie finished his biscuit and came over to us, sticky hands held out. Inga fished in her bag for a packet of wipes and sorted him.

'More choc?' he said hopefully.

'Not a chance,' I said. 'Come and help us raise.'

'I suppose,' Inga said.

We creaked to our feet. 'So,' Inga finished, 'that was the last of him.'

'That's incredible,' I said. 'I know film stars lead sheltered lives, but I can't believe she thought you'd just give up your child.'

'Me neither,' Inga said. 'I know I'm not always fussing over him and cuddling him – well, he'd hate it if I did – but she surely thought I didn't care at all. Well, she knows now. She's been told.'

'How do you mean, she's been told?' I asked. 'Did she come herself?'

Inga flushed scarlet. 'No – no – I mean, the lawyer'll have told her.' She thrust her chin forward. 'And I hope he repeated exactly what I said.'

'When was all this?' I asked.

She looked away from me. 'Two nights ago. The night before she died.'

I'd been wondering what would have taken Favelle out of Busta. Had she come to Inga's, to ask for Charlie herself? I thought I knew Inga, but now I couldn't be sure. She might be lying; she might not.

Her face puckered. 'I can't believe she's dead. Cass, do you think that lawyer will tell the police about her trying to adopt Charlie?'

'Bound to,' I said.

'But I sorted him!' she protested.

I could see she wasn't convinced, and nor was I. If Favelle had persuaded herself and everyone around her that Charlie would have a much better life with her, then it wouldn't have been hard for her to steal him. Once she'd got him in the States with a false ID or passport, Inga would never have got him back.

I'd have killed her with a motive like that, and I wasn't even Charlie's mother.

Chapter 12

I was starving by lunchtime, so I stopped at the Co-op on my way past. It was quiet, with only a couple of cars outside, along with one of those big, square camper vans. I stomped my peat-clatched feet on the mat and went in. The quiet ended there; all four aisles seemed full of children megaphoning 'Dad, can we get more chocolate spread?' and 'Mum, we're nearly out of crisps.' Dad was circular, red-faced and eyeing up the drink behind the tills. Mum had to be the woman with the full trolley. She wore a pale floral sundress and sandals, and was doggedly ignoring the shouts.

Now, I wondered. June was early for camper vans. I sidled up to the woman, shot a look at the shelf past her, and smiled. 'Sorry, can I just get you to pass me a jar of jam?'

She looked blankly at the shelf. 'What sort?'

'Oh – erm – I forgot to ask.' I gave her another smile. 'I'm involved with the film boat, you know, the Viking ship down at the pier, and catering said, if I was going to the Co-op, could I get them some jam. Don't Americans eat odd things, like stripes of peanut butter and strawberry jam?'

'Here, love, on you go,' she said, squeezing back to let me pass. Her accent was pure Geordie. I picked two jam-jars off the shelf at random and stood in comparing pose. 'We saw the film boat as we passed. There were a whole lot up filming on the hill two nights ago an all. Parked next to us, they did.'

Bull's eye.

'Yeah, they were filming the sunset.'

'So they said.' Her eyes went round. 'One on them was that Ted Tarrant. Eee, he's good looking, he is. Poor man, losing his wife like that. We 'ad the police round about that an all.'

'Oh?' I said, encouragingly.

'Police asked us, had we seen anyone take the van out, and I said no. Well, I sleep that badly, I'd've heard. I did hear them taking out bits of equipment, but the van never moved an inch, and that I'll swear to.'

'The cameraman was called Michael,' said one of her offspring, appearing suddenly beside us. 'He let me look through his lens. Mam, we need more chocolate spread.'

She put it into the basket without looking at the child. 'Then there was another one, quieter, an older man, with dark hair too, but much shorter.'

James Green.

'And later, in a separate car, there was a blond girl fussing over a clipboard, but I don't know what she had to do with anything. I didn't mention her to the police – well, they didn't ask.'

'Oh,' I said, surprised. 'I hadn't realised Elizabeth was going with them.'

'She looked the sort who wouldn't let anyone else do anything without her to keep them right.' The woman sniffed. 'Reminded me of my supervisor at work. She arrived just after eleven, in one of those little red Fiestas.'

Did she, indeed?

'She was looking for them,' the child added. I gave him a second look. He had a fashionably long mop of brown hair around a thin, white face almost entirely brown with freckles. His blue eyes were sharp and alert.

'You were in bed,' his mother said tartly.

I thought of the beds in the roof of that sort of camper van, with a nice little hatch above that someone this skinny could easily slip through. I crouched down to the tinned custards and said softly, 'Did she find them?'

'She found Michael,' he said, 'because he was right at the top, in the little house. He didn't know where the others were. He said they were about, on the hill, and she looked around at all the boulders and made a face and went off.'

'That's a load of nonsense, our Jimmy,' the mother said. 'Go on, go and get some crisps.'

I straightened up. 'They can be a bit driven when they're filming,' I said. 'I hope they didn't disturb you, banging about.'

'No, no, lass, no disturbance. They all arrived just after I'd got the bairns into bed, and I thought there'd be fussing about, but no, the two cameramen just shouldered their gear and Ted Tarrant strode off, and that was them.' A sudden cackle. 'Off into the sunset, eh! And the woman, well, she must've had the consideration to roll off down the hill, for I never heard her leave, and if she'd started the engine then I would have. She was gone in the morning, I can tell you that.' She looked disparagingly at the jar of blueberry jam in my hand. 'That's not what you want, love. The striped stuff, here, that's it.' She plucked a jar from the shelf. Maybe Anders would eat it.

She thumped a last packet of Angel Delight in her trolley, turned to me. 'You a reporter, are you? Because if you're going to use what we've said–'

'No,' I said hastily. 'I really am from the film lot. I'm actually the skipper of the longship. Cass Lynch.'

She considered me for a moment, eyes grown suddenly shrewd. They flicked from my peat-dust smeared face down to my tanned, practical hands and back up. 'Playing the coal-man for this scene, love?'

'Helping my mate raise her peats,' I said. 'You know, the turf they burn as fuel. It's a messy business.'

'Sooner you as me,' she agreed. 'The boys'd love to get a look around that ship. Any chance you could do us a guided tour?'

'Not today,' I said, 'because the police are still all over her, but come down another day, and I'll show you round.'

I walked back to the boating club thoughtfully, nursing my jar of revolting jam. Well, well. So Elizabeth had seen Favelle off to bed, then headed up to Ronas Hill to spend the night watching the sunset with Ted, only she hadn't found him. She'd departed quietly, rolling her car down the hill. She'd driven above the marina, she could even have come into it if she'd seen Favelle walking towards it. Furthermore, she hadn't told the police about that little excursion. That was somewhere between stupid and sinister.

ᛋ

When I got back to the boating club I headed for a long, hot shower, and emerged clean, pink and smelling of strawberries. Then I moved *Khalida* back to her berth. I was going to get rid of every last trace of the police intrusion. My first priority was to deal with the grey fingerprint powder. There weren't that many prints, because I'd polished all the woodwork the day before Favelle had arrived, but they included a few Rat-prints; I hoped that had puzzled them. Half an hour with a wet cloth on the white and Pledge on the wood made my home my own again. Then I went rapidly through the lockers, emptying each and re-stowing the contents.

I'd just finished and was boiling the kettle for a cup of tea when I heard Anders' step on the pontoon. *Khalida* swayed; he came aboard, moving heavily, as if he'd not had enough sleep. His kitbag was in one hand, and Rat was on his shoulder, a lump under his checked shirt. His face was grey under the tan, and he had dark circles under his eyes. His neat beard was straggly, as if he hadn't trimmed it for a couple of days.

'Tea?' I said.

He nodded, swung his kitbag forrard, and folded himself down between the bulkhead and the table, huddling into the corner as if for security. Rat oozed out from his collar, took up his favourite station on the shelf edge, and began washing his whiskers. I put a mug of tea in front of Anders and fished out the ship's brandy. 'You look as if you need that.'

'I do,' he said with feeling.

I gave myself one too and sat down opposite him. 'Me too.'

Yes, he'd changed, grown from Loki to Thor, engine hand to chief engineer, and my equal, in his own sphere. I leaned back, reassured. Whatever reason he had for lying, it would be one I'd understand. He would tell me in his own time.

He took a long gulp of tea and looked across at me. 'Are they going to continue filming, do you think?'

Two seamen, talking together of what needed to be done next. 'Ted's hoping to get filming again tomorrow. I spoke to Mr Berg straight after it happened, and again yesterday. He seemed to want that too. I suppose it'll make loads of money.'

'Favelle's last movie.' He cupped his hand around his mug and drank, then set the mug back on the table, holding on to it still, as if for warmth.

'So we should finish our contract,' I said. 'Then, I suppose, the plan as mapped out. Sell *Stormfugl.* I wonder if the Heritage Centre will still be interested.' We'd had a group from Unst, the northernmost island, wondering about making her the centrepiece of their Viking exhibition.

'They would not be able to afford her now,' Anders said. 'The boat Favelle died on.' The words made a little silence. I hadn't thought of it, but the minute he said it I knew it was true. No wonder Mr Berg was rubbing his hands. No longer an ex-film prop they'd practically have to give away to save storage fees, but a gruesome relic of the mysterious death of a star. If he put her on eBay he'd get an amazing sum for her. I grimaced.

'People are strange.'

'Yes,' Anders agreed, and fell silent again. I waited. We were partners. He would tell me in his own time. I was reminded, though, of the question I wanted to ask.

'Anders, have you ever heard anyone speaking, on set, or afterwards, of anonymous letters?'

I could see that he had. 'Yes, but not before Favelle died. Now, they are all talking about them, and a dangerous stalker. I think it is exciting for them.' He drew a long breath, set the mug aside. 'Cass, I need to explain to you. About the cops. I did not mean to get you into trouble. I was nervous – I did not want to fall foul of them, and so I–' He spread his hands out, palms down. 'They were asking questions about where I was, and what Favelle was doing here.'

He trailed to a halt.

'Yes,' I said, when I saw he wasn't going to start again. 'I thought perhaps she was looking for Maree.'

Anders shook his head. His blond hair glinted. 'No. She was looking for me.'

I stared at him incredulously. 'For you?'

He reddened. 'We had – well, it was an assignation.'

I couldn't believe it. 'You had an assignation with Favelle, aboard *Stormfugl*?' Elegant Favelle, arranging a one-night stand with one of the hired hands in an open cabin aboard a ramshackle Viking longship? That was slumming it with a vengeance.

'Many women,' Anders said stiffly, 'find me attractive, even if you don't.'

'I didn't mean that at all,' I protested. 'I meant – well, you know, her and Ted, Hollywood's golden couple. Then she's sneaking off to an assignation with you, in *Stormfugl*'s shack. I just wouldn't have expected it of her.'

'Nor I,' Anders said. 'It was all very strange.' He relaxed back against the bulkhead, turning his head away so that the sun slanted down his moulded cheekbone. 'She always smiled at me, you know, I think she thought I was Charlie's father, because of the colouring, and us both being on board that first day. Then at lunchtime she began to come on to me, leaning against me and asking questions – how I liked it here, and which room I was in. I told her that I was not in the hotel, that I slept as night watchman aboard the ship. She smiled at me, and said that maybe she would visit me one night.'

I tried to imagine it, and couldn't.

'I did not know what to say,' Anders continued. 'To make love with Favelle – it is a bit like getting an offer from Garbo. She didn't seem like a–' He paused, trying out descriptions in his head. 'A woman who would sleep with just anyone, for kicks. Yet it wasn't that she had fallen in love with me. And she smiled and patted my hand, and said no more, as if she'd decided, and so it would happen. I didn't like that either.'

'Haven't you ever had one night stands?' I asked.

He shook his head. 'Not like that. It's different, Cass, you know it is.' His fair skin flushed. 'Sometimes, when you go off in a group, and you become friends, then, at the end of the time, and you know you're not going to meet again–'

I knew what he was trying to say. You climbed the mast together, and watched the sun rise scarlet above the sea, and when you arrived at your destination, well, perhaps for that last night you might be lovers.

'You've done that too,' he said, 'even you, cool, remote Cass who walks by herself.'

Was that how he saw me? 'Yes,' I said, 'I've done it too.'

'We weren't friends, Favelle and I. I felt–' He paused again, remembering. 'It was almost as if she was acting. A sort of determination. I felt uneasy. Then the rock gave her a fright, so I hoped she would not come to *Stormfugl*. All the same, I asked you if I might desert my post. I thought I would prefer not to be there, just in case.'

'In case she came?'

'In case it was some kind of set-up,' he said. 'I was afraid that we'd be disturbed by a photographer from the papers, or the angry husband. I hoped most that after the rock she wouldn't come.'

'But she did,' I said. I asked the big question. 'Where were you then?'

'In the club house.' He leaned forward. 'I saw you go out. I had another couple of drinks and then I went down to *Stormfugl*. It was late, eleven o clock, but of course there was still daylight. I thought that it was too late for her to come, and so I went to bed as usual. I was just starting to sleep when I heard voices from above the marina, a couple walking along the road from Busta Hotel. They were just at the standing stone, up on the hill, and they had paused to talk. The man was trying to persuade the woman to do something, he was speaking like that, you know, low and quickly, not letting her speak much. When she did speak, I recognised Favelle's voice, and I realised she was trying to get rid of him so that she could come to *Stormfugl*. All my uneasiness came back. I picked up my sleeping bag and went into the clubhouse, into the men's lavatories, and laid it down on the bench there. Then I went up into the bar again, and watched. She did not come.'

'But–' I began.

'I *watched*,' he repeated. 'I waited in the bar until Alan closed it. I thought about asking if I could sleep on one of the couches there, but I thought it would be against the insurance, and I was not able to explain why.' He mimicked himself. 'Well, you see, I do not wish to sleep with the famous Favelle.'

'So you did sleep in the men's toilets,' I said.

He nodded. 'Then when I saw her, that next morning, dead, I panicked. I thought we could give each other an alibi, if I said we had taken *Khalida* out together, and I had stayed on board. I realised, after I had said it, that they were interviewing us at the same time, but then I thought if I took it back it would sound very suspicious, so I got out of the way and kept quiet.'

'They didn't believe you anyway,' I said. 'You're going to have to go back to them and tell the truth.'

'It was stupid,' he repeated gloomily.

'But what you saw was important,' I said. 'Don't you realise? You probably saw Favelle with the murderer.'

He shook his head doubtfully. 'She died later. Why should they argue for all those hours?'

'But it could have been. Who was it, could you hear?'

'Not to be absolutely certain,' Anders said. 'But I think that it was the teacher who has been filming the filmers. Kevin.'

At that point my mobile rang. It was Dad's number.

'Is that you, Cassie? Lass, I don't know what way up I am.' It was Jessie Matthewson, in a high old state of agitation. 'That lass dying on the boat like yon, well, that gave me a rare fright. We were having lunch, Gibbie and I, when it came on the news, and Gibbie, he went as white as a sheet. 'That's that Favelle wife died on our boat,' he said. I thought I was going to have to call the doctor.'

'It gave me a shock too,' I said, pointedly.

'And then we had the police round. I was that glad Gibbie wasn't working late on the boat last night.'

He'd worked late on the boat very few nights, so I wondered why Jessie was mentioning it. *A strange man's footprints, leading below decks…*

'He wasn't on board at all that evening?" I asked.

'Not he,' said Jessie, and changed tack. 'I'm had a phone call from your mother. She's wanting me to go in and make the house shining clean and put flowers all over. She says she's giving a press conference in the sitting room, so it's to look like a room in the *Hello* book.'

Since Maman regarded all forms of *Hello* magazine as unspeakably vulgar, I took this to be a sop to Jessie's frame of reference.

'I'm done that, and your dad says it's fine, but I'd've liked it fine if you'd been able to pop over and have a look. You ken what men are. They have no eye for a house.'

I wasn't sure I did, just by virtue of being female. I glanced at my watch. Quarter past four. Yes, I could come over, admire, and just go with Dad all the way to the airport, instead of him picking me up at the marina.

'I'll do that, Jessie,' I said. 'Do you have plenty of flowers, should I pop into the Co-op?'

'Na, na, no need for that, for I have tulips in my own garden, and the last of the Shetland lilies, and the first of the Batchelor Buttons, and enough bluebells to paint the sky.' Another pause for breath, and I knew that what she really wanted was coming up.

'And I'm to make up her bed, she said, and I didn't quite like to ask your Dad – that is, Cassie, I was wondering if she meant her own bed, or the spare room. After all, it's been a while, and there's this young lass, so I just wasn't sure–' She trailed off into a well-earned silence.

I'd been too busy looking at rigging to distinguish ropes. Yes, what exactly was Maman up to, sweeping home like this? Dad had seemed pleased enough, but was this the grand reconciliation, or was she just being extra rational, the goddess descending in the machine to put everything right?

'I don't know,' I admitted. 'Why not play safe, and put clean sheets on them both?'

'I'm done that,' she said. 'And I've put a chicken casserole all ready in the oven, and a bottle of her white wine chilling in the fridge, and there's a cold rhubarb crumble that you can just pop into the oven when you get home.'

'That sounds great,' I said. I remembered Jessie's rhubarb crumble.

'So that's you all set. Now, how are they getting on with the investigations? I saw you had to get your boat searched.'

'Yes,' I said. 'Jessie, I was wondering–'

She was already powering over me. 'What would you be attacking her for?' she asked with heart-warming indignation.

'They say I thought she was Maree,' I put in swiftly. 'In fact, I was wanting a word with her–'

'That you'll no get,' she said, 'for she left that same evening, with just a note on the dresser to say she'd be away for a few days, and no address to get her by.'

'You don't know what time she went?'

'Before nine o clock, for I was over at Jeannie's, you ken, Inga's man's mother, and when I came back the news was just finishing on the wireless.' Jessie had the odd habit of leaving the radio on to keep the house company while she was out; her own small contribution to global warming. 'Your Dad came over yesterday morning in a terrible state, looking for her. Have they quarrelled, now?'

There was no point in denying it. 'Yes.'

'Well, that's a good thing,' Jessie said warmly. 'She was likely a fine enough lass, I'm no saying she wasn't, but far better if she's taen herself off and your Mam's coming home.' She took a deep breath and changed tack again. 'But that was a bad thing, a bad thing, that poor lass gone like that. Do they even ken what time she was attacked?'

'If they do, they're not saying.' Elizabeth had said good night at half past ten; Favelle must have gone straight out, for Anders had seen her at dusk, eleven o clock, and kept watch after that, and she still hadn't come to *Stormfugl.* Where had she been?

Jessie and Gibbie's house was just above the marina.

'She died just before four,' I said, and waited to see how she'd answer.

'Aye, well,' Jessie finished off. She was trying to sound casual, but I could hear the relief flooding into her voice. 'I'll tell Gibbie he has no need to worry, then, for he was certainly home and in bed by then, and that I'll swear to.'

'Oh,' I said casually, 'was he out earlier?'

'Oh, you ken, he has sheep to look to and all that.'

Right enough, he did, but Jessie should have known that I'd know he wouldn't need to be looking to them at this time of year. I was left convinced that Gibbie had been out, and tinkering with *Stormfugl*. The first chance I got I'd be aboard looking to see what he'd been up to.

In the meantime, I had twenty minutes. Maree. I opened my copy of the *Shetland Visitor* and considered. She'd stormed out at eight fifteen. She'd gone back to Busta and opened her *Shetland Visitor*, just as I was doing. Accommodation. Map of Shetland.

If I wanted to get where nobody could get at me, I'd go to an island. I found the ferries timetable and considered her chances. The remote isles were out. Maybe Bressay, the long island that made a sheltered harbour of Lerwick, but she'd been to Lerwick with Dad, and knew that she wouldn't get lost in the teeming crowds of the big city. She was far more likely to walk into someone she knew the first time she poked her nose out of doors.

Whalsay, to the east, was a possible, and there were several ferries she could have taken. The best bet was the northern isles, Yell and Unst. She and Dad had done a day-trip to Yell, so it was slightly more familiar. Furthermore, the ferry terminal to Yell was only ten minutes drive away. I consulted the ferry timetable. She couldn't get the ferry to Yell sooner than 21.05, by the time she'd gathered her stuff and phoned a B&B. I had a look at Unst, two ferries away from her problems, but she wouldn't arrive there till nearly midnight – hardly inconspicuous, and a bit complicated even for a jet-setting American. I'd start with Yell.

Nothing beat local knowledge. I'd talk to Dodie, ferryman on the *Daglion*, who'd come to look at *Stormfugl* that first day. One of his jobs was to beckon the cars on to the ferry, and then he'd go along each and every car, saying hello to the person inside, mentally noting who they were, where they were going and why (and asking them if he couldn't work it out, or his mam would be after him when he got home), taking the fare and issuing a ticket. If he'd been on shift last night, I was home and dry. I flipped through the *Shetland Directory*, found his number and dialled it. I was doubly in luck; he was at home, and he'd been on just that ferry, the 21.05.

'We're looking for one of the film people,' I explained. 'She'd have been an American wife on her own, in a Bolt's Fiesta. She might have been wearing sunglasses, and a headscarf.'

There was a long pause. If you left him alone to work at his own pace, you could bet your last mooring rope on his answer.

'Yea,' he said at last. 'She was the third car down, in the middle, and she came from the unbooked lane.'

I thanked Dodie warmly and promised him a sail aboard *Stormfugl* if ever the police let us back aboard. Maree was safely holed up in Yell, had been there long before Favelle's death. She would keep. For now, we had to go and get Maman.

When I came into the house I felt I'd stepped back twenty years. Maman's flower vases were filled to the brim with artfully dangling bluebells below a haze of bachelor button, the carpet was immaculate, and her piano was polished within an inch of its life. Had Dad kept it tuned? I plinked the C all the way up, and it sounded okay. The table was laid English-style in the dining-room, with a white damask cloth, red tablemats, the best silver, cut-crystal glasses and another vase of flowers in the centre.

'It's beautiful,' I assured Jessie, standing in the middle of it. Her eyelids were reddened, and her features dragged that blurred way they go when you have a heavy cold. When Dad opened the bathroom door she started, and gave a nervous look over her shoulder.

Dad was looking good too. His hair was sleeked, and his face pinkly excited above his crisply ironed shirt. He'd gone for the casual look, dark trousers and open neck, laid back but distinguished, like an RN Commander off-duty. The laid-back didn't extend to his behaviour though; he was fussing about like the owner of a newly painted yacht on a crowded start-line.

'I wouldn't want her to think I'd let the place go to rack and ruin, now, would I, girl?' he said. 'Does it look fine, do you think?'

'You look great, Dad,' I assured him. 'Let's go and get her.'

Chapter 13

It was a bonny drive to Sumburgh, the main airport. We threaded eastwards, the Atlantic at our backs, skirted Olnafirth with its lines of mussel rafts, then swerved to the highroad south. We drove for seven miles through dark green heather moor, with boggy patches of olive-green grass hazed white with bog cotton, and pools of water turned seaweed-rust with waving marsh grass. Being there reminded me.

'Dad, this wind farm of yours, where's it to be built?'

'Here,' he said. 'And over there.' He took one hand off the steering wheel to wave towards the west. 'There's not much happening here, so nobody is too bothered about this bit.'

'Won't it mean a fair bit of road building over the peat?'

'Jobs, girl. Jobs for Shetland folk.'

'That's a yes, is it?' I persisted.

'We'll need roads to get the turbines up there, and to service them once they're up.'

I looked up at the furrowed hill. Not much happening for people, sure, and not good grazing for sheep, but I'd seen an oystercatcher pecking into the earth not far from the roadside, and further over, in one of the larger lochs, a diver bobbed to the surface, tilted its bill and dipped under again. 'What about the birds?' I asked.

'They'll move away for a year or so, while we're building,' Dad said. 'But they'll come back once there's peace again. For the divers, we've commissioned a special survey – from the RSPB, we're being absolutely transparent about this – and we'll make sure we don't site any turbines on their flight paths.'

The more often he said he was being transparent, the less I believed it. 'Why the divers, specially?'

'Because they're special, girl.' Dad settled into lecturing mode. 'This is a unique environment, we fully appreciate that. Eighty per cent of the world's diver population nests here.'

I gawked at him. 'Eighty per cent?'

'Sounds amazing, doesn't it? But it's true. They need to be able to walk out of the water to nest, see. This is one of the few remaining places they can do that.'

'Flight path,' I repeated.

Dad ducked his head away slightly. 'Birds, y'see, they don't expect hazards in the sky, so they're not tuned into them. So we'll site the turbines so they don't fly into them.'

In short, turbines were liable to make mincemeat out of any birds environmentally unaware enough to use their airspace.

'What about the other birds?' I asked.

'Oh, there are plenty of them,' Dad said, 'and they're smaller, and faster flyers, so we don't expect the losses to be as severe. And besides,' he added honestly, 'it's the divers the bird folk are making the fuss about.'

I looked out again at the hills, jigsawed over with dark lines where rain had furrowed its way through the ancient peat. 'How deep's the peat here? Can you just lay roads over it, like the gravelly tracks up the peat road to the banks?'

'Well, no. It needs to be proper roads. Each of the turbines, see, it'll weigh a good bit, and then it has to have a proper concreted stand, so there's a lot of material to be taken up there. The quarry will be jobs too, of course. The turbines will be in groups, but each group'll need its own road – look, now, as we come round this hill here, you'll get a better idea.'

We rounded the last of the brown hills and came into greener country, hills rippling with feathered grass, and the North sea on our left hand. Ahead of us was fertile Tingwall Valley, where the Norse settlers had held their parliament. On the hill above the loch were five white towers with three-bladed rotors turning lazily. They stood out in the landscape, but not horribly; elegant, gleaming white, thin-bladed, they were more like a modern sculpture than an industrial complex.

'The first of their kind,' Dad said, 'and the most productive windfarm in Europe. People come from all over, girl, to look at them. We've got clean, unbroken wind, see, and lots of it. It's a rare day those turbines aren't turning. The problem, see, is that you don't get all the potential energy, with renewables. If you put up a 2 Megawatt turbine down south, you'll be lucky to get 0.75 megawatts. Up here you'll reliably get 1, maybe 1.3 megawatts. Over 50%, that's really good. The middle one, Betsy, she's the most productive single turbine in the world.'

I kept watching them as we drew nearer. These five were bonny enough in their gleaming white, but I imagined the bare hills we'd come from filled with them, and criss-crossed with grey roads. 'How close together will they be, the new ones?'

'Not as close as these. They're twice the size, see. Twice the height, twice the diameter. The bigger the better. Folk have to be weaned off their dependence on fossil fuels, and the only way to do that is by giving them a cheap alternative.'

As we came down the hill and towards the golf course, they towered above us, dominating the sky. Double this size – I couldn't imagine it. 'Will that do all of Shetland's electricity, then, and for free?'

'Well, no.' Dad focused on the curve. 'It can't. For a start it's not allowed to. Not more than 20% can come from renewables. And you can't store electricity, you see. You'd still need a power station here in Shetland, for the days the wind's not blowing, or for when it's blowing too hard, and the turbines have to be stopped from turning. No, what we want to do is sell the electricity. Turbines like the ones we want, you could power half of Scotland. All we need is the cable connection, and we've got the go-ahead for that. We pay half, Scotland pays half.'

'So,' I said slowly, 'there's no real benefit to the community here. Not free electricity, anyway.'

In short, they were going to hack roads across Shetland's ancient peat, erect huge turbines along the skyline and destroy the wildlife that made it so special for the benefit of consumers south. I began to have more sympathy with Kevin Manson's point of view. I began to see, too, why Favelle was so important. Favelle talking of the need to sacrifice our landscape for the greater good of the planet could have been a clincher. An unbalanced anti-windfarm campaigner could well be desperate enough to resort to sabotage. Kevin Manson, the anti-windfarm campaigner, who, according to Anders, had talked to Favelle up at the standing stone on the night she died.

I needed to find out more about Kevin. I'd ask Inga – no, I wouldn't. Her enthusiasm came back to me, the long story of how badly he'd been treated by his wife, what a talented and intelligent bloke he was. She was obviously well on his side: the maternal urge, I supposed, after his experience with the clean-him-out wife. It was always Inga the littlest primary bairns ran to when they were being teased. No, I'd need to ask somebody else. Magnie would know all the gossip.

If I lived here, I wondered, if it was my hills that were going to be disfigured to give more electricity to folk who wanted to keep their on-all-the-time lights and televisions and power showers, would I be ruthless enough to kill in their defence?

Would Kevin?

4

Instead of taking the Scalloway short-cut to the airport, Dad came around the hill with the golf course below us and climbed up towards Lerwick.

'Hey?' I said.

'I can't have my own family talking like that,' Dad said. 'We've got time for a detour.'

I sat back, puzzled, as we drove into Lerwick.

'Station Garage,' Dad said as we passed it. 'A herring station, not trains. The Town Hall up there, and all the big houses. That was Shetland's prosperity then, the herring boom.'

He swerved around a second mini-roundabout, down a narrow street and stopped in front of a building I'd never seen before, with great angled wings like the red sails of the herring smacks who'd founded the town.

'This is our new museum, Cassie. It's an amazing place, well worth a visit. And this, see, this is our new cinema and music venue. Two screens and a performance space, with a 170 seat auditorium. When the SNO comes up, they won't have to play in the sports hall any more.' With a jerk, we were off again, back along the waterfront, up the hill and along the Hillhead to go past the old folks' home.

'Care for the elderly,' Dad said. He came back down and round the roundabout to Lochside. The Clickimin Sports Centre crouched before us. I didn't remember the red running track and rugby pitch before it, or the swimming pool alongside, with flumes twisting around the walls.

'This sports hall,' Dad said. 'New swimming pool. One of eight in the isles. We've got a sports centre for every secondary school.' He gestured towards the opposite side of the road. 'The Education department. You can count the new schools as we pass them on the way to Sumburgh.' He paused to negotiate the roundabout at the new Tesco. 'Council houses. More being built now, look, up on the ridge there. Sound school. Sound public hall. And on the other side, all these new houses. That's prosperity, girl. Shetland's the richest authority in the UK.'

'Yes.' I agreed.

'And where does it come from?' He left a rhetorical pause. 'Oil. See, Cassie, we're the only small place in the world that's actually benefited from oil coming to it. Other places visit us to see how we managed it. The oil made Shetland rich. From the cradle to the grave. You had as good an education as any thousands-a-term boarding school.' His face clouded over as he remembered what use I'd made of it. Luckily he was in full flood of Irish eloquence. 'If you needed a doctor, you saw him that day. The dentist came to the school – now, do you have a filling in your head yet?'

'No,' I admitted. I couldn't afford to go to dentists, but nothing was hurting at the moment.

'Even your boating club, it was Sullom Voe built that for their men. Those showers downstairs, now, they were put in by the Council for the Inter-Island games. The football pitches your pal Martin played on. The road we're driving on – have you been to the West Highlands, girl, driven on the roads there? When I get that I'm not managing for myself, well, I'll get a home help and meals on wheels, and there'll be a place in the care centre. Or sheltered housing like that.' He waved a hand at a row of little houses by the road, looking out across Cunningburgh meadow to the sea. 'Oil did all that, and it's oil money that keeps it running. So what's going to happen when the oil runs out?'

I looked out at the landscape and saw the prosperity he was talking about. New house after new house; neat gardens filled with plastic swings and little houses for the children. The school had a play area with tyres hanging from chains and a log climbing frame. The house just past it had a gleaming black 4x4, parked beside a new conservatory.

'Is the oil going to run out?'

'Production's down to a third of what it was,' Dad said. 'Ten years, and it'll be almost gone. Fossil fuels are history. The world needs new sources of energy. Tide's good, but it's not as developed as wind, and wind's what we've got here. If we want to keep this prosperity, we've got to do this. I know it'll make a mess of the countryside, although we're working with local people to try and minimise the effect. We'll site the turbines as sensitively as we can, but it's money for Shetland, girl, enough money to keep the way of life we've got.'

'And we need to save the planet,' I said. I thought of the little flocks of guillemots and puffins that used to watch my boat as I approached them, and of the two solitary puffins I'd seen this year. I imagined chicks choking on pipe fish because that was all their parents could find them, and bare ledges where the kittiwakes used to nest, and beaches emptied of swooping terns.

Dad nodded. 'We need to stop filling the atmosphere with poisonous gases, and use clean energy. It may be too late, but we've got to do something. If that means sacrificing some of our bonny views, well, that's the way it's got to be.'

We drove on in silence through green farmland now, with brown and white cattle grazing, and long rigs of Ness tatties. We glimpsed the new Dunrossness primary school, the neat rows of new boats in the equally new Grutness marina, came across the airport runway and around to park in the big new car-park at the terminal. New, new, new. The oil wealth.

4

Maman must have insisted on a rear seat, for she was almost last off, unmistakeable and elegant in her black and white chic. She paused for a moment at the top of the steps as though waiting for her photographer, then descended steadily and began crossing the tarmac. She had at least five of those plastic suit-bags on hangers over one arm.

I waved through the glass and moved to the doorway. Maman came in on a wave of *Je reviens* and stood on tiptoe to greet Dad briskly, two kisses on each cheek. 'Dermot, you are looking very well. Cassandre.' She kissed me in the same way. 'I have clothes for you. You can change here, and then we will be ready for the press. My agent has contacted them. We will give an interview when I arrive in Brae.'

Behind us, the carousel began to wheel its caterpillar sections. I grabbed Maman's luggage for her.

'Ten minutes,' Maman said. 'Dermot, if you wish to go for a cup of your dreadful English coffee, we will be back before you have to drink it.'

She whisked me into the ladies' toilet and began laying the bags out. I tried to think how long it was since I'd seen her. Six years. The ship I was on was stopping at La Rochelle, and I'd phoned her to say I'd be there. I'd wanted family. Not that she'd known about Alain, particularly; I hadn't told her or Dad, and if they'd seen the fuss in the newspapers, they'd had the tact not to mention it. I'd just wanted to say hello, that was all. We'd gone out to dinner, and I'd told her about the ship I was on, and my plans for the coming season, and she'd told me about her latest production. It had been civilised and cordial, and after that I'd phoned occasionally.

She hadn't changed. Her swept-back hair was black as ever, elegantly coiled into a Callas chignon, her pointed eyebrows perfectly plucked, and there were no wrinkles on her powder-smooth cheeks, no dark circles under the hazel-green eyes that reviewers called 'expressive' and 'commanding'. They were bright and alert as ever, and her long mouth was smoothly outlined in burnt scarlet. Only the sweeping, studied grace of her every move made her fifty, not thirty.

I'd never been able to read what she was thinking, and I couldn't now. She was too busy, too driven, her total attention on unpacking the things she'd brought for me, each parcel precisely positioned, as if she was decorating an altarpiece for the gods. Then she looked up at me and I realised she was nervous, eyes searching my face as if she wasn't sure how I might react. For the first time I wondered if she felt the same about me as I felt about her, that I was elusive, practical, too busy doing my own things to have time for her; if this was her chance to be a mother for me.

In the same instant, I realised I'd never asked her for anything before. She'd given, I'd refused. I hadn't wanted pretty dresses, a girl's bedroom, an expensive private school, I'd wanted freedom, and torn myself out of her grasp. It would have served me right if she'd stayed in her acoustically perfect salon and left me to claw my own way off this lee shore. It couldn't have been easy to drop everything, pull strings, do all this shopping and get on a flight so soon. I resolved to be convincingly grateful for the pretty dresses, to be a girl for once if it would please her. I leaned forward and gave her another kiss on the scented cheek.

'Thank you for coming, Maman.' I made a joke of it. 'You're our goddess from the machine to sort everything out, and organise the happy ending.'

She gave a French shrug at that, but smiled too. 'In opera it is easier. Here in Shetland you are not so well organised. The papers are whirling, whirling. My agent shrugged at first, and said 'Keep out of it' and then when I insisted she said it would be good publicity in the end, the mother to the rescue. She has done a press-release, but it is the interview that counts. They have seen you as the captain of the ship, and the one who found the body, and perhaps a love interest for this Ted Tarrant.' She said the name French-style, with a disapproving intonation. 'Now we will do the young girl with her family around her.'

She'd laid a litter of parcels out on the space around the three washbasins. 'I have brought everything. I had to guess, but you are far too active to put on weight, so I hoped. Let me see.' She fished out a swathing of pink patterned tissue paper. Resolution, Cass. I began taking my comfortable jeans off. 'Underwear.' I hauled off my t-shirt as well and undid my bra strap. I'd forgotten this French passion for getting clothes right from the skin outwards. The bra was not only underwired but padded upwards too, and it gave me the sort of cleavage I normally only saw on garage calendars. The knickers were like little shorts, silk, and not very comfortable. 'And do not pull at them,' Maman said severely, forgetting the new entente cordiale. After that, a slip, silk too, mid-thigh length. It had probably cost as much as new jib sheets. 'Stockings. Do you never go out without your legs covered?'

'Too cold,' I said. 'This is Shetland, remember.'

'You would need to wax,' she said. 'How can you attract a man if you do not take care of yourself?'

'I don't need to attract a man,' I said.

'Of course you do not need to,' Maman said. 'That is like saying you do not need to listen to music. You will not die without it, but you may want to listen. Life is much more full with it. With a man, too. Stockings.'

I was horrified to find she actually meant stockings. 'Not even tights?'

'They are not elegant.'

This was taking ages; I could see poor Dad having to drink nasty English coffee after all.

'Nearly done,' Maman said. 'Sandals.' I buckled them on and was instantly two inches taller and standing model-straight. She cleared the last of the paper into one of the carrier bags and brought out her make-up case. 'Can you do this yourself?'

I looked at her immaculate skin and the smooth swathe of dark eyeliner above the long lashes. 'No,' I admitted.

'Sit down on the washbasin. I hope I have matched your colouring. I took it that you would be more tanned than I.'

I looked myself in the eyes. Smooth, brown skin, the freckles across the bridge of my nose. Cutting my face in two was the long scar on my cheek, slanting from just below the cheek-bone to just above my upper lip, the width of a snail's trail and ruler-straight, with rumpled edges creeping onto the line of thin, shiny skin. The strip-lighting made it more prominent.

Maman unscrewed the lid of the tube. 'A little, only.'

Now my face was flattened, smoothed out, except for the indented line. Blusher, eyeshadow, to put the contours back. It took an effort not to shy away as Maman steadied my face with one hand on my cheek, the hazel-green eyes close to mine. 'Look up.' A little brush scrubbed at my lashes. 'Look down.' The eyeliner stick, stroking along my eyelid. The other eye. 'Good. Finished – no, do not look yet.'

She unzipped the suit cover and brought out an armful of black material with a swirling tracery of grey-green foliage over it. It was a sleeveless dress, fitted to the waist, with a scooped neck, and a flaring skirt of a floating material that hung in demure folds.

'Georgette,' Maman said.

'Your own dressmaker?' I guessed.

'The material. Good. No, do not look yet. Your hair. Did you bring your hairbrush?'

Of course not. 'I didn't think of it.'

'No matter.' She rinsed her own comb out at the sink and handed it to me. 'I am glad you have kept your hair long. I was fearing a bad cut in the boyish style.'

'Long hair's easier to keep out of your eyes,' I said.

Maman smiled at that. 'A touch of the feminine at last. Your hair is very beautiful.'

She tied a strip of the dress material around it, like an Alice band, and tucked the ends in. 'There now.' She turned me back to the mirror. 'Look.'

A stranger looked back at me. Taller than I was used to, and slimmer in the elegant dress that swirled around her ankles, she wasn't pretty in the English style, but chic, very French, with her eyeliner, and her smooth, creamy skin, unscarred now, and her dark hair tumbling down over her shoulders. I couldn't have guessed her age; fifteen dressed up as forty, or forty dressed down to twenty. I wondered what Ted Tarrant would think if he saw me like this.

'It is still Cassandre, you know,' Maman said. 'Cassandre *en fille*. You are old enough to understand that now. Look at her eyes, and the stubborn chin. Definitely my Cassandre.'

We smiled at each other in the mirror. 'Thank you, Maman.'

She insisted that I go out first, so that I could have the fun of seeing Dad's jaw drop. It did, too; he didn't recognise me at first, then his eyes widened, and he stood up. 'Well, Cassie, look at you. You're as beautiful as your mother. Eugénie, my dear, congratulations.'

He offered us an arm each to escort us to the car. We drove past the sand dunes, where cobalt and saffron flowers clustered side by side, and out by the wide sweep of sea where the waves tumbled white against Horse Island. Maman drew a deep breath.

'I had forgotten how it was beautiful. How I loved it in summer, when the wild flowers fill the roadsides, and the sea is the colour of aquamarine. Dermot, chérie, we should have had a migratory life, Poitiers in the winter and Shetland in the summer.

This barbarian child would have had her sailing and culture as well.'

'Never too late to change,' Dad said cheerfully.

In the back seat, I was having difficulty believing it. Not even a goddess could just sweep back in like that...

Chapter 14

I'd dreaded another press rush, but there was only a photographer and two interviewers, for the *Times* and the *Guardian*. Maman, Dad and I sat in a row on the couch, and were photographed as a happy family, then Dad and I listened while Maman rippled off a short aria. Dad leaned his head against the couch, eyes almost closed, smiling, contented. Had he really believed, all this time, that she'd come back some day? *Never too late to change* –

More photos, of me this time, posing against the window, chin up, head tilted away. I hoped that they'd use one that wasn't too revealing.

Then they began the questions. Maman was serene and confident. 'Of course I have had to live a lot in France, but Cassandre and Dermot and I have managed to meet up in spite of that. Cassandre, as a ship's captain, travels all over the world, and Dermot for his firm. However with this distress my place is here.'

Her calmness was infectious, and when the *Guardian* woman leaned forward to me and asked, with a meaning look, 'How did you get on with Ted Tarrant?' I managed a touch of girlish enthusiasm, 'It was amazing working with someone who was my childhood heart-throb.' I even smiled. 'He and Favelle were a very devoted couple. You saw for yourselves how devastated he was by his loss.'

'What do you plan to do now, Cassandre?' the *Times* man asked.

'It depends on Berg Productions Ltd. They own the ship,' I said. 'As Ted said, the filming was almost finished aboard. I don't know about the Shetland Eco-Energy publicity.' An over-to-you gesture to Dad.

'Favelle was going to do publicity shots for our projected wind farm here in Shetland,' he explained. 'The directors of the company are discussing whether we'll still use the ship – it's a question of sensitivity.'

Back to me. 'How would you feel about modelling for your Dad's publicity shots, Cassandre? Launch a new career?'

I shook my head. 'Favelle's record in eco-activism was what was important. Her support would have meant a good deal worldwide.'

They went back to Dad. 'Is it true there's a growing local resistance to your plans?'

'We're in discussion with the local community,' Dad said. 'We're listening to the people who live here, the people who'll have a stake in the wind farm, if it goes ahead.'

It seemed to go on for ages. We kept smiling until we'd waved them out, then sank back on the sofa.

'Well done, both of you,' Maman said. 'That went very well. Very positive.'

Dad was opening the wine. 'Your good health. Santé, Eugénie. Welcome home.'

I didn't believe it.

After we'd eaten I drove back to *Khalida*. I parked the car above the boating club and considered going in for a nightcap, but it was too bonny a night to be indoors, clear and very still, with the light thickening around me, the streetlights flickering on, red in their first moments, then dimming to ugly sulphur orange. The air smelt of mown grass and salt. On the moor, a snipe flapped its wings with an eerie drumming sound, houb-boub-boub, and below me on the shore the water shushed on the pebbles.

Besides, I wasn't dressed for the boating club. The people in there were folk I had come to know, who'd accepted me in my old jeans and jumper with the casual cameraderie of one sailor to another. I was just about to slip quietly along to *Khalida* to get changed when I heard a whistle from beside *Stormfugl*. Anders was sitting on the jetty, a pint glass in one hand and Rat on his shoulder like a pirate's parrot, contemplating the darkening sky over the western hill. His fair hair was slightly tousled, his cheeks flushed. Behind him, *Stormfugl* was criss-crossed with police tape which shone in the last glimmer of light. No entry, crime scene. At least the spacemen had gone for the night, although there was no sign of Sergeant Peterson's promised officers-on-patrol keeping an eye on her. Maybe they were going to wait until the pier-head skippers of the boating club had gone home.

'Ssssh!' I cast a quick look up at the boating club windows. It wasn't too dark for anyone to look out and recognise me..

He didn't whistle again, but I could feel his eyes on me.

'Maman,' I explained, wobbling my way down the jetty. One heel caught between the planks. If I took the sandals off I'd ruin the stockings. 'I must go and change.'

He stretched one arm out for me to sit beside him. 'Now you are head-turning, belle Cassandre. These film stars will need to look to their laurels.'

'I'm your relief watch,' I said crossly. These wretched clothes.

'I thought you might be staying at home, since your mother has arrived.'

'This is home,' I said, too vehemently.

A pause. Anders fished behind him and produced a half pint glass. 'Have some of this beer, and tell me what is wrong, if you like.'

'Nothing's wrong,' I said. He tipped half of what was left of his pint into the spare glass and handed it to me. 'Skol.' I sat uncomfortably against the angled wood, not wanting to lean back, and keeping a clear space between us. The water trickled soothingly along the clinker hull. 'No, I mean that, there really is nothing wrong. In fact everything is working out nicely. Maman is home and she and Dad are being all matey as if she'd just gone off for a fortnight's holiday instead of being away over sixteen years, and I just don't understand people.' It came out as a wail. I took a deep breath, steadied my voice. 'Here's Favelle dead and Maree missing, and Dad ought to be sick with worry about her, and instead he's just welcoming Maman home as if – as if–' I spread my hands, almost slopping some of the beer over Anders' foot. 'I don't get it, I don't.'

Anders put up a hand for Rat to run down. 'I have been thinking about you, Cass. You're a very good sailor. You know what's to be done, and you choose the best people to do it: the one to put on the helm, the one to send up the rigging. People's sea abilities, you assess those very accurately.'

'Oh, yeah,' I agreed. 'I can do that. I'd put Dad as the owner, the businessman planning the voyages, and Maman on plotting our course. She'd get us in spot-on, too.'

'Think about them like that, then,' Anders said. 'That is the way you think. What course is your mother plotting? Where does she want to end up, where are the rocks?'

I answered immediately, 'She doesn't want us to get arrested.'

'That is a negative. What does she *want*?'

'Us to be safe. Both of us.'

'Well, then. No, Rat, be still.' He put him on *Stormfugl*'s gunwale. 'What are the hazards she must steer around?'

'Bad publicity. DI Macrae arresting us.'

'Your father's girlfriend.'

'Her too.' She was the goddess from the machine, looking down at the crosses on the chart, spreading her respectability over us. I wondered what she planned to do about Maree.

'So. She is protecting you and your father. Now, here is the question you do not wish to ask. Why?'

I shrugged. 'She cares about us.'

'She *loves* you, Cass. What is so wrong with admitting to being loved?'

He left a silence for the question to echo in, and I heard the answer echo bleakly in my head. *Because I don't deserve it.* I took another swig of his beer and felt the warm nuttiness of it soothe my throat. 'Do you think of your parents as people on a ship?'

'Recently, I have begun. I need to know, you see, why my father wants for me what he does, and how I can get what I want in a way that will not disappoint him.'

Dad had wanted a university education for me. Maman had wanted an elegant French daughter. 'I disappointed both of mine.'

'No,' Anders said. 'No. At least, I do not know your mother but your father is very proud of you, do you not know that? When we met in the Co-op it was of you he talked. I would bet you anything that he could tell you everywhere you have been, every ship you have been on, and for how long.'

I considered this one. I thought of the way he'd known where Maman was singing and suddenly felt sorry for him, knowing how his family was doing through an advert on-line here, a mention in a blog there. I imagined him at his desk googling our names, with Jessie gone home to cook tea for Gibbie and the house quiet around him, and felt guilty.

Anders gave me his glass, rose, held out a hand to Rat. 'Anyway,' he said, 'not everyone needs to be good at people. You are very restful, Cass, you just accept people as they are and do not ask questions.' Sometimes people need that too.'

I felt myself going red again, shrugged the compliment away.

'Well, if you are taking over, I will go. But you will be careful? I am used to think of you as being as tough as any man, but now you look very small and fragile.'

'Looks are deceptive,' I said briskly, 'and the sooner I get out of these clothes the better, if they're going to turn you into a fuss-pot.'

Anders shrugged. 'No hurry.'

There was every hurry, if people were going to start treating me as a girl. I gave him a minatory look. 'Did you talk to the police?'

He shrugged, spread his hands. 'I'm going to. They've been along at Busta all afternoon, interviewing everyone, from the best boy's runner upwards. Michael had an hour with them, he said, re-living every moment of the rock falling, and then the night on the hill. Where had he been, where had the others been, who had he seen, who had the minibus keys, could he prove any of it? Then they asked Ted and James Green all the same questions.'

'I wonder,' I said, 'if Michael mentioned that he saw Elizabeth up there?'

'He didn't say. The cops spent until after eight along there, and then they headed back to the station, in a convoy, and did a mass order from the Indian takeaway.'

'Anders,' I said abruptly, 'what was between Michael and Maree? Were they lovers?'

His face closed against me. 'I do not know. It is none of our business.'

True, although I didn't see why he was so defensive about it. 'Off you go and get a decent night's sleep,' I said. 'I'll watch from *Khalida*'s cockpit, and call the police from behind the washboards if there's trouble.'

He laughed out at that, throwing his head back. 'You will come charging out, a tigress defending her cub with whatever weapon is to hand.'

Physical courage was easy. 'I've got more sense.'

'Good. I do not wish to have to bail you out from the police cells in Lerwick for assault.' Anders yawned and fell back to his proper age. 'You will phone me on my mobile if anything happens?'

I nodded. 'Good night.'

'Good watch.'

He turned to go, then paused and spoke so softly over his shoulder that I barely caught the words. 'You should wear make-up more often, Cass. You do not need to use your scar as a barbed-wire fence.'

He walked swiftly off. I watched him climb the steep gravelled drive beside the boating club, turn to the left, and head along the road that led to Busta House. He grew fainter until the dusk swallowed him, but I was pretty sure that he hadn't turned into any of the houses along the roadside. My last glimpse of him was a moving shadow walking quickly along the empty stretch of road between the last house and Busta itself.

Busta. I wondered which of the super-slender groomed Californian blondes was his friend. I couldn't envisage him with any of them, yet what did I know? Talking tonight was the closest we'd come to intimacy: *You don't need to wear your scar as a barbed-wire fence.*

It wasn't a barbed-wire fence. It was the mark of Cain.

I stip-stepped my way back to *Khalida* to change out of this womanly gear, hung the dress up beside my oilskins, and sat down in the cockpit to think. There were too many feelings jostling in me, and they were driving out rational thought. I shoved them away: Maman, Dad, Anders. *Think the way you can think. Then ask why, ask why.*

Favelle first. Wasn't the victim the most important point in a murder, the key to it all? I'd put her as a deckhand, and make sure she had a sympathetic and patient watch-leader. She'd be willing, but only able to carry out very precise orders. Her last day. We'd done the entry into the Hams all morning, so she'd have spent the morning at Jessie's. She couldn't have annoyed Gibbie with her pro-eco stance, for Gibbie had been on board ship. Late morning, the limo took Maree away and brought Favelle back. Lunchtime: flirting with Anders. That was the only thing that lent colour to an otherwise improbable story - she had seemed very taken with him. Taken to the point of sneaking on board *Stormfugl* for an hour of steamy passion? Okay, Anders was a very good example of a handsome Norwegian, but she'd filmed with Brad Pitt, for goodness sake. I had to choose, though. Either Anders' story was true or he was our killer, and I didn't believe that.

What, I wondered, did we public really know about our film idols? What the publicity machine chose to show us was Favelle, the intrepid activist. What I'd seen was the woman of principle who thought as simply as a two-year old, the action woman who was so unsteady on boats that she had to get her sister to stand in. Was the cosy Ted and Favelle marriage just as fake? Anders had thought it was. Maybe leaping into bed with the hired help was a Favelle habit. I was sure though that Ted hadn't acted that grief. If he wasn't truly and genuinely shocked and devastated by her death I'd give up the sea and take to rabbit farming in the middle of a desert.

Noise; I heard a scrunch on the gravel by the boating club. My head whipped around. Someone was moving in the dimness, coming down towards *Stormfugl.* I froze. Only movement would give me away, shrouded in the dark of *Khalida*'s cockpit. It was a man's height and walk. As he came into the street-lights, I saw that it was Ted Tarrant. He went straight to *Stormfugl*'s jetty and stood there, gazing across the criss-cross of police tape at the deck where Favelle had died. It was too dark to see the expression on his face, but I turned my head away. It must have been ten minutes he stood there. When I heard his footsteps again I looked round. He was coming around the long curve to the marina gate, head turned towards *Khalida*. I stood up, and he put a hand to the locked gate.

'Coming,' I said. I swung the heavy gate open, and we walked down together in the soft air, with the water rippling under our feet. The tide had ebbed away all evening, and was now flowing again, and the sliver of returning moon hung in the navy sky. I gestured him on board *Khalida*.

'Have that cushion to sit on. She's not quite the luxury yacht you're used to.'

'She's your home,' he said. 'The luxury yachts I've been on've mostly been for tax avoidance. Bought by people who didn't know whadda get next. This one–'

'Come and look,' I invited. I went further into the cabin, so that he could descend without the embarrassment of brushing against me. He'd have plenty of girls inviting that. Beautiful girls, tall, tanned Californian girls, rich prep school girls. I was practical Cass, the one you called if you needed a longship sailed. I struck a match and lit the tea-light in the little brass lantern. Immediately the cabin was bathed in flickering golden light.

'She's neat,' he said. His face was bone-white under the tan, his eyes shadowed, but he managed a smile. 'I love all the wood, and the brass, like a real ship.'

'Tea, coffee?' I asked.

He shook his head. 'I won't sleep.'

He didn't look like a man who was going to sleep much anyway.

'I've got herbal tea.'

'That'd be neat,' he agreed, and folded himself down on the seat, at the head of my quarterberth. I filled the kettle and set it on the hob, then busied myself with the mugs and teabags.

'How far have you taken this baby?'

The phrase grated. *Khalida* was a fellow adult. 'Antigua, for the cruising season, then I got out before the hurricanes began.'

'By yourself?'

'By myself.' I turned my head to smile at him. 'It uses less stores. You'd have difficulty storing water for two for two weeks aboard. Two litres a day, four times fourteen – fifty six litres. No margin for missing the Trades and drifting for a fortnight.'

'And you just plan and then go?'

'Well, yes,' I said, thinking of the struggle to save enough just to buy food for the voyage. Once I was there I'd always found work; it was the getting there. 'Mostly.'

He leaned back with a sigh. 'I'm envious. Do you know that? I truly am. No snoopers, no cameras, nobody worrying about me. Even now, I hadda tell half a dozen people I was off for a walk, and at least two of them followed me.'

I made a face.

'It's what you pay for fame; I know. I wouldn't give it up.' He smiled at me, and I felt a sudden sense of shock that he was here in my cabin, like a film come alive, with me the heroine. 'You're very easy to visit with, Cass.' A sudden wash of pain distorted the smile. 'Favelle surely liked you. She said she felt safe aboard, you knew what you were doing. Oh, God–' He dropped his head into his hands, and the chestnut hair fell forward to hide his trembling mouth. A moment's silence, then he raised his head again. 'You recognised Maree, that last day. The police Lieutenant asked about that.'

I sat down opposite him. 'How did it come about, the swapping?' I asked.

'Favelle couldn't swim,' he said simply. 'It was a phobia, you know? She was terrified in swimming pools. Her parents wangled extra dancing lessons in the school swimming times, just so she wouldn't be teased about it. A teenager standing on the steps at the shallow end, shaking with fear.'

'So how, why, put her into it? Why do all the activist films?'

'It was an accident,' he said. 'He pushed his hair back in one smooth hand movement. 'I met the producer, and the screenplay just seemed made for Favelle. A new image, to get rid a the teen-movies stuff. It's the hardest move, you know? So I accepted it. She didn't wanna tell me how shit-scared she was, so she tried to get over it by herself. We had a pool in the grounds, and day after day she went in. And then one day I came home early and found her standing up to her waist in water, with the tears streaming down her face. She'd worked herself into such a state that I phoned Maree and asked her to come and stay. Maree always soothed Favelle. We all knew that Favelle couldn't do it, so we worked out a way to double. And then the public liked it.'

'But–' I said, 'how come nobody noticed? Or does everyone know but the punters?'

'Hardly anyone knows,' he said. He sighed with a simmering anger that surprised me. 'We're movie stars. We spend most of our time with people who don't know us. Fans, coming for an autograph. Other actors, on the lot for two days. Cameramen and make-up people who're hired for six weeks. They all know what Favelle looks like, and they know how they expect her to behave, and part of the expectation is that she'll behave differently every day, depending on what part of the movie is being shot. Romantic heroine, action girl. An actor makes them two different people.'

'So for anything that required action,' I said slowly, 'you planted Maree in some nice anonymous motel, between your house and the film lot.'

His eyes rose swiftly to mine.

'I guessed,' I said. 'That's the location of Jessie's house, where she's staying. Nicely between Busta and the marina. You and Favelle drove to the lot together, and on the way Favelle hopped out and Maree hopped in.'

'I guess that's about it,' he agreed. 'How did you tell, though?'

The kettle began to whine gently. I switched the gas off before it could move to full whistle and poured the boiling water into the cups. Steam misted a curve on the plastic window, shutting out the darkening hills opposite. I slotted the little table into its plastic hinges and set the mugs on it. 'Biscuit?'

'A cookie? No.' He shook his head and cupped his hands around the mug as if he wanted to crush it. 'How did you know about the substitution?' he repeated.

'Maree came over one evening,' I said. 'The way she swung herself onboard then – well, you can always tell someone who's used to boats. Sometimes Favelle was like that, and other times she was really awkward. The graceful one was only in long shots, and the awkward one did all the close-ups. If it hadn't been for knowing about Maree I wouldn't have guessed anything so bizarre.'

His lids flickered, as if he was weighing options, then his hand came across the table to cover mine. 'Favelle's dead. You won't say anything to spoil her memory?'

'I won't say anything.'

'That's my girl.' His hand curled briefly around mine, then withdrew delicately and cupped his mug once more.

I thought of what I'd been working out earlier. 'Where was Favelle, that morning, while Maree was filming?'

He looked up. 'Why?'

'When someone dies, like that, then the reason is supposed to be in them. I wondered what Favelle had done that day.'

His face froze, expression unreadable, and I feared that I'd really put my foot in it. Then he smiled again, eyes crinkling. 'She spent the morning at Jessie's house. I expect she was knitting, or telling Jessie stories about the movies, or just flipping through a magazine. There's nothing Favelle would have done to annoy anyone. She was so gentle. Everyone loved her. I think it must have been the maniac who sent the letters–' He spoke bleakly to the pale green infusion. 'I can't stay long. I just wanted to ask what Favelle was doing out that night. What she was doing aboard *Stormfugl.*'

I couldn't say it, with his trembling hands clutching the mug so tightly that the knuckles jutted like tacks on a seaman's chest. I took a deep breath.

'I wasn't here. I took *Khalida* out for a sail. While I was out I had a text from Maree. She and Dad had had a row, and she wanted to talk to me. Maybe when she couldn't get me, she phoned Favelle instead.'

Ted nodded. 'Of course, she couldn't come to Busta, and Favelle couldn't go to her lodgings. The two of them could never be seen together. They needed somewhere like *Stormfugl* where they could talk in private. Where's Maree now?'

Something prickled down my spine. 'I don't know,' I said. It was true enough, if we were talking exact co-ordinates. 'But I think–' I jerked my head around. 'What was that noise?'

He was on his feet instantly, and out of the companionway. I would never have thought such a big man could move so swiftly. I swung out of the forrard hatch and onto the foredeck. The night was dark now, with the silver half-penny of moon painting the masts with ghostly highlighting. There was a long pause while we both stared into the darkness.

At last Ted shook his head. 'Nothing.'

'Over there,' I breathed. 'Against the beach, on the far side.' Something was moving in the shadows. Hooves clattered on pebbles, sheep startled into wakefulness. 'One of your minders?'

He shook his head. 'They're in the bar.'

I was very aware of his breathing, quicker now as he looked around. He gave a last sigh. 'I gotta be going. Thanks, Cass. We'll need to get together to talk business – tomorrow maybe. I wanna finish this movie. Favelle's memorial.'

'I'm at your service,' I said formally.

He looked quickly around, then bent his head to mine. I was breathing in the scent of his aftershave. Nobody else could have heard his voice in my ear. 'Maree. Got to find her. Where do you think she is?'

But I wasn't going even to whisper the answer, here in the night where sounds carried across the water. I stepped back, and spoke clearly, for any listeners. 'I don't know where Maree is.'

He stepped back. 'Yeah, mebbe you're smart. We'll talk tomorrow. What time would suit you?'

'You're more likely to have calls on your time,' I said. I would need time to find Maree. 'I'll be around all day.'

'I'll call you.'

I let him out of the marina and watched him go back up the drive. I heard the click of the limo's door, then the purr of its engine making its way around the curve, along past the standing stone and over the little bridge to Busta. A last snick echoed back, the door closing, then there was silence again.

I brought my downie and under-cushion up from the cabin and dozed in the cockpit. I had half an hour of sleep, then I was woken by people leaving the club in a babble of drunken, cheerful voices. They reminded me that I had to talk to Magnie tomorrow. I stayed awake long enough to hear all the footsteps receding, then, once the barman had cleared up, the door banging and his car driving away. Once the silence had returned I slept again, but not deeply; on my next waking I surfaced suddenly, with the sense of something wrong.

It was too early for law-abiding people. I closed my hand around my mobile and listened. I heard nothing, but there was the echo of a splash in my head. I laid the downie aside and sat up. From very far off there was a sharp snap, like a breaking twig. Someone on the shore? What air there was stirred from the south-west, so the sound must have come from the Busta road. Would I really have heard a twig cracking among the Busta trees from here? Perhaps, if the little bay hidden from me behind the cat's-paw of headland had amplified the noise. There would be wood on that shore, dry and brittle enough to snap like that underfoot.

There was something else faint on the wind, a smell of burning. Had it been the crackle of a fire I'd heard? If it was by Busta, the headland would hide the glow. Yes, burning paper and wood, then a sudden whiff of an acrid smell, and with the smell a reflection of light in the water, so faint that I would never have seen it if the sky had been lighter.

Anders was at Busta. I called him, but there was no answer. Either he'd seen it and was dealing with it already, or was too sound asleep to wake. When the voicemail cut in I breathed a message: 'Cass here. Someone's up to mischief on Busta beach.'

Now what? This could be our chance to catch someone red-handed. Nobody would be carrying out legitimate burning of old tyres at this hour. I was dying to jump into the dinghy, but either by fast, noisy outboard or slow, silent oars they'd be gone before I reached them. I had to get somebody on the spot to check it out.

I called Ted, and he answered on the second ring. 'Cass?'

'Somebody's up to something on the beach. I can smell burning.'

'I'll check it out.'

'Not on your own,' I said, alarmed.

He didn't reply. I laid my mobile down and put shoes on. This was my post, guarding *Stormfugl*, and I wouldn't desert it. Fires were classic diversionary tactics. I padded softly round to the shelter of the boathouse, where *Stormfugl* lay dark beneath her spider's web of glinting tape, but all remained still in the marina.

It was fifteen long minutes before my phone shrilled: Ted's voice, brief and curt. 'He got away. Either off along the beach or back mingling with us. Sabotage. I'll tell you all about it tomorrow. Thanks, Cass.'

The light was dissolving the darkness now, the water gleaming blue instead of black. I went slowly back around the marina curve and pulled my downie over me. The first ripples of the turning tide began to tap on *Khalida*'s hull. I'd be no good in the morning if I didn't sleep again now, but my heart was racing, as if I'd been with Ted chasing that shadowy figure along the beach. More sabotage...

CHAPTER 15

At eight, the sounds of the day began again: cars moving around, the snicks and clatters of the new house being built above the road, the bleep of a truck reversing. I shook myself awake and headed for a hot shower to chase the stiffness of the night. I was just eating breakfast when Anders tapped on the window.

'Good morning, Cass.' His fair hair was damp and brushed, and his neat beard jutted out with a satisfied air. 'Is the kettle boiled?'

'Not yet,' I said. 'Go you.' I fed Rat a couple of crispies and let him run up my arm to my shoulder. His warm fur was comforting against my cheek.

'How did you enjoy Ted's visit?' Anders said.

'Now how did you know about that?' I asked.

'I was talking to his minders,' Anders said. 'The odds are mixed on you.'

A crispie went down the wrong way as I took a deep breath. Rat leapt for the bookshelf; Anders considerately thumped me on the back, against all the best First Aid practice. 'Mixed?' I asked when I could breathe again.

'Half for you and half against you,' Anders said precisely.

'I know what mixed means,' I retorted. 'I don't know why there should be odds.'

Anders shook his head. 'Cass, really. Odds on you consoling him. Half of the crew think you would be a good match, the ordinary one to keep his feet on the ground. The make-up girls agree they could make you into a beauty.'

'They won't get the chance,' I said. 'What about last night, at Busta?'

'Yes,' Anders said. There was a long pause while he poured the hot water into the mug and turned to set it down. 'There has been more sabotage.' He sat down. 'Someone has destroyed all the videotapes of the film shot here in Shetland.'

For a moment I thought I'd misheard. Then I remembered the smell of burning plastic on the air. 'Destroyed? All the film taken in Shetland?'

'No, not the film,' Anders said. '*Stormfugl* will still be a star. The video copies. It will delay the film a bit, I gather, because Ted will need to edit again what he had already done, but the original footage is safe.'

'Good,' I said. 'So tell me what happened.'

'In the middle of the night, Ted saw a fire on the beach. You will not agree, I

expect–'

I glared, and he raised his hand. 'I just wondered how he happened to see it.'

'He saw it,' I said, 'because I phoned and woke him. I smelt it.'

'You did not phone me?' Anders said, disconcerted. 'Cass, surely you do not think that I am something to do with all this?'

'I tried,' I said. 'Your phone was switched off.'

He looked blankly at me. 'But it was not. I did not turn it off. It did not ring all night.'

There was no point in arguing that one. 'So what happened?'

'Ted awoke his minders and went down, and found a heap of videos burning. They were all kept in their cases, labelled, in one of the stores at Busta, so that Ted could make a start at editing. The cases had been opened, then closed again, so that the store looked normal, but the videos were gone.'

'Interesting,' I said. 'So they could have been stolen bit by bit at any time.'

'More or less,' Anders agreed. 'The actual film was developed in London, there is only one firm that does it, and they sent back a video of it by courier, so that Ted could watch it in his suite each night. There was no great security, why should there be?'

'But it doesn't stop the film being made,' I mused, 'because the originals are all in London. Who would know that?'

'All of them,' Anders said with confidence. 'Even down to the make-up girls. It is the standard procedure on all movies, and they all know how it works.'

'So,' I mused, 'the saboteur wasn't a member of the crew.' Kevin. Gibbie. Inga.

'But,' Anders said, 'it would have been somebody who'd seen the news on television last night, where Ted said he was determined to finish the movie.'

'Favelle's memorial.' I took a couple of sips of tea, thinking. *Khalida* creaked on her moorings as Anders leaned back and stretched his legs across the cabin. 'I was thinking that her death might be to do with the windfarm, to stop the publicity shots, but that doesn't fit. If anything, the movie would benefit the anti-windfarm campaigners, by showing Shetland as an unspoiled place you wouldn't want to erect turbines all over.'

'It is a pretty weak motive,' Anders said. 'Just to stop the publicity shots.'

I nodded. 'But destroying her memorial, that looks vindictive. Maybe killing her was personal. I'm going to go and see if Kevin's up. I want to talk to him.'

Anders looked alarmed. 'Cass, you mustn't. Suppose he's our murderer?'

'Girl insists on going into lonely house,' I murmured.

'It's a bad idea,' Anders said firmly.

I jutted my chin at him. 'Favelle died on my ship, and I'm going to make sure it's sorted out. If it'll keep you happy, I'll phone you.'

'No,' he said, his face grave, 'I'll phone you. You phone me the minute you arrive with the car at his house, and I will call you back in five minutes, once you are inside. You tell me loudly and clearly that you are at Kevin's house, and then he will know that I know.'

I had to turn left out of the marina. My right-hand look for traffic showed me a police car, indicating to turn down to the boating club. I shot out before it and slowed down around the curve to look back. It slithered down the gravel hill and stopped beside Anders. DI Macrae got out. His lips moved, and Anders straightened. I pulled over to look properly. Inspector Macrae gestured, and Anders preceded him towards the club, shoulders slumped.

'You'd better tell the truth this time,' I mind-projected at him. At the door of the club, he paused, gestured towards the north. I could read his lips, plain as plain: 'I have to phone Cass. It is really important.'

He'd explain why, and Macrae would be up here to stop me. I checked over my shoulder and shot off.

Kevin lived several miles north of Brae, on the road that led towards Ronas Hill. His house looked like a fifties town semi, grey-harled with a small porch projecting in the centre. It was facing the fretted dazzle of sea, with a grassy foothill of Ronas Hill rising to the blue sky behind it, and a marsh-marigold fringed burn running though the middle of the valley below. The impact of the natural scenery was diminished by a white picket-fence enclosing an empty stretch of lawn: no children's toys scattered, no deck chairs or plastic tables, nothing to show anyone lived in the house. The gravel before the door was as empty as the grass, with none of the usual impedimentia of normal Shetland living, boots or oilskins hung out to dry, bags of peats on their way in or black rubbish bags on their way out. It looked the tourist accommodation it was, but with the last family moved out and the next not yet arrived. Kevin's car was parked by the byre, but there was no sign of movement behind either of the downstairs windows.

I called Anders' mobile, gave it two rings and cut the connection. It rang back immediately. I didn't pick up. Instead, I swung the car door open and got out.

I stood for another moment looking around, and listening. There was still no sign of life, but a prickling in my shoulder-blades suggested I was being watched. I didn't want to do anything as obvious as tilting my head to the dormer windows. I opened the door and walked in, calling in traditional fashion, 'Is there anybody home?'

The hall was as tidy and as impersonal as the exterior. There was a row of brass hooks dangling one fawn Burberry and one green anorak, and a pair of Hawkshead walking boots underneath, set toes to the wall. A dusty mirror reflected me framed in the doorway. At the end of the hall was the stair to the two upstairs rooms; on each side of the stair was a door. I called 'Hello' again, louder, and opened the door to the left.

Good guess. It was the kitchen, all fake-wood cupboards and beige tiling. An upturned pan crouched on the stainless steel draining board with a wooden spoon beside it. At the other end of the room were two armchairs, each with a modern throw in a rainbow-colours stars-and-moons design which only pointed up the blandness of the fawn and grey swirled lino. There was a wooden table by the window, with the inevitable pile of jotters, a pile of A4 paper, used, and a widescreen computer with a scanner on one side and a printer on the other. If I'd been a proper private eye I'd've headed straight for it, downloaded all the sensitive information directly into my own memory stick, and scarpered.

Lying beside the computer, as if it had been taken off by someone coming to sit down at the table, was Inga's red scarf. I was just stretching out a hand to it when there were footsteps on carpet above me, then creaking down the stairs. I retreated to the doorway and turned. 'Hiya.'

'Cass,' Kevin said, without noticeable enthusiasm. He was wearing his school clothes, a white shirt covered by one of those green army jumpers with the elbow pads, and a pair of dark grey trousers in a style which made his legs even longer and skinnier. The pinkness of his cheeks suggested he'd had a go at shaving what whiskers he had, and his heron's comb hair was sleeked back in a newly-washed style, showing off the receding patches. His watery eyes surveyed me with suspicion.

'I hope I'm not bothering you too early,' I said, and launched into the story I'd thought out on the way over. 'I was passing, and I'd been thinking about you – about the windfarm.' His mouth relaxed slightly, but his eyes were still wary. 'Dad was talking about it last night, and I hadn't realised the scale of it – I thought it was just two or three, like the ones above Lerwick.' The phone in my pocket rang again; we both jumped. "Anders calling" the display said, but I'd have betted my best mainsail that it wasn't.

'Anders?' I said innocently into it.

'Ms Lynch,' said DI Macrae, 'I'd like you to return to the marina right now.'

'Oh, Inspector,' I said. 'I've just got to Kevin's house. I'll see you down at *Stormfugl* in about half an hour.'

His voice would have iced up a running engine. 'If you're not back here in ten minutes I'll be sending a car to fetch you.'

'Yes, sir. I'll see you soon.' I snicked the phone closed and smiled at Kevin. 'Sorry about that. Yes, the scale of the windfarm. I thought it'd be small.'

'That's what a lot of us thought,' Kevin said. I could see him working out what a feather it would be in their cap if Dad's own daughter came over to their side. 'Have a seat.' He gestured towards one of the armchairs. 'D'you want a cup of tea?'

I didn't, but no chat can take place in Shetland without one. 'Yes, please.' I went over to the chair, back to him, which gave me the chance to give the scarf a really good look. It was loosely knitted in reds and ambers, mixing cashmere and mohair with narrow, shiny ribbon, and if it wasn't Inga's she had one very like it. I wondered if there was any way I could slip it into my pocket and return it in a casual fashion, to see her reaction.

He filled the kettle and switched it on, still giving me suspicious looks.

'So,' I rattled, 'I've only heard Dad's side, you see, and I saw you offering leaflets around, and thought I'd like to read one or two, you know, just to get the opposition point of view.'

'I can certainly give you that,' Kevin said. 'Milk? Sugar?'

'No, thanks,' I said. I put on a look of alert intelligence.

He sat down on the other chair and fished in a khaki bag that hung over its back. 'We're a shoestring outfit so we don't have glossy leaflets, but we do have fact-sheets and a website.'

He handed me a couple of pages of very closely printed A4. 'This top one is mostly looking in more detail at various statements made by Shetland Eco-Energy, and the one underneath is other detailed ecological arguments against the windfarm. Ecological arguments. We mustn't let ourselves be swayed by the moral blackmail of 'needing to do our bit.' We're not questioning that the world needs alternative sources of energy. It does, and badly. We're not disputing, either, that the Shetland windfarm up at Burradale is already out-performing every other windfarm in the world. The problem is, whether that energy generated in Shetland can be transported elsewhere economically.'

He sat down on the other armchair, fixing me earnestly with those watery eyes. The red corners and the stare reminded me of a weasel trying to mesmerise a rabbit. The scarf lay like a fiery ribbon just behind his shoulder. 'See, now, the first question is the connector with the mainland. They're talking in terms of a joint project between the Scottish Electricity Board and Shetland Eco-Energy. Problem 1: the cost of the cables. Enormous. The wind turbines have a projected lifespan of twenty-five years, and they'd spend that paying that cost off. No benefits for the consumer there, no benefits at all. Problem 2: every time you run electricity through cables, you lose some of it. Of the 100% you put out at this end, only 40% would reach the Scottish mainland. That's an appalling waste of resources.'

'It certainly seems it,' I agreed. Inga had had the scarf on the day we'd filmed aboard the longship, with Charlie. I remembered her almost losing it as Charlie threw his tantrum. She'd worn it on Saturday too. Suitable attire for a Shetland beach on a bonny June day: scarf, woolly hat, gloves.

'So that's the first big problem,' he summed up. 'Over half of the energy created by these turbines wouldn't even reach the consumers on mainland Britain.'

'That's such a waste,' I said. That meant she'd been here on Sunday or yesterday.

'The next problem is financial too. Did your father explain how the company works?'

'Not really,' I said. There was no reason why Inga shouldn't have called in, but the way that scarf was lying suggested someone making herself at home.

'Okay.' He was really getting into his stride. 'Well, it was set up as an independent company, but then it was taken over by the Shetlands Islands Council. To fund the wind turbines they'd need to use money from the Charitable Trust – you know, the oil disturbance money which was to be set aside for the good of the people of Shetland. That's the money whose interest runs the leisure centres and care centres and all that. It'll be hugely expensive, so it'll take all Shetland's nest egg for a rainy day, and with this looming recession and dwindling oil in the North Sea that rainy day could come soon.'

'Dad seemed to be saying the returns would be huge, though,' I said. 'Enough to fund our prosperity for the next two decades.' Just how far had this affair gone?

'Oh, theoretically,' Kevin agreed. He shuffled some papers around and produced a glossy brochure with a picture mock-up of Busta Voe with the wind turbines topping the hills on the front, found a page of graphs and spread it open. 'This is their brochure. Problem is that it is totally theoretical.' His voice boomed again, as if this was a speech he'd used several times at meetings. 'Until they know the cost of the cable, the returns on the energy sent south, and the subsidy the government's going to give them – and whether it's going to continue, can you imagine the same government staying in power for 25 years? - then their sums aren't worth the paper they're written on. It's all speculative, and it could go spectacularly wrong. See?'

I nodded, meekly.

'The big thing though is the destruction of our environment.'

This conversation was too one-sided. I pushed Inga right out of my mind and made myself focus. 'Absolutely,' I agreed. 'It's partly the filming – you know, the reactions of the crew – that's made me realise what a unique landscape we have here.'

'Absolutely,' he echoed. I gave him a sharp look from under my prettily cast-down lashes, but he didn't seem to be being sarcastic. 'This mock-up doesn't start to give the impact of it.' He brandished Shetland Eco-Energy's brochure. 'It'd be pretty rare the turbines would blend into the clouds so well – you'd get them either black or white against the sky.'

'Like the Burradale ones,' I agreed.

'Don't forget, though, that they're twice the height. Twice the visual impact, huge blades spinning. The Burradale ones, you can see the flicker of their shadows down on the golf course and right across the Tingwall valley, nearly a mile away.'

That rang a bell. We'd once had a trainee aboard the *Dauntless* who'd had an epileptic seizure through squinting at the sun past a flapping flag. 'Wouldn't that have an effect on people with epilepsy?'

'There are all sorts of health risks spoken about, though wind turbines are so new nothing is really proven. Dizziness, nausea, headaches – they make a noise, you know, a low thrumming that carries through the earth, or in mist. Disrupt TV signals too, though most people have satellite these days.'

I didn't want to get too far from the film. 'Ted insisted on using Shetland because it could be all the locations he needed,' I said. 'If he can finish the movie, other film-makers would see what can be done here. It could be a whole new industry, but not if there are huge turbines along the hills.'

'You're right, it could be an excellent industry for Shetland, excellent. We have the infrastructure to cope with it, but the turbines would kill it stone dead.' He rose and went over to the window, sweeping one arm outwards and lifting Inga's scarf with the other hand behind his back. My peripheral vision caught a glimpse of him tucking it behind the computer screen. 'That hill there, there are going to be half a dozen in sight. Up there, another ten. And from the front door–' He motioned me before him. 'A dozen turbines there.' He turned, looking down across the greener hills behind the first corner of Brae. 'All the way down to Eid. More on Scallafield there. There won't be anywhere in Shetland that you won't be able to see at least three or four.'

'So that really would scupper filming,' I said.

'Scupper it entirely. But it's not just the visual effect. What do you know about peat?'

'It bends your back, cuts your hands and dries your skin out,' I said promptly. His solemn mouth curved in a smile that improved his face hugely.

'You suffered too, as a child.'

'We all did,' I said, diving promptly into this promising opening. 'We didn't have any peats of our own, but I helped Inga's family – do you know Inga Nicolson, no, what's her married name? Em – em–' I'd genuinely forgotten it, so the blank look I gave his suddenly watchful face must have been convincing. 'You know, peerie Charlie's mum. The wee boy in the movie.'

'Anderson,' he said.

'Yes, that's it. Anyway, I'd go and help her family. I was even up on her bank yesterday morning.'

'Yes. Well, here in Shetland the depth varies, but it can be very deep indeed, several metres, and it absorbs carbon dioxide. You know, the gas that causes global warming. Our peat is a great help to our struggling planet.' Handy slogan. He went back to the lecture. 'If the turbines go ahead, not only are we going to lose that absorption medium, but the digging work will release the stored CO2, thus worsening global warming – the very thing we want the turbines to fight against.'

'It's mad, isn't it?' I paused for artistic effect, and to shift my position so I could see his face. 'Wasn't Favelle concerned about that? I know you spoke to her about it.'

He jumped as if I'd run a marline spike into him. 'You weren't there.'

I decided to really chance my arm. 'Anders overheard you talking that evening. She was really nice, Favelle. I'd have thought, if you explained it all to her–'

'I did,' he said. His voice became curt, as if he was regretting telling me this much. 'She said that if I'd bring the literature down to the set the next day she'd read it, and consider.'

'Ah,' I said. 'So she was maybe going to think again about doing the windfarm publicity?'

'I'm sure she was,' he said. His very positiveness struck a false note. 'She couldn't help but see, once she'd heard both sides of the story, what a disaster this would be for everyone if it went ahead.' He paused, pulled himself up to his full height and prepared to make his winning tack. 'And of course I'm happy to say that her changing to our side totally removed any motive malicious people might have used in suggesting windfarm objectors might have been responsible for her death.' The smug expression he wore to contemplate this truly awful sentence made me wonder if he really rated my intelligence that low. All Favelle had done was fob him off: bring me the leaflets, I'll read them.

'Of course,' I said instantly. 'I can't believe anyone would really suggest such a thing. I'm sure the police don't think it.'

He darted me a sharp glance. 'I have not as yet talked to the inspector.'

'How did you come to meet that evening?' I asked.

'I had heard – that is to say, I was told that she has a habit of going for a run most evenings, just at dusk, along the Muckle Roe road.'

I closed my lips firmly on the 'But–' I'd been about to utter. It hadn't been Favelle who went running, but Maree.

'So I went out,' he said, 'and hung about, just half way round the Busta turn-off there, by the standing stone, and waited for her. She wasn't actually running, just walking briskly. I gave her a bit of a fright, stepping out in front of her, but she was really happy to listen to me, and she said if I'd bring her the literature tomorrow, she'd have a look at it. I thanked her, and offered her a lift back to the hotel, and she said no thanks, and off she went.'

'In what direction?' I asked.

He gave me a blank look. 'Towards the main road.'

That meant towards the marina. 'You know,' I said, 'I think you should be telling this to the police. You could be a really important witness.' The thin shoulders swelled a little; the weedy chin went up.

'Well–'

'For example, one of the people you passed on your way home could have been the murderer.'

'But that was at dusk,' Kevin objected. 'Eleven o clock. She didn't die until very much later.' The watery eye bent on me was suddenly shrewd. 'I heard just before ten to four, when you came in.'

Bang on, but how did he know that? He wouldn't have seen me from here.

'I drove away from her at just after eleven. She wouldn't have hung around all that time. She must have gone back to the hotel and come out again. Anyway–' I saw him thinking about it. 'No, I didn't pass any cars. You don't think about it, of course, but I'm pretty sure I didn't. I have a vague impression of someone on a bike, coming towards the marina, just after the Busta turn-off.' He gave me a long look, bit his lip uncertainly, then lifted his head and gave me that unexpectedly likeable smile again. I wondered suddenly if he was simply rather shy with strange women. 'Look, I don't want to interfere, but I wondered how well you know your mechanic, the young Norwegian. It's common knowledge he's been sleeping aboard your longship some nights. Well, she could have been visiting him. He's a bit – well – who knows what he could be up to?'

'Not committing murder,' I said vehemently. But why hadn't he heard his phone last night?

Kevin shook his head, his disapproving upper lip lengthening, and took a step back into his doorway. 'Well, I must be going, or I'll be late for school. Now think about what I've said, Cass, and if you agree then come along to our next meeting. We've all got to stand together to stop this happening. Otherwise Shetland will be desecrated because of apathy. Desecrated.'

'I'll think about it,' I promised. He whisked back inside and I put out a hand to stop him. 'One last question. Did you know about Favelle wanting to adopt peerie Charlie?'

His face darkened; his eyes narrowed. His hand on the door jamb clenched into a fist. If looks could kill they'd have been choosing the sail for my shroud. 'You're not the police,' he snapped, and slammed the door.

Well, well. I walked back to the car. He was, of course, being far more positive about what Favelle had said, but he had good reason for that. What he'd said did fit in with Anders' account: they'd met at the stone, he'd been trying to persuade her, and she'd been wanting to get rid of him, so that she could go to Anders. She'd said she'd look at the stuff, and he'd gone, according to his account.

That last spurt of temper was unexpected. I wondered how he'd have reacted if she'd flatly refused to discuss the windfarm and told him to go away and stop bothering her. Might he have struck out at her? Then there was Inga's scarf that he'd whisked away as neatly as a sail-maker stowing his knife. That sleight of hand could have lit a fuse in the gap between two stones without anyone noticing.

In spite of that last spasm of sympathy I really couldn't see how Inga could bear him. It was something about the combination of gangly height and straggliness that made him feel like a human spider. I wouldn't have had an affair with him for all the tea in China. However it seemed that Inga might be, while big Charlie was away at the fishing, and in her own house too, because although Kevin wouldn't have seen me coming up the voe from his own bedroom window, he'd have had a grandstand view from Inga's.

ᛋ

I was almost back at the marina when a police car passed me. The driver clocked me, did a U-turn and escorted me to the marina. DI Macrae got out, his easy-going face grim.

'Now, Ms Lynch, while Mr Johansen is giving his new statement to one of my colleagues, I think you should tell me what that little bit of play-acting was all about.'

'Over a cup of tea?' I suggested.

His eyes narrowed. There was a long stillness, broken only by the light breeze ruffling the curls in his short hair. Finally, he nodded. 'Why not?'

I'd had enough tea for one morning but at least it would give me something to do with my hands, or I could follow DI Macrae's lead and knock up a monkey's fist while he tied flies. He surprised me, though. 'You can handle this boat alone, can't you? How would you like to take me out, if you haven't any more mischief planned for the morning?'

'Oh–' I said, startled, then bluntly, 'Why?'

He considered me gravely for a moment. 'It's easier to talk on a boat at sea. Haven't you noticed that?'

I had.

He nodded. 'I want to stand away from these people. Get out in the loch, the voe, and look at them from a distance.' He looked straight at me. 'And I want to pick your brains. You're smart, and you're involved. I want you on my side. You know what a loose cannon would do to a ship.'

'Smash straight through the side on its little wheels.' He was being straight with me. I looked straight back at him. 'If I can, I'll help, but I don't want to betray anyone, or send you off on wrong trails after someone I care about.'

'I need all the bits of the puzzle before I can make it,' he said.

'It's not a game,' I said.

'No,' he agreed. He turned and bent to speak into the police car window. 'Ms Lynch is going to take me out around the loch. I'll be about an hour. Go on with the door to door, from Busta to the main road. Any cars or pedestrians seen.'

He made himself at home in the cockpit, peaceably looping little circular weights on his line, while I started the engine and cast off.

'Did you know there's a special variety of Arctic char, found only in Shetland?' He lifted his head and smiled at me, and suddenly we were both at ease. 'Now, if we can get this murder solved, I'll be able to go and try for one. The Lerwick shop hires out rods, though I wish I'd brought my own. How would you feel about taking me out sea-fishing?'

'I don't know the best places,' I said, 'but so long as I can help eat what we catch, I'm up for it. The Rona was always a good mackerel spot.'

As soon as we were out of the marina I turned head to wind and got the mainsail up. It was a westerly wind, a nice reach both ways. I unrolled the jib and we were gliding along with only the chuckle of the waves at *Khalida*'s forefoot. 'Want to take the helm?'

'No. Helming you can only think about the boat. I want to let my mind run free.'

We settled down, one at each side of the boat. I was aft, with my hand on the helm; he was by the echo sounder and wind reader, auburn hair dark against the white fibreglass curve of *Khalida*'s cabin, and lifted by the wind coming through the slot between the sails. His head was bent over his line still, but his grey eyes lifted every ten seconds to look outwards: up at the standing stone first, then forward towards Busta. Alain had done that too, concentrated on some task yet aware of every move the boat made. The brown hands continued to work, not needing sight to tie the knots, delicate and assured on the green wool of his lap. I wondered what he'd be like as a lover and shoved the thought away. 'Where do you come from?' I asked.

He caught the absolute sense I'd meant. 'A farm six miles from a little village in the shadow of Ladhar Bheinn. We had to go to school by boat.'

The light brown rectangle of the boating club receded as we followed the shore to Busta. There was a blackened ring on the beach, with a couple of white suits crouching beside it.

'Do you think you'll get any clues to the saboteur?' I asked.

He shook his head. 'Unlikely. It looked as though the videos had all been dumped in one rubbish bag and just fired. We may get prints from left-over plastic, but I doubt it.'

'How about prints on the cases?' I asked.

'The last person to handle each of them wore gloves. Probably male, by the size of the hands, but only probably. Did you phone Tarrant the moment you smelt the burning?'

'Oh, yes. Within a minute, anyway.'

'Dawn's a good time. Light enough not to need to draw attention to yourself with a torch, dark enough to hide who you are.

The hotel, of course, doesn't keep anyone up all night, and the doors are open. Guests just come and go as they please.'

'Nothing to stop an outsider coming in,' I said. 'Do you know when the videos were stolen?'

He shook his head. 'Not accurately enough. It could have been any time in the last couple of days. Everyone's been too distressed by Favelle's death to worry about editing.'

'And nobody saw anyone near the bonfire?'

'Elizabeth thought she heard a mobile ringing, and she looked out. She saw a dark figure against the flames, but lost it as soon as it moved away from the fire.'

'Male? Female?'

'She couldn't say. You didn't hear anyone scrunching along the beach? Coming towards here?'

'No. Definitely not.'

He considered me for a moment. More questions; I gripped the tiller a little tighter and felt *Khalida* quiver beneath me.

'How did others get on with Favelle, do you think?'

I remembered what I'd said to Anders that morning about personal dislike. It seemed DI Macrae was thinking along those lines too. 'She wasn't quite on this planet,' I said, 'but you couldn't dislike her. It would have been like disliking a beautiful child.'

'Was she happy?'

'Oh,' I said. I hadn't thought of that, gave a knee-jerk reaction. 'No.' A happy woman wouldn't want to adopt another woman's child.

'She had no children of her own,' he said, slowly, eyes on his knots once more, 'and several observers have mentioned how very taken she was with little Charlie Anderson. Taken with him, in fact, to the extent of wanting to adopt him.' The stag-red head came up. the eyes that could have been Alain's met mine, except that Alain had never looked at me with that grave disappointment, that I wouldn't help him. 'I spoke to her lawyer last night. She asked him to phone and offer to adopt the boy. The mother refused, and threatened adverse publicity if she was approached again. The lawyer advised Favelle to re-think the idea.'

'Inga told me about that,' I said. 'She was very angry, of course, but she believed, she truly believed, that she'd put a stop to it.'

'Why do you think Favelle was so taken with the child?'

Odd question. 'Oh, our Charlie's very cute, blonde curls, engaging lisp, all that. There was the part of her child in the movie. It had been cut, and when she met Charlie she insisted on putting it back in.'

'Nobody's mentioned that,' he said. He added a weight to his line. 'According to the lawyer, she accepted his advice without arguing. You think she couldn't have children, or was just wanting to have one?'

'Maybe she wanted to be a yummy mummy, like all the other film stars these days, but Ted wanted her to keep going with her career. Anders thought–'

That was what came of talking on boats. I bit the sentence off.

'It's all right,' DI Macrae said. 'He's told us version 2 now.' Then he used my words. 'Favelle, the beautiful international star, slumming it with a Norwegian engineer. Do you believe it?'

I couldn't lie out here, with *Khalida*'s tiller alive under my hand, and the white mainsail stretching above us. Perhaps he'd counted on that. 'I don't know. She was being really flirty with him at lunchtime, that day.' Then it all began clicking in my head. 'What day was it she tried to adopt Charlie? Hang on–' He waited silently. I kept feeling my way. 'Inga said the lawyer said she was ill-treating him. It was the day before. He'd been a total pain coming out of the boat, and she'd skelped him. The next day they used another boy in the morning shots, and Charlie was a right pain in the afternoon. I thought he was making Inga bad-tempered, but it was the other way round. She was in a bad mood and it spread to him. So Favelle had been told no the night before.'

I paused for a moment. Favelle's first words to Anders: *Hi there! Is this your little boy?* 'Favelle thought,' I said slowly, 'that Anders was Charlie's father. When they first met, the day she arrived. The same blond hair and blue eyes. Anders said that too. *'She always smiled at me – I think she thought I was Charlie's father.'*

Dominoes were falling in my head. *It would be like sleeping with Garbo*, Anders had said. I remembered our tough Vikings watching her shadow as it fell across their bare knees. 'She wasn't sexy. She was beautiful, like Garbo, romantic. Our Vikings were all protective about her. Helping her out of the boat, pulling the sail round so the sun wouldn't spoil her complexion. Anders sensed it. She didn't particularly want to sleep with him, she wasn't bothered about sex. She didn't want *him.* She wanted Charlie.'

DI Macrae finished the thought for me. 'She wanted him to make her pregnant.'

CHAPTER 16

We were approaching the end of Busta Voe now. The heather-dark back of Linga was abeam, the Rona opening out ahead. Strom was on our starboard side, with Magnie's house tucked in under its hillside. He was out of his bender now; his front door stood open, and a thin trail of blue peat-reek trailed up from one chimney.

'Magnie might know something,' I said abruptly. 'He was there that evening. He wouldn't talk to you, though, he'd just say he was too drunk to remember.'

DI Macrae's mouth hardened. 'We wouldn't believe him.'

'He won't be leaned on.' I laughed at the idea of Magnie caving in to the police. 'He was a whaling man in South Georgia, for goodness sake. He's endured storms and icebergs and shipwreck and hunger, and even the rum rations running out. He might talk to me.'

'Have you mentioned this to anyone?'

'No.'

'Don't. Just go along as casually as you can. Let me know when you're going. I'll give you my own number.'

'My mobile's below,' I said. 'Put it in under contacts for me.'

He went into the cabin, programmed it in, and returned. 'Phone me when you get there, and then again when you leave. If you find anything out, tell me it straight away.'

I looked him straight in the face. 'I can't promise. If it doesn't harm anyone I love, then yes.'

He didn't challenge that, just turned his face away and looked out at the ocean for a moment. 'Do you know how Favelle died?' he asked.

I shook my head. 'Only that she was hit on the head.'

'Yes,' he said. 'She was hit on the head not far from the standing stone. We found the place. She was still conscious when someone shoved her down into the ditch beside it, to hide her body from passing cars.' His voice was even, detached, making the image more shocking. 'We know that because there are the marks of her hands clinging on in the wet earth, and traces of that same earth under her fingernails.'

I raised my eyes to his, shaken. 'Still alive–'

'She was still alive when she was picked up from there and slung into the back of a car or truck to be brought to the longship. There are the traces of one person's footprints – only traces, nothing to help us. Someone carried her to the deck and left her to die. Perhaps not conscious, but if she'd been given help then she might still have been saved. She died as much of cold as of the head injury.'

I felt sick. 'The gulls–'

'Yes, still alive even then. Don't you remember the blood? Dead women don't bleed. When you found her, she'd only just died.'

I turned my face away. The water dazzled below my eyes.

'She was lucky,' that soft, implacable voice went on. 'Her murderer had left her face down. Otherwise it would have been her eyes.'

'Ms Lynch.' He leaned forward. 'I have to be her voice. That's my job. The man or woman who did that chose to abandon their humanity and do that to her.' He paused for a moment, looking out at the blue sky and the ocean horizon past the Vementry guns, then turned his head to me once more. 'You have a choice too. To join them, or to join me.'

We sailed on in silence. I was thinking, and he left me to think. 'I'm not sure I have any puzzle pieces you haven't found for yourself,' I said, at last.

'What did Ted want, last night? That's a new bit.'

'He wondered what Favelle was doing aboard *Stormfugl*. I didn't tell him. I didn't want to hurt him. And he wondered if I knew where Maree was.'

'Do you?'

'She's on Yell. I don't know where exactly.'

He lifted his head, and I explained my reasoning, and Dodie the ferryman's recognition of her description.

'Thanks,' DI Macrae said. 'That's useful.' He lifted his mobile and spoke briefly into it: 'Ms Lynch believes Maree Baker could be in Yell, probably in a B&B. Can you put the local man on to it? Thanks.'

I hoped the local man wasn't busy at the other end of Unst.

'Did you get anything useful from Kevin Manson?' Now he was treating me as one of his officers.

'He admitted to having talked to Favelle on the night she died, around eleven, at the standing stone, just as Anders said. He was trying to persuade her not to do the windfarm adverts.'

'And?'

'He said that she was very positive; told him to bring her the leaflets, and she'd read them and think about it. I thought it sounded more like she was fobbing him off to get him to go away.' Favelle's torn hands hardened my heart. 'I think he and Inga could be having an affair. She'd told him about Favelle wanting peerie Charlie. When I asked him about that he shut the door on me. I think they were together that night, at Inga's. He knew the time I'd come in.'

He nodded to himself again. I looked ahead. We were almost at Vementry. Time to turn around. 'Tacking – stay still.' The boom swung smoothly over our heads; *Khalida* leaned to the other side and gathered speed again.

'The last thing,' I said, 'is that Elizabeth was out and about that night. The boy of the caravanners saw her up on Ronas Hill, in her own car.'

'If Favelle was brought to the longship by car,' DI Macrae said, 'did you hear a car? See any sign of life as you came up the voe?'

'Only Magnie,' I said.

There was a silence. I turned my head to meet his eyes, and knew it had come, at last, as I'd known it would. I'd courted it in offering my boat as a place to talk. He said, very gently, 'Tell me how Alain Mouettier died.'

I couldn't lie, not with those eyes on me. My lips felt stiff.

'I killed him.'

ᛋ

It had been in the mid-Atlantic, in July, ten years ago. We were a thousand miles from Boston, a thousand to the outer Hebrides; twelve days out, twelve to go. *Marielle* was rolling along on the great green breakers, with the red and white cruising chute poled out on port and the mainsail on starboard. We'd settled back into our shipboard routine of rising, checking, eating, relaxing. Four on, four off watches, like a tall ship. It had been my watch, four till eight, the graveyard shift. When Alain had woken me it'd still been dark, with the waning crescent making ghosts of the sails. Now the first streak of creamy green-blue showed in the east. The moon dipped into the sea; the stars faded as the darkness did, until only the steady lamp of Venus remained. The sun rose slowly, veiled by mist, blood-red with a broad orange stripe across its centre, and the mist stayed across it so that when it came up above the horizon it looked like a montgolfier hovering above the waves.

Alain was still sleeping below as I went forrard to have a good look ahead: for whales, for floating rubbish, for clouds on the horizon that might mean storms or calms, for any changes in the limitless ocean. Sea, and sea and sea. Our little ship and us, the only people in the universe. I'd stopped believing in crowded Boston so far behind us, and the Hebrides were a mirage somewhere in the future. There was only now, with the smell of the waves that splashed over the deck, the vast silence of the ocean broken by the sounds of the ship, the mast settling against its steel-wired stays, the cruising chute flap as it lost wind and filled again, the caress of the great rollers against the stern, the slap as her bow found itself free of the water, on the crest of a wave, and the long shooosh as she slid down into the trough.

There was a smudge on the horizon that could be a ship steaming towards us. Nine nautical miles away. It could be making twenty or thirty knots, even more in these smooth conditions, which gave us fifteen minutes to take evasive action. I lifted the hand-bearing compass from its string around my neck and took a sighting, then went back to scribble it in the log. Ship sighted, 95 degrees. I left it for five minutes then I checked again. 95 degrees. Bearing unchanged; collision course. I gybed the mainsail, then wrestled the chute across. We were on a broad reach now, headed down to starboard of the approaching ship, a course change that had us pointing for Spain instead of Scotland.

All that had taken five minutes. Now she was on the sea instead of floating on the horizon, a big cruise-ship trailing black smoke. I could even feel the throb of her engines through *Marielle*'s decks. I took a bearing again. 80 degrees. We'd get her wash, but she wouldn't run us down without even noticing. 77 degrees. We'd clear her.

I fished the binoculars out of their locker to get a proper look at her. She was called *Sea Princess,* and steaming at a good speed, as if she'd been delayed by bad weather and had time to make up. It was strange suddenly to have other people in our world: people waking to sex in a double bed with crisp white sheets, or a shower before taking a turn around the decks, people coming into an almost stable restaurant for their bacon and eggs, people taking a swim in the pool, then spending their morning chatting to strangers. There'd be a buffet lunch with fresh fruit, then an afternoon spent relaxing in a deck chair, watching the waves go by from over the top of a throw-away paperback. They'd dress for dinner then dance until dawn. It was a whole other world. I wasn't really envious – except of the food, after five days of eating tins, soya mince and fish, and, yesterday, the last banana. I envied them the romance too, for I wasn't dizzily in love with Alain any longer. He was keen to try living together ashore, but I was resisting. Maybe it'd be fine; if you can get on well in a thirty-foot boat, you'd think you could get on well anywhere. We'd not done a lot together in Boston, though; Alain had gone off to look at the bars and the nightlife, and I'd wandered through the old part of the town and imagined Sam Adams and his friends stealing through the night dressed as Indians, hatchets in their hands and liberty setting their brains afire. I didn't want to spend a lifetime ashore doing interesting things by myself.

I was just about to resume our heading when I heard Alain's alarm clock from below. Half past seven. Then he rang the ship's bell, seven tings, followed by clattering about in the galley. I'd finish my watch while he made breakfast. We'd eat together, do the handover, then I'd go back to sleep.

The wind had risen while I'd been watching the ship passing. The rolling waves wore white crests now, and *Marielle* was beginning to tilt to leeward. It was time to put the chute away and unroll the jib. I loosened the sheets and went forrard. The chute had a snuffer, a long tube which pulled down over the unruly half-parachute of red and white nylon. I wrestled it down at last and dropped it into the forepeak, then hauled up the jib and went back to the cockpit to sheet it in. The wind was definitely rising now, and shifting a point too. We'd need a reef in the mainsail.

Alain was half-way up the companion-way ladder with a plate of porridge in each hand when a gust picked up the boom and threw it over. I felt it go, and ducked instinctively, yelling 'Gybe!' He didn't have a chance to dodge it, only to turn his head away and duck a little; it hit him square on the back of the head, a metal boom with the strength of a force 5 gybe behind it. I didn't hear the crack of bone at the time, lost in the judder of the boom falling, but I heard it in my dreams each night afterwards.

The boom would come back again if I didn't grab the helm and steady the ship. I pushed the tiller from me. *Marielle* surged forwards, off course, but it didn't matter. I'd get us back on track after I'd looked at Alain.

The plates were still in his hands, but the porridge had slid out of them onto the cockpit floor. He gave me a queer, blank look from eyes that were focused on something in front of me. There was a trickle of blood coming from his nose, and he licked his lips and swallowed, as if it was running backwards into his mouth too. He spoke first. 'I'm okay – I'm–'

The plates slithered from his hand and fell with a plastic thud. 'Better sit down. I'll be fine. I–' That licking movement again. 'I'll get some water.'

'Sit still, I'll get it.'

'No. We need to reef.' A deep breath, a wince of pain. 'I'm fine.' Suddenly, irritably, 'Don't *fuss*. It's my watch now. A reef in the mainsail, and put that preventer back on.'

Captain's orders. He brought us head to wind while I let the main down and secured it round the ram's horn. I came back to pull the slab reefing lines in, tightening the new bottom of the sail, winched the halyard drum-tight and reached up to thread a line through the eyes in the mainsail.

I kept looking back to the cockpit. The dead white of Alain's face terrified me. 'We just passed a ship. We could call her up.'

A smile touched his bloodless lips. 'Panic measures, Cass. Have a look at my pupils. Even?'

'Even,' I admitted. He winced as I turned his head around. 'No sign of blood on the back of your skull.'

'Well, then. Breakfast.' He bent forward to examine the porridge, and I saw him wince as he straightened. 'What do you say, scrape it up or make new stuff?'

I didn't want it, with that crash as the boom went over still echoing in my ear, and the whiteness of his face sending slithers of dread around my stomach. 'You stay at the helm. 95 degrees. I'll get some oatcakes.'

I kept glancing up at him as I fished the oatcakes out of their tin and buttered them. His colour was coming back again, and there was no more blood trickling down his upper lip. It had been a hard crack, but he had ducked a little, maybe that had helped ride the blow, and there was no obvious sign of injury. It hadn't even broken the skin.

He'd made the tea already. I passed the mugs up through the companionway, then followed them with the oatcakes.

'Here.'

He ate two, and he seemed alert enough. 'I don't think it'll blow much harder.' He looked at me and smiled, the last smile I saw him give, but I didn't know that then, and it reassured me. 'Cass, you're dead on your feet. Preventer, ma fille, then sleep.'

I obeyed, yawning fit to break my jaw. Below, I crawled into my quarter berth in my top and long johns, eyes closed, and out. I didn't sleep well, though; I lurched from one confused, anxious dream to another. Each time I awoke, Alain was sitting by the helm still, eyes looking ahead. At half past eleven, he reached in and rang seven bells. I opened my eyes properly.

'How are you feeling now?'

'A headache, and a touch dizzy, but nothing more. When you're ready, come and take over, and I'll have a lie down again.'

We did the usual handover things, a look at the log, an update on course and wind. I left the course and the reef alone but bent on the larger jib, and Alain went to bed, leaving me alone with the sea. I got the fishing line out, more in hope than expectation, and trailed it behind us; I checked the rigging again and let the sheets out a little more, then unhooked the windvane and steered by hand for a bit, feathering up the waves and bearing away down their backs, so that *Marielle* was surfing. I felt Alain moving about below, and then suddenly the forehatch opened, and he swung out on deck. He was dressed in shorts and a t-shirt, feet bare, and his gun was in his hand.

It was pointed at me.

ᛋ

'Delirium?' DI Macrae asked.

I nodded. 'He thought I was pirates. He was seeing double – that's a standard skull fracture thing, I found out later – so he didn't realise there was only one of me. Didn't realise it was me.' I spread my hands. 'I know it sounds mad. But pirates really are a problem for travelling yachts. Alain had been boarded once, in the Gulf of Mexico, and the first thing he'd done when he got ashore was buy a gun. So when he awoke and saw two people – as he thought – on board–'

The scene had unrolled before my eyes a thousand times since. Alain, his face still paper-white, but his eyes blazing, and the little pistol in his hand, black mouth towards me. I knew it was loaded.

'He told me to get off the boat. Motioned me towards the side. He didn't know me.'

'Alain–' I'd said, but he didn't even seem to hear, just took a step towards me, repeating, 'Get off the boat, or I'll shoot you. Get off. Off.' His legs were unsteady, but the pistol mouth was unwavering.

We seemed to stand there an endless moment, staring at each other. I was half standing, the tiller by my hand, he was shaking but implacable. 'Off. I'm warning you.'

I raised my hands. 'Alain – I'm Cass - you're injured – it's me, Cass–' The pistol jerked. His eyes were as black as its muzzle, his mouth set in a hard line. I stepped up onto the cockpit bench. The guard rail was just above my knees now, and the dark green water swirled below.

'Off,' he said again, and when I didn't go, he fired. I felt the bullet scorch my cheek, heard it hit the water behind me, like a thrown stone. My face stung as if someone had drawn a red-hot wire across it. I lifted one hand, and the fingers came away bloody.

I looked at his face in startled disbelief, and saw my expression mirrored in his, as if he hadn't quite believed he could do it.

'Alain–' I said again, and I thought his expression wavered. I took a step towards him, speaking as if he was a frightened animal. 'Alain, it's me, Cass. You've been injured–'

'Keep back,' he said, and gestured with the gun again. His eyes were flicking from me to a space to the right of me, in the cockpit. 'Keep back, both of you. I'll shoot.'

My face hurt, and I was terrified. I was afraid of having to throw myself over, to watch *Marielle* sailing away as I choked in the waves; afraid of another bullet, breaking bone or touching a vital organ; afraid of a slow, painful death out here in the middle of the ocean.

'He fired at me once.' I reached up to the scar. 'That made him pause, but he still thought there were two of me. Maybe if I'd kept trying to talk to him I'd have got through. I'll never know. I just felt this sudden flood of hatred that I didn't even try to fight. I kicked the helm over, hard, then grabbed for the jibsheet and let it go.'

Marielle tacked sharply, and Alain went from the up side of the boat to being tilted downwards. I saw him stagger and regain his balance, then the jib I'd released so abruptly flapped over like a striking wing, pressing him against the guard rail and tipping him towards the sea.

'The jib knocked him off the boat. He fired again as he went over – I found the hole in the mainsail later. It was that that convinced the Ballantrae police that it really was self-defence – that and this.' I touched my cheek again, feeling the shallow, uneven indentation. 'He went straight down. I was watching. Once I'd done it, I hoped that maybe the shock of the cold water would bring him back to himself. I swung *Marielle* round straight away, but I couldn't find him. His head never surfaced again. Three hours, I waited and circled. I put a danbuoy down. I tried to get another ship on the radio. The *Sea Princess* that had just passed us must have heard me, I called them by name, but they didn't respond. They had a schedule to keep. Nobody replied.' I swallowed, met his eyes directly. 'In the end I knew he had gone, and I just had to sail on.'

A thousand miles of ocean, reliving the scene over and over again. I'd sailed alone through the day and night and day again, snatching sleep as I could, warming up tins from the ship's stores.

'And you fetched up in Ballantrae. Why Ballantrae? It's not the obvious port of entry.'

'A local fishing boat guided me in. I met them coming home, and they gave me a lead in.' I smiled. 'I had to ask where I was.'

'You didn't know?' he said, surprised.

I shook my head. 'It was ten years ago. Do you know how boat electronics have changed in these ten years? We had a VHF radio and the very earliest, most basic GPS. I knew I was seeing the north coast of Ireland, and that was it. I'd done a season doing RYA coaching around Dumfries, so I preferred that as a landfall. And then – well, I was going to have to explain Alain's death. I wanted to be in Scotland, among my own people.'

'I phoned PC MacDonald at Ballantrae. He remembered you very well.'

I remembered him too. I hadn't had to feign distressed exhaustion. He'd persuaded the local B&B to put me up free of charge until I could make some money, and he'd taken my statement like one seaman listening to another. 'He was kind. He took me to the Procurator Fiscal, to decide whether there was going to be a trial.'

That interview in the Procurator Fiscal's office had been gruelling. 'Can you tell us exactly what happened? How do you know what the wind speed was? Who was in charge of the boat at the time?' They'd gone over *Marielle* with a fine-meshed net, and a doctor had examined the ragged, healing graze on my cheek. Journalists had waited to waylay me, and they'd written headlines like 'Lassie's ocean ordeal' and 'No comment from Cassie' until a new sensation had taken my place.

The Procurator Fiscal had been a little, round-faced man with shrewd, compassionate eyes. He'd taken the decision not to prosecute. He shook my hand as I left, and said, 'Now, Ms Lynch, you let the memory fade.'

I hadn't taken the advice.

'He was kind too, the Procurator Fiscal. He'd have liked it better, though, if I'd been a man. Then it would have been regrettable determination, or acting decisively. Peerie lasses aren't supposed to keep their heads in that kind of emergency.'

'Do you mean,' said DI Macrae solemnly, 'that it would have been more womanly if you'd let Mouettier shoot you?'

I nodded, smiling, and the smile must have put me off balance, for when he added, very gently, 'But why do you feel so responsible? Why, to you, is it murder?' I found myself blurting out the answer that I hadn't managed to articulate even to the Ballantrae priest in confession.

'I didn't enjoy the sex. And he wanted us to stay together when we landed.' The words were awful, but as they came out of my mouth I knew they were true, and turned my head away, miserable and ashamed. The knowledge that once we'd taken sightings, set sails for the afternoon and had lunch, he'd slide an arm around me in the cockpit, start caressing my back. It was part of the encumbrance of being a couple. I'd kiss him back, and be quiescent, when what I really wanted to do was pull away, insist I was too tired, not interested. I didn't want his weight on me on the slatted cockpit benches, or forrard on the cold, salt-scurfed fibreglass of the foredeck. I wanted to be my own woman again, free in my narrow berth. That searing pain across my cheek had crystallised all these other discomforts into one focused lance, and I'd kicked the helm over like a Fury who saw the chance of revenge at last. 'I had that split second of choice, and I let the resentment take over. If I'd have kept talking to him, maybe–'

Maybe his parents in Yell would still have had their son. That had been when I'd really confronted the enormity of what I'd done. PC MacDonald had phoned to ask the local constabulary to break the news, but after that I had to write and explain how it had happened. I'd asked PC MacDonald's advice for what would comfort them best. 'That he died quickly,' he said.

I wondered what PC MacDonald had said to DI Macrae about me. I wasn't going to ask.

He told me. 'PC MacDonald said the law wouldn't touch you, but you'd be your own punishment.' He gave me a long look, pitying. 'It's time you moved on.'

I could accept friendship, but I didn't want his pity.

The breakwater was coming towards us now, the grey rock walls waiting to enclose us again. This wind, we could sail right into the berth. We negotiated through the entrance, past *Stormfugl* and into the marina space, then ghosted into the berth. DI Macrae stepped neatly on to the pontoon and then handed me the mooring ropes, brisk again.

'Thanks for the sail. Now, you have my phone number. When were you thinking to go and talk?'

I glanced at my watch. Twelve-ten. 'Now, if nobody else needs me.'

'Let me know immediately if anything turns up.'

I nodded, and meant it as a promise. He gave me a long look. They were not Alain's eyes any more, but his own, filled with that uncompromising Scots uprightness. *It's time you moved on –*

I tied *Khalida* up and stowed the sails. I'd meant to go to Magnie's straight away, but instead I found myself slumping down onto my helming seat, shaking. Surely the grief and guilt ought to be over. Ten years was a long time ... it was only yesterday. I could see Alain's face as the boom went over, that queer, stupid look, hear the crack I hadn't noticed at the time. Then I wondered if love lasted as long as guilt, if the years before Maman left felt as vividly yesterday to her and Dad; if ghosts really could rise and walk again.

Chapter 17

It was time to talk to Magnie. I'd leave Maman and Dad to do whatever reconciling they were up to, and leave Maree in Yell. She'd be safe there from film people, if it was one of them; they didn't have the contacts to find her. A local person, though, that was different. A local person needed only one phone call to whoever they knew in Yell to start the search, and they'd have the information within an hour. Inga or Kevin, or both working together. I was glad I'd told DI Macrae where to look.

I was just going to cast off again when a gaggle of children in a neon-yellow rowing boat came jostling through the marina entrance. I'd vaguely noticed them earlier, off Busta House. The one on the oars backwatered when he saw me, and shouted, two of the others waved excitedly, and the fourth one yelled, 'Cass!' I waved. There was a quick bit of full-volume discussion like seagulls on a roof, which ended in several voices saying 'Ask her!'

I went down and caught their boat. I knew all the faces from the junior sailing group, although I was shaky on the names now they were mostly dry and clad in jeans and t-shirts instead of wet suits. The girl was Inga's oldest lass, Vaila. I knew the oldest of the boys by his Mohican plume of white-dyed hair. Drew was twelve, and mad as a South Sea second-mate. He had the makings of a very good sailor if he managed to stay undrowned. He naturally took on the role of speaker.

'Cass, we found this thing–'

'I found it!' put in one of the smaller boys. He was freckle-faced with spiky blond hair, either John or Rhys.

'Ye, John found it. His hook caught on it.'

'Just along at Busta pier,' John added. 'We were fishing off the end, in the skiff.'

'Oh, yeah?' I said. It seemed a bit of a coincidence that they should just happen to be there, after last night's fire, when the beach was swarming with policemen searching the blackened circle.

'Yeah,' Drew said, with his cheekiest grin. 'Well, we were off in the water, not on shore under their feet.'

'Mam said we weren't to bother them,' Vaila added, 'but we couldn't see how us just watching from the water could be a bother.'

'They weren't doing anything interesting anyway,' Rhys said. 'Just picking up burned video tapes and putting them in plastic bags.'

Either they were very close to shore, or – yes, he had a pair of spyglasses hung around his neck.

'So we went offshore a bit, and got the wands out, and I thought I'd caught a neesik, it was that heavy. Or a huge, huge fish. But it's just wheels.'

Drew and John fished among the ropes and bouys that littered the bottom of the boat and brought out a tangle of shining metal.

'But,' I said, surprised, 'that's a folding bicycle.' I unfolded it and locked the frame. John leapt on it with a whoop of delight, and did a quick circle round the gravel, raising a plume of dust.

'It works!'

'That looks new,' I said, eyeing the chrome of the spokes and the tread of the wide tyres.

'It is,' Rhys asserted. 'It's no been there long at all.'

'Finders keepers,' John said, and did a tighter circuit.

'John, stop for a minute, will you,' I said. 'This could be important.' The film crew's joint alibi, the wild party, when nobody had been gone for long enough to walk to *Stormfugl* and back. But with a bicycle –

'It's mine, though,' John said. 'I hooked it.'

'My boat,' Rhys said.

'Oh, shut up, you two,' Drew said. 'Cass doesn't want to listen to you sharging at each other. Cass, we found it off Busta, where all the movie folk are. Do you think,' he asked, totally failing to keep the uncool excitement out of his voice, 'it could be something to do with the murder?'

'I can't think of any other reason why anyone would throw away a perfectly good folding bike,' I said. 'These things aren't cheap.' Kevin had seen a cyclist. *I have a vague impression of someone on a bike, just before the turn-off–*'How far off Busta? Would you need a boat to drop it?'

'Yes,' John said.

'No,' Drew said. There was instant disagreement from the others, but he persevered. 'We've been doing shot-put in the school, and you can throw pretty far if you're strong in the arm. See, those camera folk, they're used to lifting heavy weights. And it'd skim too, folded like that. I reckon it could have been thrown.'

'I don't suppose you took meids, did you?' I asked. 'Bearings on the shore, so you could find the spot again?'

There was another instant babble of disagreement. Eventually they trailed to a halt in a welter of 'Fifty metres off the pier–' 'No, twenty–' 'The pier was on our *right*–'

'The police will want to know the exact spot.'

Drew's eyes flared. 'You really think it might be the murderer's? Cool!'

'I really think it might be,' I said. I flicked open my mobile and found the new number: Gavin Macrae. Gavin. He answered straight off.

'Ms Lynch?'

'I have some bairns here,' I said, 'with a folding bike, brand new, and fished out of the sea off Busta House.'

A pause. 'Interesting. Are you still at the marina?'

'Just leaving.'

'Can you stick with them? I'll be ten minutes. I don't suppose there's much hope of fingerprints, but get them not to touch it any more.'

I relayed the message on, and got a foursome of mutinous faces.

'It's mine,' John said, gripping the handlebars tightly.

'I've not had a shot yet,' Vaila said, 'and they're going to take it off us. Etterscabs.'

'Whats?' I asked.

'Etterscabs. It's a new Shetland word we learned at the school.'

'They'll need to take your fingerprints too,' I said. 'To compare.' They went straight into arguing who had the most interesting whorls while I watched for the police car coming along the road.

Gavin Macrae was good with them. I wondered if he had children of his own. He half-sat on *Stormfugl*'s side and listened in patience while Drew told their story, with a generous spattering of interjections from the other three. He took possession of the bicycle, and invited them all down to the Brae station (escorted by a parent, naturally; the faces fell a bit at that) to get their prints taken. Then he sent them away with sincere thanks for their help. This could be a vital clue in solving the murder, and they weren't to mention it to anyone but their parents – no, not even their brothers and sisters.

The faces brightened again. They dictated their names and addresses to Sergeant Peterson and swaggered off to mystify younger siblings. Gavin handed the bicycle over to the Sergeant too, then turned to me.

'Do you think we could take the oldest one out this afternoon, to see if he can pin-point the spot? We'll have to try dragging, or put a diver down.'

'You could ask the sub-aqua club, if there's no police diver handy,' I said. 'The water's pretty clear there – well, it used to be, though the salmon farms may have changed things. I may have to meet Ted Tarrant to discuss what's happening next, but the windsurfing lot can drive the inflatable too, they use it on club nights.' I eased myself off *Stormfugl*'s gunwale. 'I'll speak to you later.'

It would be bad policy to take the car with them watching me. I'd pushed my luck already today. I headed around to *Khalida,* flung her ropes ashore and backed her out of the marina.

ᛋ

Magnie's house, Strom, was set in its own little bay, sheltered from the western ocean by a cliff headland, and with a proper boat noost, a hacked-away section of grassy bank just the right size to slide a boat into before the winter storms began. The bay was reddish gravel, with a curve of seaweed tide-line like thick black rope ringing the pebbles, and water so clear it looked ankle-deep instead of the several metres you knew it must be when you looked at the drewey lines twisting down and down. We were not far off slack tide. I dropped anchor in three metres depth, launched *Khalida*'s dinghy, and rowed ashore.

This was a proper crofthouse, with house, byre and barn all in one line, just as the Norsemen built theirs. It had a black-tarred roof with two dormer windows, and whitewash so thickly plastered on that it glowed in moonlight. Each door had a fresh coat of blue paint, the colour called 'regatta', which happened to be the shade of his boat. He had several sheds, acquired through the years: a bus, a large sheep trailer whose wheels had been removed, an accommodation block from the Sullom Voe building camp, and a large green agricultural shed like a giant's tin can sliced along the middle. Apart from the hens fussing it was beautifully silent, real country silence with a hundred sounds in it: the sea shushing only fifty yards away, the trickle of the burn by the house, and a lark up on the hill. If ever I came ashore to live I hoped it would be in a house like this.

I'd barely opened the door when Magnie came out to greet me. He was in a dark blue boiler suit and tartan slippers, and surprisingly trim for someone who'd just come out of a three-day drinking spree. His yellow hair was still damp, curling a bit as it dried, his cheeks red and shining, and his chin smoothly shaven.

'Now, Cass, is dis dee? Come in, come in, du'll tak a cup o tay.'

'I'm not holding you back?' I asked, looking at the tushker propped by the door.

'Lass, the peats'll keep. Come you in aboot.'

I followed him into the kitchen-living room, dominated still by the cream enamel Rayburn that had been cooker, hot water and heating system combined for most houses in Shetland until the oil came. Magnie went straight to it and shifted the kettle to the hotplate over the fire end. 'Now, you'll take a cup o tay.' He turned to smile at me, weathered face wrinkling. 'All the neighbour folk got rid of their Rayburns for this oil, and they're all laughed at me for keeping it and working with the peats, but I'm getting the last laugh now, for the price of this oil's risen that much that they're all getting the tushkers out again and speaking o converting back.'

'As bad as that?' I said, startled.

'Dip dee doon.' Obediently, I sat down in one of the low-slung sixties armchairs beside the Rayburn. Its arms were polished from use. A stripey cat jumped up on my knee, turned around and settled down, purring.

'This young eens'll never ken how to begin.' He gave a cackling laugh, like one of his own hens. 'I'm offered the school a night class in handling a tushker.' The kettle boiled; he poured the water into the teapot and sat it back to stew while he buttered a couple of water biscuits and carved slices off the hunk of cheddar with a clasp knife. 'There now. I'm glad you came by, for I was wanting a word with you, but have your tay first.' He poured me a mug of tea so strong you could trot a mouse on it, as Granny Bridget would have said. 'And what's all doing with you?'

'Oh,' I said, 'nothing much. There's no filming going on for the moment. The police are swarming all over *Stormfugl.*'

The knife paused. 'The police? Why, what's the matter?'

Of course, Magnie'd been dead to the world since Favelle's murder. I said slowly, 'A woman died aboard.'

The knife stilled for a long moment, finished its slice and was laid aside. His shoulders were rigid under the blue cloth. 'I hadn't heard that, now. That'll be what the police car came to the door for, earlier. I didn't bother to answer them.' He added oddly, 'It can be cold these nights, for all it's warming up through the day.'

'Yes,' I agreed, and waited. He brought over the plate of biscuits and cheese. I suddenly remembered it was past lunchtime and launched in.

Magnie took a bite too. 'Aye. These youngsters all drink too much, I ken he's got a bee in his bonnet about it. All the same, he shouldna have left her there. I thought that at the time, and then I thought, well, it's no far off morning, she'll wake up and go home. So she never woke up. Poor peerie lass.'

He shouldna have left her there – The breath left my body with a jolt, as if someone'd punched me in the stomach. Dear God, Magnie had seen –

'Who shouldn't have?' I said, forcing myself to speak calmly. 'Who's *he*?'

Magnie paused as if he was surprised that I didn't know, jerked his head forward to peer at me, like a turtle coming out of its shell, and jerked back. There was a long pause; his pebble-round eyes watched me, doubtfully.

I put my chin up. 'I'm the skipper,' I said, 'and she died on my boat.'

He laughed at that, a wheezy laugh that ended in a cough. 'So you are, lass. So you are.' He shook his head and fumbled in his pocket for a tin of tobacco, began making himself a roll-up, and I knew that he'd tell me now. A skipper had the right to know what happened aboard his own vessel. But he'd tell it in his own way, and in his own time.

'*He*,' he said at last, mimicking my tone, 'was that great streak o ill-tempered misery you have aboard to make mischief. Jessie's man. Gibbie o Efstigarth.'

'Gibbie,' I repeated. I made my voice very matter-of-fact. 'Can you tell me what happened from the beginning, Magnie?'

He began to laugh again, shaking his head. 'Man, to think I'd see the day. I'm fairly blyde I'm no one of your deck hands. You're a right wee tyrant. A man wouldn't be allowed to sneak a drop o rum while he was on watch aboard your ship.'

That made me smile too. I'd been fitting other faces among skippers I'd known, and now he was doing the same with me. 'The Vikings had a bottle aboard, after we'd done the filming.'

'Ye, ye, I heard all about that. And you keeping an eye on it as it went round.' He wheezed again, and took a draw on his cigarette. 'They said you kent what you were about.' From a Shetland seaman to a slip of a lass, it was a compliment that made a warm glow of pride swell within me. 'Keep eating, lass. I'm had my dinner.'

I took another biscuit, which kept me quiet with mouthfuls of flaky crumbs for a couple of minutes. Come on, Magnie...

Honour was satisfied. Having made it clear he was telling me only of his own good will, he patted his knee for the cat, got it settled under one of his gnarled hands and began. 'Well, Cass. I bought a half bottle before the club closed, and I got into the car, ready to drive home. I had a mouthful–'

I'd seen Magnie's idea of a mouthful, a quarter-bottle swig.

'– and then I just sat back in the car and dozed for a bit. Then something wakened me.'

'A car?' I asked. Someone bringing the body?

Magnie shook his head. 'I dinna think it. Footsteps, more like, I'd say, but I wasna paying attention.'

'D'you have any idea of the time?'

'Not far off dawn, though it was still dark. Two o clock, maybe. There was this lass stumbling down towards the marina, plain as plain under these new street lights. I wondered for a moment what she was doing there, and then I remembered your young lad, and I thought, well, she's been drinking at the disco and she's come to try her luck with him.' He let out a great cackle of laughter. 'For all they're so clever, these bairns, they can't see what's under their noses. Lasses, going after him!'

I gave him a puzzled look. 'He's very good looking.'

Magnie cackled again. 'Reminds me of a mate we had once. We had to warn all the young boys about him.'

'Anders?' I said, startled. 'He doesn't go after young boys! At least, I don't think so.' I thought, horrified, of the sailing classes we'd done, tried to remember if he'd ever gone in the changing rooms with the boys, and breathed a sigh of relief. No, he'd always stayed out, standard RYA practice, chatted to parents and helped tie the boats down.

Magnie gave me an old-fashioned look, and didn't explain further. 'Fairly fou, she was, stumbling and only just keeping upright. She got herself as far as the gangplank when she laid her length on the floor.'

It was only then I realised it was Favelle he was talking about. I remembered how Alain had stood after being struck, and spoken; how he'd lain down, then risen again, swaying. Favelle had been struck beside the standing stone, made unconscious, tumbled into the ditch. She'd come to again. We'd got the movement in the wrong direction: not someone else shoving her into the ditch, but Favelle hauling herself out, leaving those handprints. She'd stumbled down towards the marina, where she knew there would be people. *There are the traces of one person's footprints – only traces, nothing to help us,* DI Macrae had said.

'Well, she never got up again. I was just about to go and see if she'd hurt herself, when who should come up from below decks but Gibbie o Efstigarth. He lookit around and saw her, and came over wi a face like someone'd just cracked open a bad egg under his nose. I thought he was maybe taking on night watchman while that young lad was off with his pal. Ony road, there he was.' He grinned. 'I thought I'd have a fine time the next time I saw him, asking what he was up to smuggling young lasses aboard while Jessie's back was turned. He looked that affronted at her being there.'

He paused to open his tobacco tin again, clumsy-looking hands deft as any girl's. 'He bent doon ower her, an I saw him thinking, clear as clear, 'Serve her right if she lies there aa night.'

He gied her a shake, and she didna waken. He stood up again and lookit again, and then he crouched down and hauled her over.'

'Recovery position,' I said. No wonder it had looked familiar.

'That'll be it. And then he nipped back down below and brought up his box of tools, and steppit over her and headed for his car, and off he geed. I thought, 'You're not been watchman this night. You're creating mischief. I'll warn Cass when I see her to check every inch o that hull. And then I slept again, du kens the way, and when I awoke, well, it was first light, and I was cold from sleeping in the car, and I never minded me about the lass, I just started up the car and came home.' The stubby fingers paused on the roll-up. 'Lord forgive me. Did I leave her there to die o cold?'

'No–' I said. 'No.' The anger was still burning within me. 'She'd been struck on the head. By the time you woke again, you couldn't have saved her. But Gibbie could, if he'd not been so miserably against anyone having fun.'

No wonder Jessie had looked so upset. She must've known he'd been out that night, been afraid of what he was doing to me, to *Stormfugl*, yet unable to stop him. And then, when Favelle had been found murdered – what sort of life did she lead with him? Did she know he was capable of murder?

'She was hit on the head,' I said, 'not drunk. She'd been struck up beside the standing stone.'

Magnie rose, paced to the door and back again. 'If I'd no so much to drink I'd've gone and seen if she was all right. A head injury – they could've saved her, in the Gilbert Bain, or in Aberdeen.'

I couldn't tell soothing lies to Magnie. 'Maybe. But she'd been injured a while before.' That time gap was falling into place now. Like Alain, she'd been unconscious for a while, then come to. *Just after dusk … I waited but she didn't come.* 'Just after dusk. Eleven, eleven thirty.'

'Eleven thirty,' he repeated. 'Yea, three hours earlier, four.' He stopped then, shaking his head. 'Well.' The long sound held all he wanted to say of regret and guilt.

'If it's anyone's fault it's Gibbie's,' I blustered into the silence. 'He left her. Just put her into the recovery position and walked off and left her there to die.'

If that ship which had been in such a hurry had answered my frantic calls on the radio, 'Mayday, mayday, Sea Princess, *mayday–'*

Magnie considered me again, round eyes narrowing under his heavy lids. 'He didna ken, any more as me.'

'But he didn't hit her,' I said. 'You saw him come out from below decks.'

'No he,' Magnie said. 'He was up to other mischief.'

I remembered Gibbie's cat-with-the-cream expression of that lunch at the Hams, when Favelle was swarming all over Anders. He'd heard Favelle's invitation, and assumed that Anders would go to her. Favelle, slum it aboard an open boat? His gloating had been because he'd expected *Stormfugl* to be unguarded.

Now, how did that affect our timetable? Perhaps Favelle, too, had expected Anders to come to her. When he hadn't arrived, she'd set out, just after half past ten, when Elizabeth had said good-night. She'd met Kevin at the standing stone around eleven. Anders had grabbed Rat and his sleeping bag and headed for the clubhouse; our murderer had come along on his bicycle and struck Favelle. She'd been lying in the ditch when Gibbie had strolled quietly down the grass, swung over the wire fence onto the marina curve, and headed for *Stormfugl.* He'd gone aboard and worked away for a couple of hours – what the devil had he been doing, in all that time? I had to get aboard *Stormfugl* to look. Then he'd heard footsteps stumbling towards the boat, on the gangplank. He'd heard her fall. He'd come up and seen what he thought was a drunk girl looking for Anders. He'd felt a brief flash of conscience towards a young lass unable to help herself, and put her in the recovery position. Then he'd gathered up his tools and legged it.

'Lass,' Magnie said, watching me, 'you canna come up wi answers when you're running round in circles. You need to sit on the top o the hill and joost think. I'll walk you half the way.'

So we walked up the Ward together as far as his peat bank. I left him there casting, and climbed up until *Khalida* was a toy boat moored in a half-circle of pale green water.

Then I thought. I thought about triangles. Dad, Maree, Maman. Dad, Maree, Michael. Ted, Favelle, Elizabeth. Ted, Favelle, Anders; even Ted, Favelle, me. I thought about peerie Charlie, about Favelle walking briskly along in the dusk to meet her lover, dreaming not of him but of his child, trying to keep her errand secret and being waylaid by Kevin talking of windfarms. I thought of someone coming silently up behind her on rubber wheels. Brake, strike, roll the body into the ditch, fast, fast, in the half-light, before someone looked out of a nearby window, too fast to really check the shallow pulse, turn and pedal away. I thought about letters: anonymous letters, beginning long before the world knew about the plan for Favelle to publicise the windfarm, a letter from a sperm analysis lab stuffed in a coat pocket. I thought about a rock tumbling down a green hill, and a heap of video tapes burning in the night. When I put it all together I began to see a pattern confused only by doubles: Favelle and Maree, Maree and Favelle. It was a pattern with one ruthless brain behind it.

I had to talk to Gavin Macrae. I pushed myself up from my rock and set off down the hill. Before that, though, I was going to look at my ship. I needed to know what Gibbie had been up to on board.

It took less than half an hour to sail the two miles back to the marina, and five minutes more to tie *Khalida* up. *Stormfugl* was still festooned with ticker-tape and swarming with people in spacesuits. I paused by the gangplank and called, 'Hello?'

A couple of heads looked up. I called again, and put a foot on the gangplank. Immediately one came over.

'Sorry, miss, nobody's allowed on the ship. This is a crime scene.'

'I understand that,' I said. 'I am the skipper of this vessel, Cassandre Lynch. I have reason to believe someone has been attempting to sabotage her, and I'd like to check she's safe for you to be on.'

He was from south, didn't know me at all. 'We can't let you aboard, madam. DI Macrae is in charge of the case. If you have concerns, or of course any information, he'll be very pleased to discuss that with you.'

'I'm concerned about your safety,' I said. I tried a smile, an appeal to fellow-feeling. 'Look, if she sinks under you it'll be my head on the block.'

'We'll look out for water, madam,' he said. 'Now, if you don't mind.' He made an ushering movement.

I stood my ground, fished out my mobile and called Gavin Macrae. 'Hi, it's Cass. Listen, I really need to check *Stormfugl*, but your forensic officers won't let me aboard.'

'Oh?'

'I'll explain when I see you. Can I go aboard?'

'How urgent is it?' He sounded harrassed. I could hear a woman's voice in the background, giving orders.

'I won't know till I've looked.' I wasn't going to read out sealed orders in front of the forensic deck-hand. 'Look at it as an insurance problem,' I said. 'Who's liable?'

Now I heard him smile. 'The words that guarantee instant attention from any official. What kind of sabotage could someone do that would endanger people working on the boat?'

'Really dangerous stuff?' I reflected, then spoke at the watchdog. 'Drill a hole in the boat, and fill it with something that would dissolve over time.' Gibbie was more accustomed to working with wood and rope, he'd go for those before going for the engine. 'Cut part-way through one or more ropes so that the mast or yard fell when the last one snapped. Weaken a plank so that it would give when someone stepped on it.'

Of course he might have done something totally different that would only cause havoc when the boat was moving. He hadn't expected a murder to keep her in port, he'd expected the final day's filming. He could have sawn through the rudder straps, or split a plank and plugged it with something that would come out at speed, or weakened the mast so it would crash down when the sail filled.

'Okay. Obviously I'll warn them to get out fast if she starts filling with water. Can you check as much of the rigging as you can from the shore?'

'If your officers will allow,' I said pointedly.

'Give me five minutes. When you've done your check, come over and tell me what you've found out.'

He rang off. I waited, scanning the sky airily. Within half a minute the intercom on the officer's belt buzzed. There was a short conversation, consisting mostly of 'Yes, sir'. He put the set back and turned to me.

'You have permission, madam, to examine the ship visually from the shore. Please do not touch anything.'

He watched me as I went slowly along the pier, looking hard at each of the leather blocks. Then I went across to *Khalida* for my spy-glasses and looked across at the other side, then up the mast. There was nothing visible. I couldn't tell from here if the yard's wooden pulley was intact. There were no breaks in the hull above the waterline, and the mooring ropes were secure and un-frayed.

I called Gavin back. 'Cass again. It looks fine, but I wish you'd let me aboard to make sure.'

'They need the rest of today. Can you tell me anything they shouldn't do, for safety reasons?'

'Touch any of the ropes. Tell them not to undo them, loosen them, lean on them or use them to steady themselves.'

'I'll tell them. See you soon, Cass.'

I said goodbye politely to the watchdog, happy to leave him casting worried glances up at the mast, and headed round to *Khalida*. I'd go round and tell Gavin Macrae all that I'd learned in a minute, but I was sleepy, so sleepy. I'd been up most of the night. Ten minutes, just ten minutes ... I lay down on *Khalida*'s starboard seating and fell asleep.

Chapter 18

I was only out for half an hour, not enough to start anyone worrying. I felt refreshed as I headed back to the car and drove around to Brae proper.

The incident room had been set up in Brae Hall. A young woman was on duty at a table just inside the door, and past her I could see Gavin Macrae, with a group of officers gathered around him. He was setting up a notice-board covered with photographs and post-it notes, and there was a flipchart easel beside him.

'Yes, madam?' the young woman said.

'I was wanting to see DI Macrae,' I said. 'It's Cass Lynch. Don't disturb him, I'll wait outside. Can you tell him I'm here once he's free?'

I could tell by the way she looked up that she'd heard of me. 'Yes, madam, I'll tell him. Will you be in your car?'

'Thereabouts,' I agreed.

I left her making a note and strolled back out into the sunshine. The air was filled with the smell of cut grass. The low wall around the back of the hall was the obvious place to wait, back against warmed brick, watching the waves playing with the seaweed at the shore's pebbled edge. There was a wriggle underneath, a small explosion of water, and the smooth back of an otter curved over and dived again, to re-surface ten yards on. The cat-face popped up to look warily around, but the hall behind me hid my silhouette. Reassured, she ducked under again in a scuffle of crinkled kelp. I was following her progress along the shoreline and wondering where her cubs were when I heard Sergeant Peterson's voice floating from the window above me.

'A few useful comments, sir. A car went along around dawn, someone called Magnie o Strom. I tried his door, but there was no reply. Several people saw Cassandre Lynch's boat going out at the time she said.'

'She and the Norwegian working together,' put in a male voice. It was DI Hutchinson, the one who'd interviewed Anders. He had a very definite I-am-right air which made me take against him immediately. 'He took the boat to give her an alibi, while she did the murder.'

'There was that odd 'we', sir, the first time she spoke of it,' Sergeant Peterson said. 'We sailed.'

Another voice spoke, Glaswegian. 'Why deny his alibi later?'

'Rogues fall out,' Inspector Hutchinson said promptly.

Sergeant Peterson continued smoothly. 'One woman saw 'one of these film folk walking along the road' just at dusk, but she couldn't positively ID Favelle, just said it 'could a been her or the other one staying at Efstigarth'. Nobody saw anyone on a bicycle.'

'How about the people up Ronas Hill?' Gavin Macrae's voice was crisper with the soft Highland lift almost gone, the police officer at work.

'The campers are certain that the film people's minibus never moved.' This was a young man's voice, with a Lerwick accent. 'They'd have heard it. A number of people saw Ashcroft and Green, both with cameras, and Tarrant roaming about the hill taking photographs, but the times are too vague to help us. I've done a list, giving approximate times, and I'm certain that none of them was gone long enough to get from Ronas Hill to Brae on foot.'

'Could they have done it on bicycle?'

'A professional cyclist could, sir. They'd have to be good.'

'News on the burned videos, Ewan?'

'Just fragments, sir, although we might get a print off them.' That was the Glaswegian officer again. 'No footprints at the burning site – the entire hotel clustered around and trampled.'

'The bicycle?'

'Ted Tarrant's, sir. He always packs a bike in case he gets the chance to do a bit of exercise. That's well known among the film crew so someone else could well have borrowed it. He kept it folded up under the bed in his room. The case was still there, with marks of gloved prints over Tarrant's; average to large male size, or large handed woman.'

'My money's still on Tarrant. The husband.' It was Sergeant Peterson again. 'The perp in 96% of cases is the husband. All this heartbroken stuff is just crocodile tears. He's an actor, remember.'

'Not a very good one,' Inspector Hutchinson retorted.

'He could be lousy on screen and brilliant off it. He suspected his wife of having an affair with the hired hand–'

'If you accept the Norwegian's version two.'

' – came back and caught her at it.'

'Don't forget the profile,' Gavin said. 'Ruthless, emotionally cold. Efficient. That doesn't fit with your scenario of a man catching his wife being unfaithful.'

Ruthless, emotionally cold, efficient. Yes, the murderer was all of those.

Sergeant Peterson wasn't going to be kept down. 'It spoils Jim's scenario too, ma'am. Dermot Lynch killing Favelle in mistake for Maree.'

'96% is husband *or lover*.' Perhaps Mr I-am-right was trying to rise above so commonplace a name as Jim. 'We've only got Lynch's account of what the row was about, and it's about as implausible as they come. Why on earth should she get his sperm tested? No, she told him she was leaving, taunted him with his age, and he wanted revenge.'

'One at a time,' Gavin said. I could hear the scribble of a pen. 'Any more new information on Tarrant?'

A new voice spoke. How many officers did he have in there? 'His finances are sound, sir, ma'am. He gave me full access to his stockbroker in the States. And as he told us himself, his wife was his star. His films will be much less valuable without her.'

Answer: as many officers as it took to uphold the honour of the Scottish police and fend off demands for Scotland Yard. To step aside for the English would be the ultimate failure.

'So if Tarrant was responsible his likely motive was his wife's infidelity.'

'How could he have found out about it, Gavin?' That was Inspector Hutchinson again. 'Nobody we've questioned has him anywhere near the lunch tent. He was up on the hill with the camera-man talking about shots while she was propositioning the Norwegian.'

I felt another surge of anger. Anders had a name.

Gavin side-stepped that one. 'The bicycle was his and he knew where it was kept. He's certainly capable of bicycling that short distance quickly. Opportunity without motive. Keep working on that, Sergeant – texts, calls, notes from Johansen to Favelle or vice versa that he might have found. How about his relations with Maree?'

'No hint of anything wrong there, sir. She visited the house regularly, according to the housekeeper, but never when Favelle wasn't there. Her stand-in work was generally with Ashcroft, not with Tarrant.'

'Very well then. Dermot Lynch.' A flap as he took a new page. 'I don't like your quarrel scenario, Jim, but I agree that his business record shows he can be ruthless.'

I hadn't thought of Dad as ruthless. I remembered the way I'd been packed off to France, the way he was planning to carve up Shetland, and wondered with a sudden sense of panic if I'd got it totally wrong. Magnie'd taken ten times the drink Dad had and still managed to drive home.

'The other possible motive, sir,' Sergeant Peterson said, 'is that he wanted his wife back, and Maree was getting in the way. Putting her body on the longship confused the issue, involved the film folk.'

'And his own daughter.'

'They quarrelled bitterly fourteen years ago and she hasn't been home since,' Sergeant Peterson said. 'What does he owe her?'

'She says he was too drunk to drive.'

'The blood readings don't agree with that,' Hutchinson stated. 'Illegal, yes, but not incapable.'

'Very well. Motive for killing Maree, possible. We need to talk to Maree.'

Sergeant Peterson said, 'The local man was dealing with something on Fetlar when we phoned, but he said he'd get off there by the next ferry. Radio Shetland is doing an urgent call on their 5.30 bulletin. She may not be listening to the wireless, but her landlady will be.'

'Good. Lynch's opportunity, yes. Motive for killing Favelle?' Gavin asked.

'None, ma'am. She was his pin-up girl for the windfarm,' McDonald said.

'Very well. Lynch, possible motive of either revenge or elimination to kill Maree, opportunity good. The speed his wife arrived here at suggests she suspects one of her family.'

Hutchinson's voice turned contemptuous. 'She was sweetness and light this morning. No interest in what Dermot was doing with another woman; she is his wife. Her Cassandre is strong, but little. She could not possibly have moved a heavy body.'

Poor Maman, poor Dad, not even allowed a morning together.

'How long have she and Lynch lived apart?'

'Sixteen years.' A rustle of notebook. 'They've met up occasionally in that time. They seem to keep on friendly terms. Phone each other every couple of months. No suggestion whatsoever of them getting back together until now, according to the Poitiers flic I spoke to.'

'When did she book her flight over?'

'Exactly when she said. Phone call from the house on Muckle Roe, 9.25. Flight booked from the Poitiers flat after a couple of other calls, 9.55.'

'Very well. Next suspect.' It was Gavin's voice again. He didn't even pause before saying my name. 'Cass Lynch. Motive: jealousy. She's come home expecting her father to welcome her, only to find a woman in his bed. The same age as she is but pretty, charming, glossy, everything she's not.' The words stung like a loaded rope lashing across a bare arm. 'She admits Maree telephoned her, but nobody's spoken to Maree since. She knew Maree could be coming along that road, for her evening run, but she didn't expect Favelle.'

'Why move the body to the longship?'

'Same as her father, to focus attention on the film, not the personal. She could have sent the anonymous letters too, she's been around the film lot long enough to be a familiar face. She's got a computer and a memory stick, so all she needed was twenty seconds alone in the office. She was one of the few who knew about the windfarm when the first letter came.'

'Or,' the quiet voice said slowly, 'she could have known about Favelle and Johansen. She's Johansen's skipper, and he was worried about it. He could have confided in her. Maybe it was Favelle she meant to kill. I've been talking to the film crew, sir, and the general feeling is that Ted thinks highly of her, and she's pretty starry-eyed about him. An affair?'

I felt sick.

'She'd have to be stupid. Think he'd go for her, after Favelle?'

'Obsessed women are stupid.' Sergeant Peterson had an edge to her voice that suggested she'd been there.

The bile rose in my throat. If they were going to decide I'd done it, they'd find the simplest things and count them against me: my memory stick and a couple of jokes shared on deck after the day was over.

'Opportunity: yes.' Gavin Macrae's voice was coolly matter-of-fact. 'We've no exact time for the blow, only the death. The doc suggested earlier, but it could be as late as when she got in.'

'She's got form, sir.'

The bastard didn't even pause. 'Yes, Mouettier's death. I agree with the Fiscal's conclusion at the time; no jury would have convicted. No point in even trying. That bullet across her cheek was fired by someone else, and there were no signs of other violence aboard. Her story was simple and convincing. But yes, she had the ruthlessness to get him overboard after he shot at her.'

I'd half-wanted to go to prison for Alain, but I wasn't going to let them frame me for Favelle's death. Testing each stone before I put my weight on it, I retreated back along the shore and across the tarmac parking space to my little car. I had to nail the real murderer, and fast.

Although she didn't know it, Maree had the evidence I needed. The police officer at the door was looking the other way. I slid into the car, eased the door shut and drove off. Yell.

4

The ferry terminal had changed completely. The small motor-boats were still riding nose to waves in the bay formed by the pier, and the same obelisk marked the end of the sewer pipe, but there was a huge turning space where the old ferry had docked, and after that a yellow gate keeping the general public from the end of the breakwater. Ahead of me stretched a smooth two-lane highway into the jaws of a huge dark-blue boat with a white superstructure.

I took my place in the unbooked lane and fished for my purse. Three day-glo yellow jackets were waving the booked cars on. They had their hoods pulled up, so that I couldn't see if one of them was Dodie. As my line crawled forwards I spotted him taking the money with a machine slung around his neck, like an old-fashioned bus conductor. I just had to wait till he got to me.

He flushed pink under the yellow hood when he peered into the car. 'Cass! I was hoping you'd phone again. I'm found your lady.' He gave a quick look over his shoulder to assess the number of cars packing in. 'I'll meet you up in the cafeteria, in mebbe five minutes.'

'Thanks, Dodie. See you in five minutes.'

He nodded and slipped off to the next car. I squeezed myself out in the foot between me and the car on my right, and headed for the steel door marked 'Lounge.' It was palatial, with rows of maroon seats, like a huge aeroplane, and picture windows framing the grey, tumbled water. I bought a hot chocolate from the machine, and sat down.

Dodie didn't keep me waiting long. He eased his spray-stained jacket off with a glance at the pristine seats and slid apologetically into the seat beside me. His fair hair was tousled, and his cheeks rosy from the wind. 'Now then. I'm found her,' he said. 'I asked me Mam if she could ask some of her pals that had B&B or self-catering, and she did a bit of phoning around. Your wife's up at da Herra, in a house there.'

'Dodie, you're a star,' I said.

He beamed. 'Is this the wife the police is looking for? It was on SIBC just half an hour ago, saying if anyone kent her whereabouts they were to ask her to contact the police.'

I nodded. 'Yeah. She's the sister of the wife that died.' I grimaced. 'I'm going to have to tell her.'

His cheery mouth turned down. 'Do you ken da Herra?'

'Turn left just before Windhouse.'

'That's it. Joost keep going along the road, almost to the end. It's called Grimister, the hoose, and I think there might even be a sign, for tourists. It's a big grey and white house, wi a brown wood porch. You'll no miss it.' He looked at his watch. 'She's been walking a fair bit, the wife, but she'll likely be in for her tea ee now. If she's no there, try the Old Haa, down at Burravoe. She likes their fancies. Eating for two, Agnes that runs the cafe said.'

I liked Yell. Seventeen miles long, seven across, the island was shaped rather like Bart Simpson with a squared off head, big grin (the long inlet of Selli Voe), one arm pointing skyward and short legs. In spite of the satellite dish on every house and the new prosperity of food stockpiled in freezers, it was essentially Shetland as it used to be. Nearly every one of the thousand folk was related to at least five hundred of the others, and everyone was concerned in everyone else's business. I had no doubt, as my car trundled off the ferry, that each person who raised a hand from the side of the road knew exactly who I was and where I was going. Details of the why would have to wait until Dodie finished tying the ferry up and phoned his mum.

I rattled over the metal ramp and on to the road running along the low hill that rose on my right, dark green with heather. On my left, the land fell away in a long slope down to the sea. A rust-red tanker waited in the Bay, taking its turn in the queue for Sullom Voe jetty. I passed a fishing loch, with a boat pulled up at one end. The peats here were newly cast and hadn't started drying yet; the bank was black and smooth as an oiled whetstone. Just beyond it was the sign I wanted: Whalfirth Grimister Herra Raga.

I drew in. Above me brooded Shetland's most haunted house, Windhouse, a gaunt ruin that raised gap-toothed battlements to the sky. I'd lost track of the number of people supposed to have died there, including a man driven to death by the devil and a baby whose skeleton was found behind a nailed-back shutter. Dodie had had a fine fund of stories to tell as we'd all camped at the regattas. The most impressive among the faceless monks and disappearing white things was a simpler one. He'd gone up there one day to herd a dozen sheep that had got into the grounds, and everything had been fine at first. Then he'd started to feel uneasy. His dogs began darting at the sheep with whitened eyes and flattened tails, and cringing away from the ruined walls. They'd got the sheep away, and it was just as he was fastening the rickety gate behind them that the lead dog turned and stared at the empty driveway leading to the door-less opening. 'I saw the hair on her back rise, just like that,' he told us, 'and then she gave a howl like

I've never heard and bolted, with the other dog following her, and the sheep scattering before them.'

'Did you see anything?' Martinhad asked breathlessly.

'Nothing. I stood my ground for a moment, then I had to get oot o there an aa. I turned and began walking, but my feet went faster and faster, and by the end of the gait I was running, trying to pretend I was chasing after the sheep.' He took a disgusted swig of the red tin we'd managed to sneak from the bar. 'Faerd o nothing.'

I'd known that story was true because Dodie loved embroidering. If he'd made it up there'd have been a headless spectre at the very least.

I looked up at the old house, much more of a ruin than it had been when we'd come up to Mid Yell regatta and taken time between races and prize-giving to go and look around it. It had a new owner, Dodie had said, a builder who'd bought it for £1 on condition he restored it. I felt a sudden surge of rebellion. Why did everything old have to be kept? Be-damned to that, for once. The ruin above me was a memory of a house, fit only for tearing down. Demolish it, ghosts and all, back to bare green hill, and let a new family build in the space and bring happiness.

I turned my back on it, and scrunched along the track to the Herra, a community of thirty souls spread around a corner of shelter for the fishing boats, with the wild Atlantic beating at the door.

Dodie was right; I couldn't miss the house. It was an old manse, or built by a merchant who'd profited by the herring boom. It had a square frontage, a thin porch with a window each side, and three windows above. The brown of the porch was echoed in visible stones on the front, set in white cement, and the battlement pattern around the windows was painted grey. The view of the Atlantic was breath-taking. I hoped it had done Maree good.

Dodie had also been right about her being in. She met me at the door, opening it wide and stepping back into the carpeted hall with a resigned air. She was dressed in a big jumper and jeans, and her feet were socked, as if she'd just left her walking boots at the door. With her short hair tousled and her cheeks rosy she looked like someone I'd like. I was sorry at the way she'd got entangled with us. I hoped she wouldn't mind too much if Maman was home to stay.

'Hiya, Cass,' she said. 'D'ya want a cup of coffee?'

'Yes, please.'

She showed me to a comfy sitting-room, dominated by a gleamingly white mantelpiece, navy-tiled, with a real grate under the arch. It smelt gently of rose pot-pourri. I sank down on the couch and prepared to break the news. I heard her footsteps approaching across a wooden dining-room floor, then silencing for the thick carpet of the hall. The door was pushed open by the tray in her hands.

She came in talking, as though she was determined not to let me break her peace. 'You did well to find me – how'd'ya manage? I guess everyone knows everyone here. Still, I've had a coupla days of solitude. I even switched my phone off, can you believe it? But I guess it's time to get back to real life. Does Dermot know I'm here?'

'No,' I said. 'I've not come about that. Maree, everyone's been trying to get hold of you. Favelle's dead.'

The hand pouring the coffee stilled, then set the pot down, cup half-filled. Her mouth opened and her eyes stared blankly. She sat down on the couch behind her. Her mouth shut, opened again, shut. She swallowed, tried again. 'Favelle? But she can't be, she was fine – she can't be–'

Her hand came up to her mouth, fell again and gripped its pair in her lap; she watched them as if they could tell her the answers. 'How?'

'They're investigating that,' I said. 'The police.'

Her eyes flew back to mine. 'An accident.'

'No,' I said. I looked away, to let her react in privacy. She made a little, stifled sound, rose, and went to the window. It seemed a long time before she spoke, and her voice was harder.

'Do they know who did it?'

Then feeling penetrated through numb shock. She began to cry. I sat beside her and held her hand, as if that would comfort her for losing a sister. When at last she stopped I drew back and poured the coffee.

'I need to get back to Brae,' Maree said.

'Yes,' I agreed. 'There's something else, though. There's a suspicion that maybe Dad was so angry with you that he killed her, thinking it was you.'

Her mouth fell open. 'Dermot? He was lucky I didn't kill him. Reading that letter in my pocket, and jumping to conclusions, well, I was so mad I wouldn't have explained even if he'd given me the chance. How dared he think I'd do something like that behind his back?'

'The thing is,' I said, sticking to my guns, 'Maman's come back.'

She was startled but not desperately upset, I was relieved to see. 'Like in, come *back*?'

'I think so.'

'Oh.' She rose again, went back to the window. 'Oh. Well, gee – You think it'll work?'

'I don't know,' I admitted.

Maree sat down. 'Look, this is a shock. I can't think – Do the police know who?'

'They've got several suspects,' I said, 'and no proof. You have, though, if you still have it.'

She looked at me blankly. 'Have what?'

'The letter,' I said. 'The letter that Dad threw such a fit about.'

'Not here, though,' she said. Behind the blank, shocked look in her eyes I could see her calculating. 'It's at Jessie's house.'

I just hoped our murderer hadn't known about it. 'Good,' I said.

'But I don't see–' she began.

'It's the key to the whole thing,' I said. 'Our evidence.' She was still looking puzzled. 'Because, you see,' I finished, 'it wasn't your letter at all. Was it?'

She shook her head. 'No. It was Favelle's.'

Chapter 19

I wanted to take Maree back with me, but she refused, and her determination to play a lone hand chimed in with mine. I was worried all the same. 'Keep your phone off; don't give them the chance to talk to you. The local policeman's looking for you too.'

'Honey, there's no mobile reception here anyway.'

'That worries me,' I said frankly. Then I had a better idea. I drove back to the main road and phoned Dodie. Did he have a spare room, and could he possibly take a visitor for the night? He did, and they could, and his Mam would be delighted to look after her. He'd make sure she got safely on the ferry in the morning.

'And come straight to *Khalida,*' I said. 'Seven o clock, while they're all eating breakfast at Busta.'

'Check.' We hugged like conspirators, like sisters, and parted.

I drove back slowly southwards and took the West Sandwick turning. Alain's family. I should have come before. As I bumped gently along the road into the village, I had misgivings. I pulled into the last parking place and sat there, looking at the old schoolhouse. Someone came out of the back door, a woman with a basket of washing. I watched her stoop and stretch, shaking out each item before pegging it up: a blue shirt, a green shirt, a pair of jeans, one sock and space left for its neighbour, a grey jumper, back for the second sock. She was tall, with bobbed brown hair; she wasn't Alain's mother. Perhaps the family had moved away to another part of Shetland, or back to France.

Ten years. I had no right now to come looking for forgiveness.

The woman hung up the last pair of socks, picked up her basket and went inside. I turned the car around and drove away.

ᛋ

I spent the ferry journey reading the texts I'd missed. The first was from Maman, saying good morning. One was from Anders: where was I? One was from the Norwegian office: Flying over this pm Berg. It had been sent at 10am. I presumed he'd pulled strings and got an oil-man flight. The last three were from DI Macrae. The first two were curt and official: please contact at your earliest convenience. The third had a nice touch of worry: Concerned re yr safety reply as soon as u get this. I sent a terse reply: 'perfectly safe. C'. and switched the phone off.

It was after seven by the time I got back to Brae. I headed straight for Busta, with an automatic slow-down as I passed the boating club entrance. *Stormfugl* was still, the white ants gone. Only a lone figure remained as sentinel. I was glad the police had left a guard, but it meant I wasn't going to be able to inspect her more closely. Then the dark figure turned, and I saw that it was a man in a business suit. Mr Berg.

I skidded the car to a halt, rearranged my face and strode on down past the waiting luxury taxi. He turned to watch me coming.

'Mr Berg.'

'Ms Lynch. You got my text? Do you know how long it will be before the police will allow the use of the longboat?'

'DI Macrae gave the impression they were almost finished.'

He grunted. I gestured towards the boating club. 'Can I offer you a drink?'

'No. I will go back to Busta Hotel, where I am staying.' He gave me a long look, the skipper assessing which pieces of cargo had to be jettisoned. 'There has been a good deal of comment in the Norwegian papers. My fellow-directors and I are concerned.' His briefcase was sitting by the gangplank. He reached down to it now and brought out a cardboard wallet crammed with photocopies of newspaper articles. 'I will meet with you tomorrow, 10am, at Busta Hotel. We need to minimise the damage. If the film can be finished quickly then that will be your contract ended, and all will be well.'

He handed me the wallet and walked away. I turned it over in my hands as I watched the taxi drive off, then eased open the flap, paused, and closed it again. The wallet was heavy in my hands. I wasn't going to open this in public. I slipped down into the changing room, heart beating fast, and opened it with trembling fingers.

The strip-lighting blared out on newspaper articles. The top one had a photograph of the press conference, taken from an angle that made it look as if I was sitting on Ted's lap, and a 3-inch headline: VIKING LOVE-TRIANGLE? The text steered short of libel, but the general suggestion was that I was chief suspect. The others weren't much better, and there were publicity stills of Ted and me conferring on board ship from the 'making of the movie' feature. One had me looking narrow-eyed and mean; from the background I knew I was assessing the narrow entrance into the Hams, but I looked like I was plotting half a dozen murders.

I felt like Mr Berg had slapped me in the face. I'd been tried on this mix of rumour and tricked photography, condemned in my absence. The smell of vanilla and coconut soap clogged my breathing.

I shoved the articles back in their wallet and came out into the fresh air. I took a long, deep breath, feeling the cold reach right to the depths of my lungs, and stuck my chin out. Until 10 am tomorrow I was still *Stormfugl*'s skipper. The papers might have tarnished my name but I was in command right now. I'd hand DI Macrae his murderer, and I'd sort out the sabotage aboard *Stormfugl.*

I re-parked behind the skip so the car'd be hidden from the police station windows, and walked briskly back to the boating club. The wind had fallen to a silvery fret on the water; the tide had pushed its load of dark seaweed and coffee foam up the beach and retreated, leaving it lying like wave shadows on the pale shingle. It was still light, but the blue of the sky was beginning to darken as I stepped on to the gangplank.

Ghosts everywhere. *Stormfugl* was greyed with powder. One oar had the rower's gloves lying by the handle, curved into open hands. In the centre was the blurred chalk outline of how Favelle had lain, one knee drawn up below her, head pillowed on the crook of her elbow, as Gibbie had left her, his reluctant gesture towards what he took for a lass too drunk even to walk straight. He'd been too full of his own prejudices to recognise the famous Favelle.

Now, what had Magnie said? *Who should come up from below decks but Gibbie o Efstigarth?* That figured. In these light nights, if he was going to be longer than it would take to saw a rope nearly through, he'd work where he'd be unobserved.

Below decks. I looked at the half-deck running at shoulder-height from the stern to the mast. The engine was there, but I left that for Anders to go over. He'd know without needing to start her what had been done, and where. Sugar in the fuel tank was possible. Wood, though, wood was Gibbie's passion.

The grey haze covered the lower decks too. I peered into the half dark. There were ten rowing benches, spaced so that the rowers could wedge their feet on the ship's ribs. The oar-holes shone sky-blue in the gloom. I bent double and worked my way along the ship's sides, drawing my fingers along every smooth piece, every knothole. My back was aching by the time I'd examined every inch of each side, but I was certain he hadn't spoiled the integrity of the hull. She wasn't going to sink under her next crew.

I came out into the open area again to straighten out. The rudder fixings were above decks, and the strapping holding the heavy spar that supported the sail. It had to be the mast, then. I paused to listen before going back under. Sheep crunching along the beach; football cheering from someone's Sky Sports.

He'd done it very neatly. It took ten minutes of careful feeling around the mast to find the first hole, a centimetre-wide depression neatly plugged with plastic wood. I fiddled the plug out with my pocket-knife. It was only a couple of millimetres deep, yet when I inserted my marlin spike into the hole it disappeared right in. I went around the mast to the other side, and found the exit hole, plugged too.

Now I knew what I was looking for it was easy. There were nearly twenty holes in all, nothing we'd have noticed in daylight, but the minute the wind filled the sails, the whole thing would topple like a felled tree.

I had this to take to tomorrow's meeting, at least.

ᛋ

I still don't know how the murderer managed to come aboard without my sailor's sense being conscious of the boat moving on the pontoon. I suppose I was too horrified at my mind's image of the mast falling forward among my rowers in a tangle of sail and rope. I didn't even feel the blow. I was just straightening up when my world dissolved into stars.

I staggered, and caught at *Stormfugl*'s side. Someone moved behind me, passed me. Darkness was closing in on me, but even as I felt my legs give, and my body slump forwards against the wooden planks, I knew that was all wrong. Now was not the time to give way, except that I couldn't help it, my legs were folding under me, I was crumpled down on the boards between the rowing benches, and all I wanted to do was lay my head down and let the dark take over. There was a crackling sound behind me - no, before me too, it was all round me. I was trying to struggle to my feet while my brain was still registering 'Fire!' but my legs wouldn't thrust under me.

A scarlet light was flickering around me. The fire must have been started in several places, for it was eating its way up the mast and crawling over the dragon tail. The little cabin had a ridge of flame. Smoke from the head was blowing towards me, filling my mouth. If I breathed that in, I'd die. I fumbled one hand up to my neck and pulled the rib of my jersey over my nose. If my legs wouldn't obey me, I'd haul myself out of here. While I tried again to bunch my legs below me I was working it out. Skipper caught in misbehaviour decides to sabotage boat and take herself with it. They'd bury what charred remains were left, and consider the case closed.

Maree's evidence wouldn't be enough to over-ride such a simple solution. I had to live and tell my tale.

I took firm hold of the ladder. Mothers of trapped children could lift a car. It was a cliff to me now, the ratlines of a tall ship. I could do ratlines. Up to the crow's nest. I clenched my hands around the rough tarred rope. If the flames reached the engine it would explode. *Hurry. Lord, help me.* I hauled my feet under, then I heard shouting, and cars skidding on the gravel. The running feet were salvation. A dozen hands reached down to me and I was lifted into the air, swinging light and being caught, landing on the wooden jetty with a crumpling of knees; out cold.

ᛋ

When I came to, I thought it was Up Helly Aa, the red flames lighting the sky. Then memory returned and I pulled against the hands that supported me. '*Stormfugl*–'

'They're having to tow her out,' Anders said in my ear. 'To save the boats in the marina, to save your *Khalida*.'

Later he told me how the Delting sailors had launched their rescue boats, attached two grapnels to *Stormfugl*'s dragon prow and towed her out to sea. I didn't hear the engines at the time; all I knew from the cage of restraining hands was my ship moving away from me, her dragon head wreathed in fire, the sparks rising up into the midnight air and reflecting in the still water. Her mast fell with a crack, the red and ochre striped mainsail catching and burning in an instant. She blazed like the funeral of some Viking chieftain of a thousand years ago, the flames hissing in the water, and then the fire reached the engine at last. There was a dull 'boom' that flung burning timbers up into the air, then the darkness closed in.

I turned round then and saw the crowd on the pier. There were several cameras on tripods; Michael and James, with Ted beside them, as well as the Shetland news team. The police were in the middle of it, of course, with DI Macrae being briskly official. 'What happened?'

'Someone hit me,' I said. 'I was just examining below decks – examining the mast.'

Stormfugl was gone. There was no point in talking of sabotage now.

He turned my head, shone a torch on it. 'The skin's not broken.'

'Someone hit me,' I repeated doggedly, 'and I went down, then I realised she was on fire.'

Sergeant Peterson lifted one of my hands, turned it over, bent her head to smell it, slowly, methodically. She repeated the procedure with the other one. 'No smell of inflammables, sir. Just smoke.'

I gave her an outraged stare. 'Somebody else set her on fire, with me aboard.'

'Have you any idea who?'

I started to shake my head, thought better of it. 'No.'

'Size, bulk? Were you hit with a downwards stroke?'

'I don't know,' I said, 'It was someone who moved very smoothly, used to boats. I didn't feel her rock at all.'

'How long ago?'

'I don't know,' I said. 'The people who pulled me out, ask them.'

He checked his watch. 'Sergeant, go over to Busta and get everyone together in the long room. Macdonald, you interviewed Kevin Manson, didn't you? Phone and see if he's in. If he's not, go over and wait until I call.' A look around; his gaze fell on two more uniforms. 'Sergeant, you do the same with Inga Anderson; you, Sergeant, same with Mr and Mrs Lynch. Insist on speaking personally to Mr Lynch.' He turned back to me. 'Did you hear how your assailant arrived?'

'Not by car, I don't think. I thought there were sheep on the pebbles of the shore – it could have been a walker.'

DI Macrae's gaze returned to his crew. 'I want alibis for the last hour, and particular note of anyone who arrives late, or looks breathless. I'll join you at Busta once the doctor's seen Ms Lynch.'

I was about to say that I didn't need a doctor when I realised it was for him, not me. A doctor would see if I'd really been hit, and how hard.

'Can I sit down?' I said. Anders walked solicitously with me to the bench overlooking the marina. DI Macrae was talking into his intercom; to the doctor, no doubt. Maree should be at Dodie's by now, and her phone would work there. I grabbed my own mobile, and got her on the second ring.

'Developments. Come now, next ferry – to the marina.'

'Will do.'

With luck, she'd be here in forty minutes, an hour at most - before the gathering at Busta had broken up.

ч

Forensics came first, to take sticky-tape samples from my hands, then the doctor, who didn't say anything conclusive. 'None the worse for wear. You're tough, you sailing types,' he said cheerfully to me, then went to confer with DI Macrae, low-voiced. I saw him shake his head. DI Macrae gave me a long, dubious look then turned his back, drawing the doctor round so that I couldn't guess what they were saying. Then DI Macrae came back to me.

'What are you going to do now?'

I was going to play possum, play ghosts. 'Have a cup of tea,' I said, 'and take an aspirin. Lie down.'

'Aboard your boat?'

'Yes.'

He frowned. 'I'm not entirely happy about you being alone on her. Can you lock her from inside?'

'Yes,' I said, carefully keeping any suggestion of '*of course*' out of my voice. *Khalida* was a sea-going yacht; she could be secured against a storm from inside.

'Lock yourself in, then.' He paused, as if he was going to say something else, then nodded, turned away. He'd just reached his car when Maman brought Dad's 4x4 skidding to a halt at the top of the gravel drive. She leapt out and enveloped me in a flood of motherly concern. 'Cassandre, what happened? We just had a phone call–'

'I'm fine, Maman. Really I am.'

She didn't notice the space by the jetty where *Stormfugl* had been. She hadn't even seen my first command.

'Maman,' I said, 'I need your help. It's really important, to get this cleared up.'

She smiled with affectionate condescension, as if I was five again. 'You are going to stage the final scene, in the library, as in all the best detective stories.' Then she shook her head. 'This isn't a story, Cassandre. Leave it to the police.'

'They're getting it all wrong,' I said. 'Besides,' I gestured at the jetty where *Stormfugl* had been moored over her own reflection, 'the murderer knocked me out and burnt my ship, and I'm going to nail the bastard. Will you help me?'

She gave me a long look. I don't know what she saw, the travesti hero perhaps, Orpheus on his quest, Orestes, but it was something she recognised as an irresistible force. She nodded gravely. 'What do you want me to do?'

I explained quickly and left her to get the things we'd need for Maree at Jessie's: lighter clothes, her stand-in wig and her make-up. I was feeling a bit shaky, but no worse than I'd have felt after a day of sea-sickness.

'Where're you going?' Anders asked, as I started walking up to the car.

'Busta House.' Anders was part of this too; he needed to be there at the finish. 'Will you drive me?'

'Of course.'

'I left the car behind the skip.'

'I will get it.'

ᛋ

We were doing Favelle's last journey in reverse. She'd stumbled down to the jetty on the gravel slope we were walking up now, to fall unconscious on the deck and be left there by Gibbie. She'd gone past Magnie's car, parked where Anders had drawn mine up. It took us less than a minute to drive around the corner to the standing stone, but it must have taken her far longer, alone and in pain, her vision blurred. She'd staggered along this dim road between grass verges without any friendly arm to support her. I almost expected to see her white-faced ghost hauling herself out of the ditch by the standing stone. Here, Kevin had waylaid her and talked to her of wind turbines and the environment. She'd stalled and promised anything that would get him to go away and leave her to her desperate enterprise: sleeping with a stranger in the hope of a child like Charlie.

The car bumped along the mile of road to Busta. I wondered if she'd had any misgivings as she'd walked briskly along here towards *Stormfugl* where she was to meet Anders. Was she naive enough to think her reputation would rise above the scandal, if he decided to kiss and tell? Yes, I thought she probably was. I didn't think she'd have minded about Ted, either. She'd have told him the child was his, and maybe he'd have believed it.

Poor Favelle, going to an accidental death. I hoped she hadn't seen her killer's face.

We parked above the House of Commons gargoyles, gaping their distorted beaks in pitted faces. I drew Anders through the car park and down between trees to what had been the main gate, a tall double entrance of iron curlicues that opened on a flagged path leading past the Long Room. The official front door faced the beach where the video tapes had burned in the night and the stone jetty the bicycle had been thrown from. I tugged Anders down a little, so that we'd be below the first wall of the terrace, and we came silently up to the house. Through the window I could see the heads turned attentively forwards; DI Macrae must be standing at the fireplace end, below the portrait of Thomas Gifford of Busta, to lay down the law.

I eased the front door open and heard Ted's voice. 'Are you, Lieutenant, linking this latest outrage with the earlier sabotage?'

'It's probable they are connected, yes.'

'Perpetrated by somebody who is out to stop the film? The person who sent the letters?'

I nodded to Anders to follow me, and slid into the Long Room. If Thomas Gifford had come back, he'd have known his salon, for it was lit only by firelight, as I'd hoped, and still furnished in eighteenth-century fashion. There was a polished half-moon table and a mahogany bookcase at this end, and occasional tables and half a dozen easy-chairs at the other, old-fashioned chairs with wide, curled arms and upright backs. The air breathed lavender, beeswax, old books; the parquet was slipper-smooth under our feet. Family portraits still glowered down on the present-day visitors: Thomas and his wife, Madam Busta herself, the termagant who'd stolen poor Barbara Pitcairn's son and set her ghost haunting.

Nobody turned to look at us. They were all focused on the far end of the room, with DI Macrae facing them in front of the amber light of the peat fire glowing softly in the hearth. He had one elbow on the white Adam mantelpiece, entirely at home, the other hand gesturing as if he'd just made a point. His face was tipped towards Ted, a metre from him in one of the curved-arm easy-chairs. Ted sat very upright, his head tipped back to show off the moulded nose and strong chin. Behind him was Mr Berg, wary and watchful, with his pinstripe suited lawyer on an upright chair at his elbow. Opposite Berg was Michael, the Cavalier poet in his ruffled shirt, dark hair gleaming against the pale brocade. They were sideways on to us. Between us and them were half a dozen rows of upright chairs: the cameramen, the make-up and costume girls, the set design people, the runners. DI Macrae's eyes flicked up as we came in, and his mouth straightened, but he didn't speak.

Immediately behind Michael was Elizabeth's platinum-smooth head, the only one that was turned to a different angle. She didn't care what the police had to say. Her gaze was fixed on Ted.

It was Ted who was speaking. As we arrived he leaned forward. 'I find that more plausible than that my wife had a personal enemy. Everyone loved her. Your investigations, your interviews, will all bear that out.' He repeated it like an elegy: 'Everyone loved her.'

'The burning of the longboat certainly suggests that someone is determined to stop the film being finished,' DI Macrae agreed.

'I shouldn't have said how much I wanted to finish it,' Ted mourned. He looked straight at DI Macrae. 'We get so many crank letters, and these were so vague. I wish–' He stopped there.

Michael leaned forward. 'But if that's really true, then we must all of us be cleared.' There was something slightly stiff about his diction that I recognised now. He'd picked up Anders' English-speaking speech habits. 'We've all worked hard on the film.' I sensed the wave of relief that ran through the crew, heard the held-breaths let out in a soft rustle. Only Elizabeth remained tense, her whole attention on Ted. 'It would have been–'

'Will be,' Ted cut in. Elizabeth leaned forward slightly. He cleared his throat. 'Will be a feather in all your caps. I said to–' His eyebrows drew together as he tried to remember, but my name had gone from his memory. 'I said, 'You'll be putting this on your CV in thirty years time, and people will say, 'Wow, you worked on that movie?' There are shots I'd have liked, but we can reconstruct them or do without. This movie is going to be finished.' He gave a wintry smile. 'If, Lieutenant, you can find the person responsible–'

'Ah, yes, the person responsible,' DI Macrae agreed. He raised his head and looked evenly round the room. 'Someone who was there to plant the anonymous letters.' For a moment I wondered if he too had found the answer, seen the face. 'There to put the fuse under the rock; there to fire the longship. Now that was within the last hour, so you should have no difficulty in remembering where you were, and who with. Thank you for your co-operation. Those of you who have already given your statement to Sergeant Peterson may go. I'd ask those of you who haven't to stay behind here.'

Even in that short time the last of the light had gone, and the moon's rays were trickling in through the windows, falling like cold sunlight on Michael's face, icing Elizabeth's platinum hair. DI Macrae nodded to Sergeant Peterson. Her hand was just on the light-switch when the French door at Michael's elbow opened, and a chill breath of sea-air touched the room. Favelle slipped in from the moonlight outside, and stood there, her eyes fixed on us. Her face was the blanched white of old paper, her eyes hollowed and the lids reddened; her lips were bloodless above her pale trouser suit. There was a heart-beat pause, then she moved on silent feet into the room with us.

Chapter 20

The moment seemed to last forever. We could hear the sea washing on the beach a hundred yards away as we stared at dead Favelle and saw her expressionless eyes look back. That cold sea-breath stirred the red-gold hair and let it fall again. She took a step towards us. A gasping breath, and then Elizabeth gave a high, thin scream, and dropped in an untidy bundle on the floor. Ted didn't speak, or move, but his eyes stared in wild horror at the apparition, and I saw the blood drain from his cheeks, leaving his face an unhealthy greenish-brown. Michael stared, then gave a little nod. He knew Maree.

A long instant, then DI Macrae dropped to his knees beside Elizabeth, ignoring Favelle. That broke the spell. Even as Ted rose slowly, as Sergeant Peterson's hand found the light switch, Maree was pulling off the wig and shaking her own dark hair free. The flood of brightness dazzled for a moment, then illuminated the clown-white pallor, the half-circles of dark shading under the eyes and the frosted lipstick. Maman had done a good job. The entrance had caught them.

Ted was the first to speak. 'Maree! Where have you been?' He paused, swallowed. 'Did you know – you must have heard–'

'I heard,' she replied, and the words fell like stones thrown into deep water and left a spreading silence behind them. DI Macrae rose slowly, whole body tensed. Maree turned and looked around the semi-circle, right around, a short, intent look into every face. 'I heard that one of you in this room killed my sister.' Her gaze went down to Elizabeth, lying open-mouthed on the floor with legs spread in an ungainly sprawl, came forward to Michael and returned to Ted.

DI Macrae's glance flicked across to me. I could read his disapproval but I'd banked on his being too good a policeman to let a chance like this slip. He didn't speak, just watched Maree and waited.

Her left hand slipped into her pocket and brought out the envelope I'd handed her that day at the Hams. It was white with a typed address, just the way I'd described it to DI Macrae, as Ted had confirmed the envelopes he'd found had been. Maree looked at it, turned it over in her hand. 'This is what killed Favelle. This is what made her go along to the longship.' She opened the envelope, drew the letter out. The lawyer made a movement of protest, as if to take it off her, and was stilled by Berg's hand lifting.

It was a lengthy letter, almost a whole page of A4, but she read out only one sentence of it. 'We confirm, therefore, that the subject is unlikely to be able to father children without IVF procedures.'

The letter Dad had found in Maree's pocket, testing an anonymous man's sperm. No wonder he'd been so angry, so unwilling to explain himself to the police. The letter had said he was infertile.

I'd been sure Ted hadn't known about the letter. There hadn't been time. I'd put it into Maree's hands, and she'd given it to Favelle. A quick read, then it was thrust into Maree's pocket. It wasn't a letter to leave lying around the set.

He recognised that it was talking about him, though. He must have known he couldn't father children, although he hadn't admitted it to Favelle. Maree had told me he'd just insisted that she was at the high point of her career, there would be plenty of time to have a family. He moved forward now, taking the letter from her to read it. She continued as if he hadn't moved.

'You'd told Favelle you'd been tested and everything was fine. After two years of trying she didn't believe you, and she got her own test done. That was the result.' Now she turned to look at Michael, then down the room at Anders. She took a deep breath, ready to mix lies with truth, as we'd worked out, up in Yell. Maree wasn't going to let Favelle be dragged down with her murderer. 'She was upset about it – she couldn't sleep, so she came to talk to me. That's what she was doing on the road, visiting her sister.'

The directors all these years ago were right; she wasn't the actor her sister had been. I hoped the accusation to come would over-ride the lie.

'You didn't expect her to be out. I was the one who ran every evening. All you had to do was come up behind me on your cycle, stop, hit me hard on the back of the head. Problem solved.' She took a step forward, so that she was standing over Ted. 'You meant to kill me, and instead you killed Favelle. You. You killed her.'

Then there was pandemonium as the lawyer leapt to his feet with vehement protests, and Mr Berg advised Ted to say nothing, anyone could see Maree's head had been turned by the loss of her sister, and Ted himself just stood there with the letter in his left hand, shaking his head gently and smiling at Maree. 'Maree, honey, this has been an awful shock to you, so I'm not going to even try to believe you mean that.'

But his back was rigid, and he didn't ask the natural question, 'Why? Why would I want to kill you?'

I'd heard the answer to that too, floating down from the green field by the standing stone. *I'm going to tell her. She has the right to know.* I saw him working out that Maree had come back, ready to tell the truth about that conversation, then he smiled again. 'Honey, we sure were worried about you.' His eyes went across the room. 'Michael, I'll leave you to talk to Maree. Try and get her to lie down, maybe take something.'

Michael came forward, hand stretched towards Maree's elbow. She jerked away from him, suddenly uncertain. 'It's true! Doesn't anyone believe me?'

DI Macrae stepped in then. 'I think, Ms Baker, it would be better if you came and talked to us in private. These public accusations help nobody.' His face was grim. 'You too, Ms Lynch.'

He paused to murmur something to Sergeant Peterson, and she and the other officer moved smoothly to where Ted was already in discussion with Mr Berg and the lawyer. I hung back to make sure they were all leaving the room together.

ᛋ

DI Macrae wasn't happy with us. 'If you had information then you should have come to the police, Ms Baker.' Then he cut to the important bit. 'Have you any proof whatsoever that your brother-in-law was responsible for your sister's death? Can you explain why he wanted to kill you?'

'I told him,' Maree said simply, 'that I was going to have a baby.'

Not anonymous letters, as I'd guessed and Ted had pretended; it had been much more important news. Maree was pregnant. It was her freedom from being Favelle's stand-in. She wanted a life of her own.

Ted had known what it would do to Favelle. She'd longed for a baby to the point of madness. The knowledge that Maree had succeeded where she'd failed would have pushed her over the edge. Maree had to go.

'Favelle wanted a baby,' Maree said. 'All these yummy mummies all around her, in every paper – that's what she longed for, so much that nothing else mattered. She almost had a nervous breakdown over it. They hushed it up, then she tried to steal a baby in a trolley at a supermarket. The mother turned away to get something from a shelf and when she looked back the baby was gone. They stopped Favelle at the door, and the baby wasn't hurt or anything, but it sure gave us all a fright. That was just before the filming of *The Sea Road* started. There should have been a child in that, and Ted cut the part. We were all so scared, you know–'

'But you'd have had to tell her,' I said, 'about your baby. Yours and Dad's.' I thought of the conversation I'd overheard. *It'll tear her apart* – and Maree's reply, *I've got to tell her.*

'I told Ted. I guess that was when he decided I'd got to go. Only–' Her voice shook.

DI Macrae nodded. 'Okay, that's motive. What about the anonymous letters?'

'There weren't any,' I said.

He raised his brows at me.

'None of the film crew had heard anything about them,' I said. 'Not even Michael, and if Maree had really known then he would have known too. Just Elizabeth, and she knew there was something wrong about them. No envelopes, no postmarks, just Ted's story. Those two he showed us could have been printed yesterday – have you got a test that can tell? I bet they're no older than two days old.'

'Explain why,' DI Macrae said.

'Like Maree said, after she'd told him about her baby, he decided she had to go. But he wanted to be clever about it. What we were all meant to think, when Maree was found dead, was that someone was trying to kill Favelle. The classic set-up, that the understudy had been killed by mistake for the star.' My head was aching; I hoped I was being clear enough. 'So he wrote some anonymous letters. He told Elizabeth they'd started a while back, and left one for her to find. Stars like Favelle often have stalkers, so that was plausible. But he didn't want Favelle to feel threatened, so nobody else knew. Okay. Then the next step. The rock.'

'A dangerous trick for throwing dust in our eyes.'

'Well, yes and no,' I said. 'That was what made me think. If it was a real saboteur, it was a stupid way to try to sabotage a film. For a start, there was no certainty you'd hit anyone, let alone anyone important, although Ted made a good case for making out that it was aimed at Favelle. But it was Ted himself who made sure that it wouldn't harm anyone. He kept everyone down at the beach until he knew it was about to fall, just to make sure the actors weren't too close. To make doubly sure he gave Favelle Anders to take care of her, with his seaman's reactions. Anders wasn't supposed to be in the film at all. At that point Ted and Favelle should have been walking up towards the old house, arm in arm. Ted placed himself ahead, so he could see the rock going. Once I thought about it, I even remembered that he shouted before the rock moved. There was the bang, then he yelled, 'Clear set!' He'd been expecting it.'

We'd looked at it the wrong way round. The anonymous letters that Favelle never saw, the falling rock that didn't hurt anyone. They'd been meant to look like attempts on the star, so that when the understudy died it would be a mistake.

'He organised himself a nice alibi,' I said, 'up on Ronas Hill. James and Michael worked the cameras, and he was director, roving between them, and taking footage with the hand-held. He had his fold-away bike in the back of the minibus.' One of his first films had been as a long-distance cyclist, and he'd done all the stunts himself. He'd have done the ten miles between Ronas Hill and Brae in unexpectedly little time. 'As soon as it was dusk, he took it out, pedalled fast to the Busta road, and waited with a stone in his hand for Maree to come along on her evening run.'

He just hadn't known that Maree had quarrelled with Dad and gone to Yell; that Favelle had taken advantage of his absence to go to Anders.

'Then,' I said to DI Macrae, 'he saw you searching *Khalida*. Well, I'd no motive to kill Favelle. You were arguing that I'd meant to kill Maree – that I'd made the same mistake that he had, killed the star for the understudy, and he had to stop you thinking along those lines. He produced the letters, then he came to set me up.'

'To set you up?' Maree echoed.

'To start gossip about him and me.' I'd known even then that I wasn't the heroine of his movie, however much he smiled at me. 'All that stuff in the Norwegian newspapers, the crew taking bets on whether I'd console him. He set that going. Even allowing for newspapers making smoke without fire, there was nothing, nothing, for anyone else to start that up. He stopped at the end of the day to check over the next day's arrangements, and that was it. So I was suspicious when he came visiting, as if we were friends. He was giving me a motive for killing Favelle.'

DI Macrae nodded.

'As well as that,' I continued, 'well, he said he'd come to ask why Favelle had come to *Stormfugl*, and he did want to know that, genuinely, but much more important was where Maree was hiding. I pretended I heard someone listening, so as to have an excuse for stalling, but he knew from what I said that the police were still suspicious. So that night he burned the videos. It was like the rock; lots of visible damage, but no real harm. The actual footage was safe in London. All he'd lost was the time he'd spent editing, and I bet there's some kind of back-up of that. It looked good, though. He'd announced very publicly that he was going to finish the film, and here was somebody trying to stop that. The saboteur who'd killed Favelle was still going.'

'Plausible, but no proof,' DI Macrae said.

'I'm pretty sure it was a splash that woke me,' I said. 'The folding bicycle going over Busta pier, maybe. When I smelt the burning I phoned Anders. He was at Busta too, but I couldn't get through, because there's no signal there. I should have remembered that. I tried Ted, and got through straight away. Ergo, he wasn't in his room at Busta. He was outside, where he'd get a signal. He sounded breathless, too, as if he'd just sneaked down with a folding bicycle in one hand and a heavy bag of videos in the other.'

'Why get rid of the bicycle?' DI Macrae asked.

'To keep you from thinking of his alibi? To make it look like someone from the Busta end had done it? Maybe in a day or so he'd have discovered it was missing. This is important, though: Kevin passed a cyclist, at about the right time. Well, Kevin wouldn't have passed someone from Busta, he came from the other direction. So that cyclist was coming from the Ronas Hill direction towards Busta, towards where Favelle was.'

'Ted's folding bike had smaller wheels than a regular bicycle,' Maree said. 'He might have noticed that.'

'Possible.' DI Macrae made a note. 'The signal thing is a better bet, though. You're certain a mobile can't be reached in Busta House?'

'Positive. And then Mr Berg arrived, with Norwegian newspaper clippings of Ted and me, and a general suggestion that I'd killed Favelle for love of him. That brought on tonight's episode. He was lucky to find me aboard *Stormfugl*, but if he hadn't he'd have made some excuse to take me there.' I could hear his voice in my head: *Cass, honey, I wanted to go aboard in private before tomorrow – will you come with me?* 'Knock me on the head and fire the boat. My last sabotage, as good as a confession. Case closed.'

'I wouldn't have believed it,' DI Macrae said. I gave him a long look; he smiled at me. 'Your suicide as a confession was one thing, but nothing would have induced you to fire your boat.'

'Gudrid didn't die in the original script,' I said. 'But maybe this version of the movie would have included a Viking funeral. James and Michael were both filming away.'

'It's still illogical,' Maree said. 'To think that me having a baby would drive her haywire, but my murder, her sister's murder, wouldn't.'

I wasn't sure that Favelle was connected enough to other people to be deeply distressed by the murder of even a sister, but there was no need to say that now. 'A baby was her obsession,' I said. 'And he was conceited. He knew she had him to console her, so that made it all right.'

I wondered if prisons had an editing suite.

ᛋ

I half thought Anders would stay over at Busta, but he put a proprietorial hand under my elbow and steered me out, turning to ask Maree, 'Can we give you a lift home?'

'To Jessie's yeah,' she said. She was looking drained. 'Do you think they'll get him?'

'He'll do his best,' I said.

We dropped her off at Efstigarth and came on down to the pier. I was knackered, and my head ached. Anders undid the washboards, shoved the hatch open. 'Have you eaten?'

I shook my head.

'I'll make something. You sit still, Cass. You've had a hard day.' He gave me an anxious look. 'Perhaps I should take you to the hospital, for a head X-ray.'

'No. I'll be fine.' I slumped onto the starboard berth and leaned my head against the wooden bookshelf. Rat came to curl around my neck. I closed my eyes, then opened them again to look thoughtfully at Anders. 'Was it Michael you were with, at Busta?'

The back of his neck went scarlet. 'Yes, but it was not – we are not–'

'There's nothing wrong with being attracted to other men,' I reassured him.

He turned and glared at me. 'I am not in the least attracted to other men. Really, Cass, you can be very obtuse.'

'So what were you up to?' I asked.

He went crimson again, and I wondered what he might be so embarrassed about. Porn movies? Masonic meetings?

'I had better show you,' he said. He went forrard and rummaged in his kit-bag for a roll of green baize, which he laid on the table between us. I undid the ties and gradually began to unroll it. The thick material enclosed something knobbly, no, a lot of little somethings, each in its own pocket of baize. I drew one out. A knight in futuristic armour, beautifully hand-painted.

The pair of them were Warhammer addicts.

I knew he was a nerd.

ᛋ

'Not boat,' Peerie Charlie said, leaning in a dangerous fashion over *Khalida*'s side to look over at the jetty where *Stormfugl* had been.

I took a firm hold of the back straps of his dungarees. 'Gone,' I agreed.

He leaned over, looking down at the water and humming to himself. Inga re-settled her red-amber scarf around her neck and looked at me quizzically.

'Yes, I saw it,' I said.

'That anti-windfarm leaflet is hopeless. I was making up a new version, with pictures, and Kevin has a far better scanner than ours. Don't even think of joining Jessie in believing the worst.'

'So what was he doing tooling around Brae at 4 am?'

'*Ah*,' Inga said. She started to laugh. 'Filming otters, Simon King style. You know, getting up at dawn and creeping around the hills in a camouflage jacket, instead of just sitting quietly by the shore like everyone else.'

Peerie Charlie wriggled back between the guard wires and slid down to stand on the cockpit floor. 'Velle gone too.'

'Yes,' I said. 'Favelle's gone too.'

'But you can still see her,' Inga said. 'On the telly. I'll get you the video to watch, and when you're big you can tell everyone Favelle loved you.'

ᛋ

Mr Berg didn't apologise for his suspicions when he came round that afternoon, but he paid me in full. I didn't ask if he'd give me a reference. After he left I walked up to the standing stone and stood with my back to it, staring out over the water. My first and last post as a skipper wouldn't bring other employment, as I'd hoped. I was back to the hand-to-mouth business of a summer here, a deckhand job there, trapped in this round of summer in the Med making sailing instant fun for overweight brats, and winter waitressing.

It was a bleak prospect.

ᛋ

Maree saw me standing there, and came out from Efstigarth to say goodbye. 'I'm going back to the States. It wouldn't have worked, you know. Dermot was just too old for me. I think I was using him as an escape route out of the movies. And then, you know, he reminded me of my own Pop.'

'A classic,' I agreed. Alain's energy and certainty had been like Dad too.

Maree blinked a couple of times, mouth working. 'I don't need to escape now. My poor sister.'

'What about Michael?'

'He was an escape chute too. I didn't have to worry about giving myself away. He'll soon get someone else.' Maree looked across the glimmering water and took a deep breath. 'Even now, maybe I was wrong about Ted. I thought he was just hitching his falling star to her rising one, but he loved her enough to kill for her. Kinda romantic, even. He made her the star she'll always be. Favelle, honey.' Her chin tilted defiantly. 'Good luck, Cass. I'll see you at the trial.'

I reached out a hand to stop her. 'Maree, what about the baby?'

She didn't look at me as she shrugged. 'False alarm. Just as well really. Your Mom and Dad are better together. Same generation, all that history. Best kept together.' She turned away. I thought about the way the green velvet dress had draped across her rounded belly. *Eating for two*, Agnes of the Old Haa cafe had said. The son Dad had longed for, my little brother.

I asked, 'Will you give me your address?'

She stopped then, shook her head.

'I'd make a cool half-sister,' I said. 'Even though I'm so much older. Exciting even, blowing across the Atlantic to say hello. Children like that.'

Maree took a step back to me. 'So they do.' A long pause, then she turned away again. The words whispered across the grass. 'I'll write you.'

Maybe she would, maybe she wouldn't. When the time was right, I'd need to talk to Dad. I watched her go and thought about parents and children: about my father who'd driven me to so many regattas, and about Maree and Favelle and their mother, who'd wanted two stars and had to make do with one. I thought about

Favelle, who'd wanted a baby so desperately, and about Maree, who was having one, and about Ted, who'd killed to stop her.

Maree, who'd always been her sister's stand-in. I wondered how she'd manage on her own.

I'd barely got back to *Khalida* when Maman came stepping delicately onto the marina pontoon. She scanned the boats, biggest ones first, then, finally, her gaze came round to the smaller ones. I stood up in the cockpit and waved.

'Here, Maman.'

Her eyes went along *Khalida*'s sides, doubtfully, and came back up to my face. 'Salut, Cassandre. I've come for a cup of coffee with you.'

'Come aboard.' I held out a hand to make it easier. 'Foot up on the side, then swing the other leg over.'

She managed it with her usual competent elegance and then stopped on the top step to look around the small cabin. I saw dismay in her face, but she spoke with her usual calm. 'He is handsome in the summer, but how do you heat him in the winter?'

I grimaced. 'A flowerpot on the gas ring, a warm sleeping bag, and mooring near a heated swimming pool.'

'You are very resourceful.' She sat down on the berth and said no more until I was facing her, our coffee steaming up the window. Then she took a deep breath. 'Listen, my Cassandre. I've been doing a lot of thinking recently. When we are young we do things, follow priorities, but as we get older we start to see more clearly.' The selkie wife finding fish harder to catch, and wondering if she should have chosen the security of old age ashore. 'You are not young any more, and perhaps you should look at your life and see if this is how you wish to continue, while you are still young enough to change it.'

Now I was old enough to tell the truth. 'I've been thinking that too.'

'You see,' she continued, as if she'd learned her lines and was going to say them, 'I let you down when you were little. I wasn't there. Oh, yes, my body was in the house, but my mind wasn't there for you. I was longing for singing again.' She paused, her long, dark-lidded eyes scanning my face. 'When we tried again, in France, I didn't realise that you were longing.' She looked out at the sea glinting in the marina. 'Longing so much you had to run away.'

'Yes,' I agreed. 'As you did.'

'I was unhappy, you know,' she said. 'Unhappy staying, unhappy going.'

'You left all your dresses,' I said. 'I thought you'd come back.'

'I thought I'd come back too,' she said.

The water rippled outside: time, flowing in a never-ending stream.

'It doesn't matter now,' I said.

She shook her head. 'It matters. What I did then has made the Cassandre who's sitting here now. It has made the Eugénie and the Dermot too, but we will work on those. I want to talk of you.'

I shrugged, and she made a distressed movement.

'Cassandre, you aren't happy. I can see it, feel it. Listen to me. I have a talent for singing, just as you have a talent for the sea. I'm a director's first choice for Rameau. There is not a significant production without me. Rameau, he's a great talent, but not the greatest, and I'm not the greatest either. For these little talents, I sacrificed you and Dermot.'

It was funny, I thought, how you could get away with saying that kind of thing in French.

'We wouldn't have been any happier if you'd stayed and been miserable,' I said, and realised that it was true. The weight of blaming her shifted and lightened, and I could feel that in a short time, when I'd got used to the idea, I'd walk away from it.

'I thought I could justify it,' she said. 'If I became famous, you'd know it had been worthwhile. Then the time comes when you realise you're only a star in a very little sky, and your heart aches for what you threw away that was ultimately more important: love, companionship, vows, children.'

She blinked and turned her face away so that I saw only the smooth cheek.

'Can you and Dad make a go of it again?' I asked.

'Perhaps not. I would like to try.' Her dark eyes were on me again. 'But I wish to talk about you, Cassandre.' She took a breath then asked simply, 'Did you love Alain Mouettier very much?'

I didn't know. 'No – yes.'

'You cannot keep punishing yourself. He would have to hate you very much to want that. Besides–' She shrugged. 'If the Church is right, he is sleeping here on earth and waiting for the Resurrection in our time, and already in the Holy City in God's. If the Church is wrong he is nowhere.'

I winced at that. I needed the Church to be right, so that I could meet him again. If he was nowhere I could never ask forgiveness.

'Either way, he would not want you to turn your life into ashes.'

I thought of Alain, laughing over the fish twisting and glinting in his hands. I remembered him coming into the cabin with his scarlet oilskins running water and smiling apologetically at me as he dripped past, or pulling me into his arms and holding me there in the cold nights. Only the Alain who'd fired at me had been a stranger. I felt this burden shift too.

Maman set her mug down and rose. 'Will you think about it, at least, Cassandre?'

I nodded. 'I promise.'

I lay in my bunk that night and thought, as the tide turned, as the sun came up to catch the gold flecks in the wood along the front of my pilot books. I lay snuggled in my sleeping bag with my head cradled in the pillow that smelt slightly of damp, and thought about life on land. I tried to imagine being home, where everyone knew me and all my past deeds were behind. I tried to see myself marrying and having a peerie Charlie of my own.

I couldn't live on land yet. I was still longing for my ocean, for the tides and currents, and the rushing waves, but I didn't want to be a nomad any more. Maman was right. I was punishing myself for Alain's death, and it was time I stopped. What I'd done had been very far from Ted's calculating ruthlessness. I'd reacted from pain and shock and fear. If Alain had surfaced again, I'd have saved him. He might still have died from head injuries on *Marielle*, as Favelle had died on the longship. I would make another confession, a good one, with all the hate and confusion I'd felt, then accept forgiveness. I'd allow myself to go into my own society, into the closeness of a floating world.

I'd cut myself off from that too, with my stubborn teenage will that wouldn't let Maman and Dad know best. I could have returned to France and been educated there. I could have come back and applied for college here. Pride, deadliest of the seven. It wasn't too late to turn that around.

I wriggled quietly out of my berth, hauled my jumper and jeans on and started up the computer.

When I drove along the next morning they weren't very long up. Dad was relaxing in his favourite old jumper and Maman was in her floating dressing-gown, humming as she made coffee. I paused for a moment in the doorway to watch them, and hoped that the trying worked out.

Maman poured me a coffee and I sat down at the table, mouth too dry to drink.

'Maman, Dad, I want to ask a huge favour.'

Dad's eyebrows shot up. 'Ask away.'

'I want to go to college, and I can't afford it.' His eyes widened, then half-closed in satisfaction. Maman's hand came to his shoulder. I was determined to go the whole way to them. 'Would you pay me through?'

He was smiling so hard he could barely manage the business questions. 'What college, and what courses exactly?'

'The North Atlantic College, here in Shetland. I can live aboard *Khalida* in Scalloway. I want to get my ticket, so that I can get permanent work afloat. I want to belong on a tall ship.'

ᛋ

Gavin Macrae came to see me before he went back south. I was peaceably below, re-splicing a worn mooring rope, when I heard a knock on *Khalida*'s side. He was standing on the pontoon, waiting. I kept the guard rail between us. 'Hi.'

'I came to say goodbye,' he stated. He looked down at *Khalida*'s cockpit benches. 'Can I come aboard?'

I shrugged and stepped back. No, he wasn't here to apologise. *I did my job,* his eyes said, *and if you didn't like it, tough.* I tried to transfer that thinking to a ship. If someone told me in confidence that he had epilepsy and was liable to seizures, I'd have to tell the other officers. Catching a murderer was the kind of ship that took priority.

If I hadn't told him about Alain's death, I wouldn't have been able to go to Yell. I wouldn't have felt cleansed at last. In time, I'd be grateful.

His first words dispelled future gratitude quite nicely. 'That was a risk you took for Maree. How did you know Tarrant wouldn't silence her?'

'Not in front of so many people,' I retorted. 'He wasn't stupid. He was calculating. Lie, get an expensive lawyer, pat Maree on the head and say she's distraught, unbalanced by her sister's death.'

'Exactly what he is saying.'

'Do you think you'll nail him though?' I asked.

His jaw set. 'The crime was committed here, he'll be tried here. I have faith in Scottish justice.' He gave me a long, steady look. 'You know you'll be one of the key witnesses for the prosecution?'

'The conversation about the baby?'

'Write down what you heard now, word for word, and learn it off by heart.'

'I didn't know policemen were supposed to give advice like that.'

He looked away from me, his lower lip pulling in against his teeth. 'I've seen all Favelle's movies. When I got this case I even thought that I might meet her.'

Instead, he'd had to look at her body.

I wasn't a suspect any more; we were equals now. I looked him straight in the face, seeing his own grey eyes, not Alain's any longer. 'I won't let her down,' I said.

He nodded and stood up. 'I'll see you at the trial.' Suddenly he smiled, and held out his hand. 'And if you take off in a tall ship and insist on being at sea, I'll personally run you in for everything I can think of the next time you set foot on Scottish soil.'

I smiled back, and was just about to shake hands on it when Rat swarmed out of the cabin, whiffling with interest at the stranger. He had the timing of a rock star. Gavin Macrae gave him a level look, entirely unfazed. 'We can start with him,' he said.

'He belongs to Anders,' I said.

'I know,' he retorted, 'but the skipper's responsible for those on board her ship. You'd need to make sure that Sergeant Peterson doesn't see him.'

I set Rat up on my shoulder. He took one turn, like a cat, then curled his tail around my neck for balance. His whiskers whiffled my cheek.

'I'll see you at the trial,' I said.

A NOTE ON SHETLAN

Shetland has its own very distinctive language, *Shetlan* or *Shetlandic*, which derives from old Norse and old Scots. Magnie's first words to Cass are,

'Cass, well, for the love of mercy. Norroway, at this season? Yea, yea, we'll find you a berth. Where are you?'

Written in west-side Shetlan (each district is slightly different), it would have looked like this:

'Cass, weel, fir da love o mercy. Norroway, at dis saeson? Yea, yea, we'll fin dee a bert. Quaur is du?"

Th becomes a *d* sound in *dis* (this), *da* (the), *dee* and *du* (originally thee and thou, now you), *wh* becomes *qu* (*quaur*, where), the vowel sounds are altered (well to *weel*, season to *saeson,* find *to fin)*, the verbs are slightly different (quaur is du?) and the whole looks unintelligible to most folk from outwith Shetland, and *twartree* (a few) within it too.

So, rather than writing in the way my characters would speak, I've tried to catch the rhythm and some of the distinctive usages of Shetlan while keeping it intelligible to *soothmoothers*, or people who've come in by boat through the South Mouth of Bressay Sound into Lerwick, and by extension, anyone living south of Fair Isle.

There are also many Shetlan words that my characters would naturally use, and here, to help you, are *some o dem*. No Shetland person would ever use the Scots *wee*; to them, something small would be *peerie*, or, if it was very small, *peerie mootie*. They'd *caa* sheep in a *park*, that is, herd them up in a field – *moorit* sheep, coloured black, brown, fawn. They'd take a *skiff* (a small rowing boat) out along the *banks* (cliffs) or on the *voe* (sea inlet), with the *tirricks* (Arctic terns) crying above them, and the *selkies* (seals) watching. Hungry folk are *black fanted* (because they've forgotten their *faerdie maet*, the snack that would have kept them going) and upset folk *greet* (cry). An older housewife like Jessie would have her *makkin*, (knitting) *belt* buckled around her waist, and her *reestit* (smoke-dried) *mutton* hanging above the Rayburn. And finally... my favourite Shetland verb, which I didn't manage to work in this novel, but which is too good not to share: *to kettle*. As in: *Wir cat's joost kettled. Four ketlings, twa strippet and twa black and quite.* I'll leave you to work that one out on your own... or, of course, you could consult Joanie Graham's *Shetland Dictionary*, if your local bookshop hasn't *joost selt* their last copy *dastreen*.

The diminutives Magnie (Magnus), Gibbie (Gilbert) and Charlie may also seem strange to non-Shetland ears. In a traditional country family (I can't speak for *toonie* Lerwick habits) the oldest son would often be called after his father or grandfather, and be distinguished from that father and grandfather and perhaps a cousin or two as well, by his own version of their shared name. Or, of course, by a *Peerie* in front of it, which would stick for life, like the *eart kyent* (well-known) guitarist Peerie Willie Johnson, who recently celebrated his 80th birthday. There was also a patronymic system, which meant that a Peter's four sons, Peter, Andrew, John and Matthew, would all have the surname Peterson, and so would his son Peter's children. Andrew's children, however, would have the surname Anderson, John's would be Johnson, and Matthew's would be Matthewson. The Scots ministers stamped this out in the nineteenth century, but in one district you can have a lot of *folk* with the same surname, and so they're distinguished by their house name: *Magnie o Strom, Peter o da Knowe.*

GLOSSARY

For those who like to look up unfamiliar words as they go, here's a glossary of Scots and Shetlan words.

aa: all
an aa: as well
aabody: everybody
ahint: behind
allwye: everywhere
amang: among
anyroad: anyway
auld: old
aye: always
bairn: child
banks: sea cliffs, or peatbanks, the slice of moor where peats are cast
bannock: flat triangular scone
birl, birling: paired spinning round in a dance
blootered: very drunk
boanie: pretty, good looking
breeks: trousers
brigstanes: flagged stones at the door of a crofthouse
bruck: rubbish
caa: round up
canna: can't
clarted: thickly covered
cowp: capsize
cratur: creature
crofthouse: the long, low traditional house set in its own land
darrow: a hand fishing line
dastreen: yesterday evening
de-crofted: land that has been taken out of agricultural use, eg for a house site

dee: you. **du** is also you, depending on the grammar of the sentence - they're equivalent to thee and thou. Like French, you would only use dee or du to one friend; several people, or an adult if you're a younger person, would be you.
denner: midday meal
didna: didn't
dinna: don't
dis: this
doesna: doesn't
doon: down
drewie lines: a type of seaweed made of long strands
duke: duck
dukey-hole: pond for ducks
du kens: you know
dyck, dyke: a wall, generally drystane, ie built without cement
ee now: right now
eela: fishing, generally these days a competition
everywye: everywhere
fae, frae: from
faersome: frightening
faither, usually **faider**: father
fanted: hungry, often **black fanted**, absolutely starving
folk: people
gansey: a knitted jumper
geen: gone
greff: the area in front of a peat bank
gret: cried
guid: good
guid kens: God knows
hae: have
hadna: hadn't
harled: exterior plaster using small stones
heid: head
hoosie: little house, usually for bairns
isna: isn't
joost: just
ken, kent: know, knew
kirk: church
kirkyard: graveyard

knowe: hillock
Lerook: Lerwick
lintie: skylark
lipper: a cheeky or harum-scarum child, generally affectionate
mair: more
makkin belt: a knitting belt with a padded oval, perforated for holding the 'wires' or
knitting needles.
mam: mum
mareel: sea phosphorescence, caused by plankton, which makes every wave break in a curl of gold sparks
meids: shore features to line up against each other to pinpoint a spot on the water
midder: mother
mind: remember
moorit: coloured brown or black, usually used of sheep
mooritoog: earwig
muckle: big - as in Muckle Roe, the big red island. Vikings were very literal in their names, and almost all Shetland names come from the Norse.
muckle biscuit: large water biscuit, for putting cheese on
na: no, or more emphatically, **naa**
needna: needn't
Norroway: the old Shetland pronunciation of Norway
o: of
oot: out
ower: over
park: fenced field
peat: brick-like lump of dried peat earth, used as fuel
peerie: small
peerie biscuit: small sweet biscuit
Peeriebreeks: affectionate name for a small thing, person or animal
piltick: a sea fish common in Shetland waters
pinnie: apron
postie: postman
quen: when
redding up: tidying
reestit mutton: wind-dried shanks of mutton

riggit: dressed, sometimes with the sense dressed up
roadymen: men working on the roads
roog: a pile of peats
rummle: untidy scattering
Santy: Santa Claus
scaddy man's heids: sea urchins
scattald: common grazing land
scuppered: put paid to, done for
selkie: seal, or seal person who came ashore at night, cast his/her skin and became human
shalder: oystercatcher
sho: she
shoulda: should have, usually said sooda
shouldna: shouldn't have
SIBC: Shetland Islands Broadcasting Company, the independent radio station
skafe: squint
skerry: a rock in the sea
smoorikins: kisses
snicked: move a switch that makes a clicking noise
snyirked: made a squeaking or rattling noise
solan: gannet
somewye: somewhere
sooking up: sucking up
soothified: behaving like someone from outwith Shetland
spew: be sick
spewings: piles of sick
splatched: walked in a splashy way with wet feet, or in water
swack: smart, fine
tak: take
tatties: potatoes
tay: tea, or meal eaten in the evening
tink: think
tirricks: Arctic terns
trows: trolls
tushker: L-shaped spade for cutting peat
twa: two
twa-three (usually twa-tree): a small number
vee-lined: lined with wood planking

voe: sea inlet
voehead: the landwards end of a sea inlet
waander: wander
waar: seaweed
whatna: what
wasna: wasn't
wha's: who is
whitteret: weasel
wi: with
wir: we've – in Shetlan grammar, we are is sometimes we have
wir: our
wife: woman, not necessarily married
wouldna: would not
yaird: enclosed area around or near the croft house
yoal: a traditional clinker-built six-oared rowing boat.

Acknowledgements

I would like to dedicate this book with affection and thanks, to all the "boaty folk" of Aith and Brae who have encouraged me in my passion for sailing.

In Aith, there's the Regatta Committee: Jim and the Moncrieff boys, Wilbert and the Clark boys, John Robert Hay, Trevor, Ian and Robbie Anderson, Peerie Ollie, David Nicholson and the late Jamie o' Roadside. Thank you for letting me mess about in committee boats and guard boats, and for cheering me over the finish line. Thank you, Jim, Victor and *Pattibelle* for some cracking sails. Thank you to John, George and John for fishing me out at Vementry; thank you to the lifeboat crew, particularly Kevin and Luke – I hope never to call you. Lastly thank you, Gunner Cheyne for bringing the cannon to the pier to welcome *Karima S* home.

In Brae, there are my fellow dinghy sailing instructors, Joe, Hughie (owner of the Standing Stone), John, Ewan, Ian, Richard and Graham. There are the cruising sailors, including Drew, Frank, Hamish, Charlie, Peter, Willie and Scott, who've shown me new horizons. Most of all, thank you to Joe and *Cynara* for some truly memorable expeditions.

I hope you all enjoy this tale of improbable mayhem in our home waters.

On the literary side, thank you to my agent, Teresa Chris, for her support and encouragement – in print at last! Thank you, Anselm and Eloise of Attica Press, for making the process easy, interesting and fun. To my fellow Westside Writers, thank you for all the fun evenings – it's your turn next!

About the Author

Marsali Taylor grew up near Edinburgh, and came to Shetland as a newly-qualified teacher. She is currently a part-time teacher on Shetland's scenic west side, living with her husband and two Shetland ponies. Marsali is a qualified STGA tourist-guide who is fascinated by history, and has published plays in Shetland's distinctive dialect, as well as a history of women's suffrage in Shetland. She's also a keen sailor who enjoys exploring in her own 8m yacht, and an active member of her local drama group.